MARK SCHWEIZER

faintinggoat
press

To the guys who read this first—
Mark, Ken, Jay, Tim, Richard, and Phil

And the gals who waded through the football
to get to the good parts—
Donis, Beverly, Liz, Kristen, Karole, and Betsy.

Dear Priscilla

Copyright ©2011 by Mark Schweizer

Published by

faintinggoat press

an imprint of
SJMPBOOKS
P.O. Box 249
Tryon, NC 28782

ISBN 978-0-9844846-1-4

Jacket design by Chris Schweizer

Taking a Chance on Love, © 1940
by Vernon Duke with lyrics by John Latouche and Ted Fetter

Chicago, © 1916
by Carl Sandburg

A Charm
by Thomas Randolph (1605-1635)

Chicago, 1943

She stood in the hazy glow of the yellow lights, rummaging through her handbag for a nickel, but the porter, who had tossed her suitcase rudely onto the platform, had already given up on his tip and stepped back onto the steps of the Pullman as the train began to move. She looked up, startled and frowning, as if the railway schedule should grant deference to a woman who needed a few extra moments to collect herself after two bumpy hours on a train. Her fingers closed around the coin and she held it aloft. The porter motioned for her to toss it and she did, but she was not adept at throwing things—a source of amusement to her boyfriend—and the nickel bounced off the side of the metal car with a ting and disappeared into the gap beside the tracks. The porter waved her off in disgust and disappeared into the car. She sighed. A prettier girl would have gotten better service.

It was her routine to take the Wabash into Chicago every other weekend, but tonight her schedule had been altered through no fault of her own. Her supervisor, a spiteful, bitter old spinster named Eunice Twitman, had given her a meaningless task and it caused her to be late leaving work. Then, having to take a later train, she missed her connection in Joliet. Now it was close to midnight and she'd been the only one to disembark.

1

In fact, looking around, it seemed to her as if she was the only one in the station.

She wasn't.

She smoothed her skirt over her thighs, and quickly admired her manicure. It was a splurge. She'd never before used nail polish or, in fact, done anything with her nails. She gave a tug at the hem of her jacket and tried to do the same with her blouse. The new gray tweed suit had cost the better part of two weeks salary. The blouse was pale blue silk, and had been borrowed from her friend Louise with a stern warning not to get any of her red lipstick on it. She'd skip breakfast tomorrow, she thought, and maybe lunch, too. A smallish dinner and then the same on Saturday. That should take her down about five pounds. She wasn't fat, but she wasn't exactly thin either, and she wanted to look her best this weekend. Five pounds off her hundred and sixty wouldn't make a huge difference, but if she had to shed her clothes and get into bed with her boyfriend, and she suspected she might, at least she'd feel better about it. Yes, she'd feel better about it—but she wasn't looking forward to it.

She gave the suitcase a nudge with her foot. Heavy. On previous visits, she'd stayed in Chicago for only a couple of days, three at the most, and packed light. This time, she hoped the trip would be different—an extended stay—and she'd packed accordingly. If she decided to remain in Chicago, it would be a pleasure to send Miss Eunice Twitman a letter telling her to suck on a light socket. Then she shook her head, took a deep breath, closed her eyes, and listened again to her mother's nattering. Pride comes before a fall. First things first. Don't burn your bridges.

She lifted the bag with two hands, swung it sideways (banging it painfully against her shins), and started lugging it toward the exit where she hoped it wasn't too late to find a taxi.

"Need some help with that?"

She started and dropped the suitcase, turning around in surprise.

"Sorry. Didn't mean to frighten you."

"That's okay," she said with a nervous laugh. "I thought I was

2

the only one to get off the train."

He gave her an even-toothed smile and picked up her heavy suitcase as if it was a pillowcase full of feathers. He slung his own duffle over his shoulder.

"Are you home on leave?" she asked, eyeing his uniform.

"Yeah," he said, then smiled at her again, a reassuring smile, a friendly smile. "How about you?"

"I'm visiting my boyfriend," she said, pointedly squelching all intentions that this gentleman, however dashing, might have of asking her out while she waited for the taxi. Her mother had warned her about GIs on leave.

"He's a lucky guy. I have a girl, myself. Would you like to see her picture?"

Without waiting for an answer, he set down the suitcase and the duffle, and pulled a snapshot out of his wallet. He handed her the photograph. A girl with darkish hair wearing a swimsuit and standing on a beach looked back at her without expression.

"She's very pretty."

"We're getting married," he said. "Sometime this spring, but we haven't set the date yet."

She relaxed and twirled a finger through her brown hair. "Me, too," she said. "Actually, that's sort of why I'm here. Wedding plans."

He returned the picture to his wallet and picked up the two bags. "Nothing like a wedding to take your mind off the war," he said good-naturedly. "That's what Jenny's ma says. Me? I'd rather face the Japs!"

She giggled.

"Listen," he said. "You're never going to find a cabby at this time of night and Jenny would never forgive me if I left you here by yourself." He lowered his voice. "This neighborhood is full of coloreds. How about if I give you a lift?"

She didn't think too long, having also been nattered at by her mother about the coloreds. "It's just a few blocks. That is, if you don't mind."

"I don't mind a bit."

MARK SCHWEIZER

1

It was hot and I was sweating like a fat kid in a candy shop.

"Cahill! Get your sorry ass in here!"

I kicked the wooden chair back from the desk on its creaking iron casters, yanked my partner's report out of the typewriter, and dropped my half-finished smoke into my half-finished coffee. Around me, three heads immediately lowered, as if reading some old Chicago Police circular was going to be as interesting as my can getting chewed for the third time this week. I looked up at the calendar hanging on the squad room wall, chiefly to appreciate Betty Grable's million-dollar legs, and because there wasn't anything nearly as compelling on my desk. Betty looked back and gave me the wink, one hand resting daintily on her bare knee, the other pointing toward the date. October 1943. Six years on the force. Twenty-four years till retirement. I couldn't start collecting my pension till I was fifty-nine. But then, I'd gotten a later start than most rookies.

"Cahill!" came the second bellow.

Captain Stanley Sherman's bellows came in threes. If you showed up early—after the first bellow—you were still bound to get the other two. Stan really didn't like it if you showed up before that third bellow. Bad form.

I shuffled a few papers on my desk, rolled my shoulders free of the tightness that a couple hours of typing police reports always produced and wished I hadn't thrown my cigarette away so early.

"Wait for it," muttered Tilly, mopping his sweaty brow with his handkerchief.

"Cahill! I ain't gonna call you again!"

I glanced over at Tilly and in keeping with my halfsy theme for the morning, gave him a half-nod and a half-grin, then placed my hands flat on the desk and hoisted myself into a standing position. Being confined to a desk wasn't doing my knee any good. My long legs didn't fit underneath the standard issue furniture and I didn't have enough scratch to buy my own. As I rose, the quads in my right leg tightened to compensate for the lack of any functioning ligaments. After six years, this muscular contraction was now as automatic as the process of gingerly shifting my weight every time I rose, involuntarily testing the tolerance of the joint. My knee always loosened up after a few minutes of walking and I didn't much think about it anymore.

"Going for four?" asked Tilly, under his breath, still pretending to be interested in his wanted poster.

"Nope. Three's plenty."

I reached Stan's door just as he was winding up.

"Ca-..." He stopped abruptly and glared at me over his litter-strewn desk. It was tough to tell by looking at Stan's desk where police work ended and garbage collection began. As on my previous two visits this week to the inner sanctum of Precinct 26, I noticed several unfinished cups of joe, two overflowing ashtrays, a growing pile of petrified cheese sandwiches stacked in a weirdly artistic white and yellow mound, strewn folders, loose reports, a top hat, assorted pistols and ammunition, and three-quarters of what might be a lemon pie. That the black-flies weren't hovering in swarms was a testament to Stan's new penchant for keeping the windows shut tight, even in the dead heat of August—or now, the dead heat of early October. The hottest October on record so far, even though we were only eight days in. He saw me eyeing the stack of sandwiches.

"I hate cheese sandwiches. Bessie packs me two of them every goddamn day. Lemon pie, too. She makes me one every Monday morning. The plate goes home today. You want a slice?"

It being a Friday, I shook my head. "No thanks."

"Don't blame you. It tastes like something the cat threw up. Bessie ain't the best cook, but she tries hard. Hard to make lemon pie with no sugar. Course, this rationing may be her best excuse."

"How about crackin' a window, Captain? We could use a breath."

"Ain't gonna happen. I already told you guys about that."

I wiped some sweat off my brow and nodded. Bessie Sherman, a hypochondriac as well as a bad cook, had been reading an ongoing series in the *Times* about the imminent dangers of recent epidemics. During the past six weeks, she'd been frantic about the possibility—or rather, the *probability*—of catching either polio, influenza, measles, even more virulent measles, tuberculosis, or syphilis, and maybe all of them at once. It didn't help matters that Stan had come down with the latter. After he'd managed to convince Bessie it was a medical fact that syphilis was, in fact, "borne upon the breezes of Lake Michigan," she'd made him nail all the windows shut. It was the least he could do.

I pushed a pile of Stan's civvies off of the only other chair in the office and sat down. "Well, if you don't like the cheese sandwiches, why don't you ask her for something else? Meatloaf, maybe?"

"And break her heart? Damn, Merl, you are a cold piece of work."

"Yeah," I agreed. "Cold."

"I think you oughta get married. Then you'd understand the delicacies of keeping a wife happy."

"That's what I was thinking, too," I said, though in fact I was thinking about the Bears opening home game on Sunday and where I could score a couple of tickets. Being on the desk wasn't all bad news. At least I had weekends free.

"You're off the desk," said Stan. "Your gun and buzzer are

here somewhere." He hauled his six-foot frame out of the chair with some difficulty.

Stan Sherman had been captain of the precinct when I started coming through the ranks. He'd been in pretty good shape then, but now bore a remarkable resemblance to William Howard Taft, complete with mustache and side-whiskers. He rooted through assorted papers, knocked over his stack of sandwiches, and bumped one of the ashtrays onto the floor before finally coming up with the appropriate gun and badge, then shoved them across a mountain of trash in my direction.

"Did the D.A. drop the charges?"

Stan snorted. "You ain't going to jail, so don't worry about it. Those charges was bunk anyway."

I nodded. "Thanks for going to bat, Chief."

Stan waved me off. "You ain't the first to punch some punk in the mush. The commissioner says you're off the desk."

"Yeah, great," I grumbled. "Can't you wait until Monday to reinstate me? Maybe pretend I was out sick or something? I've got tickets to the Bear's game."

"I'll take 'em," said Stan, grunting back into his chair and holding out a porcine hand accompanied by an evil grin.

"Well, see, I don't actually have the tickets *per se*. I was going to pick them up tomorrow."

"*Per se* this, college boy. There's a dead colored woman over in Stanford Park."

I waited for a couple of beats. "And?"

"And you need to get over there and investigate," said Stan, his irritation showing. I was pretty sure it was the heat.

"Yeah," I said. "I was just wondering if there might be any other consequential details which might aid in our erstwhile investigation."

"I'll 'erstwhile' you, smart ass. There's a dead girl. She's *dead*. Dead, in the park. So unless she fell over dead while walking her poodle, you've got work to do."

"Got it. Dead girl. Poodle."

Stan ignored the comment. "Pick up Biederman on your way and get on over there."

He gave my gun another push with a piece of fossilized bread just as his telephone rang, the bell muffled by a stack of papers.

"That's it. Now get the hell out of my office and back to work."

I collected my piece and my badge before they disappeared for good, retreated, and left Stan to find his missing telephone.

"Fish been in this morning?" I asked, after I'd made my way back to my desk.

"Yeah," said Tilly. "He came in about nine, then checked out. I'm covering for him."

Tilly Brown was as thin as a split fence-rail and just as tough. He looked at me through wire-rimmed glasses, sporting a hangdog visage. His salt-and-pepper hair was cropped, sides and top, military-style. Even though he'd only been in the squad room for an hour or so, his tie was already loosened and his shirtsleeves rolled up to his bony elbows. He kicked his chair back from the desk. "Glad you're off the hot-seat. Got something?"

"Body over in Stanford Park. Colored girl. Stan doesn't have any more than that. Maybe a poodle involved."

Tilly smirked. "Yeah, I had a poodle once. They're tough. Hey, you hear we're getting a dame in the squad?"

"Hmm...a female detective? Didn't hear that." I laid my badge on my desk and started checking my gun for any unwanted food products that may have made their way into the works.

"Yep. What I heard was that the whole city is hurting for recruits, so we're promoting broads. Can you imagine? A dame with a badge and a gun? What if she like—goes nuts or something?"

"It's a caution," I agreed. The Colt Police Special was as pristine as when I'd tossed it in disgust on Stan's desk four days earlier. I slid open my bottom desk drawer, took out my holster and a box of lugs, opened the cylinder of the ·38 and carefully slid each bullet into its housing. Then I flipped it shut and gave the gun one revolution, cowboy style, on my index finger. It felt good. I had a backup piece as well—one that wasn't registered

with the department. Another Colt, this one a ·45 automatic that
I usually carried in a holster under my arm. I'd have been happy
with just the ·45, but the mayor made some sweetheart deal with
the Colt company, and we were all issued the ·38. No rule against
carrying both though. Not yet.

"I'm the only one without a partner," Tilly said. "A dollar to a
donut hole I'm gonna be stuck with her."

"Maybe she'll be a looker," I suggested, standing up to put the
holster back onto my belt.

"Maybe she won't. And even if she is, how's that gonna help
me in a dust-up?"

"She might distract the criminal element long enough for you
to shoot them."

Tilly nodded. "Yeah, maybe. It's all right for you. You're a big,
ugly mug. But me…" He ran a hand through his short hair.

"Yeah, you're a real Errol Flynn," I said. "Gripe all you want.
I'm going to collect Fish. I'm off the desk and I've got a case.
Things are looking up." I headed for the door.

"Probably not for the poodle," said Tilly.

2

I paused long enough to pull on my jacket and my new hat, a fedora that cost the better part of a week's salary, then gave a nod to the poor saps still stuck inside the sweltering office, and took my ugly mug onto the street.

Maxwell Street was a mile-long stretch of open-air market, the likes of which could be found nowhere else in Chicago; or for that matter, as far as I knew, in the whole country. Immigrants needing quick cash headed for Maxwell Street, set up booths and hawked their wares to passersby in Polish, Italian, Russian, German, Yiddish, and a few languages I didn't recognize. You could find anything you wanted on Maxwell Street—legal or illegal—cars to shoelaces, eyeglasses to live chickens, prostitutes to dope and a whole lot worse.

The morning was already warm, but definitely an improvement over the steam bath in the squad room. I stood on the station steps, surveyed the street from under a low brim, and saw Larry the Dip working the other side of the street. We didn't worry about Larry. He'd pick some pockets and run a grift or two, then come over every Monday with our squad's cut. I gave him a nod when he spotted me, then pulled a deck of Camels out of my shirt pocket, banged one loose on my sleeve, and tugged the cigarette out of the pack with my lips. I lit the smoke with one hand cupped against the breeze, at the same time noticing a large bill plastered on most of the wall of Sullivan's Deli across the street. The bright advertisement announced in no uncertain terms, that Camels were the cigarettes that doctors recommended, combining both good taste and a smooth smoke. It felt good to take a doctor's advice for once in my life. I hadn't taken the doc's advice about my knee. I hadn't taken his advice about the bullet lodged behind my lung. So I figured taking a doctor's advice about Camels made it all jake. If I could just stay out of the syphilitic breezes of Lake Michigan, I was on the road to wellness.

I took a long drag on the smoke and felt health racing through my body. Dead girl. Stanford Park. Murdered, probably, or someone thought she was. Stanford Park wasn't a particularly bad area, but we weren't usually called out for accidents.

I stepped into the street and was immediately hit from behind by a rack of suits being pushed by a fat little man with an Adolph mustache. He backed the rack up and gave it another shove, but I didn't budge. I knew cussing when I heard it, even if I didn't understand the language. By the time the shopkeeper had gotten his face out of the merchandise and looked up, he knew he'd made a mistake. At six-feet seven inches tall, if I wasn't the biggest, meanest looking sonofabitch he'd seen since he landed on Maxwell Street, I was a close second. I gave him a hard look. He offered me an apologetic smile, showing a set of badly made false teeth, and quickly dollied off in the opposite direction, deftly dodging other racks of suits, coats, furs, and various dry goods being wheeled to and fro by street peddlers eager to sell their daily quota.

Happy to be walking, I imagined the scenario at Stanford Park. Killed in the park or somewhere else and dumped. Business always picked up around the precinct when the temperature rose, not that it wasn't brisk to start with. The war didn't put a damper on crime. On the contrary. Everybody, including the cops, was trying to make a buck.

An old lady, wearing a babushka and badly in need of a shave, lunged at me from a booth and waved a length of purple cloth in my face. I brushed it aside, then stopped and dropped a nickel into the clarinet case sitting open in front of a five-piece klezmer band. Not a tune I recognized, but I wasn't an aficionado. An Arab woman pushed a dish of rice and some kind of meat on a stick at me as I passed, and jabbered something unintelligible. It smelled great—street food always smells great, but I moved on.

As I traveled up Maxwell, the distinctive, old-world sound of the Jewish-gypsy klezmer music became the Negro jazz of two middle-aged black men playing guitars and singing on the next corner. I didn't have another nickel to spare, so I tipped my hat, pushed past a businessman carrying a briefcase, and jaywalked against the light. A car laid on its horn and some mug shouted, "You dumb bastard! You wanna get killed?" I ignored it.

At ten o'clock on any given Friday morning, Fishel Biederman was most likely to be found on the eastern end of Maxwell Street conducting business. Not police business, because, although detecting criminals was his primary occupation, the City of Chicago's paycheck was not his primary source of income. In fact, his departmental take currently ranked number three on the list of Fish's weekly revenues. Second place belonged to the Congregation Achavas Achim. Friday nights found Fish canting at the synagogue on Newberry Street. Fishel Biederman's lilting tenor was second to none and he could make every Irish cop on the West Side cry like a baby just by *offering* to sing *Danny Boy* at a police funeral. Still, singing services was a distant second in the catalog of Fish's weekly compensation. Friday nights were appropriated for holy matters, but Friday mornings were, generally speaking, reserved by Fish to collect his book for the week. Number one, Fish's book.

I was half-sure that Fish would be holding court at the corner of Maxwell and Union along with his two regulars. His place of business was a shoe-shine stand in front of Rubenstein's Grocery. The stand sat under an awning and was run by an ancient Negro named Cecil. Fish would be sitting in one of the two customer's chairs, three feet up off the pavement, surveying his subjects like a little King Solomon perched on a wood and leather throne. The other chair would be occupied by one or another of Fish's customers, probably Irish, and usually there just long enough to hand Fish a wad of cash, or in some rare cases, an excuse. It almost never worked the other way. Fish didn't pay out much. It was against his business principles. Most times, he'd collect his vig, pat his customer magnanimously on the back, ask about the wife and kids, take the sap's next bet, and send him on his way feeling as though they'd just had an audience with the archbishop himself. If the customer did happen to hit once or twice, it didn't really matter to Fish. The chances were good that he was already into Fish for more cash than he'd ever be able to win back.

My partner was just where I thought he'd be. As I walked up, felt my jacket start to catch a warm breeze and decided that fastening a couple of buttons was smarter than flashing my gun to a bunch of nervous plungers. There wasn't a man on the corner that didn't know we were coppers, but even so, there was no need to make anyone unduly nervous.

"Merl!" called Fish. "Thought you were still in the hot seat."

"Apparently not."

"Glad to hear it. Stan send you over?"

"Yeah. We've got a body in Stanford Park. You almost finished?"

Fish gave me a lopsided grin. "Yeah, but I already know about it. In fact, I already solved the case." He pointed at the Packard parked illegally across the street from the shoe-shine stand. Uniformed cops drove the black and whites. The members of our elite detective squad drove whatever car we'd managed to impound. I looked past the traffic and saw the head and shoulders of someone sitting in the back seat. I couldn't make out any features from where I was standing.

"Is that the guy?"

"He admitted as much," said Fish. He lifted his chin and gestured toward the car. "I've got him cuffed to the door. He's not going anywhere." Being a criminal himself in no way impeded Fish's effectiveness in collaring crooks.

"Wouldn't hurt for you to bide on your partner," I grumbled, then lit another cigarette and leaned against the corner of the grocery store, disappointed that my case had been solved before I even showed up, but still glad to be off the desk. A pint-sized black and white mutt looked at me from his haunt in the alley, bared his teeth, and gave me a miniature growl. I flicked the spent match at him, gave him a growl in return, and he disappeared.

"Justice don't wait for you to be let out of your playpen," said Fish.

The shoe-shine stand belonged to Fish and, to be sure, he always took his cut, but Cecil didn't do any business on Friday mornings, so Fish would always slip him a fin. Cecil would be in attendance for appearances sake, his derby askew on his bald head, his apron covered in various hues of shoe polish, and brushes in hand.

"You need a shine, boss?" said Cecil. "Be happy to fit you in."

"Nah. Thanks, though." I looked down at my shoes. Ten years old and resoled twice already. A shine wouldn't do them a lick of good.

Cecil would pretend to stay busy through the morning, but customers came and went so fast that even if he wanted to, he wouldn't have time to give them anything more than a spit shine. Added to that was the fact that when these particular customers were finished doing their business with Fishel Biederman, most of them didn't have enough jack left for a piece of penny candy.

In addition to Fish and Cecil, there was one other regular at the corner of Maxwell and Union, a thug named Little Eddie Nowak. Fish's muscle.

I tipped my hat to a uniformed beat cop as he stopped briefly to choose an apple from Rubenstein's fruit bin before meandering down the sidewalk. Fish gave the cop a wave.

"Morning, Sweeney," he called. "Hope that apple isn't poisoned."

"I'm expectin' it will be one o' these mornin's," laughed the flatfoot in a hard Irish brogue. "How's business then, Fishy?"

Fish's book was well-known and well-protected.

15

"Better and better," answered Fish. "Stop by McGurty's this afternoon. I'll buy you a drink."

"Well, bless your little heathen soul, I will. And I expect there will be a wee bit more than a drink coming my way."

"Barukh ata Adonai Eloheinu melekh ha olam, bo're pri hagafen," said Fish with feigned piety. "Blessed are You, Lord God, King of the universe, who creates the fruit of the vine."

"Amen," said Sweeney, with a laugh. "A worthy sentiment. Sure, and it's a shame that you'll be burning in hell with the rest of your pagan race."

Fish gave a smile that faded as soon as the cop continued on his beat. Then he spat and muttered *"Putz!"*

My partner's next "appointment" had been sitting next to him during this entire exchange and was now shifting uncomfortably in his chair. Fish finally turned his attention to his customer. He opened his black book and ran a finger down the page.

"Lester Rafferty," he said sweetly. "You don't mind if I call you Lester, do you?"

Lester shook his head. He was a family man. You could always tell by the clothes. His shirt was clean. His jacket had patches on the elbows, sewn by a loving hand. His shoes were covered in whatever passed for poor-man's shine these days, probably axle-grease. His thin hair, oiled and combed, had obviously been cut by a family member. None of this mattered to Fish.

"Do you have my money, Lester?"

He shook his head again. "I can get some of it by this afternoon. Here's the thing. My wife..."

Fish waved a dismissive hand. "Lester, you're a new customer and I need you to understand that I can't let this kind of thing go on. It's bad for business. You *do* understand, right?"

Lester nodded. "Yeah, sure, but..."

"It's not so much. You owe me what?" Fish shrugged his shoulders and raised his splayed fingers.

"Fifty bucks," Lester said.

"Fifty bucks today, which you don't seem to have."

"Yeah, no problem. I'll get it to you next Friday. I swear on my mother's..."

"Don't swear," said Fish. "It's never good to swear. I'll tell you what." Fish put a comforting hand on his customer's leg. "I'll give you till next Friday. You'll bring me a C-note next Friday."

"A C-note? I don't owe you no C-note!"

I was listening to the exchange, but watching the car across the street. Anyway, I'd heard it all before. So had Fish. The figure in the back seat of the Packard hadn't moved. I took a long pull on my cigarette.

"I understand your confusion," Fish said to Lester. "It's what we call *vigorish*—the interest on the loan. Just sit here with me a minute." He looked around and, spotting Little Eddie, waved him over to the stand.

Little Eddie Nowak wasn't little. He was bigger than I was (which was saying something), and just a little smaller than his brother, Big Eddie, but none of us had seen Big Eddie for a while. We all thought Big might be dead. There was a third brother Eddie as well, and he went by Just Plain Eddie to avoid confusion. In this family of psychopaths, Just Plain Eddie was the meanest and worst of the bunch, but Little Eddie was the strongest. I'd seen him lift the back end of the Packard once and hold it up so Fish could change a flat. His eyes had all the cunning and intelligence of a halibut, but Fish didn't keep him around for his smarts.

"Little Eddie," said Fish. "You know my friend Harold Darke, the florist?"

"Yuh," grunted Little Eddie.

"Harold owes me a C-note. That's a hundred clams. He was supposed to come and pay me this morning, but he didn't show up." Fish turned and smiled at Lester—still patting his leg—then shifted his attention back to Little Eddie. "I need you to go and find my friend Harold and break his left thumb and three other fingers. You can choose which ones."

Little Eddie was good at breaking stuff. I broke stuff, too, but not for Fish. Fish's business was Fish's business. What I broke was my business. If he was in a jam though, a mug would have to come through me first.

"Thanks, boss," said Little Eddie.

"On his left hand," said Fish, shaking a warning finger. "Not his right hand. He's got a flower shop and he needs to be able to trim his posies." He studied Little Eddie's face. "You know which hand is your left hand?"

Eddie held up both his huge mitts and looked at them in consternation.

Fish motioned me over to his chair, and when I walked over, reached up and plucked the cigarette out of my mouth. He put it to his lips, inhaled deeply, then blowing the smoke out through his nose, took Little Eddie's left hand and ground out the cigarette in his palm. Little Eddie grunted but didn't flinch.

"That one's the left," said Fish. "Got it?"

"Yuh," grunted Little Eddie, looking stupidly at the dark smudge on his hand.

"Go on then," said Fish with a smile. "You do what I told you, Little Eddie."

I looked over at Lester. He had gone white.

"Aren't you...aren't you a copper?" he said in a hoarse whisper.

"I most certainly am," said Fish. "One of Chicago's finest. Detective second class. So's my friend here."

I nodded at the introduction and brushed the brim of my hat with my forefinger.

"But that really has nothing to do with our business arrangement, does it?" said Fish happily. "I'll see you here next Friday?"

"Yeah, umm... sure... I guess."

The smile left Fish's face, his face darkened and his eyes narrowed to dangerous slits. When he spoke, his voice was low. "I don't believe you understand the temerity of an unwise decision in this matter." Fish consulted his book. "According to my information, you work for the city water department and live at 435B 18th Street with your wife, Sylvia, your mother, Rose, and your three children, Chester, Patrick, and Mary Margaret. A fine Catholic family. It'd be a shame for them if something happened to the bread-winner so he couldn't work. Think of Chester and Patrick picking pockets just to help the family get by. Maybe little Mary Margaret on the street selling pencils. Or worse." Fish patted Lester Rafferty's leg. "Now, that's not something I'd want on my conscience, if I were you."

"You can't..."

"Shut the hell up." Fish growled. He lowered his voice and put his mouth close to Lester's ear. "Here's the order, Lester," he said with a snarl, holding up one finger at a time, in front of Rafferty's terrified face. "Fingers, arms, legs, back..." He paused for a moment, then raised his thumb. "Dead."

I saw Lester gulp.

"Even then, you're not off the hook," Fish snarled. "After 'dead,' Little Eddie visits your family. And the vig doubles every week. You understand me?"

Lester Rafferty's eyes were wide with fear. He nodded.

"See, Lester," said Fish, sitting back, his jovial visage and demeanor returning, "we can all be friends here. We can live side-by-side, Jewish and Catholic, Hebrew and Irish—even big dumb Lutheran Polacks like Little Eddie. It's what makes this country great." He straightened his tie, clapped his hands together and stood up. "You can stay and get a real shine if you want," he said to Lester. "On the house."

"Little Eddie is no Lutheran," I said, as we crossed the street to the car. "There aren't any Polish Lutherans in Chicago. He's as Catholic as the pope's pecker."

"But a damn sight more useful," said Fish. "I know Little Eddie's one of you mackerel snappers. I was just making a point."

"You ever get to 'dead?'"

"Once," admitted Fish. "You only have to do it once. And, quite frankly, he had it coming."

Fishel Biederman might have cut an unusual figure in most cities. In Chicago, on Maxwell Street, he fit right in. More than a couple inches short of his self-proclaimed five foot eight, Fish had an affinity for well-tailored, silk jackets and little regard for the clothing rationing that was happening across the country. That his choice in fabric was now considered contraband by the War Production Board had little effect on Fish's pre-war fondness for the material, and it didn't take him long to find a tailor that didn't mind supplying my partner with his illicit suit jackets in any color he chose, as long as it was pale yellow. According to Fish, Seymour Weissman had a warehouse full of pale yellow silk straight from China.

"Weissman says the army's after his silk for parachutes," he told me, "but they don't want to pay him."

"No skin off my nose." I said.

"I'd offer to hook you up with one of these fine jackets, but it wouldn't be right, both of us wearing the same thing. Somebody might think we're a couple of *faygelehs*." He thought for a moment. "I could get you some drawers, maybe."

I declined the offer.

Dark gabardine trousers and Fish's trademark black homburg, set at what Fish considered the optimum angle for ogling skirts, completed his outfit. Altogether, he was a notable individual, even among the colorful characters who populated the lower West Side.

"I saw the girl he croaked," said Fish as we walked up to the Packard. "Pretty girl. Colored, but maybe half Puerto Rican or something. Strangled her and left her in the bushes next to the fieldhouse. Beat cop came and got me. I stayed with her till the meat wagon showed up, then started nosing around." Fish pointed at the figure behind the glass. "Genius here hadn't gone far."

"Did you call the captain? Tell him you got the guy?"

"Nah. Not yet. I've been busy."

I opened the back door and a young colored man, maybe eighteen years old, tumbled out, dragged by the handcuff that secured his wrist to the door handle. He blinked a couple of times and lifted his free hand to shield his eyes from the sun. His shirt was grubby and his brown canvas trousers looked like they hadn't been washed since Roosevelt's first term. He might have needed a shave— it was tough to tell. A well-worn tweed cap fell down over one eye.

"Get up," ordered Fish, giving him an ungentle nudge with a highly polished shoe.

The boy struggled to his feet and adjusted his cap.

"You do this thing?" I asked. He nodded sadly.

"He was hiding in a tree," said Fish in disgust. "In a *tree*, for God's sake. I had to shoot him out of there."

"He doesn't look shot."

"Well, I shot him in the hat. He jumped down after that."

"Were you aiming for the hat?"

"Hell, no. I was aiming for his head."

"How close were you?" I asked.

Fish beetled his brow. "Maybe eight feet."

I nodded. That seemed about right. Fish was notorious for his inaccuracy with his snub-nosed ·38.

"Why'd you do it?" I asked the kid.

"Got drafted. I'm leaving this afternoon." He shrugged and continued. "So last night I call Josephine and tell her I love her and will she wait for me and she says we gotta meet in the park. Then, when I get there she gets sour on me and tells me to blow 'cause she's with Ray now."

"That's her name?" I said. "Josephine?"

"Josephine Scott."

"So you killed her?" I said.

"I hate that Ray. Anyway, I'm leaving today. Got drafted."

"Good news, boy," said Fish. "You ain't drafted no more."

3

The dogs found her first, a pack of three smallish strays that had been working this particular block of Maxwell Street for a couple of years and were as street-savvy as any of their two-legged counterparts. The smallest, a black and white mongrel that may have had some border collie in his ancestry, stood as sentinel at the mouth of the alley, a lookout against intruders, while the other two worried the grisly package. His turn would come. Except for one quick growl, they were all quiet as mice.

4

Fish punched the starter on the Packard. "I am worn out! High Holy days will put a crimp in the old vocal cords. I've been singing nine days straight."

I nodded in sympathy.

"You get my reports typed?"

"Most of them. There're a few left."

"Think you could finish them up for me? You know I hate to type."

"Yeah," I answered. "I've got nothing going on. But let's string Genius along for a few more hours. I don't want to go back yet. I've been sitting at that desk all week. "

"Suits me. It's almost lunch time, anyway."

I gave a half turn and addressed the occupant of the rear seat, still handcuffed to the door.

"You have a name?"

"Yeah."

"Like to tell me what it is?"

"Okay."

I sighed. "What is it?"

"Henry."

I turned all the way around and smacked him hard on the side of the head.

He yelped. "What was that for?"

"Henry," I said, "I do not care for one word answers. I want to know your name and I want to know your address. Now, I am a man of infinite patience, but my partner here, is not. He might not be able to shoot you in a tree, but he sure as hell won't miss you in the back seat."

Fish pulled out his gun and waved it in the air. Henry's mouth dropped open in surprise. Then the gun went off and we had another hole in the roof and probably another stain on the back seat.

"Jesus, Fish!" I groused. "I've only got one set of ears! Tell me when you're going to do that!"

"Ah, sorry," said Fish. "I get carried away sometimes. You want me to shoot the kid, or not?"

"Henry Clarence Goldberg Junior the Third," yammered the kid in a stream of syllables. "My momma calls me Clarence, since Henry Junior the Second was my daddy's name, and when he was around she didn't want to keep yelling 'Henry Junior the Third,' but I goes by Henry now 'cause Daddy left and Clarence is *no* kind of name for a cat. I'm staying with my sister at 435 West 14th Street, apartment three. Her name's Flo. I used to live with my momma off of Roosevelt till about a month ago, but she throwed me out for coming home drunk on a Sunday morning when I was s'posed to be singin' in church. That was the morning that and me and Ray went down to the stockyard and got some shine from a guy named Stink Eye. You want his address, too?"

"Nope," I said, turning back around.

"You want Ray's address? I hate that Ray."

I ignored him.

"Goldberg, eh?" said Fish, pulling into traffic. "You're not Jewish are you?"

"Baptist."

"Too bad," said Fish. "I was going to let you go if you were Jewish."

"I might be half Jewish," offered Henry. "I've been circumscribed."

"Doesn't count," said Fish.

"How about Jim's Original for lunch?" I suggested.

"Sounds good to me," said Henry Clarence Goldberg Junior the Third, settling back. "I could really go for a Maxwell Street Polish. I haven't had anything to eat since noon yesterday."

Fish and I looked at each other and laughed.

"What's so funny?" asked Henry. "You gotta feed me, right?"

"No, we don't," said Fish. "And to tell you the truth, I wish you'd shut your pie hole. I rather prefer you less chatty."

Jim's Original was on the corner of Maxwell and Halstead and, according to their advertising, had invented the Maxwell Street Polish, a polish sausage sandwich topped by fried onions, peppers if you wanted them, and a smear of mustard. We drove up to the stand, parked the car, disembarked and left Henry handcuffed in the back seat.

"I don't want any peppers on mine!" hollered Henry as the front doors slammed shut.

"I've changed my mind," I said. "Let's take him in right after lunch."

Fish nodded. "I didn't get a formal statement," he agreed, "so we might as well get it over with."

"We got a confession. It shouldn't take long."

"Let's pretend we didn't," suggested Fish. "I'm starting to feel like he needs a tune-up."

"Perhaps next time, you'll endeavor to shoot a bit straighter."

"I would have got him with the second shot. He jumped out of that tree too fast."

"Yeah," I agreed. "Your second shot is usually pretty good."

We could hear Henry yelling from inside the car, something about extra-mustard. We ignored him.

"You want one or two?" Fish asked me, taking his turn at the counter.

"Two."

"That'll be four originals and two beers," Fish ordered.

"Dressed." He slapped five dollars on the counter, then handed me my half of the order, picked up his own, and followed me over to a bench after tossing a "keep the change" over his shoulder.

"Nice day," he said, settling into one of the sandwiches. "Glad you're off the hot-seat."

"Me, too." I unwrapped one of the sandwiches, and savored the delicious scent of grilled sausage, onions, and peppers.

"Did they clear you?"

I shrugged and took a bite. "I guess," I said, chewing and talking at the same time. "The commissioner himself put me back on the beat."

"Bah," said Fish in disgust. "That guy was resisting arrest. What were the chances he'd be some alderman's kid?"

I popped the remainder of the sandwich into my mouth. It didn't take me long to finish a Maxwell Street Polish. Three bites. Two, if I was hungry. "I have been suitably chastened," I said, then took a long pull on the beer bottle. "And perhaps I *was* a tad heavy-handed."

"Don't second guess yourself," said Fish cheerfully, carefully licking his fingers before starting on his second sandwich. "Anyway, he was out of the hospital in a week. No real harm done. Well... maybe that plate in his head."

"When you're right, you're right," I agreed.

Being Fish's partner hadn't always been easy. When I started on the force, he didn't exactly welcome me with open arms. His last partner had been shot during a gambling raid, and the word around the city was that Fish was somehow involved. I asked, Fish denied it, and I never brought it up again. Still, it took eighteen months and a lecture from his wife, Ziba, before he trusted me enough to back his play with a couple of thugs from Little Italy. After that, we were jake. I made it clear from the start that I didn't want a cut of his book. He was my partner and you look out for your partner. Besides, who was I to throw the proverbial stone?

"You have anywhere you need to be this afternoon?" he asked.

"Nope."

26

"So let's dump Henry Junior the Third at the station and see if we can make a couple races at Arlington."

"You got some interest?"

"Yeah," said Fish, already planning our escape. "There are a couple of ponies I'd like to get a read on. Of course, we'll need to book him and file the official report before we take off. It's our sworn duty as detectives."

"Yeah."

"And, as you know," he said, "I can't type."

"If I have to type it, I want half the credit for the arrest."

"What did *you* do? Walked up and had a smoke, that's what."

"It was a long walk," I said. "Dangerous. Some car honked at me."

"Yeah. Okay," agreed Fish, with a grin. "Half credit, but you're buying the beer later."

5

Henry sat in the chair across from Fish's desk. "I sure wish I had me one of them sandwiches," he said. "I'm hungry as a hoot." He blinked some sweat out of his eyes. "Man, it's hot in here."

"Shut your yap," said Fish, "and sign right here on this line. You can write your name, can't you?"

"Course I can."

"Then do it."

"Don't I need to call a lawyer or something?"

"Plenty of time for that later," said Fish. "Just one more to sign." He looked over at me. "You finished yet, Merl?"

"I'm typing as fast as I can," I said, my fingers banging away on the keys. "I'll be finished in a minute."

"Where'd you learn how to type anyway?" asked Tilly, pushing his chair back from his desk and resting his feet on the blotter with a thud. "The rest of us are pecking away like a bunch of punch-drunk pigeons."

"College boy," said Stan Sherman, overhearing the question on his way back from the john. He was still trying to tuck his shirt back into his pants and not having much luck.

"I went to college," said Tilly. "They never taught *me* to type."

"I took a class," I said. "Had to." I rattled off another line, heard the bell, and banged the carriage back to the left. "Football scholarship. I was an English major, but I had to take either typing or short-hand to fill my schedule."

"So, it was like secretary school?" smirked Stan, interrupting his trek to take a jab. "Remind me. What kind of nancy college was this, anyway?"

"Notre Dame."

Stan blinked and the side of his mouth gave a small twitch. Tilly hid a smirk.

"Hey, Stan, didn't you go to Notre Dame for a semester or two?" asked Fish.

"Yeah, well...best damned college in the country," said Stan with a sniff. He turned his back on the conversation and waddled off. "You mugs get back to work," he barked, giving his door a perfunctory slam for emphasis. The door banged shut, didn't catch, and bounced back open to its original position. The telephone rang in Stan's office.

"Done," I said.

Fish grabbed the paper out of the typewriter and slapped it down in front of Henry. "Sign it."

Henry shrugged and wrote his scrawl across the bottom of the paper.

"That's it then," said Fish. "Now, Henry Clarence Goldberg Junior the Third, it will be our pleasure to drop you off downtown."

"Can I get something to eat? I'm feeling a little sick."

"That's probably just a little clap you caught from a wayward zephyr," said Tilly, mopping his brow with a soggy handkerchief. "Don't worry. You're safe enough in here."

"Huh?" said Henry.

"They'll feed you downtown," I said.

"Cahill! Get your sorry ass in here!" came the bellow from the bowels of Stan Sherman's trash heap.

"What now?" I sighed.

"Biederman! You, too!"

"Does that count as one or two?" asked Fish.

"Now!"

"That's three," said Tilly. "Better go on in."

Fish put on his hat and gave me the eyebrow. I followed suit, snugging the brim down across my forehead. Better for Stan to remember that we were on our way downtown. Maybe he'd cut us a break and give whatever this was to Ned and Vince when they got back to the station.

"Dead girl," said Stan, seeing us standing in the doorway.

"We already solved it," said Fish, carefully avoiding a pile of dirty shirts and stepping over what might once have been angel food cake. "You saw the bum sitting at my desk. Name's Henry Clarence Goldma..."

"Not *that* dead girl. There's another one. This one's bad."

"Huh," I grunted. "The first one was dead. This one is *worse?*"

"Yeah. Worse. In the alley beside Rubenstein's grocery. Maxwell and Union."

"Hey, wait a minute," said Fish. "That's where my stand is."

"Yeah," said Stan. "Exactly. Tilly can take your collar downtown. You get on this thing."

6

We drove up to Rubenstein's and parked across the street in Fish's usual illegal spot. Cecil had a couple of well-heeled customers and was busy buffing and shining. The grocery was bustling as well, Fridays being payday. Most of the working class on the West Side headed home for lunch after getting paid, cashed their checks, and paid their tabs at whatever local bar they patronized. Then, grudgingly and not without a few snide comments about the expense of female companionship, legal or otherwise, they dutifully handed the rest over to their wives.

There was a small crowd of people gathered around the opening to the alley beside the store, the side opposite Fish's shoe-shine stand. Most of them were cops, but I also recognized Pete Flambeau, crime photographer from the *Times*, and another reporter whose name I couldn't remember. There were some gawkers as well, but the police line kept them well back of the entrance. Fish and I muscled our way through the assembly, and spotted a sergeant named Dougherty. He waved us over.

"This one is bad."

"That's what Stan Sherman said," said Fish. "But he didn't elaborate. So? How bad?"

"Chopped up and left in an army duffle bag bad," said Dougherty.

31

Fish's eyebrows went up. "Chopped up?"

"A white girl. Torso, legs, arms. I didn't see her head, but maybe it's at the bottom. I didn't dump everything out."

"Jeeze!" said Fish, making a face.

"Official army duffle?" I asked.

"Looks like it. No stenciling though," said Dougherty. "Could be a fake, I guess, but I don't think so."

"Who found her?" I asked.

"First off, a pack of dogs," said Dougherty. "Then Esther Rubenstein saw the blood on the pavement when she brought some trash out. The dogs took off. The bag is over behind the bins."

"Okay," I said. "We'll take it from here. Can you guys stick around till we get everything cleaned up?"

"Yeah. No problem."

"And get that shutter-bug out of here," said Fish.

"He'll leave or I'll run him in," said Dougherty.

The narrow alley was a cut-through linking Maxwell Street with Liberty and was just wide enough for a fat couple in love to saunter down hand in hand, though only one of them at a time would be able to squeeze by the trash cans. There were no shop doors opening directly onto the passage—just two blank brick walls and four metal cans. The Rubensteins, or maybe their neighbors on the other side, kept the alley clear. Except for the reddish smears on the pavement, there was nothing remotely ominous about this location. Quite the opposite. It was clean and relatively well lit—at least during the day. There was a bare bulb hanging under a green metal shade about eight feet up on the right side, just above the trash cans, but it wasn't on.

Pete Flambeau held up his Rollei and was doing his best to get a shot of Fish and me when Sergeant Dougherty bumped his arm rather egregiously.

"Hey! Watch it!" yelped Pete.

"Aye, sorry there, laddie," Dougherty said, accentuating his heavy brogue as the Irish cops were told to do when dealing with the public. Our police commissioner thought it made them seem friendlier. "Sure, and we need to have a little chat, you and me."

"Hey, just one second..." I heard the photographer stammer.

We passed by without looking at him and found the army duffle, stretched to its length behind the trash cans, out of sight of the bystanders. The upper half of the bag was a familiar olive green. The lower half was a color that had once been the same green, but was now a soggy, blackish mess. Bluebottles had discovered the feast and were now clustered around the bottom of the duffle. Fish squatted down and waved them off and they hovered for a moment, buzzing angrily, only to land again a few seconds later.

"You want to open it?" asked Fish.

"Not especially. Dougherty already spoiled the surprise."

"Yeah. Me neither." Fish tugged at the top of the duffle bag. It came open and he gave a cautious, sideways glance inside, then immediately made a face. "Aw, Jeeze!"

I squatted down beside him and looked inside the bag at fingers and toes and a lot of meat. *"Holy Christ!"* I tasted bile in the back of my mouth and swallowed hard, then pushed my hat back on my head and wiped my brow with the back of my hand. "Jesus, Mary, and Joseph!"

I'd seen worse, but not much worse.

"The blood's all right here," said Fish, looking around the alley. "At least the dogs didn't drag it all over the place."

I couldn't take my eyes from contents of the bag. One of the bloodied hands was half-clenched, but one was open, the manicured feminine fingers extended in supplication. A piece of broken ecclesiastical statuary complete with stigmata and nail polish. Her feet were visible as well, although pushed further into the bag, and her toe-nails exhibited the same bright red color that I saw displayed at the ends of her fingers. I swallowed hard, then let the bag fall closed.

"There's no blood trail leading in," continued Fish. "Probably the duffle was dumped out of a car sometime last night."

I stood up, looked around, and agreed with Fish's assessment. "Yeah. Back the car in, open the trunk, dump the bag. Easy." I poked around the outside of the soggy canvas, then pulled out a handkerchief and wiped the blood off my fingers. "I don't feel anything that might be her head."

"Well, we're not dumping it out here," said Fish. "Let's get a tarp and haul this down to the morgue. We don't want to wait for the bus."

"Be easier to put it in a trash can and make sure the lid's on tight," I said. "We can stash it in the trunk. No, wait a minute. Let's check the cans first. If her head's not in the bag, maybe it's in one of the trash cans."

"Aw, Jeeze!" said Fish again. "I don't want to find a head in a trash can."

"Me neither. Make our job easier, though."

1

To say that McGurty's on any Friday afternoon was busy was akin to saying that W.C. Fields liked his gin. Fish and I wandered into the bar at four o'clock after dropping the body at the morgue, returning to the alley to spend a useless hour going over the scene, and another at the station twiddling our thumbs. Now we were heading back to talk to the saw-bones. McGurty's was on the way.

It was clear to almost everyone in the place that we weren't in a good mood. Word of the dead girl had already gotten around the precinct, and the two or three cops that had just come off duty gave us a deferential nod and plenty of space. We walked directly up to the bar and leaned on it. Joe McGurty had two double scotches in front of each of us before we'd taken off our hats.

"Good to see you, boys," he said. "Heard you had a rough day."

"Yeah," said Fish. He pulled out a deck of Luckys, tapped a smoke halfway out of the pack, and offered it to me. I was a Camel man, but I didn't care. Lucky Strikes, Camels—hell, I'd even smoke a Chesterfield if someone offered it. I lit up and watched Fish repeat the exercise, lighting his own cigarette from the pack of matches sitting on the counter. He flicked the spent match absently into the mirror behind the bar. I looked up and watched it bounce off the yellowed glass, then squinted and ran a hand absently through my shock of black hair, smoothing it back with the help of the Wildroot I'd put on this morning. Violet, the girl I'd gone with for the better part of a year, had gotten me the hair tonic last summer and I dutifully applied it once a week. Every Friday.

Violet was right. I was scary looking. I checked to see if my nose was really as crooked as it appeared or if maybe the mirror was cracked. I moved my head to one side. The mirror was fine. Every morning I took the time to shave, more or less, but by one in the afternoon, I had enough shadow to pass for a Punjabi. Accentuating this rough visage was a scar that traveled jaw to eye—a white trail, barren of any growth, in a field of stubble. I gave a crooked grin and put a finger where one of my eyeteeth should have been. Actually, I had more of my own teeth than most retired pro-footballers.

"You seeing Vi tonight?" asked Fish.

"Think so. I don't know for sure. I got a letter Tuesday."

"She still in Peoria?"

I nodded and knocked back one of the drinks. "Still working in the lab. If she shook loose, she'll be on the eight o'clock train, but she might have to sit with her grandma. I'll head down to the station just to see."

Fish slapped a hand down on the bar, lifted it up, sneered at what was left of the cockroach, and wiped his hand on what passed for a napkin. McGurty's was a hole. The booze was watered down. The lights were so dim that it was difficult to see the menu, much less the occasional rat scurrying along the back baseboards. The pretzels were week-old at best and months-old at worst. Still, the price was right for most of these working stiffs and Joe didn't mind running a tab. He didn't like to spend undue cash on upkeep or furnishings, but the essentials were there: usable tables and chairs, a dart board, a wall full of hooch, and a black marble bar that stretched the length of the establishment. More importantly for me, this was the watering hole of choice for Chicago Bears players—the older ones, anyway. I'd been patronizing McGurty's since I came to Chicago ten years ago and it felt good to keep in touch with the players I'd been friends with, the ones still playing. Made me feel like I still belonged somehow. If Fish had another bar he'd rather frequent, he didn't say so. A good partner, Fish.

On Fridays and Saturdays and Sunday afternoons, both Joe and his son, Oscar, would be filling glasses as fast as they could. Weekdays found either one or the other on duty. Sunday morning they were closed, supposedly to clean up the joint.

I picked up my hat and my unfinished scotch and moved away from my spot towards a table across the room, then felt a tug on my arm. I stopped walking, and turned to see a big, squinty-eyed flatty, still in his police uniform, hanging onto my coat.

"You Merlin Cahill?" he said.

"Yeah." I didn't recognize him. He wasn't one of ours.

"You're a big boy, ain't you?"

I pulled my sleeve loose from his fleshy fingers. "Yeah." I saw Fish watching me from the bar.

"I saw you when you was with the Bears. You were a tackle, right? Saw you play against Washington in '37, the year we lost the championship."

"That's nice," I said, making a move away from the table.

"Why ain't you in the army?" he called after me. I didn't need to answer the lush, but I'd had a lousy afternoon and so I turned back.

"Four F. Busted up my knee in '39."

I didn't ask why Flatty wasn't doing duty. They weren't taking forty-year-old out-of-shape drunks. Not yet, anyway. He grinned at his companions, all cops, none of whom looked familiar. Then he stood up, faced me and pushed a finger into my chest. The top of his head came up to my nose.

"I'm six feet tall," he slurred, "and I boxed heavyweight in the Navy. Course you wouldn't know anything about that, you being a slacker. How much you weigh, anyhow?"

I put my drink on the table, but didn't answer. The bar had gone quiet.

"Cahill was one of the biggest guys on the Bears team in '39," said one of Flatty's tablemates. "Six-seven and two-eighty. Course it looks like he's gained a few pounds," he guffawed. "Or maybe just got a little tubby."

"Tell you what, Merr-lin," said Flatty, dragging out my name in a particularly discourteous fashion. "Why don't you buy all of us a drink, and we'll tell everyone what a swell homo you are?"

I could always feel the onset of the rage. First, a slow burn at the base of my skull, then, if I paid attention, I could feel my jaw clench and my shoulders knot. In a moment, and just for a brief second, a red haze would drift over my vision. Fish said that my eyes went from gray to black, something the court-mandated police psychologist attributed to abnormal pupil dilation.

"Tell *you* what, asshole," I said, putting an open hand in Flatty's face and shoving him back into his chair. "You sit down and shut up and maybe you'll walk out of here."

He jumped to his feet, his hands clenched and his face beet red. "You goldbricking sonofabitch! You can kiss my..."

I hit him so hard, I thought for a moment that his head had come off. It hadn't, but in the morning, he'd wish it had, or, if he wasn't awake by then, as soon as he regained consciousness. Flatty's three companions hadn't moved. I was quite ready to mop the bar with any or all of them, but they stayed put. Fish walked up to the table and put a hand on my arm.

"As long as I've known you, Merl," he said with a grin, "I've never heard anyone finish that sentence. How does it end? You can kiss my...what?" He looked down at the cop. "You want to hit him again? I can hold him up if you want."

I rubbed my hand, then picked up my drink and shook my head. "Nah."

"You think he's dead?" asked the cop that was the Bears fan.

"He's still breathing," said another.

"Jesus, look at his jaw. There's bubbles coming out the side."

"That's 'cause it ain't attached no more," said the first.

Fish took a puff on his cigarette. "What are you boys doing on this side of town anyway?"

"It was Al's idea," said the Bears fan, pointing at the now-gurgling flatty. "He heard about Cahill tuning up that alderman's kid. He's bucking for sergeant and thought it'd be a good career move to get a little payback." He looked up at me. "He heard you were big, but that you were a candyass."

"Guess what?" I growled.

"What?"

"I ain't."

Fish gave Flatty a nudge with the point of his shoe. "You boys need to pick up your friend and take him home." He gave a closer look. "Or maybe to a hospital." Fish turned to me. "You ready to go?"

"Yeah. Let's come back after we see the doc. I'm not feeling sociable just now."

I downed my drink in a gulp, then looked back at the cops. They were taking Fish's advice, but not, I noticed, before they finished their beers.

8

The morgue was run by a grizzled doctor named Claude Everette. He'd been a prominent surgeon in his day, but thanks to a fondness for morphine, was now relegated to the basement doing autopsies and screaming obscenities at nurses who avoided him at all costs. Dr. Everette was short and squat, had a permanent three-day beard, a rarely-combed shock of white hair, and a lighted cigarette between his nicotine-stained lips at all times. I'd even seen him light up two or three and puff on them simultaneously. His eyes had the wild, furtive look of an addict; the troll who lived in the basement of St. Luke's Hospital on Michigan Avenue.

Dr. Everette had placed the pieces of the poor girl out on a metal table, hosed them off, and arranged them, more or less, in the correct order. Seven pieces counting the torso. The arms had been removed at the shoulder and separated again at the elbow. The legs were intact, but had been taken off about six inches above the knee. It was a clean job. Surgical.

"You don't have her head?" asked the doc, lighting a fresh cigarette with the glowing butt of his previous smoke.

"Does it look like I've got it in my pocket?" said Fish with irritation.

"No head," I said.

"Hmm. Probably has part of her neck with it," said the doc, pointing at a piece of gristle sticking out of where the throat began, then abruptly terminated. He poked at it with his pencil. "This here's the first thoracic vertebrae. Cervicals are up higher, closer to the brain." He rolled the torso slightly and looked thoughtfully down the neck. "It's a nice clean cut though. Same with the limbs."

"She looks young to me," I said. In reality, the body, still glistening with water, looked neither old nor young, but like something in a butcher shop; pale, bloodless, and marked at fifty-eight cents a pound. The red fingernail and toenail polish standing against the white flesh only seemed to make, to me at least, the dismembered corpse even less human.

"Probably early to mid twenties," said the doc. "Well fed. No children, I'm betting. I can let you know what she had for dinner after I open her up. I was just gonna do that. You want to wait?"

"Nah," I said. "We can come back."

"I'll check for sexual activity later."

"We appreciate that," said Fish. "The 'later' part."

"Any idea who she is?" asked the doc.

"Nope," I said. "Of course, we haven't started nosing around yet."

"Ain't gonna be easy," said Fish, "unless someone comes up missing."

"Fingerprints?" asked the doc.

"We can take 'em," I said, "but it won't do any good unless we have prints to compare them with."

"Well," said the doctor with a shrug, "it seems to me that what you have here is a woman between nineteen and twenty-eight, with brown hair, probably five foot six or seven and around one hundred fifty pounds. Ring any bells?"

"Yeah," said Fish. "Every other skirt in Chicago."

"Of course I could be wrong about her age, her height, and her weight. I'm pretty sure about the hair color though."

"Huh?" said Fish. Doc Everette rolled his eyes and tapped her just below the equator with his pencil eraser. "Ah," said Fish with a nod. "Brunette. Got it."

"Cause of death?" I asked. "For the report."

"Lack of head," said the doc.

9

We were back in McGurty's an hour later. The cops were gone, but the bar had filled up with regulars. I nodded toward four guys at a table in the back and they waved us over.

"Afternoon, Merl," said the largest man at the table of large men. "I heard from Joe that you haven't lost your way with people." George Musso was a bull, and about fifty pounds heavier than the next biggest, and most famous of the Chicago Bears' quartet sitting in the back of McGurty's, Bronislau Nagurski. Bronko.

"One of our brothers in blue. Some beat cop. He was being rather..." I searched for the right word. "Rude."

"So we gathered," said the lean, muscular guy, straightening his tie. "Sorry we missed the show." Sid Luckman was the Bears' quarterback, only slightly shorter than Bronko's six-foot two, but significantly slimmer. Being the quarterback, and having his picture plastered across anyone of Chicago's rags on any given day, he cut a well-known figure on Chicago's East Side.

"How you doing, Merl?" Bronko said. "We heard you fellas had a bad day. Sit down. Have a drink." He pointed to a bottle of whiskey on the table. Bronko wasn't nearly as physically imposing as Musso, but in his day, he was the most feared player in the National Football League. Even now, on or off the field, he was a force to be reckoned with.

"Don't mind if we do," said Fish, as we pulled up a couple of empty chairs. Fish, diminutive in most settings, looked positively elf-like sitting at the same table with me, Musso, Bronko, Sid Luckman, and Woody Sugarman. I'd played alongside all of them. Bronko, Woody, and I had all been at Notre Dame together during Knute Rockne's glory days. Bronko had joined the Bears in 1930. I graduated two years later, but laid out a year and came in with Musso in '33. Sid joined the team in '39, the year I got hurt. Elwood "Woody" Sugarman had been a journeyman tailback and, after a stint with semi-pro teams up north, had played for the Rams, the Eagles, and the Redskins before being traded to Chicago earlier in the summer. He was bigger than Bronko, with shoulders you could hitch a plow to, blonde hair, and a smile that always stood him well with the ladies.

"Woody," I said, giving him a nod. "Good to see you again."

"You, too, Merl," said Woody. "You're as pretty as ever."

Bronko pushed the bottle across the table toward Fish. "Help yourself."

"Thanks," said Fish, pouring himself a couple of fingers. "Thought you retired and became a pro wrestler."

"Yeah," said Bronko. "I did. Been doing it for five years."

"You like it?" Fish asked.

"Sure," shrugged Bronko.

"He's heavyweight champion," said Sid. "But Hunk Anderson needs the Bronk for one more season. Most of the squad's either enlisted or been drafted."

"You know the season's been cut to ten games?" said Woody. "Ten games and a championship. We're down to eight teams as well. The Cleveland Rams have shut down. Pittsburgh and Philadelphia merged."

I nodded. "I read about it."

"I'll bet you didn't read about *this*," said Musso, in disgust. "The league says we have to wear helmets. *Helmets,* for God's sake." He looked as though someone had shot his dog.

"I'm sorry, George," I said. "Let's have a drink to the good old days."

"To the good old days," said Sid, raising his glass.

"The good old days," echoed Bronko.

"When men were men," said George sadly, "and the game was played by giants."

We all drank.

"Speaking of Giants, how about getting seats for the home opener on Sunday?" I said. "Do any of you fellows happen to have a couple of extra tickets you haven't given away?"

"We're playing the Cards," said Woody. "The Giants aren't on the schedule until sometime in November. Hey, I have a thought. They brought Bronko out of retirement. How about you?"

I shook my head. "The knee's bad. Got a bullet behind my lung, too."

"Not to mention your hair stinks," added George.

"Violet likes it," I said defensively.

"I've got some tickets," said Sid. "I'll leave them at the gate. How about you, Fish? You need any?"

"Just one of Merl's," said Fish.

"You laying any points on us?"

"The Bears are a three touch-down favorite," said Fish. "The Chicago Cardinals are a joke, but they have a following, and with a twenty-one point spread, I'm getting a lot of action. When you win, win big."

"We'll do what we can," said Sid. "Sorry about that girl, too." He shook his head.

I got to the train station at seven forty-five. The eight o'clock from Peoria came and went.

Violet wasn't on it. I stopped by the precinct on my walk back and called Mabel Guthrie's rooming house in Peoria. No answer.

10

"Hell of a game," said Tilly. "Did you see it?"

I was trying to shake a doozy of a hangover, courtesy of a Sunday night post-game shindig at McGurty's. We'd spent Saturday back in the alley beside the grocery going over what little evidence we had, then knocking on doors until late in the afternoon. Police work—gotta love it. We came up empty, then took Sunday off.

"Yeah," I grumbled. "Hell of a game. Talk a little softer, will ya?"

"I'll bet Biederman ain't happy. He never should have given twenty-one points. That's a tough spread."

"He was close. Twenty to zip ain't bad." I closed my eyes. "Man, this is no way to start a Monday morning."

"Know what works for me? A Bloody Mary."

"Yeah," I said. "I just don't know if I want to start with the vodka at eight o'clock."

"Hell of a game," called Ned Mansfield, banging through the office door. "How about that Luckman? What a quarterback! I think we can go all the way this year."

"They tied with Green Bay in the first game," I said, "and barely beat Detroit."

"I don't care. I think they can do it," said Ned, hanging his hat and coat on the rack. "Hey, could one of you guys go ahead and bust open a window before Stan gets in here?"

"Too late," Tilly answered. "He was here when I came in a half hour ago."

"Christ!" said Ned. "I'm starting to sweat just *thinking* about how hot I'm gonna be for the rest of the day. Vince here yet?"

Ned and Vince Hogan were partners. Had been for years. They were like an old married couple—fought like hell, finished each other's sentences, even dressed alike: brown trousers with braces, white shirt, gawd-awful tie, ugly jacket, cheap, stingy-brimmed fedoras. Of course, that was the uniform of ninety percent of the detectives in the city. No surprise there.

"Nope," said Tilly. "Not yet. You looking for him before noon?" It was a question that didn't expect an answer.

Standing up for the fashion-conscious ten-percent of Chicago's finest, Fish was the next to appear, dressed in his pale yellow silk jacket, a light gray overcoat hanging from his shoulders like an impresario's cape, and, of course, his beaver-felt homburg.

"Greetings, gentlemen," he chirped happily. "I trust this morning finds you all doing well."

"What are you so happy about?" asked Tilly. "You were giving twenty-one points."

"And so I did," said Fish. "But you know, it's not *all* about the final score. There are hundreds of side bets."

"For instance?" Ned asked.

Fish shrugged. "People bet on anything: how many first downs will be made in the last two minutes of the game; how many yards Bronko will rack up; in what quarter will Hunk Anderson throw his hat onto the ground and stomp it; whether or not the opposing quarterback will bang our head cheerleader in the visitors locker room after the game. All these bets make for a delightful and profitable afternoon. And before you ask, the answer is no, he didn't. I had a little talk with Ruthie at halftime."

Ned snorted. "So the fix was in?"

"Heavens no," said Fish, walking over to his desk. "How's your boy doing, by the way? Any news?"

Ned put both his hands face down on his desk and pursed his lips.

"We haven't heard anything for a few weeks. The last letter we got was right before the 5th Army landed in Italy."

"Anything in the news?" Tilly asked.

"Some. They're clearing the passes to Naples, but unless there's a hell of a battle, nothing much gets reported."

"Augie'll be fine," said Vince. "He's got a good head on his shoulders." Vince's own son, Lee, was married and on the force. He even had a kid. He was waiting for the draft to catch up with young fathers, but it hadn't so far. Not yet. Augie had enlisted in the Army as soon as he was out of high school.

"Cahill!" came a bellow.

"Oh, man," I groaned, holding my head with both hands and resting my elbows on the desk.

"I'll go," said Fish, "but I'll let him yell another couple of times first. You need a Bloody Mary or something?"

"Maybe some coffee," I grumbled. "Anyone make any coffee?"

"Not me," said Tilly. "I'm off coffee."

"You ain't off coffee," I said.

"Clara read that it isn't good for you. It's addictive."

I ignored him and walked over to check the coffee pot. When I looked inside, I judged the muck in the bottom to be just slightly older than one of Stan's petrified lunches. I poked at it with a pencil and could have sworn it moved.

"Anyone clean this thing out in the last decade or so?"

"Nah," said Ned. "Nietzsche said it best. 'What doesn't kill us makes us stronger.'"

"Nietzsche never drank this."

"Get your hat," called Fish, exiting Stan's office. "We have a clue."

"Ooo," said Tilly. "A clue. I'm all aquiver. Think I could come with you detectives and see what you do with it?"

Fish grunted. "It'll probably die of loneliness. You stay here in the sweat-box. We'll call you if we need you. Anyway, your new partner is on the way down."

"Oh, yeah?"

"Stan told me your partner's name. Kingston." Fish grinned. "*Gloria* Kingston. Hell of a name for a bruiser."

"That ain't funny," said Tilly, in disgust. "Christ! I *knew* it'd be a dame."

I followed Fish to the station door, retrieved my hat and overcoat, and traipsed after him out onto the street. I took a deep breath and the fresh air helped to clear my head just a bit. Maxwell Street was just starting to jump.

"What's the deal?"

"We're going to the *Times* newsroom over on Wacker Drive. Stan just got a call from the editor. They got a note from the killer."

"Our killer?"

"Unless there are more girls stuffed into duffle bags, he's ours," said Fish, taking the time to light a smoke. "It was pretty specific." He offered me the pack. I took one and lit up.

"You gotta switch to Camels," I said.

"Yeah, I've been meaning to. But I know this guy who knows a guy who owes me money. He's paying me off in Luckys. Twenty packs to the dollar."

"Sweet deal," I agreed, opening the car door and climbing behind the wheel. "You want to stop somewhere for bite? Maybe some coffee and a donut would help this headache."

"Might as well," agreed Fish. "That girl ain't going to get any deader."

11

The Chicago Times building was a bustling place. We entered the lobby, walked past the guard, and climbed the stairs to the second floor; then, barely dodging three women coming out of an apparently very busy powder room, entered the newsroom through the glass double doors. We'd wandered through the newsroom and into the editor's office before someone bothered to ask us who we were or what we wanted. That person was the editor.

"Where's my secretary?" he sighed, when we showed him our badges. "Where's security? What going on out there?" No one seemed to be paying him any attention. Fish and I sat down in the two armchairs across from his desk and I introduced us.

"Now," I said, "what's this about a note?"

"It's here somewhere," he said, knitting his brows. "Where have you been? I called hours ago." He rifled through some papers on his desk and then came up with an envelope. He shoved it at me.

"My name's Stewart, by the way. Russell Stewart." Stewart was a kid that looked to be in his early thirties, hungry and eager, his sharp, bright eyes looking at us from behind rimless glasses. "I'm the managing editor."

"We gathered as much," said Fish, looking at the note I pulled out of the envelope. "Says that on your door."

I unfolded the paper and we read it at the same time. It was written in cursive script—a spidery hand—with a pencil.

Dear Priscilla,
This is my third time of writing you and still I have no reply. I need your help. You should look in the bag in the alley.
E.P.

"Who's Priscilla?" I asked, passing the letter to Fish.

"That's our lonely hearts column. It's called 'Dear Priscilla'."

"Priscilla have a last name?"

"There's no Priscilla," explained Stewart. "It's written by a gal name Amy Rogers. She's the one who brought the letter to me. It was in the stack of mail she was going through. I called downtown. They sent you."

"You know why?"

"Nothing official, but I heard. We're a newspaper, you know. Amy's really scared."

"She oughta be," said Fish. "Where is she?"

"At her desk would be my guess. I'll get her." Stewart walked out of his office into the busy newsroom.

"What do you think?" asked Fish.

I looked at the envelope. It was addressed to Dear Priscilla, *Chicago Times*, Wacker Drive.

"Postmark says Thursday," I said.

"Yeah. Day before we found her."

"Was she already dead on Thursday?" I wondered. "Or did he send the letter in advance?"

"If it's him," said Fish.

"It's him."

Fish nodded his agreement just as Amy Rogers came into the office followed closely by Russell Stewart.

"I'm quitting!" said Amy. She spun around and pointed a

piece of paper she had clenched in her hand right in Stewart's face. "Don't try to stop me!"

Amy Rogers was a fidgety waif of a girl with bobbed dark hair and huge glasses that made her look like an excitable bug.

"Calm down," I said, getting to my feet. "Here. Have a seat."

"I'm quitting!" she said again, brushing her bangs away from her face with the crumpled paper. "You're not talking me out of it."

"Fine with us," said Fish. "We couldn't care less."

That seemed to shut her up. She sat down and crossed her arms.

"Miss Rogers," I asked, "when did you find the letter?"

"I'm quitting," she said, this time less forcefully, her lower lip starting to quiver.

"So what?" said Fish. "Quit. No skin off my nose. When did you find the letter?"

"Umm...I guess around six. I usually come in at four in the morning and work till about lunchtime. We have a ten o'clock deadline." She frowned and looked at her watch. "I went down to the mailroom a little before six."

"They deliver the mail that early?" Fish asked.

"No. That's the mail from Friday and Saturday."

"You read the mail every morning at six?" I asked.

"Not always. I had my column about half finished and decided to take a break."

"And you came across this letter," Fish said.

"Yeah."

"You know what this is about?" I asked. "Why we're here?"

"I heard about the girl in the duffle bag," said Amy. "Pete Flambeau said he saw her, but he couldn't get a picture because of some big, dumb cop."

Fish gave me a wink. "How about the other two letters? The first two he sent. Where are they?"

"I don't even remember getting them," Amy admitted. "'Dear Priscilla' gets about three hundred letters a day. Most of them get thrown right in the trash. I look through all three hundred in about an hour and a half. That includes the time it takes to open them. If one catches my eye, I'll put it in a file and read it again later. Most of them, though, get tossed almost immediately."

"Why do you toss them?"

"We get so many. I scan for something that sparks a little interest. Maybe smacks of innuendo. That's what keeps the readers coming back. If I used the vanilla letters, nobody would bother to read the column."

She seemed to notice, for the first time since she walked into the office, the piece of paper clutched in her hand. She held it in my direction. "Here. Look at this."

I took it, smoothed it open, and read it aloud.

Dear Priscilla,

My husband comes home from work, eats supper, then sits himself down in front of the radio and listens to war reports until its time for bed. Then on Sunday, he listens to a ball game, turns on the war and falls asleep in his chair. What can I do to get him to take me out?
Signed,
Ready to Dance

"Looks okay to me," I said, handing it back to her. "You using it?"

"Nope," said Amy. "Boring. That's the same letter I see fifty times a day. Mostly it's more of the same. The kids won't behave, my husband doesn't understand me, my boss is coming on too strong, that sort of thing. I look for the letter that pops."

"That's her job," said Stewart. "And she's good at it."

"So it's not about giving advice," I said.

Amy pushed her glasses up her nose. "Of course not. It's about selling papers."

"Did you look back through your file?" asked Fish. "Maybe you kept one of E.P.'s letters."

"Nope." Amy shook her head emphatically. "I would have remembered."

"Why didn't you toss this one?" Fish asked, holding up the letter Stewart had given us.

"It was the second one I opened this morning. I saw the words 'look in the bag,' and then I quit skimming and read it very carefully. I took it back to my desk, put it in my folder, and waited for Mr. Stewart to come in. Then I brought it straight up."

"Look," said the editor, "we're going with the story about the body in the duffle bag. It'll be in the paper this evening."

"You do what you have to do," I said, "but we'd appreciate you not saying anything about this letter."

Stewart shrugged. "What's in it for us?"

"How much detail do you have on the corpse?" asked Fish.

"Not much," admitted Stewart.

"I might be able to help," said Fish, with a grin. Stewart matched his smile, tooth for tooth.

"Good," I said, then faced Amy Rogers. "I need to look at your desk. Could you show me where it is?"

"Yes," she said. "Then I'm quitting."

The newsroom was a-clatter with the noise of typewriters, telephones, reporters, columnists and copywriters—all working feverishly to make the ten o'clock deadline for evening publication. Amy's desk was situated at the far end of the room, away from the windows, nestled in a cluttered corner. There was a picture of a G.I. in a wooden frame sitting next to her Underwood. Other than that, and a blue colored pencil, the desktop was bare. The typewriter had a piece of paper in the carriage that was half-filled with typewritten text.

"Where are your files?" I asked, sitting in her chair without asking permission.

"Bottom drawer on the right."

I pulled open the drawer and lifted out a file folder maybe six inches thick. I dropped it onto the desk and opened the file.

"These are the letters you're going to use?"

"Not all of them. I'll go through them again. I only use two or three a day."

"You must have a couple of hundred here."

"I guess."

I looked at the first letter in the file. It was from a woman who had to live with her mother-in-law while her husband was overseas. I flipped it over, looked at the next one, and stopped cold.

P.S. Dear Priscilla,
I can't stop this from happening.
E.P.

"Amy," I said, "you remember this one?"

Amy looked over my shoulder and started shaking. *"No, no, no, no,"* she whispered. "That wasn't there."

"Look around the room," I said quietly. "Anybody you don't recognize?"

"I don't know!" whispered Amy, looking around the room, close to panic. *"I don't know!"*

"Okay, calm down," I said. "Since you came in this morning, when did you leave your desk?"

"I don't remember," Amy whimpered. *"I don't remember."*

"Stop it," I said, standing up and towering over her. I turned her away from the hubbub of the newsroom and locked onto her gaze. "Look at me. When did you leave your desk?"

"Umm...I went down to read the mail. Then I opened two letters."

"In the mailroom?"

"Yes. I open the letters in the mailroom. There's a desk down there."

"Are the other letters still there?"

Amy blinked twice and nodded. "All the letters are there. That's the second one I opened." Thursday's aren't there though. They go to the incinerator after I go through them."

Amy paused for a moment, stuck her tongue in her cheek, and looked as though she were concentrating. "I came back up and put the letter in my folder. After that I went downstairs and got some coffee. Then I came back up. I was maybe gone twenty minutes. I wandered around for a little while and nobody said anything and I was too creeped out to do any work so I went home and fed my cat. That was around seven."

"You went home?" I asked.

"I just live a couple of blocks from here. I was back at maybe seven-thirty, quarter of eight. I took the letter to Mr. Stewart. Then on the way back, I stopped and was talking to Jeanette." She pointed across the room. "She's got the desk closest to the door. Then you guys showed up. That's it."

I broke my gaze with Amy and looked across the newsroom.

"Wait a minute!" she whispered. "He knows who I am! He knows where I work!"

"I don't think so," I said. "Sure, he knows where you work, but look. The letter says P.S. It was probably stuck in with his other letter."

"It wasn't!" gasped Amy.

"You just didn't see it."

"I'm going to be sick!" said Amy, now wide-eyed with terror. *"I'm going to be sick!"*

"Hang on a second!" I said, but she was already weaving her way toward the newsroom door.

"Ah, Jeeze." I flopped back into the chair and took off my hat.

I pulled open the middle desk drawer. Two pencils. The two drawers on the left, nothing. The drawer above Amy's file drawer, an apple and some typing paper. I pushed the drawers closed and picked up the photograph on the desk, turning it over and sliding it out of the frame. No name. No inscription. I put it back the way I found it and looked at the paper sticking out of the typewriter.

Dear Priscilla,

I'm in terrible need of advice. My boyfriend has joined the Navy and is getting his training at the Great Lakes Naval Station. I've been writing to him every day. He writes to me too, but only once a week. Now he's getting a weekend pass, and in his last letter he says he wants

me to go all the way with him. He says he could be sent to war any day. I really love him. What should I do?
Signed,
In Love But Not Ready

I grinned in spite of myself. Amy had already answered this one.

Gracious Reader,
Your signature says it all. Priscilla is not a devotee of going all the way with any sailor, boyfriend or not. It can only lead to heartache or worse. Wait until you have a wedding ring on your finger before you let him put the dingy in the boathouse.

I read the next letter.

Dear Priscilla,
I have reason to believe that my husband is fooling around with a floozy masquerading as his secretary. She can't type, she can't take dictation, she can't file, and to make matters worse, she won't put my calls through to him when I know he's in. She just sits at her desk and buffs her fingernails.
Yesterday, my husband left our bankbook sitting on his desk and when I went through it, I found that he's been paying rent on an apartment in Lincoln Park. I can't divorce him. We're Catholic. What can I do?
Signed,
At Wit's End

The rest of the page was blank. Dear Priscilla hadn't managed an answer. She'd left to feed her cat. I didn't mind helping out. The style was easy to mimic. Address the letter to Gracious Reader. Refer to Priscilla in the third person. Make it cutesy. No problem. I clicked the carriage return a couple of times and started typing.

Gracious Reader,

This seems to be a common problem with husbands, especially those with secretaries. Although Priscilla abhors violence in almost every instance, it is clear that drastic measures are called for. My advice is as follows:

Wait until your dear husband is fast asleep, then sneak into the kitchen, get the biggest knife in the drawer, and walk back, pitty-pat, to the bedroom. Pull down your husband's pajamas, (trust me—he will be delighted) and as he smiles at you in gratitude, grasp his wandering appendage in your loving hand, pull tightly and place the knife edge directly at the root of the problem.

At this point, you may feel free to present your grievances. Priscilla suggests that certain threats be made and certain assurances extracted upon promises of a future visit by Mr. Carrot Chopper. If you play your cards right, the resident floozy will be looking for employment elsewhere, your bankbook will be back in balance, and your happy home will be restored.

I'd just finished typing when Fish gave me the high sign from the door of Russell Stewart's office. I stood up, put my hat back on, and was getting ready to wave him over. He'd appreciate the joke. Maybe Amy might appreciate it as well, once she got back from the powder room.

"Where's the column?" asked a voice behind me.

"Huh?" I turned around and saw a kid in his early twenties with ginger hair, freckles, and a sport coat that looked as though some Scotsman had vomited plaid all over it. He had a stack of papers in his hand.

"I need the column. Deadline's in two minutes. Gotta get it down to typesetting."

I shrugged, not understanding.

"Ah, there it is," he said with a grin. "I knew Amy wouldn't let me down." He reached across the desk and pulled the paper out of the Underwood. "Thanks."

"Wait a min..." I started, but it was too late. He was already at a dead run, dodging newshounds, and heading towards the door.

I let out a slow breath. "This can't be good," I said to no one in particular.

As we waited for Amy to return, I filled Fish in on the second letter I'd found in her desk and together we quizzed the rest of the newsroom, but it had been near deadline and no one had time to notice anyone out of place, lurking or otherwise.

"I think the P.S. was in with the other letter," I said.

"Probably. But if not, maybe he works here," suggested Fish. "If he didn't, how would he get in here without being noticed?"

"We did it easy enough."

"True," agreed Fish.

"Let's go find Amy. She went to the head to throw up, but she's been there a while. I've gotta give her a heads-up on a possible problem."

Fish straightened his tie and jacket and set his homburg back to its usual fashionable angle.

"And stop by the mailroom and pick up the rest of those letters," he said.

12

Amy Rogers was no where to be found and after we'd gotten her address, I pointed out to Fish that it was still my turn to drive.

"Fine, drive," said Fish. "We should stop by Everette's office after we check on Amy. See if he's got anything."

I nodded.

"You got any thoughts on this?"

"Maybe. I don't think that Miss Rogers will be working at the *Times* any longer. She was pretty spooked."

Fish shrugged. "So?"

"Maybe this guy will send another letter. We ought to keep him on the hook if we can. It's the only lead we've got."

"Makes sense," said Fish. "What do you suggest?"

"We need to talk to Stewart again. Find out who's going to take Amy's place if she quits and make sure they stay on the lookout for another letter."

"I agree," said Fish. "Pull over for a second, will you?"

I rolled the Packard to a stop, running the two right tires over the curb and up onto the sidewalk. We were a couple of doors away from Darke's Flower Shop, an establishment made conspicuous by tables of fresh flowers adorning the storefront. Fish opened the car door, stepped out, and disappeared into the entrance of the shop after first pausing to choose a white chrysanthemum for his lapel. I waited in the car. He reappeared two minutes later, flipping through a stack of greenbacks.

"Harold Darke was most accommodating," Fish said. "Of course, he's going to have to get himself a part-time worker. I distinctly told Little Eddie 'left hand'. You heard me, right?"

"I heard you." I pulled back into traffic.

"I've got to get better help," said Fish in disgust. He waved an idle finger at the windshield. "Off to the morgue, Watson."

"Watson? I'm the sidekick? I thought you were the sidekick."

"No, you're the sidekick. Everyone thinks so. The big, strong, good-hearted galoot with a hair-trigger temper."

"I've got that under control. Anyway, I'm the smart one."

"You *ain't* the smart one," said Fish. "And I don't care what that psychologist says, breathing exercises ain't gonna help that dander."

"I'm probably the good looking one."

"Not on your best day."

Amy wasn't home and half an hour later we were getting an earful from Dr. Everette, although his profane tirade was essentially aimed at a quickly retreating nurse.

"I need some morphine," he said when he saw us. "I'm out, and they won't let me write any more script." His clenched teeth snapped his cigarette to attention with every word. "Give me a smoke, will you?"

"There's one in your mouth, Doc," I said. "I don't mean to be insensitive to your addiction, but have you got anything else on our victim?"

"No. Now get the hell out of here so I can get back to rummaging through the medicine lockers upstairs."

"C'mon, Doc," said Fish. "We know you've got *something*. Give it up."

"Jesus!" said the saw-bones, picking up a clipboard and flipping a few pages. "*Fine.* She was about twenty-five and ate chicken and rice about six hours before she was killed. I would say that she'd been dead for at least a day before you found her.

There wasn't any sign of rape, or even any recent sexual activity, although she wasn't a virgin."

"You can tell that?" I asked.

"Pretty easy to tell unless she's the Madonna. She was pregnant."

Neither Fish nor I spoke.

"About twelve weeks along. Three months. Any idea who she is?"

"Nope," said Fish.

"We haven't checked the missing persons list this morning," I added. "Maybe we'll get lucky."

"I don't know," said the doc. He shrugged. "Without her head..."

"If we find someone who fits the description, and we can get some fingerprints from her house or something, we can compare them to the dead girl's."

"So you want me to keep her here?"

"Yeah," I answered. "Put her on ice. We'll let you know."

"She'll be in the cooler when you need her."

Fish and I had been running around for most of the morning. By the time we arrived back at the station, the weather had turned and it felt almost as though autumn was upon us. This happened often in Chicago. Summer one minute, fall the next. I certainly didn't mind. Neither did anyone else in the squad.

"Leave the door open, will you?" called Ned as we walked in. "It's about time we got a little relief. And the chief wants to see you."

"Who?" asked Fish. "Me or Merl?"

"Merl."

"Good," said Fish.

I sighed, dropped my coat and hat on the hook, and headed for Stan's office.

"Did you solve the case yet?" asked Stan, seeing me in the doorway.

"Solve it? We don't even know who the victim is."

"How about the note? Anything there?"

"Yeah," I said. "Our guy wrote it. Signs with the initials E.P. He's got this thing for Priscilla over at the *Times*. We're going to go back to Russell Stewart, the editor. If this guy writes in again, we'll know it."

"What's your gut say?"

I sat down and grimaced as I flashed a mental image of the pieces of meat lying on Everette's table.

"I've got a bad feeling about this one, Stan. Bad."

Stan tapped a pencil absently on the top of his desk, and read my expression. "This isn't his first, is it?"

"I don't think so. And I doubt it'll be his last. It was too clean. Surgical. Not the work of a beginner. His note says that he's written to the newspaper twice before. Could be two victims we don't know about."

"Any other leads?"

I shrugged. "Not yet. There's not much to go on. Fish is checking the missing person reports. The duffle looks like Army issue, but doesn't have any stenciling on it."

Stan nodded. "By the way," he said, "I got a call from Captain Britt over at the 19th. Seems one of his patrolmen is in the hospital. Britt says he'll be there for a week or two and then drinking his meals through a straw for six months."

"He could stand to lose a few pounds."

"Yeah." Stan smiled. "I know that prick. Name's Gardener. We came up together on the West Side. He's been tossed out of two precincts that I know of. Anyway, Britt asks would you please not bust up anymore of his cops. He's short-handed as it is."

"Can't promise anything," I said, "but I'll do my best." I started to go, then turned back. "Hey, where's Tilly? I want to meet his new partner."

"Gloria Kingston."

"Yeah."

"They're out. Somebody burgled a jewelry store over on Halstead."

13

"We need to have a little chat," he said, putting a gloved hand on her shoulder.

"Huh?" she answered.

"I followed you from the Union Bus Depot."

She blanched a little at that. "You a cop?"

He smiled and nodded.

"Haven't seen you around."

"Haven't been around," he answered.

"Lemme see your badge."

He reached into his coat and pulled out a badge. It disappeared back into his pocket.

"What are we going to do about this?" he said.

She shrugged. "I know the drill. Where do you want it?"

"My car's as good as anywhere."

She stood up. He smiled again, showing his perfectly white teeth. This wouldn't be too bad, she thought.

"Did you get the cash out of the handbag?" he said, as they walked together toward the exit.

She shook her head. "Wasn't anything in it," she lied.

"Give it here."

He rifled through it for a moment, then tossed it onto the tracks.

14

I woke with a pounding in my head courtesy of Ned's generosity down at McGurty's. He'd finally heard from his son, Augie, and the drinks were, for the squad at least, on his tab. I opened my eyes, focused on the cracking plaster on the ceiling, and decided that the water spot now directly above my head looked more like Groucho Marx than St. Brigid. Or that maybe the patron saint of Ireland had grown a mustache during last night's rainstorm.

I eased myself up and swung my legs onto the floor, ruefully aware of the rusty springs singing that song that all old beds warble when announcing any sort of activity. I squinted my eyes against the light and bounced lightly a couple of times listening to the tell-tale creak. Violet had visited my room twice and, after having listened to the amorous going-ons of everyone else through the paper-thin walls, and then having been leered at on her way out by almost every man in the hotel, had stated, quite firmly, that she wouldn't be visiting again until I had procured a less-noisy set of bedsprings. She'd be staying with her friend Miranda.

I worked my knee gingerly in an effort to loosen the joint. My room was a dump, but I couldn't complain much. It was the cheapest place I could find within walking distance of the station.

The old rat-trap hotel rented rooms by the week, the day, or the hour, depending on how fancy you liked your accommodations. Weekly rates were seven bucks and included a dresser, a lamp, one chair, a bed, and moderately laundered sheets every Sunday. The daily rate was three bucks, and included the bed and a light on a stand. Hourlies paid a buck and a half and got a bare bulb, half a mattress, and all the bedbugs they could carry home with them.

Being a weekly renter, I kept my clothes in the dresser, my two suits and whatever laundry I could manage in the sink hanging on a wire strung between corners, and the rest of my possessions in a steamer trunk stuck in the corner.

The lavatory was down the hall. The five men who occupied the third floor, of which I was one, had worked out a system over the months we'd lived there. We could be in and out of the bathroom, shaved and showered, in four minutes. I was generally the second one in. If I overslept, I could still slide in at number three. If I was nursing a hangover, I'd be last.

I listened as the shower down the hall clanked on and then, after a couple of minutes, back off, then spent another two minutes stretching, getting my kit and towel, and limping down the hall. The door to the bathroom swung open just as I walked up. Good timing.

"How you doing, Merl?"

"Headache," I said through half closed eyes. I didn't want to chat. Bobby Molony, an ex-sailor, was a nice enough fellow, but he liked to talk, and his favorite subject was how he lost his leg on Pago Pago. I'd now heard several versions that included a heroic one man attack on a Jap machine gun nest, hand to hand combat with a Samurai, and a booby-trapped trip wire deep in the occupied jungles. The easiest one to believe was the one he'd told after he'd finished half a bottle of rotgut gin. That story ended with his buddy Bill dropping a cargo net full of used airplane parts on him after pushing the wrong button on the ship's crane.

"Looks like it's going to be another scorcher! I remember this one day on Pago Pago..."

"Yeah," I said, cutting him off. "Scorcher. Hey, I think Oscar is up and at 'em. He was talking last night about finding someone to go to the races with this afternoon. Better catch him before he leaves."

"Really? Neat-o! Great idea! Thanks!"

I shouldered past him and watched as he cheerfully hopped on his one leg, buck naked, down the hall toward Oscar's room. I wasn't lying. Oscar, who had the room next to mine, *was* up and he was *always* looking for someone to accompany him to the races.

"Hey! Merl! I forgot..."

I opened the door back up and squinted down the hall at Bobby. He was still hopping. He always hopped, he said, to keep his balance, but it was quite disconcerting to watch him from the front in his current state of undress, especially from a distance of fifteen feet or so.

"We're having a penny poker game in the lobby tonight. Just the guys on the floor. Wanna join us?"

I thought for a moment, then shrugged. "Sure. Sounds great. What time?"

"Eight sharp," said Bobby with a big grin. "And don't bring that Fish guy with you."

"I don't play poker with Fish," I said, returning his smile. "You shouldn't either."

I closed the door, noting that two of my four minutes had already expired, then turned the shower on hot, or as hot as it would go, dropped the towel to the floor, and hung my shaving mirror next to the shower head onto the nail that the management had so thoughtfully provided. The pipes clanked as the luke-warm, rust-colored water rattled up from the basement and after a few half-hearted spurts, began a steady drizzle more suited to watering a potted plant than taking a shower.

In addition to my mirror, my kit contained a bar of Swan soap, a Gillette safety razor, a styptic pencil in a plastic case, and a bottle of Wildroot, all presents from Violet. The soap I liked particularly well, it being suited to both showering and shaving.

The razor I could take or leave. I hadn't gotten used to it yet and still preferred the straight razor I kept in my trunk. The Wildroot was reserved for Fridays.

I lathered my face and hadn't scraped the blade across my whiskers a couple of times before I drew blood. Deep. "Damn it!" I said through clenched teeth, then looked in the mirror to spot the damage. I couldn't see the cut. Just blood. A lot of blood, it seemed to me, turning the soap on my face a frothy red, and dropping like rubies from my chin down to the floor of the shower.

I watched the blood swirl around the drain and thought about the girl on Everette's table. Something... I concentrated on the reddening vortex at the bottom of the shower and lost the thought.

The next thing I knew there was a pounding on the door. "Merl! C'mon! What are ya, jerkin' off? I gotta get to work."

I blinked the water out of my eyes. "Yeah. Sorry Oscar," I hollered back. "I got a late start."

"You gotta quit talkin' to Bobby in the mornings. It screws up the schedule."

"Yeah. I know. I'll be out in a few."

"Well, hurry up, will ya?"

I finished showering, dried off and, gritting my teeth, applied the styptic pencil to stem the bleeding on my neck. Aluminum sulfate. Gritting my teeth didn't stop me from howling. Nothing hurts worse than a styptic pencil and I say that having been shot more than once. I wrapped the towel around my waist, collected my kit, and opened the bathroom door. Oscar and the other two guys on the floor, Herm and Glenn were standing there, looking concerned.

"You okay?" said Glenn. "We heard you yell."

"Yeah. Thanks. Just cut myself."

"So we see," said Oscar, grimacing in empathy. "You're still bleeding. Styptic ain't gonna help that, You'd better get some plaster."

I nodded, gave a half-hearted smile, then, one hand holding

my thumb over the cut, the other holding up my towel, limped back to my room.

When I walked out the front door a few minutes later, Fish was waiting for me with a cup of joe in each hand. He handed me one of them.

"Thanks," I said.

"What did you do to your neck?" Fish asked.

"Shaving," I muttered.

"You ought to be using one of those new safety razors. I don't like 'em much, but at least you won't cut your jugular."

"You have news?"

"I have news," said Fish. "But before my news—have you seen Tilly's new partner?"

"Gloria something-or-other?"

"Yeah. Gloria Kingston."

I took a sip of coffee and grinned. "She's a dish?"

"In a word. Mrs. Tilly Brown is *not* going to be happy."

"I don't think Tilly's thrilled either. He didn't want a skirt for a partner."

"He'll get over it," said Fish. "Wait till you see her!"

"She's a dame, Fish. A *dame.*"

"Aaa, that's what I think, too, but Ziba says give her a chance. No need to rush to judgement, she says, and she's right. What if this gal's cracker-jack? The world is changing and who's to say. Look, we've got women riveting airplanes, we've got women welding ships. Ziba says..."

I interrupted, not at all interested in Ziba's view of women in the workplace. "Okay, fine. Quit harping."

"Now, it'd be different if she wasn't a looker."

I laughed. "That's the Fish I know. Now what's your news?"

"First of all, there's nothing in the missing persons list. No women the age of our victim. Not in the last few days."

"Didn't think so."

"Secondly, you read the *Times* last night?"

Yesterday's visit to the newspaper office popped back into my consciousness. "I picked up a copy on my way home, but left it down at McGurty's. I haven't read it."

"Hmm..." said Fish, pulling a folded newspaper out from under his overcoat. "Here you go. Right there on page twelve."

I flipped open the paper with my free hand, already folded by Fish to page twelve, and scanned the page. My eye immediately went to a column titled "Dear Priscilla." I recognized the second letter right away.

"Uh oh," I said.

"I *knew* you wrote it," chortled Fish. "I knew it as soon as I read it. Why didn't you tell me?"

"Some kid came and yanked it out of the typewriter while I was standing there. I figured the typesetter would know it was a joke and scrap the whole thing."

"Well, needless to say, the editor thinks you wrote it and he wants to see you. The owner of the paper wants to see you, the commissioner wants to see you 'cause he's pals with the owner, and the chief wants to see you 'cause the commissioner wants to see you." Fish took a long sip of his coffee. "Probably the typesetter's gonna want to see you, 'cause he's just been fired."

"Who's first?" I sighed.

"Maybe you should call the mayor," suggested Fish.

After a leisurely breakfast, Fish and I walked into the *Times* lobby and were immediately accosted by the security guard.

"Police," I said, holding up my badge. Fish held up his as well.

"You guys Cahill and Biederman?" asked the guard.

"Yeah," said Fish, puzzled. "How'd you know?"

"You're expected. Seventh floor." He pointed at the elevator.

"Thanks," I said, with a sigh. "I think."

We walked to the elevator and gave a polite nod to the operator, a middle-aged black man turned out in black trousers, a starched white shirt and a red bow tie.

"Seven," I said.

"That's the executive offices," said the operator. "You sure?"

"We've been summoned," said Fish.

"You're the boss."

The elevator dinged as it passed every floor and we watched as the needle swung in a clockwise arc from the "L" to the seven. The operator pulled hard on a lever and we lurched to a stop. Then he opened the door for us, smiled a smile made whiter by his very black face, and gestured toward a door across the hall.

"Right there. You all have a good day," he said, closing the elevator behind us as we exited.

I knocked on the door.

"Yeah!" came a yell from inside.

I opened the door and went inside followed by Fish at a respectful distance. He didn't want to get any of this on his suit.

Russell Stewart was sitting on a leather davenport. There was another man beside him. A sour, mousy guy. I pegged him as a lawyer, or maybe an accountant. The other guy in the room I recognized. Samuel E. Thomason. He was sitting behind a huge desk made of a half-mile of mahogany.

"You Cahill?" asked Thomason.

"Yeah," I said.

"I'm Sam Thomason. I own this paper," he said, getting up and coming across the room with his hand extended. "I saw you when you were with the Bears. You were quite a player. Saw you play for Knute Rockne, too." He shook my hand heartily. "Glad to meet you."

"Ditto."

"Fish Biederman," said Fish, appearing by my side and introducing himself.

"Fish?" said Thomason. "What an odd appellation."

"Appellation? What the hell does that mean?"

"Your name. Fish. Uncommon to say the least."

"Short for Fishel."

"Well, glad to make your acquaintance, Detective Biederman," said Thomason, shaking his hand in turn. "You gentlemen have a seat. I'd like to have a word, if you don't mind."

I looked at Fish. If he was as confused as I was, he didn't show it. He simply smiled and took a seat in one of the two huge leather wingbacks facing the davenport. I took the other. Thomason leaned against the edge of his desk and placed his hands, palms down, on the polished wood.

"We have a problem," he said. "There was a column that appeared in our paper yesterday evening. Perhaps you saw it. 'Dear Priscilla?'"

I nodded. Fish said, "Pretty good column."

"Here's our problem. The city council is having an emergency meeting this afternoon to decide on whether they're going to pull our business license for publishing that column. Apparently they feel that it flies in the face of common decency."

"They can do that?" I asked.

"*Of course they can't!*" spat Thomason, bristling and immediately defiant, glaring with the righteous indignation of a seasoned defender of the First Amendment. "I dare them to try. I'll sue them every way to Christmas." Seeing our startled looks, he relaxed. "No, our problem is that we don't actually know for sure who wrote it."

"I wrote it," I said. "I didn't think your paper would *print* it."

"I thought so," said Russell Stewart, without smiling.

"You already know Russell," said Thomason. He gestured towards the mousy guy. "This is Norman Ledbetter. He's in charge of our circulation. Norman, what's our average daily circulation?"

"About three hundred thousand."

"And what's the circulation of the *Tribune*?"

"Half a million."

Thomason raised his hands and splayed his fingers outward in a gesture of helplessness. "It's all about advertising dollars, gentleman. The higher our circulation, the more we can charge for advertising. Our paper costs the average joe three cents. That's not where our money is made. Understand?"

Fish and I nodded but didn't say anything.

"The biggest accounts go to the paper with the highest

circulation. It's only common sense. They have to pay more, but they feel it's worth it for the extra exposure."

"We get it," said Fish. "Higher circulation, more advertising money."

"Exactly," said Thomason. "Norman, how many papers did we sell last night?"

"All of them."

"Which was?"

"Well, we did two runs. Four-hundred fifty thousand."

"And?"

"And, if we reprint the 'Dear Priscilla' column like we promised, we'll sell another half million tonight."

"So, you see, Detective Cahill, your column is a smash. People are buying papers just to read it."

"Yeah," I said. "So?"

"So," said Russell, getting up off the couch, "we want to hire you."

I looked around the room. Norman Ledbetter was studying me with a steady gaze. Thomason had already sized me up, or thought he had, and settled against his desk, his arms folded and a smile playing across his lips. Russell Stewart, the editor of the *Times*—the *Chicago Times!*—looked at me without expression. I blew some air disgustedly through pursed lips. What kind of newspaper sells out for a gag of a column? I was pretty sure I was gong to cancel my subscription on the way out.

I sneered as nicely as I could and shook my head. "I've got a job. I don't want to be no Agony Aunt."

"Hang on," said Fish. "How much will you pay him?"

Thomason smiled and looked from me to Fish to me. "We can start you at fifty a week."

"Two hundred a week," said Fish.

"Don't be ridiculous," said Norman Ledbetter.

"We can go as high as seventy five," said Thomason, keeping his eyes locked with mine. I didn't blink.

"One-fifty," countered Fish. "Three columns, and he doesn't

have to come in except to drop it off. He'll also need someone to open the mail and maybe choose the letters."

Thomason nodded and glanced at Fish. "Wednesday, Saturday and Sunday. Then we can run Sunday's column again on Monday. We can do that. But not for one-fifty. One hundred twenty-five." He turned back to me. "Okay with you?"

I looked over at Fish. He smiled and nodded.

"Not quite," I said. "What about Amy Rogers?"

"She's gone. Already left Chicago. She wouldn't even tell us where she was going."

"What do you mean she's left Chicago?" exploded Fish.

"I told her to contact the precinct," said Stewart. "Those were the first words out of my mouth right after she stormed in and quit. I take it she did not do so."

"No she did not," Fish said sourly.

Thomason turned to me. "So how about it? One hundred a week?"

"I believe the offer was one twenty-five," said Fish.

Thomason smiled. "So it was."

"And just for that little dodge, he'll take a month's salary in advance."

I'd walked into the *Times* building expecting to be fricasseed by extremely well-connected big-shots. Now they seemed to be intent on making me rich. My salary with the department was just under two grand a year.

"Okay, a month in advance." said Thomason. "Well?"

I thought the offer over for about two more seconds. "Yeah. I'll do it."

Thomason clapped his hands together and Russell Stewart beamed. Even Norman looked happy.

"Great," said Thomason. "I'll have legal draw up a contract."

"Just one thing," said Russell. "You can't tell anyone. It has to remain a secret. We can't have anyone finding out that Priscilla is a man."

"No problem," I said. "You think this is something I want getting out? What about the people at the paper? Won't they squeal?"

"We're the only ones who will know about it," said Russell, rubbing his chin thoughtfully. "Tell you what. My niece is working over in fashion. I'll have her transferred and she can be your secretary. You won't have to come in at all. We'll arrange for her to drop off the letters and pick up your column. As far as everyone else is concerned, Priscilla is incognito."

I nodded. "That works for me. When do I start?"

"We're re-running your first column tonight," said Russell. "Can you have another one ready for tomorrow?"

"Absolutely."

15

"The good thing," I said, starting the car for our short ride back to the precinct, "is that we can monitor the letters that come in. We'll know if this psycho writes to Dear Priscilla again."

"No," corrected Fish, "the good thing is you've just upped your salary by more than six large a year. You can afford to get some new gabardines. You're making me look bad."

"I like this suit." I glanced down. Gray rumpled wool had always been a good look for me.

"That suit was out of fashion when you bought it fifteen years ago."

"Possibly," I agreed. "Maybe I shouldn't have bought two of them. I've been waiting for them to wear out."

"Well, at least your hat is stylish."

"I can afford better digs—that's for sure. And maybe an ice-box."

"You'll be living the highlife," agreed Fish.

"How much do you pull down?" I said. I'd never bothered to inquire before, but since Fish was now privy to my income, I didn't mind asking.

"I don't keep track," Fish lied.

I laughed. Fish knew every penny that went in and out of his pocket and he saw more of them in a month than I'd see this year, even after my bump in income. We turned onto Halstead.

"Hey! Pull over!" ordered Fish. "There's Tilly and Gloria."

"Gloria? You're on a first name basis with her already?"

"Hope to be," said Fish. He took off his hat and smoothed his hair back behind his ears. "She's got some stems, huh?"

I pulled to the curb. Tilly and his new partner were on the sidewalk just behind us, heading in the same direction.

"Need a ride?" called Fish through his open window.

"Don't mind if we do," said Tilly. He opened the back door and climbed in, then scooted across the back seat to make room for detective third class Gloria Kingston. He didn't hold the door open for her.

"Gloria Kingston," said Tilly sullenly, "this is Fishel Biederman."

Fish had already turned all the way around in his seat and was shamelessly ogling Tilly's partner. "A pleasure, I'm sure," he oozed. "Call me Fish. You have a middle name, Gloria?"

"Jill," said Gloria. "Gloria Jill."

"What a beautiful appellation," said Fish, pulling out his new two-dollar word.

"And this is Merlin Cahill," added Tilly, with a nod in my direction. It didn't take a trained detective to know Tilly wasn't happy. Gloria Kingston pretended she didn't notice. I glanced up into the rearview mirror. I could see the two passengers in the back seat, but in actuality, I was only looking at one of them.

"You're the football player," said Gloria in a dark, husky voice that I thought would make Fish faint dead away.

"Yeah," I said. I glanced at myself in the mirror on the off chance that I'd gotten better looking in the last thirty seconds or so. No luck.

"I don't watch football, but my husband did. He said you were aces. Really good till you got hurt."

"Yeah," I grunted. *Husband.*

"You have a husband?" said Fish, never one to play the wait-and-see game.

"Not any more."

"I'm so sorry," said Fish, not sorry at all.

Gloria shrugged. *"C'est la vie."*

Gloria Kingston was a blonde of the sort that made every guy who saw her wish he was twenty-six, rich, and looked like Gene Kelly on a really tall day. She was wearing a full, dark skirt, a blue cotton blouse with a matching scarf, and a long, swing coat that mimicked the overcoats that marked us as cops, but with a feminine flair that was alarmingly attractive.

"Care for a smoke?" said Fish, offering the pack across the back seat.

"Sure," said Gloria. "Thanks." A breeze came through the car and she glanced up. "Hey...you guys know you've got some holes in the car roof?"

"We like the fresh air," said Fish.

"How'd the burglary shake out?" I asked, as Fish twisted around to light Gloria's cigarette.

"It was the brother-in-law," explained Tilly. "Stole some watches last week and hocked 'em. They knew who did it from the get-go. The husband wants him thrown in jail, but the wife was crying up a storm saying it was just a mistake and they didn't want to press charges. I told 'em to give us a call when they made up their minds. How about your case?"

"Got a note from the killer. That's all we have right now. That, and the initials E.P."

"You have a note?" said Gloria.

"He sent it to the *Times*," Fish said. "To 'Dear Priscilla'."

"Did you read that letter yesterday?" asked Gloria. "It was hilarious! I don't know who that Priscilla is, but I'd sure like to meet her. She really tells it how it is. That gal's got moxie."

Fish laughed. I let a faint smile cross my lips. "Yeah," I said. "She must be something."

"We're glad you like her," Fish said. "'Cause you've got a couple hundred letters to go through when we get back to the station."

16

Fish was typing up a domestic dispute, albeit at an excruciating, glacier-like pace. I was on the blower trying to nail down a witness in a two-week-old shooting over on Taylor Street. We had a suspect. We had a gun. We had a victim. It would be nice to have a witness, but the misdeed happened during a crap game by the river and no one felt like talking about it. Too bad for the D.A. He'd have to do his own work for a change.

Ned dropped his newspaper onto his desk. "Italy just declared war on Germany."

"About time," answered Vince. "Wait a minute. I thought Mussolini was Hitler's fat little puppet."

"Yeah, but he was arrested and tossed out of power in July," said Ned. "Then, last month, he reformed his Fascist government in the north, but they... Hey, don't you keep up with this stuff?"

"Um, no," said Vince, going back to his paperwork. "Just tell me what you hear from Augie and leave me the hell out of the rest of it."

"You can tell me when it's over," said Fish.

My "Dear Priscilla" liaison—Russell Stewart's niece—was a girl named Sally Clifford. She was smart, a bit jangled, but efficient as hell. It hadn't taken us long to set up a protocol insuring my anonymity. Sally would open all the mail, choose a week's worth of letters, and pass them on to Fish. Fish would give them to me, I'd type up some answers, and mail them back to Sally in care of Dear Priscilla. We also made sure that Sally stayed on the lookout for any letter from E.P. which was why she showed up at the station on Thursday morning.

"I need to see Detective Cahill," she said, looking right at me, playing her role to the hilt.

"Yeah. That's me."

Fish looked up from his typewriter and eyeballed Sally. "Where's the K?" he asked. "I can't find the damned K."

"Next to the L," Sally said. "Right hand side."

"Thanks," said Fish, resuming his two-fingered pecking. "God, I hate typing!"

"Detective Cahill," said Sally, still in character. "I'm Sally Clifford. I work down at the *Times*. I'm in charge of opening the mail for 'Dear Priscilla.' This came in this morning."

She handed me an envelope. It was addressed to Dear Priscilla, *Chicago Times*, Wacker Drive, in the same spidery script as the envelope in my desk drawer.

"Sit down, Miss Clifford," I said. Fish had stopped his exercise in clerical futility and rolled his chair over to my desk. Sally sat down, put her hands in her lap, and sat ramrod straight, obviously terrified.

Tilly spun his chair to face me. Ned stuck his pencil absently between his teeth. Vince stopped pouring coffee in the middle of his cupful. Gloria, looked at me, wide-eyed, from her desk. All typing had stopped. Even the telephones had stopped ringing. I opened the letter and read it out loud.

Dear Priscilla,
    I would like an answer now. In anticipation of your response, I have left you another package.
E.P.

I turned the letter over. Nothing.

"I expect this gift won't be hard to find," said Fish with a sigh. "The last one wasn't."

"Didn't find the first two," I said. "If there *were* a first two."

"That's a good point," said Stan, who had come out of his office when he saw Sally enter the squad room. "Maybe we should start looking for them."

"He says he wants an answer," said Gloria. "What's the question?"

"Don't know," I said. "The first two letters were tossed."

"Maybe we could get Priscilla to ask him?" suggested Gloria, looking at Sally.

"I'm not her," said Sally. "I'm just a secretary. I can ask though."

"It'll have to be worded exactly right," said Tilly.

"Can I talk to this Priscilla?" I said.

"You'll have to ask the editor," said Sally. "I don't even know who she is."

"I'll go with you," said Fish, standing up.

"Let's get a call out to the beat cops," I suggested. "Better we find this package than some kid playing stickball."

Stan nodded.

"You need some help with this, you let me or Ned or Vince know," said Tilly. Ned and Vince nodded in agreement. "I don't like this," Tilly added. "Don't like it a bit."

I escorted Sally outside and slipped an envelope out of my pocket.

"Here you go," I said. "The column for tomorrow."

Sally nodded and dropped the envelope into her purse. "I don't mind telling you, this thing has me rattled."

"Yeah. We'll get him. Don't worry."

17

It wasn't kids playing stickball that found her. It was one of the grounds keepers at Soldier Field. Fish and I went over to the stadium in the late afternoon, as soon as the call came in. A cold front had blown in off the lake and the city finally felt as though autumn had settled in for the duration. Two beat cops had arrived at the field ahead of us and we parked them outside to keep the hyenas at bay. It wouldn't be long before word of the discovery hit the streets. We went in to find the grounds keeper. He met us just inside the main entrance. I knew him. Ernie Springer.

"I saw some crows flocking on the other side of the equipment shed," he said. In addition to working at Soldier Field, Ernie was also the assistant equipment manager for the Bears and had been for as long as the Bears had been a club.

"I went on down there to shoo 'em off. I don't like crows. Filthy."

Fish and I nodded and waited for him to continue. He looked me over carefully, recognition finally registering on his face.

"You're Merl Cahill, right?"

"Yeah," I said. "How're you doing, Ernie?"

"Jake, I guess. Been a long time since I seen you. I heard you was a cop now."

"Yep. Tell us what you found."

"Like I told you. I was making sure everything was a-okay and I saw them crows and went over to the shed. There was a canvas bag. Green."

"Army bag?" Fish asked.

"Yeah, like that. Anyway, them crows was pecking all over it. I don't like 'em."

"Did you open it?" Fish asked.

"Yeah, I did," said Ernie sadly. "I wished I didn't." A big tear ran down his cheek.

"Yeah," I said, putting a hand on his shoulder. "Where's the bag now?"

"I left it over there." He nodded toward the south end of the field and shook his head. "Who would do such a thing?"

"Don't know," I said, "but we'll find out."

"Anyone else know about this?" asked Fish.

Ernie shook his head. "Everybody's gone. I called over to Wrigley and talked to Coach Anderson. He told me to call down to the precinct. Didn't know *you'd* show up, though."

I knew Hunk Anderson. This was his first full season coaching the Bears, but he'd been my coach at Notre Dame for a couple of years after Coach Rockne had been killed in that plane crash in Kansas. Last year, Hunk and Luke Johnsos took over the coaching duties halfway through the season when George "Papa Bear" Halas headed off to war.

"We had practice down here on Tuesday. Yesterday morning, too. They were working on the turf at Wrigley." He pointed in the direction of the bag. "That wasn't here. I know 'cause I had to get into the shed."

"Thanks, Ernie," I said. "We'll take care of it. You go on home."

The bag was another army duffle, just as blood-soaked as the first one we'd found, and the brief cloudburst that had hit Chicago just before dawn hadn't helped our cause. The bag had been left on the far side of the shed, out of sight, and would have gone unnoticed for a while except for the crows. After a few days, though, the stench would have brought it to someone's attention.

"Your turn to open it," said Fish.

"I wish these guys would quit spoiling the surprise." I knelt beside the bag, dreading what I knew was inside. Ernie hadn't bothered to fasten the bag closed and it only took a glance, once I had lifted the flap that covered the open end, to see what Ernie saw.

"*Jesus,*" I said, my stomach turning over. "Goddammit, Fish. We gotta get this guy."

I took the duffle by the open end, grabbing handfuls of the wet canvas on either side, lifted it off the grass, and set it on end so we could look inside more easily. It wouldn't have stayed upright on its own, so I held it as Fish looked in, poked around, and did a quick inventory.

"Two hands, two feet. Neck and torso. Woman. No head, probably."

"Probably not," I said, looking past Fish's prodding. No nail polish this time, and the fingers on both hands were curled.

"That bag heavy?"

"Heavy enough. You done looking? I wouldn't mind setting it down."

"You notice that there aren't any drag marks?" said Fish. "In the grass, I mean. This duffle bag has to weigh, what? Maybe a hundred and fifty?"

I set the bag down. "Somebody carried it all the way in here." I said. "Not much in the way of footprints either. That shower this morning didn't help."

"Pretty strong guy," said Fish.

"Probably came in one of the side gates," I said. "Or over the fence. It's a good five hundred yards from the entrance."

"Car?" said Fish.

"Don't think so. There aren't any tire tracks and the ground isn't that hard. Anyway, once the gate is locked, a car couldn't get in. When the gate's open, someone would have been here to see it."

"So, we figure the bag was dumped last night?" Fish said.

"That's what I'm thinking."

Fish and I checked the rest of the area, but there wasn't anything to find. The equipment shed was unlocked and we took enough time rooting around to convince ourselves that it wasn't part of the crime scene. It contained bags of lime, a field striper, chains for measuring first downs, a few old footballs—stuff you'd find in any athletic shed in the city. Several college teams used Soldier Field. Even the Bears occasionally played a warm-up game here. I spotted a tarpaulin on one of the shelves and we commandeered it under the jurisdiction of "police business," then started walking the perimeter fence.

There were two other gates, both secured with chains and padlocks, and both a couple hundred yards from the shed. The fence was intact.

"Could have had a key," I said.

"Maybe," said Fish. "Something to think about. That's a heavy bag. Even if I had a key, I couldn't have carried it that far."

"He might have slung it over a shoulder. A big guy could have carried it in."

"Or maybe two guys. You think there might be two of them?"

"Never heard of it before. Two killers working together? A hit maybe, but random killings like this? Doesn't feel right. What if he used a wagon or something?"

"Wheelbarrow?" suggested Fish. "There wasn't one in the shed. And even if he had one, how'd he get the body into the park? That fence is probably seven feet high." He looked thoughtful for a moment, then asked, "Could you throw that duffle bag over the fence?"

I shrugged. "Yeah."

"Easy?"

"Easy."

"So if this guy was as big and strong as you, it wouldn't be any problem."

"True. But how many guys are as big as me?"

"Okay. Let us say, slightly smaller. What are we looking at here?"

I walked up to the fence, stretched my arms to their full

height, and mentally measured the distances, then stepped back a few paces and studied the question for a moment. "The fence is seven feet high. You'd have to go eight feet high, or maybe nine, to make sure you clear it, and at least six horizontally. That's a hell of a throw. Not to mention that the bag is probably slimy and sticky to boot."

"Yeah," agreed Fish.

"To toss a hundred and fifty pound bag that far, you'd have to be strong. The taller you were, the less strong you'd have to be. But make no mistake: if he threw the bag over the fence, this is a big boy."

"What if he stood on something?"

I nodded. "Could have done. The closest point in the fence is about a hundred yards from the shed. Let's look over there and see if we can find something."

"Okay," Fish said.

We ended up walking the whole fence again, this time looking for any blood splattered across the grass where the duffle might have landed after being tossed over, but didn't find anything. Rain.

"You want to wait for the meat wagon, or just take it ourselves?" asked Fish.

"Might as well take it ourselves. It'll end up in the same place and I don't want to hang around here and wait."

Fish and I wrapped the duffle bag in the white canvas tarp. Then I picked up the soggy package, hauled it across the football field, back through the entrance, and over to where we'd parked the Packard. Fish popped the lid and I loaded the whole thing into the trunk. The two cops were still out front, but there wasn't a crowd.

"We got rid of everyone," said the older one, tipping his hat. "If you don't need us anymore, we'll be heading back."

"Appreciate it," I said, watching them walk off.

"How's the knee?" asked Fish. "You're limping again."

"It's okay. That's a long walk with a hundred and fifty pounds of dead weight."

Fish nodded. "Let's get her down to the morgue and see what the autopsy has to say."

I sighed and nodded in agreement. "Sounds like a plan."

"And we could use a plan," said Fish.

18

"Is there a head with this one?" said Dr. Everette. He had donned his fisherman's waders—rubber boots that covered him from his feet to his armpits, and elbow length rubber gloves.

I sighed, stifling a snide comment, and said. "No head."

"I just don't get it," he said.

"It appears to be missing, doesn't it?" said Fish politely, pointing to the pieces of the body lying on the gleaming steel table. "You see, doctor, although there are seven pieces accounted for, the eighth—or 'head' as it were—is missing entirely. This is what we call, in police parlance, 'no head.' It's a technical term, I grant you, but one that perhaps you can grasp, being a medical professional."

"That's not what I meant, smart-ass," snarled the doc. "I just don't get why someone would do this. Sheesh. Allow me to wax rhapsodic once in while, will ya?" He spit a spent cigarette butt onto the floor. "And light me another smoke." He waved his gloved hands in Fish's direction. "I can't do it with these mittens on."

Fish pulled out his deck of Luckys, shook one loose, slipped it out between his lips, and lit it with his Zippo. He stuck it in Everette's mouth and the man sucked on it like it was a milkshake. Fish and I watched the ash grow to almost an inch in a matter of seconds. The doc finally exhaled, relaxed, and began arranging the pieces in front of him in the correct anatomical order—first carefully picking up and studying each limb in turn, then placing it in its correct position alongside the torso. The table was a bloody mess and once the pieces had been arranged, the doctor pulled down a spray nozzle from a retractable hose attached to the ceiling and started rinsing the body. Fish and I stood back and watched as the warm, gentle spray dissolved clots of blood, loosened matted hair and sent a river of crimson flowing off the table and into the drain located in the middle of the floor. After fifteen minutes of washing, the doc was satisfied. He gave a sharp tug on the hose and it reeled itself back into the ceiling. He motioned us back over to the table.

"Same as last time," he said. "Torso, legs, upper and lower arms. Clean, surgical amputation."

"How old is she?" I asked.

The doctor shrugged. "Mid-twenties?" He pulled out a tape measure and ran it neck to feet. "Probably five-seven or eight taking into account her missing head. Brown hair."

"Weight?"

"I weighed her when she came in." He checked his notes. "One forty-three. Add another eight to ten pounds for her head and maybe ten pounds for fluid loss. I'd say around one hundred sixty pounds, give or take. Average." He tilted his head and looked at the body. "Bigger breasts than the last one, but not what you'd call 'well-endowed'. In fact, the two girls are remarkably similar."

"Great," said Fish, in disgust. "Just great. She's not pregnant, is she?"

"Can't say, but she doesn't look like it. I'll be sure to check. Be a hell of a coincidence if she was. Look here though." The doc, held up the piece of arm still attached to her left hand. "The little finger's missing a knuckle. Old wound. Might have happened when she was a kid."

"Might help identify her," said Fish.

"You want me to open her up?"

I shrugged. "Yep. Maybe you'll find something we can use. We'll get back with you."

"I'll do my best," said the doc cheerfully. "You want I should keep this one on ice, too?"

"Yeah," I said.

"Hey," said Fish, when we'd gotten back to the car. "I've got an idea. Why don't you invest some of that big newspaper check with me? Eddie Arcaro's riding at Washington Park this week."

"I don't play the ponies," I said. "Drive."

Fish pushed the starter and the Packard sputtered to life. "How about some craps then? I keep a game going over in the back of Rubenstein's."

I took a drag on my smoke. "Nope. I've been doing some thinking. Now that I'm rich, I'm going to see if I can find some new digs. Maybe an apartment. Or even a house."

"You maybe have a roommate in mind?"

I smiled. "I guess. Maybe. Violet doesn't really like that job in Peoria. She only took it because her grandma was sick and her mother wanted her down there in case she was needed."

We pulled into traffic.

"Granny still sick?" Fish asked.

"She's been sick for years. Vi says that her mom used it as an excuse to get her to move back. Family obligation and all that. At least she didn't go back home. She's in a rooming house with a two mile buffer."

"A little guilt goes a long way," said Fish. "Maybe Mom's Jewish."

"Catholic. Now Vi has to watch Grandma whenever Mom goes out to her USO dances, which, coincidentally, almost always fall on Friday nights. Mom doesn't usually show back up until Saturday afternoon."

Fish laughed. "How does dear old Dad feel about that?"

"He died a few years ago. Then, to top it all off, Vi leads some ladies' Bible class at the church on Sunday morning. Makes for a busy weekend."

"Did she call?"

I shook my head. "Nah. I got a letter Tuesday. She won't call the station—says it's unprofessional—and the flea-bag I live in doesn't even have a telephone." I shrugged. "If she can make it, she makes it. If not, not. That's our battle plan. She's missed a couple of times. I don't sweat it."

Fish laid on the horn just in time to startle a thin woman carrying a bag of groceries back onto the curb. I watched her yell something at the car that was lost in the wind.

"So," Fish said with a smile, "you're thinking that with the extra jack you're pulling down, she could move back to Chicago. What about Grandma and the guilt? The horrible, horrible guilt?"

"I believe that ship has sailed," I said.

"You thinking about getting married?"

"She's been throwing hints around like crazy, but I just don't know. I guess we will eventually."

"She's a nice girl," said Fish philosophically. "Love can grow. Look at me and Ziba. I know dames, my friend, and I know Vi isn't moving in with you unless there is a ring on her finger."

"Maybe not, but she says she's sick and tired of Peoria. And I can help her out with her rent if she needs it. If I've got a place, at least those old bedsprings won't bother her."

"Hey! I know just the thing," said Fish, taking one hand off the wheel to snap his fingers. "There's a nice house over on Canal Street with a view of the river. Don't know why I didn't think of it before. The previous owner turned it over to one of his creditors just yesterday, due to the fact that he was very short of cash and wished to keep his limbs in working order. The *new* owner would very much like to rent it out to an upstanding tenant with a lucrative newspaper contract."

"Let's go look at it."

"It just so happens that I have a key."

"I thought you might."

"By the by, next weekend I'm off the hook," I said. "Vi's going to go down to Springfield for a wedding. One of her girlfriends. Bernice... Beulah... Blanche... something like that. "

"You going with her?"

I looked at Fish as though he was crazy. "Home game, Fish. What're you thinking?"

Fish nodded. "Yeah. I forgot."

"Anyway, we should do something."

"Something besides work, you mean."

Fish's new acquisition on Canal Street was within easy walking distance of the police station and I was pleasantly surprised. Fish was known as a slumlord, but this was a fairly new home, only a few years old at most. The house was a two-bedroom bungalow; white clapboard exterior—simple and elegant with a hip roof broken by a dormer on the front, and a bay on the left side. From the porch, there was indeed a view of the Chicago River, although if there happened to be a train going by, the view would be obscured entirely.

Fish opened the door and we walked into a spacious living room devoid of furniture.

"The previous owner got his stuff out pretty fast," I said.

"He wanted to get out of the state as quickly as possible."

"I see."

We moved through the living room, admiring the stone fireplace on the left wall, and into the dining room, lighted by the bay window I'd noticed when we walked up. The dining room opened both into the kitchen behind it and onto a hall which led to the two bedrooms and the bath. There was a back porch as well. I was impressed. I'd never lived in quite so fine a place.

"Okay," I said. "How much?"

"Ten bucks a week," said Fish.

"I pay seven now."

"So, it's a good deal."

"You could get more for this place," I said. "You could get twenty, twenty-five easy."

"Yeah. Probably. But then I wouldn't have the tenant indebted to me."

"When can I move in?"

"Tomorrow if you want."

"Suits me. Everything I own fits in my steamer trunk." I looked around. "I'll need some furniture though. My bed belongs to the rooming house. The dresser and chair, too."

Fish rubbed his hands together. "Leave it to me."

19

"We might have caught a break," said Gloria as I came in the next morning. "Sergeant Sweeney called in. He found a woman's handbag in the train station. He and his partner went through it. He says there's a photograph of a girl who matches the description of your last victim."

I nodded. "Fish here?" I asked.

Gloria shook her head. "Come and gone. He said he had some business to take care of. Anyway, Sweeney's bringing the handbag over. It was down on the tracks."

"He's on the way now?"

"He'll be a few minutes. Also, Tilly has the flu or something. He called in sick."

"No problem." I looked around the squad room. "Well, till Fish gets back anyway, you can work with me this morning."

"Glad to." Gloria gave me a smile that I felt all the way down to my socks. She was wearing a lavender skirt and matching jacket with an emerald green blouse that matched her eyes. It was a look. A great look. I gave an involuntary glance down at my own clothes. Yep. Gray. I tried to smooth out my tie.

"I've got to go through the missing persons list this morning. See if there's anything there."

"Did you read the latest 'Dear Priscilla' column?" Gloria asked. "She's a stitch!"

She opened a desk drawer, pulled out a section of the *Times*, snapped it open and started reading aloud.

Dear Priscilla,

My husband is in the navy and is in the Pacific on a battleship. Before he left, he moved his mother in with me and told me I should take care of her even though she has a perfectly good house right down the street.

Priscilla, she is a witch! She criticizes me at every turn, snoops through my bureau when I'm out, insists on using my bathroom when she has one of her own, and has now taken to ringing a little bell whenever she wants me to wait on her. In addition, she refuses to let me use her rationing coupons, saying that she'd rather give them to her friends and go without. Here's the thing. She doesn't go without. She just uses mine! What can I do?
Signed,
Sick and Tired

I smiled to myself and walked over to the coffee pot. "Sounds like a real conundrum."

"Yeah," said Gloria, with a sniff. "I'd throw the old bat out. But listen to what Priscilla says."

Gracious Reader,

Far be it from Priscilla to cast aspersions on difficult loved ones, but I will admit they can occasionally be a bit trying. Priscilla has two words for you: horse laxatives. They're quite cheap and can be gotten at any feed store--no rationing coupon required. Of course, you'll want to make sure that YOUR bathroom door is locked, her toilet seat has been removed and that all the plumbing is up to snuff. After three days, I suspect your dear mother-in-law will move back to her own house, no questions asked.

I had to admit it. I liked the sound of Gloria's voice. I closed my eyes for a second and tried to think how Violet's voice compared. I couldn't even remember it. Not a good sign.

"Horse laxatives! I swear…" Her voice trailed off in a low laugh as she put the newspaper back into the drawer and slid it closed.

"So, did you get hold of Priscilla?" she asked.

"Umm…as a matter of fact, I did."

"What's she like? I mean, I think she's great."

"She's just sort of normal. Kinda plain, in fact. Nothing special."

"Will she let you use the column to contact the killer?"

"She seemed willing to help," I said.

"He wants an answer and we don't know the question. What are you going to ask him?"

"Not sure."

"Aw, c'mon," said Gloria. "I'm here. I'm on the squad. I know you guys don't like me, but at least give me a chance."

"Okay, fine," I said, sitting down at my desk. "Here's what I'm thinking. How many questions could this pervert ask Dear Priscilla that, number one, demand an answer, and number two, are accompanied by dismembered bodies."

"He wants to meet her," said Gloria.

"Or says he does."

"Doesn't make sense. Why tell her about the gifts? She'd be terrified of him. She wouldn't agree to a meeting."

"Me and Fish think he'd be killing the girls anyway. That's not part of it."

"So why write to Priscilla?"

"He's screwing with us." I tapped my knuckles on the desk and thought for a second. "I don't know. Could be anything. Maybe, on some level, he wants to get caught. Maybe he feels guilty about it. I think he's not counting on meeting Priscilla, but hey—" I shrugged. "A lot of things could happen. Maybe the police talk Priscilla into agreeing to a rendezvous so they can catch this guy. Maybe her editor thinks it'd make a great story and she goes along. Maybe she's one of those career women who want to make a name on the crime beat." I gave Gloria a look. "Maybe she just likes excitement."

"She'd have to be crazy," said Gloria. "So, what are you going to do?"

"Send someone to meet him."

Gloria jumped to her feet. "I'll do it."

I looked at her and shook my head. "See?"

She sniffed and smoothed the front of her skirt. "That's not the same thing and you know it. I'm a detective."

"You know, 'Dear Priscilla' isn't the only Agony Aunt in the city. We should check the other papers. Maybe they're all getting letters."

"Priscilla's the most famous."

"Sure. Now. But when he sent the first letters, she wasn't. She was just one of who-knows-how-many."

"I'll start checking," said Gloria.

"Do that. Is Stan in?"

"Yeah. But he's in a bad mood."

"Never mind then. I'll wait."

I was still waiting, going over the missing person reports, when the purse came in— a nondescript, beat-up, brown leather handbag. It didn't look new, but then it wouldn't be, with all the leather in the country being appropriated for the war effort. Sweeney brought it in, brandishing his prize like a beagle bringing in a dead squirrel.

"I spotted it on the tracks," he said proudly. "This morning, first thing. I thought you'd want to see it straight away." He lowered his voice. "There's some clues inside."

"Excellent work," I said. "Congratulations, Sergeant Sweeney, you may have broken the case."

Sweeney beamed. "Always glad to do my part. You think you might be kind enough to mention me in the official report? That is, if the handbag comes to anything?"

"It would be my pleasure," I said.

"Thank you very much, sir." Sweeney saluted smartly and marched out of the squad room.

"What was *that* about?" asked Gloria.

"It always pays to encourage the help. Doesn't cost anything and I get everything first. If I want to growl at someone, I'll growl at you."

"Gee, thanks. How about fingerprints?"

"Look at this thing," I said, holding it up with a handkerchief. The purse was covered in the dirt and dust of the railroad tracks. There were spots of smeared oil and it was crushed on one end. "What do you think?"

Gloria shrugged. "I guess not," she conceded.

I opened the handbag and dumped the contents onto my desk. There was a lipstick, a broken compact, a hairnet, a fountain pen and two pencils, an empty change purse, a bottle of vitamins, a handkerchief, and a letter with an address and stamp affixed. Emma Anderson, St. Margaret's Hospital, Montgomery, Alabama. No return. There was also a snapshot of a girl in her early twenties, her dark hair pulled back in a ponytail. She was wearing a light-colored cardigan and skirt, and was leaning against the fender of a convertible with her sweater sleeves pushed up to her elbows and a bottle of beer in her hand. On the back was written "Emma, 1942."

Of more interest to me was a Willard car battery guarantee receipt. It listed the make of car—a 1938 Plymouth—and the dealer's name and address. Better than that, though, was the name and address of the purchaser. Betty Anderson of 122 4th Street, Oneonta, Alabama. It was dated a year ago.

Gloria had been looking over my shoulder, but now I was unmistakably aware of her presence. Her corn-silk hair brushed my cheek as she reached all the way across the desk, bending over to pick up the envelope. I did a double blink, willing my gaze away from the swell at the top of her blouse. It may have been my imagination, or maybe just fancy, but I sensed that she was a lot closer than Tilly might have been given the same situation. The scent of gardenias hit me like a flower truck. I didn't squirm. I could take everything she could dish out, no matter how terrifying.

She read the address aloud, then opened the letter and dropped the envelope in front of me.

"It's to Dear Sis," said Gloria, quickly scanning the letter. "Betty found a job as a waitress and found a room, too. Emma's a nurse."

"New to the city, I guess. Think you can find a telephone number for Oneonta? Maybe there's a switchboard or something."

"If there is one," said Gloria, "I'll find it."

"Seven'll get you ten that this ain't nothing," I said gloomily, scooping the contents back into the handbag and picking up the missing person reports. "Police work isn't this easy. It's just a purse that Betty Anderson lost on the tracks. Maybe we can get it back to her, though."

"Maybe," said Gloria.

"Cahill!" yelled Stan Sherman. "You and Biederman get over to LaSalle National Bank. Robbery in progress. Uniforms already on the scene."

"Biederman's not..." started Gloria.

"Dammit!" I said, grabbing my hat and coat. I looked around the squad room hoping that one of the guys would magically appear. Didn't happen.

"Get your diapers on," I said, setting my jaw. "Let's go."

20

It was a six minute drive to the bank. I made it in four. We pulled in behind two police cars positioned at opposing angles in front of the LaSalle building. Four uniforms crouched behind the hoods, pistols drawn. Gloria and I came up behind them and identified ourselves.

"There's three of them," said a very rotund officer, without relinquishing his gaze on the double front doors. He, like his partner, rested his gun on the hood of the Ford with both hands, drawing a bead on whoever was getting ready to walk out.

"How do you know?" asked Gloria.

Her voice brought his head around. "We got dames working detective now? Let's hope she doesn't get us killed."

"Ain't it a kicker?" I said, then repeated the question. "How do you know there are three?"

"Guy was coming out just as they got dropped off," said Pudgy. "He saw the guns and was out the door before they could stop him. He said there were three men. Luckily, Lee and Andy were driving by. He flagged them down."

"Lee Hogan? Vince's boy?" I asked.

"Yeah."

"How many guns?"

"Guy saw one Tommy and one shotgun. Already heard the shotgun go off. I'm betting the other one's packing as well."

"Can't discount it." I didn't doubt the witness. The Thompson submachine gun had become famous worldwide as the Chicago Typewriter during the mob wars a decade ago. There wasn't a citizen that didn't know its distinct look with its double grips, short barrel and round drum magazine. A shotgun was not as distinctive, but was equally recognizable. If that's what the guy said he saw, I was inclined to believe him.

"You send anyone around back?" asked Gloria. "You know, in case they decide to leave by the back door?"

Pudgy looked up at Gloria. "Yeah, well, I was just about to send Lee to check on that."

"Oh, they're probably still in there," I said. "Tell you what. We'll check the back. You watch the front. Don't let anyone leave. If they come out shooting, shoot back."

"Planning on it," said Pudgy with a slow smile, returning his attention to the front door.

Gloria and I went around the building and set up behind a black four-door Ford in the alley. There was one back entrance to the bank, if you didn't count the fire escape that zigzagged up the four floors. The rickety iron ladders had landings at three windows festooned with iron grates, and ended twelve feet off the ground.

"Think they'll come out this way?" Gloria whispered. She had her ·38 Police Special in her right hand. I hadn't noticed it before now. I had my Colt automatic out as well. It was bigger, faster and packed more punch. My ·38 was still on my hip.

"Yeah," I said. "This is probably their car. I didn't see one in the front." I nodded toward her revolver. "Where do you keep that thing, anyway?"

She held up her gun. "This? Lot's of places. Tell you what. I'll hide it again and let you guess where it is. "

"Maybe later," I said with a smirk, looking toward the back of the building. "You wait here."

She glared at me. "I don't think so. I'm perfectly capable of taking care of myself. Just think of me as one of the boys."

I gritted my teeth and cursed under my breath. *Dames.*

"Then try not to get shot. And, more importantly, try not to get *me* shot."

Her mouth set a hard line, but she didn't say anything as she followed me down the alley beside the bank. We cleared the rear of the building and saw two cars parked in the back lot. We took cover behind the red and white Buick coup, the one nearest to the back door.

"I'm betting that when they come out," I said, "the back door will close behind them and lock. Don't get jumpy. Give them enough time to get all the way out."

We didn't have long to wait. A minute later, the back door eased open and a head pushed out and looked up and down the alleyway. I motioned to Gloria to stay hidden and quiet.

"All clear," came a heavy whisper from the first head through the door. He came out like a mouse out of its hole, furtively, looking first left, then right, then left again. He was a little guy wearing a long coat and a bowler—the coat, presumably to hide the shotgun he was carrying; the bowler, to make him look like Edward G. Robinson in *Little Caesar*. He came into the alley, knees bent, shoulders around his ears, and angled at the waist as though being hunched over would make him less conspicuous. Right behind him was a taller man wearing another long coat, two hands cradling his Tommy gun. The third man out wore a suit and looked terrified. He had both hands on his head and shook like a robin laying goose eggs. Hostage.

The last of the bank robbers carried a large leather Gladstone that strained against the straps holding it closed. His other hand held a revolver that swept the alley, following his gaze. He stood in the doorway and surveyed the street behind the bank.

"Get in the car," the fourth man said in a growled whisper. He gave the hostage a shove toward the other car in the lot—a big, dark green Plymouth.

"Please," said the hostage. "Please don't hurt me. I have a wife. I have three children..."

Little Caesar turned and hit him in the mouth with the butt of his shotgun. The hostage gave a cry, dropped to his hands and knees on the bricks, and started to spit blood.

"Shut up!" hissed Little Caesar, "or I'll kill you right now!"

"Don't kill him yet," whispered Tommygun. "We need him."

"Get in the car," said Gladstone, one foot still inside the threshold. "I'm not gonna tell you again."

I could feel Gloria's muscles tense as though she was getting ready to jump so I put a hand on her knee, gave a slight shake of my head, and felt her relax. As soon as I heard the back door of the building close with a bang, I motioned her to the rear end of the car. I'd come around the hood where I would have the drop on them as soon as they cleared the doorway. Gloria would end up behind all four. If no one acted stupid, we'd all be home, safe and dry, in time for lunch—that is, if we could consider the Illinois State Pen these idiots' new home.

My plan might have worked like a charm had Pudgy the Cop not come bursting through the back door at that very moment followed closely by his partner. Pudgy had his gun in both hands and yelled "Police!" He may have been getting ready to yell something else, but the words never made it out of his mouth. The double-blast of the shotgun missed him, hitting the cornice just above the door and showering him with grit and spent pellets, but the long burst from the submachine gun tore through Pudgy, his partner, and most of the back wall. The man with the Gladstone calmly took a step toward the well-dressed hostage, still on his hands and knees, and shot him in the back of the head. I saw patrolman Lee Hogan peer carefully around the other corner of the building, both hands wrapped around his ·38 special.

Gloria had been moving to the back of the car and instead of stopping when the shooting started, continued on and was now in full sight of the three gunmen. Her gun was shoulder high as she assumed a classic two-handed shooting stance.

"Drop it!" she yelled.

If the three bank robbers were startled to see a great-looking blonde pointing a gun at them, they recovered in a heartbeat. Tommygun needed only a second to pull the bolt back on his Thompson. It was half a second longer than he had. I shot him in the chest and the machine-gun clattered to the bricks. Little Caesar, who had unloaded both barrels of his shotgun at Pudgy the Cop, now found himself pointing an empty gun at Gloria— although I doubted that she realized it wasn't loaded.

From where I was standing in front of the car, Gladstone was directly behind Tommygun. I had to wait for the dying man to fall before taking the shot and he was taking his own sweet time, inspecting the bright red stain in the middle of his chest even as he went to his knees. Gladstone's gun was on Gloria and he was already pulling the trigger. I fired a shot anyway and saw a slug splash into Tommygun's head as he dropped. Didn't matter— he was already dead and so was Gloria. I couldn't save her. Lee Hogan, coming around the side of the bank, his pistol in firing position, couldn't save her either. It was too late.

I heard the next concussion in slow motion, expecting to see Gloria's chest or head erupt in a shower of crimson. Instead, Gladstone's head exploded as he threw his hands into the air and fell face first over the body of the hostage.

Fish stood in the doorway, a smoking scattergun in his hands and a very serious look on his face. Little Caesar, his options fast disappearing, ran towards Gloria.

"Stop!" she yelled, but I could see her gun hand wavering. He saw it too and didn't stop. I fired one round into the back of his knee. The shotgun skittered across the bricks as the little man fell with a yelp. There was calm for a brief moment, then Little Caesar started whimpering. I walked over and picked up his gun. Gloria stood about six feet in front of the writhing body, looking dazed and watching the blood beginning to pool under his shattered leg. The whole episode—from when Pudgy had come through the back door, to five people dead on the ground— had taken less than twenty seconds.

Fish walked up to Little Caesar, looked down at him and said, "You killed two cops. I'm gonna have to sing at both their funerals."

Then he pulled out his revolver and shot him in the face. Six dead.

"Jesus," whispered Gloria. *"Jesus Christ."*

Lee Hogan walked up, holstering his gun. "You guys good?" he asked with the false bravado of youth.

"Fine," I said. "You okay, Fish?"

"Yeah."

Lee looked at Gloria and shook his head with a smirk. "Damn. Froze up. You know, I gotta say that I agree with Dad on this one. A skirt's got no business..."

Gloria snarled, whipped her gun to shoulder height, pointed toward Lee's head, and pulled the trigger.

21

We were three hours cleaning up the mess. The two other uniformed officers—the ones who had been alerted to the robbery by the customer—grimly related the tale of Pudgy's insistence on going in, despite orders to the contrary. We told our story to the chief, including Gloria Kingston's shooting of the driver, the man I'd forgotten about. It was my theory that he'd crept out of the driver's side door during the commotion, seen Fish put a bullet in his compatriot, and decided he'd have to get us all or go down trying. Whatever his motivation, he'd jumped up from behind the hood of the Plymouth, just behind Patrolman Lee Hogan, and was just about to put a slug in the back of his head when Gloria pulled the trigger. One shot. Bridge of the nose.

We also told the chief about Fish's heroic act, shooting Little Caesar just as he was reaching for his concealed derringer.

"Lucky," said the chief, with a wink. "Damned lucky you saw that pocket gun."

"Yep," said Fish. "Of course, now I've got to get a new suit." He looked down at his pale-yellow jacket. "These stains are *not* gonna come out."

Pudgy and his partner would get a hero's funeral—a half-mile parade to the church accompanied by pipes and drums, then carried down the long aisle and back by eight pall bearers, a short two-block ride to the cemetery, and six feet more as Fishel Biederman offered the lonely strains of *Danny Boy* to the grieving widows and families for the price of only ten dollars, paid for by the Chicago Policeman's Benevolence Fund.

Gloria didn't say much, nodding as we told our story first to the chief, and then to the commissioner's deputy. We praised Detective Kingston for her marksmanship, then, just for good measure, threw in some accolades about her courage during the gunfight and her willingness to draw fire away from Fish and myself.

"You want me to put her in for a commendation?" asked Deputy Sheenan, an old cop that had come up through the ranks the hard way and looked more like a railroad tramp in his rumpled suit and scuffed shoes than the Deputy Commissioner.

"Nah," said Fish, watching her walk away. "She may have been in someone else's squad room before she made detective, but she's a rookie as far as we're concerned. Her time will come."

The rest of the afternoon would be spent typing up reports. Seven dead people were cause for a lot of paperwork and it would be me that had to type it. I told Fish that I'd ride back to the station with Gloria. He said he had one more stop to make and then he'd meet us at the precinct.

"You okay?" I said to Gloria as she climbed into the front seat.

"I guess."

"You're shaking."

"I'll be fine. It's my first shoot-out."

"You did okay. Where's your gun?"

She reached behind her back and came out with her revolver. "Never far," she said. "I had it tucked in my belt. Under the jacket."

"Man," I said. "I'll bet I could have found it." I looked over at her. Nothing. So much for my attempt at humorous banter.

During the ride back to the station, Gloria was quiet. As we pulled up, she put her hand on my arm.

"Do you mind if we drive for just a while longer?"

"Fine with me."

I pulled away from the curb, turned on Clinton Street, and headed north.

"I froze out there."

"It happens," I said. "You made up for it."

"I've never shot anyone. I've certainly never *killed* anyone. And I've only been a policewoman for three years. The commissioner and the mayor decided to fast-track me because of the manpower shortage. You know—the war and everything. I just don't know if I..." Her voice trailed off. "Pull over, will you. I've got to throw up."

I did. She did. I pretended she didn't.

I pulled away from the curb and we drove by the post office. Gloria was staring out the window. The silence was uncomfortable. I figured I knew what she was thinking about. Fish.

"Look," I finally said, "Fish and me... we don't mind shooting the bad guys. In fact, I think Fish rather enjoys it. If they would have given up, sure, we'd have taken them in. But once they killed those cops and the shooting started, there was no way they were leaving that alley alive. That driver saw Fish plug that guy. He was dead already."

"Oh, I know." She turned back toward me, her eyes wide and anger showing at the corners of her mouth. "I'm not an idiot. I know the score. I wasn't even thinking about that."

"Yeah? What then?"

She shook her head and didn't answer for a minute. Then, "I didn't even have time to think about it. I just pulled the trigger."

"Exactly what you're supposed to do," I said, "Don't talk it to death."

"But, I couldn't have shot the guy on the ground."

"No one asked you to," I said, my voice taking on an irritated edge.

More silence. Just as uncomfortable.

"You saved my life," she said.

"Not me. Fish. I didn't have the shot."

"Oh. I thought I saw you shoot the man with the suitcase."

"We fired at almost the same time, but I couldn't hit him. The other guy was in the way. Fish got him from behind."

"You got the guy with the machine gun."

I nodded.

"And the other one. The one with the shotgun."

"Yeah."

Gloria thought for a moment, running the sequence of events through her mind. "You shot him in the leg. How did you know he wouldn't shoot me on the way down?"

"Shotgun wasn't loaded," I answered with a shrug. "I didn't want him to take you as a hostage. *You* weren't going to shoot him, so a leg shot was the best bet."

"Oh."

"A head shot might have hit you."

"You mean you might have missed?"

I shook my head. "No, I wouldn't have missed. But I had a ·45. You were right behind him. The slug might have gone through him and hit you."

"Wait a minute. What do you *mean* the shotgun wasn't loaded?"

"Double-barrel shotgun. You have to break it open to reload. There wasn't time. He'd emptied both barrels at the cops when they came through the door."

Gloria looked shocked, but seemed suddenly interested. "I didn't even notice. What else?"

"Huh?"

"What else did I do wrong?"

"You kept coming around the car when the shooting started. You gave up your cover."

"So did you," she said.

"Only when you did. Then I had to take them fast. No choice."

"You and Fish."

"I didn't know he was there until he shot the guy with the suitcase."

"Good thing he was," she said.

"Good thing," I agreed.

We arrived at Union Station and I turned east on Jackson, intent on making the block and coming back down Canal Street.

"Thank you," Gloria said.

"It was Fish," I repeated.

"You, too," she said, relaxing back in her seat. "Now... tell me about Violet."

I turned south down Canal and took a deep breath. *Where did that come from?*

"Vi's great," I said. "We've been seeing each other for about a year."

"How old is she?"

"Twenty-six."

"She have a last name?"

"Donovan. Violet Donovan."

"Pretty?"

"Sure. Pretty enough. I'm no prize pig, you know."

"Oh, you could be a prize pig with a little grooming," said Gloria. "What's she do for a living?"

"She works at the Northern Regional Research Lab in Peoria. Actually, she just got that job a couple of months ago. Well..." I counted in my head. "A month and a half, actually. She's helping with that penicillin thing. You know, mass production."

"I've heard about it. It's the new wonder drug."

"Well, she's on her feet all day and is bored silly. But it should help our boys overseas. I'm proud of her."

"You two serious?"

"I guess. But she hasn't been up here in a couple of weeks."

"You don't talk on the telephone?"

"I don't have a telephone. She has one in the rooming house, but none of the girls use it much. The house mother's quite the busybody. Listens in on the line all the time and is happy to tell all she knows. If I need her, I send a telegram to the lab. Penny a word. Violet comes in on Fridays if she can make it. Eight o'clock train. Then she heads back late on Saturday afternoon."

Gloria nodded and looked out the window.

"Hey, my new house is right down here. Want to take a look?"

Gloria smiled. "Sure. But then I've got to get back. I still have to find Betty Anderson from Oneonta, Alabama."

There was a truck in front of the house when we drove up. Fish's car was a little way up the block. I parked the car behind the truck and Gloria and I got out and walked up the front steps.

"Nice view," she said, turning around once we'd reached the porch. There was a slow barge making its way down the river and it gave a long bellow when the captain tugged on its horn. Two smaller boats were passing it on the near side, rocking in its wake.

"Do the trains bother you?"

"I don't know," I said. "I haven't moved in yet. I doubt I'll mind them. I like trains. Besides, it's a damn site better than where I live now."

Fish opened the front door.

"Welcome! Come in! Come in!"

I had rarely seen Fish so ebullient. He stepped aside and let us enter the living room.

"Oh... my... God..." said Gloria. "It looks like a... like a..."

"Like a whorehouse?" finished Fish. "It should. That's where I got the furniture."

There were heavy red velvet drapes laden with golden ropes, a red velvet-covered settee, several velvet-covered arm chairs, swags of velvet, festoons of velvet, and garlands of velvet, with some extra velvet thrown in for good taste. Only the dining table wasn't ensconced in velvet, it being a dark, heavy, Mediterranean piece of furniture that some Moroccan prince might have used to serve a roasted camel to fourteen of his closest friends and still have room for two fricasseed goats and a stuffed piglet.

"There's an electric ice-box in the kitchen," said Fish. "And wait until you see the bedrooms. I got a *great* deal on the bedrooms."

"How did you *get* this stuff?" asked Gloria in amazement, as we walked into the first bedroom. "And how on earth did you attach a ten-foot tall mirror to the ceiling?"

"Easy," Fish said proudly. "You just need four big guys and some bolts. To answer your other question, I happened to procure these fine accouterments from Miss Hattie's Gentleman's Club." He lowered his voice. "Miss Hattie has a gambling problem. I didn't want to shut her down entirely, but she needed to downsize her operation."

The mirror didn't hold my attention for long. It was overshadowed by the bed—a huge four-poster that had probably come over from France sometime during the last century. It was the size of a football field, elegantly carved and covered by a plush bedspread made of—what else?—velvet. The pillows were plump and large and extraordinarily plentiful. There was a bureau as well, carved in the same pattern as the bed, and adorned with a large vase full of peacock feathers.

"Nice, eh?" said Fish. "The other bedroom isn't quite as good, but it'll do." He waved us along. "This way."

"I'm not even going to *ask* what the feathers are for," whispered Gloria as we went down the hall.

The second bedroom had a large mirror as well, this one attached to the wall. The bed was smaller, but no less elaborate, and the pillows and bed covers matched the ones in the front room. The dressing table was elegant and feminine and thankfully, devoid of feathers. A thick Persian carpet covered the wooden floor.

"What do you think?" said Fish, clearly pleased with himself.

"Great!" I answered.

"I've never seen anything like it," said Gloria. "Truly."

"Ten bucks a week?" I asked.

"Yep," said Fish proudly. "Of course, that doesn't include utilities."

"Of course," I said.

"Think Vi will like it?"

"How could she not?" I said. "I expect it's every girl's dream house."

We looked at Gloria.

"I have *never* seen anything like it," she said. "Truly."

22

"Tilly's got the measles," said Ned, hanging up the telephone.

Gloria was at the side table making the third pot of coffee of the morning.

"He's got the measles," Ned reiterated. "I just talked to his wife. He can't keep his clothes on. She says he looks like some sort of spotted mollusk."

"Sounds attractive," said Gloria, hiding a smile.

"I had the measles when I was a kid," I said. "Itched like a sonofabitch."

"They're worse if you get 'em as an adult," said Ned. "At least that's what I hear."

Vince came out of Stan's office and walked directly up to Gloria. She looked at him with mild surprise on her face.

"I gotta say this in front of the squad," he announced. "Or everyone that's here at least."

"No you don't," muttered Gloria, now embarrassed.

Fish banged in the front door whistling an unrecognizable tune. It was always easy to tell when Fish had a good Friday morning at the shoe-shine stand. He was in fine fettle. "What's going on?" he called across the room.

Vince ignored the interruption. "You saved Lee's life. Lee's our oldest boy. Jane and I want to thank you."

Gloria tuned red and looked at the floor.

"As far as I'm concerned, you're jake with me," he said, awkwardly sticking out his hand. "Ned, too." He gave Ned a hard look and his partner gave him a grudging nod. Gloria took Vince's hand and shook it.

"Okay, girls," said Fish, "that was real touching. Now that your little tea-party's over, fill me in on the news."

"Tilly's got the measles," Ned said.

"Well, that's just *great!* I haven't had them yet. I hope he's not planning on coming in anytime soon."

Fish walked over to his desk. He'd changed his outfit and was looking dapper in an orange silk jacket with light floral embroidery on the cuff.

"Nice togs," I said. "I thought Weissman only had yellow."

"He got a shipment. Some guy he knows in Miami."

"Does he have black? I could use a black jacket."

"Nah," said Fish. "You can't re-dye this stuff. It comes out all splotchy. I can get you a lavender one, though."

I got busy typing reports. Fish got busy watching me and making occasional comments like "Don't forget about the part where I..." Gloria got busy on the telephone trying to get hold of anyone in Oneonta who knew a girl named Betty Anderson. She wasn't on the horn long when she came up aces.

"Got it!"

"Yeah?" I said.

"I was just on with Minnie Blackwell, the operator. Betty's mother, Edna is on a trip down to Montgomery and won't be back till next week."

"Nuts," said Fish.

"But," continued Gloria, "Oneonta is a small town and on a party-line. Minnie Blackwell just happened to know that Betty Anderson is working at the Cantwell Insurance Company on West Monroe and got a raise last week. She also happened to know that Betty is living at Mrs. Westfall's boarding house, but doesn't have a telephone, so she calls her mother from the insurance office on the QT during her lunch hour. I also found out that Betty left Oneonta because of 'boy problems' and Minnie suspects that the poor girl is in a family way although she wouldn't repeat that to just anyone. She's also pretty sure that the head of the Blount County school board is a Nazi sympathizer and do we want his home address so we can inform the government?"

"Lucky for us she's so closed-lipped." Fish said, lighting up a cigarette.

"Well, I *told* her I was a detective."

"Minnie have a telephone number for Cantwell Insurance?" I asked.

"As a matter of fact, she did."

"God bless that little blabber-mouth," I said. "Give Cantwell Insurance a call and see if Betty's been in to work in the last week."

Fridays were traditionally slow at the 26th. It was Vince's theory that Thursdays were the worst because everyone was out of money for the week and on edge. Friday was payday and most working stiffs would be feeling pretty good with a couple days off and some jangle in their pockets. Today was no exception. Gloria spent the afternoon working the buzzer while I typed up Fish's stack of unfinished reports. Fish was happy to watch, clean his gun, and offer constructive criticism.

A couple of hours later, Gloria hung up her telephone and walked over to my desk.

"I just talked to Betty Anderson. She's fine. She's off tomorrow and can come in and get her purse."

"So," Fish said, "it wasn't Bouncing Betty in the duffle."

"No, it wasn't. Listen, I'm supposed to be off tomorrow, but I wouldn't mind coming in."

"Your day off," Fish said. "You can do what you want. I'll be here."

"Me, too," I said.

"I'm going home then," said Gloria. She stood up and smoothed her skirt. Then she picked up her coat and purse and moved toward the door. "By the way, I called the editors at the *Tribune*, the *Sun*, and the *Daily News* and asked about their advice-to-the-lovelorn columns. They're not getting strange letters—well, not stranger than usual—but they were, to a man, *very* interested in why I was asking. See you tomorrow."

"I think she likes me," said Fish.

"Gotta write a column for tomorrow," I said to Fish, as soon as the squad room cleared out. "I'm thinking we should maybe try to flush this guy out."

Fish nodded. "Hmm. What could Dear Priscilla say to the man to get him intrigued enough to show himself?"

"Well, we know he wants an answer. We just don't know the question."

"You have another letter you need to answer?"

"Yeah. I thought I could answer a real one and then maybe do a note to the killer without a letter."

"Let's get busy," said Fish. "We've got to get down to McGurty's. That whiskey isn't going to drink itself."

I pulled open my top drawer and lifted the first letter out of my file folder.

Dear Priscilla,
I am at my wit's end with my brother and his wife. They live in Gary but love Chicago, and try to visit at least six times a year. When they come, of course, they have to stay with us. It's my fault. I invited them once and that was all it took. Now they stay for two weeks at a time. I've tried dropping gentle hints, but it doesn't work. My patience is at an end. What can I do?
Signed,
Befuddled

"Put something in about betelnuts," Fish suggested.

"What's a betelnut?"

"The upstairs maid chews them. Makes your teeth red and gives you a buzz," said Fish.

I shrugged and started typing.

Gracious Reader,

There is an old saying that house guests, like fish, start to smell after three days. After four days, Priscilla thinks that they should be gutted, rolled in cornmeal, and dropped in hot oil for two to three minutes per side.

If you'd rather not go to that extreme, Priscilla would be happy to recommend an alternative. It's called Priscilla's Amazing Lunatic Adventure.

First, get yourself a hatchet, a quart of pig's blood, a little soot, a cow brain, and a betelnut. Just before your brother and his lovely bride are due to arrive, go into the bathroom, tease your hair into a wild tangle, apply some soot liberally beneath each eye and chew on the betelnut. This should turn your teeth a lovely red as well as dilating your pupils to an astounding degree.

Next, when you hear them coming up the walk, Priscilla suggests you splash the blood liberally on your hands and frock (be sure to wear an old one--those stains are just MURDER!) and meet them at the door with the hatchet in one hand and the cow brain in the other. Don't say anything. Just give them each a big hug, being sure to smear them well. Then take a bite of the brains and offer the remainder of this sumptuous hors d'oeuvre to your guests. I know this flies in the face of hostess etiquette (Priscilla always serves her guests first), but the effect is truly amazing.

If this doesn't deter them, Gracious Reader, the hatchet has other uses.

"That's great," said Fish with a laugh. "Brains! Great!"

I chuckled. "Yeah. Now, what do we say to our boy?"

"I don't know. Give him something cryptic to contemplate. Invite him to dance or something. I think the important thing is that we actually answer his letter in the paper."

I nodded and typed.

Dear E.P.
    Thank you for the gift. Shall we dance?

"What do you think?" said Fish.

"Might work. I'll drop this off at Sally Clifford's place on the way home. It'll be in tomorrow's rag."

"How 'bout a drink?"

"Let's go."

McGurty's was busy. As we elbowed our way toward the bar, I caught Joe's eye. He gave us the nod and we had our double scotches waiting when we were through glad-handing the other cops in the place. Fish threw his back in one gulp and knocked his glass twice on the bar for another. I wasn't in such a hurry.

"Merl!"

I looked down the bar and saw Woody Sugarman with his arm around a great looking redhead.

"How're things with you, Woody?"

"Better and better. I think I'm starting at tailback on Sunday. We're playing the Steagles."

"Steagles?"

"The Steelers and the Eagles. They merged for the season."

"Ah. I remember. How 'bout some tickets?" I asked hopefully.

"How many you need?"

"Two."

"I've got a couple down front on the thirty-yard line. You can pick 'em up at the front gate."

"Hey, thanks," I said. "You're a pal."

Woody stepped back, put his arm around his date and swung her into view. "Rhonda, this is Merl Cahill, the world's meanest detective. Merl, this is Rhonda, the world's most flexible cheer-leader."

Rhonda gave a high-pitched giggle and snapped her gum like it was punctuation. "Pleased to meet'cha." She giggled again.

"A pleasure," I said. "Can I buy you two a drink?"

"Nah," said Woody. "We were just leaving. I've got to get Rhonda to bed early. She needs her beauty rest."

Rhonda burped. "Pleased to meet'cha." Another giggle.

"You have to excuse her," said Woody with a grin. "She's a mite inebriated." He took her arm and led the unsteady cheerleader toward the door. I looked around for Fish, but he'd already found George Musso and Bronko sitting at their usual table in the corner. I noticed Danny Fortmann, the Bear's all-NFL guard, throwing darts and stopped on my way over to the table.

"Nice toss," I said, as a dart found the second ring.

Danny turned around and a smile spread across his face. "Merl! Good to see you!"

"You, too. Are you a doctor yet?"

"Yep. Dr. Fortmann. Isn't that something?" Danny was the smartest guy I knew. He had been the youngest starter in the NFL when he was drafted in '36, Phi Beta Kappa from Colgate, and a whiz at everything he put his hand to.

"That's something all right. Congratulations."

"Thanks. I don't know if you heard, but I'm joining the Navy after this season."

"I hadn't heard."

"Well," said Danny with a shrug, "they need doctors. Over three million kids drafted last year."

"You're a good guy, Danny. We'll miss you around here."

"Hey," he laughed, "I'm not leaving yet. The season's just starting to heat up. I think we have a good chance this year."

"Yeah. Monsters of the Midway."

"That's us." Danny pointed at the dart board. "Care for a game?"

"Thanks anyway," I said, taking my drink and moving towards the back table. "I've seen you throw and I'd be lucky to even hit the board."

Fish was deep in hushed conversation with Musso and Bronko when I walked up. They stopped for a moment, looked at me as if deciding whether I was to be let in on the discourse, then George pulled out a chair and I joined them at the table.

"We have a problem," said George.

I looked as attentive as I could and waited for him to continue.

"We've got a couple of rookies that are messing around with whores and dice. I've talked to them once already, but they think they're too smart."

Bronko nodded. "Somebody like Fish gets his hooks into them and... well..." He looked over at Fish. "No offense."

"None taken," said Fish. "I know just what you mean. Some bookies are unscrupulous. Me? I'm just a businessman. I make the odds and I take my chances like everyone else. I'd hate to see games getting thrown just for a few bucks."

"You want us to have a talk with them?" I asked.

"I think it'd help," said George. "Don't you have a goon you could take with you?"

"Little Eddie," said Fish. "Yeah. We could take Little Eddie."

"We'd appreciate it," said Bronko. "I didn't come out of retirement to have two punk rookies queer the season."

"Hell of a thing about that girl at the stadium," said George. "You guys got any leads?"

"A couple," I said. "We're working on it."

We chatted for about an hour about the season, this year's roster, and the upcoming game with the Steagles who, by all accounts, had a pretty good team. They were 2 and 0 with wins over the Brooklyn Dodgers and the Giants, and their quarterback, Roy Zimmerman, was looking tough.

"Tell you what," said Fish. "I'm going out on a limb and picking the Bears plus four."

"Don't do yourself any favors," Bronko replied. "We're gonna cream these guys."

Fish headed off to the synagogue to sing. I went home to pack my belongings into my trunk and haul them over to my new house on Canal Street. Violet was in Springfield. Truth be told, I felt relieved and was surprised by the feeling.

23

Gloria Kingston was already at her desk when Fish and I walked in. Of course, we weren't exactly what you'd call early birds. If we wandered in by 9:30 on a weekend, we were doing well, especially since we had a standing Saturday morning appointment at Rita's diner. Now, well-sated with coffee, scrambled eggs, hash, and a couple of smokes, we were ready to start the day.

"Betty Anderson come in yet?" Fish said.

"Good morning to you, too," said Gloria.

"Ooo, sorry. Hi-de-ho, Detective Kingston," Fish said sarcastically. "Betty Anderson come in yet?"

"Morning," I said.

Gloria smiled her greeting, then answered Fish. "She said she'd come in around ten, so you haven't missed her."

"Whew." Fish pulled his pocket watch out and checked the time. "That was close."

I took off my coat and hat and dropped them on Tilly's empty measle-ridden desk. Then I flopped back in my wooden chair. It gave an angry squeak as my two-hundred eighty pounds tested the limits of the antique oak.

"We checked with the doc on the way in," I told Gloria. "The second girl wasn't pregnant. No evidence of rape, either."

Gloria gave a heavy sigh and sat back in her chair.

"What about the bags?" I said. "Why does he use army duffle bags?"

Fish thought a moment. "Let's see. First of all, they're the right size."

"So are mail bags," I noted.

"Duffles could be easy for him to get," suggested Gloria. "Maybe he's at a military base."

"Could be surplus," I said. "There's a lot of that. Or black market. A lot of that, too."

Fish snorted. "You can get all the army duffles you want on Maxwell Street."

"Yeah," I agreed. "Duffles and anything else. Let's not discount the army base theory, though."

We heard the squad room door open and a young woman entered. I judged her to be in her late twenties. She was easily the less attractive of the two sisters, if her sister's picture was anything to go by. She didn't appear to be pregnant—as Minnie Blackwell, the Oneonta operator, had surmised—but was on the heavy side of average and her black hair fell to her shoulders framing a square face with full lips and heavy brows. Her smile was infectious, though, and she chirped as she came in.

"Good morning! I'm Elizabeth Anderson. Betty. Is this where I can pick up my pocketbook?"

"It certainly is," said Fish. "Come in. Have a seat."

Betty looked nervous. "Did I do something wrong?" she asked as she sat down in the chair opposite Fish.

"No, no," said Fish. "No trouble. We just have a couple of questions."

"Oh. Sure."

"You lost your purse in the train station?"

"Oh, no. I lost it in the bus station. Well, that's not exactly right. It was stolen in the bus station."

"Stolen?" I said.

"I told the policeman at the Union Bus Depot." She dug into her pocket and came up with a scrap of paper. She read it and handed it across the desk. "Officer Bernard Bell. He said I could file a report down at the police station, but he doubted they could do anything."

"Whoa," I said. "Start at the beginning."

"I already told Officer Bell..."

"I know. Now tell us."

Betty let out a sigh that may have been exasperation. "All right. I was in the depot, sitting on the bench next to this other girl, waiting for the uptown bus. I decided to get a newspaper to pass the time. So I opened my purse, got some change, and went over to the newsstand and got a *Times*. I thought there might be a new "Dear Priscilla" column. I think she's just a hoot."

We nodded.

"When I turned back to the bench she was gone. My purse was gone, too. I felt like such a fool. I went straight to the policeman."

"Do you remember what she looked like?" asked Fish.

"Sure. I gave Officer Bell a description. She was... well... I guess about average. Brown hair. I don't know how tall she was. She was sitting down when I saw her. Kinda pretty. Well dressed. She was wearing a hat—one of those little ones that are all the rage in New York."

"Huh," I grunted. "Let me ask you something. Did you notice if she was missing part of her little finger? Left hand."

Betty thought for a second, then brightened. "You know. She was! I remember noticing because she was reading a *Life* magazine and I was sitting just to her left. Why? Does that mean something? Have you caught her?"

"Let's just say, we don't think she'll be stealing any more purses," said Gloria.

We gave Betty her handbag, thanked her for her time, and Fish walked her to the door.

"We still don't know who it is," said Gloria.

"Well, we know who it isn't," I said. "It isn't Betty." I stood up. "Fish and I need to go over to Wrigley Field. Can you hold down the fort until Stan gets here?"

"When's he coming in?"

"Schedule says noon."

"Sure," said Gloria. "By the way, how did Violet like your house?"

"Hasn't seen it. She couldn't make it up here this weekend. One of her girlfriends is getting married in Springfield."

"Next weekend then?"

"Probably. Unless something comes up. Sometimes she doesn't get back to Chicago for weeks at a time."

Gloria nodded and flashed me a strange little smile. "Yeah. Unless something comes up," she said.

24

The Bears were finishing up their Saturday morning warm-up when Fish and I arrived at the field with Little Eddie Nowak in tow. Hunk Anderson had them running thirty-yard sprints in full pads, cleats, and helmets—ten players at a time. He saw us, gave us a nod, and continued blasting short sharp bursts on his whistle signaling the start of each new group. I recognized the orange jerseys with the navy numbers and black arm stripes from when I played—jerseys now relegated only to practice. On game day, the team sported black jerseys with orange numbers and stripes.

"I don't miss those sprints a bit," I said to Fish. We sauntered up to the side lines and sidled up to George Musso, who had somehow escaped the exercise.

"Told Hunk I wasn't going to do it," said George. "I've got a toothache that's killing me. I'm hoping to get it knocked out tomorrow during the game. You here to see the kids?"

"Yeah," I said. "Fish brought Little Eddie. You want him to break a couple fingers?"

"Nah. Just scare them. Maybe they'll smarten up."

Fish and I nodded our agreement. "It's worth a try," said Fish.

"I hate these helmets," said George. He held up the black leather headgear with padded ear pieces. "I have to keep the ear flaps up or I can't hear the signals."

I nodded sympathetically.

"And this tooth is killing me."

"Boys," said Bronko, "this here is Merl Cahill. He played for us a few years back. Now he's a cop. Merl, this is Jeff Howard and Don Picarro."

"Pleased to meet you," said Jeff nervously. Don was quiet. Both of them were bigger-than-average guys. The rest of the team had headed for the locker room. Bronko had brought these two over to the sidelines to meet with us. They might not have been thrilled with the visit, but if you were a rookie, you didn't say no to Bronko Nagurski.

Bronko walked off leaving Fish and me to have a chat with the players.

"This is Detective Fishel Biederman," I said. "You can call him Fish."

They didn't call him Fish. They didn't call him anything. They'd heard of Fish.

"Listen," I said, "a couple of your teammates wanted us to have a little chat. It seems you've been doing some gambling. Maybe some dice... a little sporting...."

"Yeah? So?" said Don Picarro.

I kept my friendly, man-to-man tone. "Look, you guys are rookies. I know what it's like to come into some cash. You're just having a little fun, right?"

"Right," said Jeff. "Just a little fun."

"But now it's time to stop," Fish said. "You get in over your heads and the first thing you know, somebody's asking you to throw a game. That's not going to happen."

"Who the hell are *you*?" said Don with all the bluster he could summon. "We're not in over our heads, and we'll do whatever the hell we want."

"I'm the guy who just bought your markers," said Fish. "You owe me two hundred. Each."

"We only owe a hundred each," said Jeff. "We owe a hundred to Mickey Whelan."

"No," said Fish. "That was last week. I bought your markers. Now you owe *me* two hundred. Next week you'll owe me three hundred. See how this works?"

"Mickey didn't say anything about that," said Jeff, now looking scared and shaking his head.

"No way," added Don.

"See," I said, "this is what I mean. Before you know it, you're up to your eyeballs with no way out. Then an unscrupulous bookie might try to collect this debt by doing something far more sinister than just breaking your arms or legs. He'll try to get you to fix the games."

"Fuck you," said Don. "We're not paying you no two hundred."

"I understand your reticence," said Fish. "Because you don't know how these things work. That's why we brought Little Eddie."

"I think they got the point," I said as we were walking out the front gate. "I didn't know you'd bought their markers."

"I thought it would give us a bit of leverage," said Fish.

"Well, luckily they're not starters."

Fish shook his head in disgust. "You heard me tell Little Eddie before we came in. 'Don't break anything,' I said. You *heard* me."

I shrugged. "Take it easy. I've played with busted fingers lots of times. The trainer will tape them up. They'll be fine in a few weeks."

"I've *got* to get some new help," said Fish.

"Know what?" I said thoughtfully. "Those two are big boys. New in town."

"Familiar enough with Soldier Field," added Fish.

"They're on the list," I said.

Fish snorted. "Well, they're the only ones."

25

I made four purchases on Saturday afternoon. I was flush for the first time in a long while and was happy to spend a couple of hours browsing my way down Maxwell Street on what turned out to be a beautiful October day.

My first purchase was two oversized wicker chairs. Big and white, with colorful cushions, and sturdy enough not to turn to kindling when I flopped into one after a long day. I wanted to sit on the front porch of my new house, drink beer, and watch the trains and barges go by. I wasn't planning on wicker, but I'm a sucker for a comfortable sit-down, and when I dropped into one of them, I was sold.

"How much?"

"Thirty for the pair." The merchant was a weasely guy with a very thin pencil mustache resting on a prominent upper lip. His thinning hair was plastered back with some sort of hair tonic that made me want to give up the Wildroot for good.

"Nah. I saw the same chairs right down the street. I'm pretty sure I can do better."

"Carl Jensen's shop? Those chairs are *shit!* Made of grass or something. Twenty-five."

"I sat in one of his," I lied. "They were a little roomier. Fifteen bucks."

"Like *hell* they were! Jensen gets his chairs from the Japs. *The Japs!* He's a goddamn traitor. That's what *he* is! Twenty-two for the pair."

"I dunno. This fabric... what is it? Chintz or something? Seventeen-fifty."

"Chintz? What are you, a homo?" He held up both his hands. "Listen, if you are, it's none of my business. I'm just saying... This here's canvas. Same stuff they make sails out of. Lasts forever. Twenty for the pair. That's a *deal!*"

"You deliver them. No charge."

"Where to?"

"Canal Street. Three blocks."

A big smile spread across his rodent-like visage. "Done!" He stuck out his hand and I shook it. I gave him a twenty and the address and told him to leave them on the front porch.

"They'll be there in an hour or two," he said, but something in his eyes gave his game away.

I narrowed my gaze and gave him my darkest look—the one that usually scared suspects into confessing, whether they were guilty or not. "*These* chairs. These two right here. Not two you have in the back. I'd hate to have to come back and find you. You know my partner, Fish Biederman?" I didn't mind dropping Fish's name now and again when I thought it would do some good. Being big and mean was fine, as far as it went. Being Fish's friend was in a whole 'nother league.'

He went white and nodded his head. "You're Fish's partner? No problem. An hour. Did I say an hour? I meant thirty minutes. Hell, thirty minutes? I'll take care of it right now. They'll be there in ten." He went scurrying off.

Satisfied with my purchase, I went down the street looking for the next thing on my list. I didn't have to go far.

I spotted Just Plain Eddie Nowak standing on the corner looking extremely suspicious, but then, Just Plain Eddie would look suspicious to Helen Keller. Just Plain Eddie wasn't nearly as big as either of his mutant brothers, but he was meaner by half. He was dressed in a black suit, black shirt and tie, and pointed patent leathers. The shoes had been all the rage when zoots were in style, but passé for a decade at least. In style or not, I knew that Just Plain Eddie had the sharp toes reinforced with metal tips. They'd go right into a ribcage or tear a face to ribbons in seconds and Just Plain Eddie didn't mind kicking you when you were down. In addition to his psychopathic outlook on life in general, Just Plain Eddie had all the intelligence his two siblings lacked. I crossed the street and gave him a nod.

"Eddie," I said, by way of a greeting.

"Merl," he grunted.

"I'm in the market for a couple of pieces. Think you could help me out?"

He perked up. "Probably. What do you need?"

Just Plain Eddie and I had done business before and could therefore skip all the preliminary sidesteps, dodges, evasions, and veiled threats. "I need a drop gun and an ankle rod."

"I've got a sweet little Walther ·38 straight from the Führer himself. They call it a PPK. *Polizei Police Kriminal.* Say what you want about those sausage-suckers, they can *make* a gun. A guy brought it back from Africa as a souvenir after the Krauts shot his legs off. Small, unregistered. Perfect ankle piece. "

"How much?"

"Gimme fifty for it and I'll throw in a drop gun. I've got a ·38 with the serial number filed off. It's a piece of shit—one of the grips is gone and it pulls way right—but it fires okay."

I reached in my pocket and peeled a fifty off a wad of greenbacks. Just Plain Eddie watched the bills go in and out of my pocket without changing expression.

"You cops must make a better living than I thought," he said dryly. "Meet me back here in half an hour."

He turned and disappeared into the crowd of pedestrians. I pulled out my pocket watch and gave it a look. It was getting late and the shops and vendors would start closing up once the light started to fade. I continued my stroll looking for a street merchant I'd seen a couple of weeks ago. He'd had an overcoat and a hat that I'd taken a real shine to. I'd gone ahead and bought the hat—I had it on now—but I'd foregone the coat, my salary being what it was. My current overcoat had lasted me since my college days and, although it was still warm enough, it was getting threadbare. Besides, I was rich. I finally found the fellow I was looking for, although he was in the midst of hanging his wares back onto a moveable clothes rack so he could wheel them off to safety for the night.

"Don't put it all away just yet," I said.

He looked perturbed for a second, then recognized me and became all smiles and teeth.

"Ah, Detective. Good to see you again. Are you maybe interested in that coat?"

I smiled and nodded. "I am. Do you still have it?"

He was a little Jewish tailor, short, fat, bald on the top, with an accent straight from the old country, whatever country that might be. He shrugged. "So who am I going to sell it to? There's nobody else your size in the city. I could go to the circus maybe…" He laughed at his own joke, then rifled through the movable clothes rack for a moment and came out with a beautiful dark gray overcoat with a curly lamb's wool collar. I took off my own coat and slung it over the top of the rack, then allowed the tailor to hold the coat open for me while I slipped my arms into the sleeves. I gave a shrug and felt it settle onto my shoulders as if it were made for me.

"You know what a Kashmir goat is? It's a goat from Persia. Only the softest and finest wool."

"Very nice," I said. "How much?"

"For you…" He shrugged and held up his hands in the traditional Jewish "how-much-can-I-get-from-this-goyim" gesture. "For you, seventy-five dollars."

"What? Two weeks ago it was sixty-five."

The tailor smiled and spun me around, surveying his handiwork. "Two weeks ago you didn't have any money. Now you do."

"Yes, but if I don't buy it, who are you going to sell it to? Is the circus in town?"

He smoothed out the shoulders from the back, then spun me back around to adjust the buttons. "I joke, I joke. There were two gentlemen looking at this very coat only this afternoon. I fear that at least one of them will be back tomorrow and it will be gone. The coat goes splendidly with that hat, by the way."

"Yeah, I know. I'll give you sixty-eight."

"Seventy-two. My children will go hungry and my wife will beat me for a *shmendrik*."

"Sixty-nine and not a penny more."

He looked sideways at me and then pointed right at my nose as if he'd come up with the perfect compromise. "Seventy-one and I throw in an extra set of buttons."

I gave him a hard look. "Seventy. Buttons included."

"Bah! My wife will never speak to me again—which might not be a bad thing." He pretended to deliberate for a moment, then threw up his hands. "Give me two-bits more and we'll call it a deal."

"Fine," I said. "You win. I'll even throw in the old coat."

He sneered. "What should I do with that? The cat wouldn't even sleep on it."

I was wearing my new coat when I met Just Plain Eddie back at his corner. He sized up the garment in a moment and gave a little nod of approval.

"Got inside pockets on that thing?"

"Yeah," I answered, holding open both sides of the coat. Just Plain Eddie stepped in close and before I could move, had dropped a gun into each inside pocket so smoothly that I had to pat myself down to make sure they were there.

"Check 'em out when you get home, but I'm sure they'll do the trick," said Just Plain Eddie. Then he was gone.

26

The two white wicker chairs were sitting on my covered porch, as promised, when I arrived home. I skipped the pleasure of relaxing for the moment, unlocked the front door and entered into the velvety luxury of my new digs. The temperature of the house was pleasant, but on the cool side. I had set the furnace on low and left it there.

The first order of business was to check the guns. I pulled them out of the pockets of my coat and tossed them onto the settee. I went over the Walther first, checking the weight and balance, first with my right hand and then my left. I dropped out the clip, checked it, and slid it back. Just Plain Eddie had thoughtfully loaded the magazine and now I pulled back the action and watched a lug slide into the chamber. It had been my experience that an unloaded gun isn't much use. I kept both the ·45 and the ·38 Police Special loaded and ready. I didn't have an ankle holster yet, but I'd pick one up on Monday or Tuesday.

Just Plain Eddie was right about the drop gun. It was a piece of shit, but it didn't have to be good—or accurate—just be able to shoot when the D.A. found it planted on a previously unarmed suspect who had the bad luck of having been shot accidentally or on purpose. Fish had dropped our last one on the punk behind the bank. I'd try this one out at the range on Tuesday when I took the PPK out for a test run.

I changed my clothes, pulled on an old Chicago Bears sweater from my playing days, then walked into the kitchen and opened the refrigerator. It was square and white and contained nothing but cans of beer. I took one out, punched two holes in the top with my church key, and walked back onto the porch to enjoy the evening.

The sun sets in the west, even in Chicago. My new house, facing east, didn't catch any of the last rays as it dropped below the cityscape. It didn't matter. The view was great. I watched a barge, guided by a tug at its bow. Then another, this one unattended. A wooden Chris Craft powerboat roared by and the woman in the passenger seat gave a friendly wave. A train whistle sounded to the south and announced the six o'clock from Bloomington. I pulled my watch out of my pocket and looked at it. Right on time. I counted twenty cars, including the engine and the caboose. All passenger cars. The cattle cars to the stockyards took a different line.

My house sat on a block with four others facing Canal Street— smack dab in the middle, two on either side. I hadn't met the neighbors, but there were a couple of kids running up and down the street. In each front yard stood a big elm tree, probably planted by the city fifty years ago, shading the yard and half of the street. I took a sip of my beer, lit up a Camel, sat back on my new wicker throne, and surveyed my kingdom with a smile.

I was busy counting sleeper cars and had managed to get to forty-eight when I caught sight of Gloria coming up the walk. Surprised the hell out of me. She'd changed from her office attire into something more casual, but just as fetching—a navy skirt and a sky-blue sweater. Her golden hair was pulled back into a pony-tail and she looked like a million and a half bucks. She waved and I returned the greeting, beckoning her up to the porch.

"Out for a walk?' I asked, as she ascended the steps.

"Well... yes," she said. "I live about six blocks that way." She pointed to the north-west over my shoulder. "Got another beer?"

"Sure do. I'm about to have another myself. Have a seat and help yourself to a smoke." I stood and offered her the other wicker chair, then opened the front door and went in to get two more Falstaffs. When I got back Gloria had her feet up on the porch rail and was taking a long drag on her cigarette. I handed her a cold can.

"I've got a refrigerator now," I said, sitting down beside her, "so the beer is cold."

"This is great," said Gloria. "Dusk on the river. Very pretty. Did you and Fish finish your errand?"

"Yep. We took care of it. Then I went shopping."

"What did you buy?"

"These two chairs, for one thing."

"They're comfy. What else?"

"A new overcoat I've had my eye on. And an ankle gun."

Gloria nodded. It was getting dark. We sat in silence for a few minutes—a comfortable silence—then I ventured a question.

"So, why the detective squad?"

"Well, you were right. I like the excitement, I guess. I got married when I was twenty and my husband had the marriage annulled when I was twenty-five. He was from a rich family in Joliet. The Fitzgeralds. Ever heard of them?"

"I know some Fitzgeralds," I said. "None of them rich, though, and none from Joliet."

"Anyway, I needed some direction—something to do, and I didn't want to work in the factory or join the WAC. So I opted for the force."

"What was the deal on the annulment?" I asked. "I mean, if you don't mind telling me."

"I don't mind. Turns out I can't have children. I had a miscarriage and then some complications. 'Daddy' wanted grandchildren to carry on the family name and hubby was an only child, so a quick call to the Archbishop and I was *persona non grata.*"

I took a long draw on my beer and watched the silhouette of a seagull fly in a lazy circle over my elm. The moon had risen and the stars were starting to come out. "Doesn't seem quite fair," I said.

She shrugged. "It was over long before the annulment. And I got a lot of money from Daddy-in-law not to make any waves. I'll tell you one thing. I'm *never* getting married again."

"Still..."

"You have any family?" she asked.

"Nah. You?"

"Nope. I lost both my folks to polio in '37. My brother was killed last year in the Pacific. Guadalcanal."

We were quiet again, listening to the sounds of the river.

"Getting a little chilly," she finally said. "Are you going to ask me in?"

"I haven't decided yet."

"I think you should." She pulled her hair loose from the ponytail and ran her fingers through it. "Ask me in, I mean."

"Yeah, I'm thinking I should, too."

The first kiss was at the door and was the kind that made you want to major in kissing at college. A long, slow, delicious kiss that tasted of cigarette smoke, and beer, and infinite possibilities. Our sweaters came off over our heads and we kissed again. The second kiss was a slow dance that moved across the living room, past the fireplace, into the hallway, and finally, to the bedroom—eyes half-closed, negotiating corners and doorways of the unlit rooms, all the while shedding clothes and leaving them in a trail—as if they were bread crumbs leading back to the front door and business-as-usual. But not yet.

The third kiss lasted for hours. Or seemed to. As our mouths remained locked, we struggled out of the rest of our clothes and fell into the massive bed. Gloria was a woman of few inhibitions. If she had any at all, I couldn't seem to find them. And believe me, I tried.

An hour later we both lay spent on what was left of the bedclothes, me, puffing away like I'd just finished a set of wind-sprints and wondering if I'd make the whistle for the second half. Gloria seemed to be in better shape than I was, but I'd played in tougher games than this and I sure wasn't known as a quitter. After a few long minutes of catching our breath, Gloria sat up. Not me. I lay there like a slug. I'd been right. She was in better shape.

The moon had risen and was casting its light directly into the window in the bedroom, bathing the bed in a silvery glow. In the moonlight, sitting cross-legged on the bed, Gloria looked like a Victorian fairy painting—a translucent nymph, albeit sans wings and gossamer clothing, and therefore, *much* more interesting. Fish's placement of the mirror didn't hurt matters either.

"That was *something*," I said.

"You're very talented." Gloria giggled and ran her fingers down my chest. "Wow. I knew you were strong, but... just look at this chest." Her fingers played across my pectorals and settled in a quarter-sized indentation in my ribcage. "What's this?"

"That's from a ·44 slug. It's still behind my lung. The hole is where it punched through my ribs."

"Ouch." She bent over me and put both hands over my heart. Then her hands parted and her fingers slid across my chest in both directions, first coming to rest on my shoulders before slipping down my arms and wrapping around each of my biceps. I gave a flex to show off. When she bent over at the waist and kissed me on the chest where her hands had been, I felt my abdominal muscles leap to attention, then my quadriceps, followed by almost every other muscle capable of showing off without rerouting the blood from my brain.

She continued her examination. "Yikes! How about this one?" She traced a long weal down the inside of my arm, shoulder to elbow.

"Knife cut when I was a rookie on the force. I didn't search the guy well enough. He pulled out a blade and slashed at my face. Got me here to here." I pointed to the scar running from my eye to my jaw. "He slashed again, but I ducked it and threw up my arm. Mistake."

"Where's the guy now?"

"Dead."

She cocked her head without comment and looked inquisitive. "Here?" Her hand rested on white, puckered skin just below my ribs.

"Football spikes. I was on the bottom of a pile. Don't know who did it."

"So you didn't kill him?" she joked.

"Nah."

"What about your teeth? I heard professional football players had most of their teeth knocked out."

"Not me. They're all mine. I just lost that one eye-tooth."

"Lucky."

Her hand moved back across my stomach, then lower— pausing for effect, then down my right leg, stopping at my knee.

"This looks an absolute mess."

"That, my dear, is a missed block on Chet Adams of the Cleveland Rams, October 8, 1939. Ended my playing career."

Gloria grimaced and ran her fingers gently over the scar tissue. "That must have hurt."

"Oh yeah. Worse than being shot."

Her fingers crept back up the inside of my leg, stopping six inches short of my stomach. "Ready for the second half, tiger?" she asked with a smile.

"I think I'm up for it."

"Yes, I think you are."

Afterwards, I suggested we sit in front of the fire and have another beer.

"You built a fire?"

"Well, I haven't lit it yet."

Gloria rolled her eyes. "I gathered *that*. But you have it ready to light. Were you expecting me?"

"I don't know what I was expecting, but I'm pretty sure whatever it was wasn't that."

I pulled on a pair of shorts and looked around for a sweatshirt. Gloria stood up beside the bed, found her undershirt and pulled it over her head. Thusly clad, she walked out of the bedroom, knowing that my eyes were glued to her swaying backside peeking out from beneath the white cotton. I finally found a sweatshirt and then followed her like a puppy, or maybe a wolf. She'd gotten two beers out of the refrigerator by the time I'd made it to the living room.

"Start the fire," Gloria said, keying both cans. "It's cold in here. I'll have to put some clothes on pretty soon."

"I'll get it going. Let's not do anything rash."

Gloria brought our refreshment into the living room and sat on the couch, tucking her long legs underneath her, a beer in each hand. The under-shirt was thin—thin enough to see through, and short enough not to hide anything of interest. She was chilled, that much was obvious, but the flames were beginning to lick at the kindling, and a full-fledged fire was only moments away. I sat down next to her, took one of the cans from her hand and pulled her close. I could feel every curve through the thin fabric and upon discovering that delightful fact, went ahead and felt quite a few. She was still chilly, but the room was beginning to warm up. Me, too.

"Mmm. Did you read the paper tonight?" she asked, snuggling in and picking up the paper lying unopened beside her.

"Nope."

"Look here. The headline is about the second dead girl. They're calling him the 'Duffle Killer.' Chicago's version of Jack the Ripper."

"How much information does the article give?"

She skimmed the paper quickly. "Everything we know, which isn't much. It tells where the bodies were found, the condition, stuff like that. It doesn't say anything about Dear Priscilla, though."

"Good," I said. "We gotta find this guy."

"We will." She put down her beer, took the can from my hand

and placed it next to hers, then leaned over and gave me a kiss of the mind-numbing variety. "I love a fire," she whispered. "Now, let me show you a trick."

27

I slept like the dead. When I finally woke on Sunday morning and staggered out of the bedroom, Gloria was gone and Fish was in the kitchen rooting through the refrigerator.

"All you've got in here is beer," he called.

"Yep. Get me one, will you?" I fell onto the settee.

"Where's your church key?"

"Top of the fridge."

I heard the hiss of one can being opened, then another. Fish walked out of the kitchen, handed me a can of suds and flopped onto one of the opulent chairs.

"Nice porch furniture," said Fish.

"I got that coat, too. The one I was looking at."

"About time. Saw your girlfriend, too. She was on her way out."

I reached up and scratched the stubble on my face. "Yeah... well..."

"Vi couldn't come up this weekend?"

"I telegrammed her and told her not to."

"Don't dance too close to the fire, my friend," said Fish. "That's my advice." He looked at his wristwatch. "It's 10:30

now. Kickoff's at one. We could go and get some breakfast," he suggested. "Know what would go great with this beer? Waffles."

"Sure," I said, happy to change the subject. "How about Rita's? She open on Sunday morning?"

"Nope. Not till lunch. Railway Café?"

"Suits me," I said. "Let me get some clothes on."

"Don't you have to write a column?"

"Goddammit," I grumbled. "I've got a couple of Dear Priscilla letters in the kitchen. Let me grab a piece of paper and a pencil and we'll do it over breakfast."

The morning of October 17th was cold. We walked onto the porch and a blast of wind from off of Lake Michigan came swooping down across the river and rattled through our bones.

"Nice," I said, taking a deep breath, savoring the fresh air tinged with the smell of wood burning in the fireplaces up and down the street. "Great day for a ball game. I used to love a game day like this."

"Just *feels* like football," agreed Fish.

We walked up Canal Street, kicking through the leaves piling up on the sidewalk. The elms were still in their cups, decked in orange and yellow, but the leaves were starting to drop and in a week or two, they'd be as bare as one of Miss Hattie's professionals. Another wind kicked up, swirling dead leaves around our ankles like hungry ghost-cats vying for attention, and I turned up my collar against the cold.

"Now, *that's* an overcoat," said Fish, as we walked. "Can't go wrong with a coat like that. Makes you feel like a million bucks."

"Warm, too."

The Railway Café was a block from Dearborn Station on State Street, just past St. Peter's. We came up on the church just as the bells were beginning to peal announcing the eleven o'clock mass. Families were making their way into the front doors, chatting happily, and greeting each other in the way that church folks do. We heard the organ sounding in the nave as we walked past the front doors and continued on. I hadn't been to St. Peter's for a while. Violet used to drag me along on Sunday mornings when she was living in Chicago, but since she moved, I hadn't managed it, and going to weekly confession was definitely not on my list.

The train station and the café were a brisk fifteen minute walk from my new house on Canal Street. The police station was a few blocks in the other direction. All things considered, Fish had dropped me in a great location.

We got a table without any trouble. The breakfast crowd had dissipated and the lunch crowd was still in their pews confessing their manifold sins and wickedness.

"Waffles," Fish said to the waitress, as soon as she walked up. "And a glass for my beer." He set his can of Falstaff on the table in front of him. "I'll need an opener, too, if you have one."

She made a face, but wrote the order diligently on her pad.

"Same," I said.

"Waffles and beer?" she asked.

"Nope. Waffles and *two* beers." I'd carried mine in a paper bag. Now I pulled them out and set them next to Fish's.

Our waitress nodded and disappeared. The Railway Café did a brisk business on most days, catering to the folks between trains, changing lines, or maybe waiting on a late arrival. Violet and I had eaten here plenty, sometimes catching a late bite after her train came in—other times, maybe breakfast or dinner before she left on Sunday to go back to Peoria. The food wasn't bad, the coffee was usually hot, and the waitresses kept your cup filled, but otherwise left you alone.

"Get us a gat?" asked Fish.

"Yeah. Just Plain Eddie hooked me up. I got an ankle piece, too."

Fish nodded. "What kind?"

"A ·38 auto. They call it a PPK. German. I'll be leaving that Colt in the glove box."

"I've seen one of those PPKs. Nice. How about the drop gun?"

"Junk. No serial number. Half a grip."

Fish smiled. "Put it in the glove box. You never know..."

"Yeah."

The waitress came back to the table with a couple of empty water glasses and thumped them on the table, then left without a word. They weren't exactly sparkling.

"Hey," Fish called after her. "These glasses ain't clean. And how about a beer opener?" The waitress pretended she didn't hear him.

"She thinks we're bums!" said Fish. He made a face, then reached into his pocket and pulled out a folding knife. With a flip of his thumb, the blade jumped to attention and Fish punched some quick holes in the top of all three cans. We filled our glasses and sat back in our chairs.

"Can't blame her, I guess. Waffles are a nickel. We bring our own beer. She's not gonna get rich on us."

"That's not it, but I can see why she'd think that," Fish said, studying me. "It's because, in spite of your fancy new coat, you look like hell."

"Late night I guess."

"I guess. Merl, you're ugly as a mud fence, but you've got something the ladies like. Ziba says so, too." He shrugged and held up his hands. "I don't get it either, but there you are. You gonna fill me in on the details?"

"Nope."

"Didn't think so," he said with a grin. "The mirror was great though, wasn't it?"

With our waffles and beers safely under our belts, we turned our attention to literary pursuits and had soon slathered ourselves, once again, with journalistic glory. We even had time to go by the station, type up the letter, and drop it off at Sally's on the way to the game.

We grabbed a cab and got to the stadium just before kickoff. As promised, Woody Sugarman had left us two tickets at the gate and they proved to be great seats, about ten rows back on the 30 yard line. The combined Steelers-Eagles squad was already on the field, their bright green jerseys standing in contrast to the browning turf of Wrigley Field. We made our way down the aisle to our seats.

The grandstands were a sea of color and activity. Attendance had been slumping since the war, but these were Bears fans and wouldn't be kept down for long. Some donned the orange and black mufflers that had become a trademark, some carried felt pennants, some were still wearing the clothes they'd worn to church. There was a cheerfulness and a camaraderie borne of commitment to a single cause—taking the championship back from Washington. The Nazis were thousands of miles away. The Redskins were much closer.

The home team came onto the field and the crowd roared approval. Dressed in their black jerseys with orange stripes and numbers, white pants, and black-striped socks, they looked formidable, but as imposing as they looked from the stands, I knew that when you were *on* the field, they were even bigger. Every time I contemplated my early retirement decision, I'd make myself remember being hit by Bronko Nagurski in practice and think fondly of the relative safety of the Chicago Police Department. I also couldn't help but notice the proliferation of helmets. Helmets weren't new to pro-football—players had been wearing them for years, but some of the old-timers, myself included, had never bothered with them. New this year was a league rule requiring helmets and thusly compelled, each member of the team was either wearing the padded, leather headgear, or carrying it in his hand.

The Bears had tied their opener with Green Bay, but hadn't yet been defeated. The Steagles were undefeated in three games as well, and their quarterback, Roy Zimmerman, was in top form. But they'd lost a practice game to Chicago and so the crowd expected a close, hard-fought battle. They weren't disappointed— at least for the first quarter.

On the second play of the game, the Steagles scored on a sixty-yard pass play. It was a high, floating toss from Zimmerman to Ernie Steele that just barely cleared Harry Clark's outstretched hand. Steele reeled in the pass on the 20-yard line and when Harry turned to grab him, he fell and Steele trotted to the goal. The crowd groaned.

"What's the line again?" I asked Fish.

"Bears plus four. I'm not worried," said Fish.

"I'll take some of that," said a big guy behind us waving a Philadelphia pennant.

"Nah," said Fish. "Too late. I only take bets up till game time."

The Bears immediately retaliated when Dante Magnani took the next kickoff ninety-six yards to tie the score. He burst through the wall of green at midfield, and twenty thousand fans roared to their feet. Magnani tore down the east sideline, outrunning a hapless defenseman, who made a desperate lunge to stop him at the 12, but came up empty. Magnani skipped in for the score and the crowd settled back in relief.

The next 28 points were scored by the Bears and Sid Luckman, the Chicago quarterback, was brilliant. He threw to George Wilson for the second score. Then, after two drives that featured a second touchdown run by Magnani and one by Ray Nolting, completed six straight passes, topping off the drive with a ten-yard zinger to Doug McEnulty. Woody Sugarman, finally breaking into a starting position, had intercepted Zimmerman's pass to set up the score. The Bears had a half-time lead of 35 to 7, and the rout was on.

"Still want to place that bet?" said Fish, turning his head to talk to the big Steagle fan. He was gone.

"Musso's playing a hell of a game," I said. "Danny, too."

"Yeah," agreed Fish. "Hey, how about Gloria? She like football?"

"I don't know. She said her ex-husband did. Anyway, last night was a one time thing."

"That's good. A girl like Gloria can get under your skin pretty quick."

"It's done," I said.

"Got it," said Fish with a nod. "One time thing."

"And, as you know, Vi doesn't care for football."

The first scoring play of the second half was a gift for the Bears. The Philadelphia team fumbled on the Chicago 19 yard line and Harry Clark scooped up the ball and ran eighty-one yards to the north goal. Sid threw one more touchdown pass to open the fourth quarter. Then, with the score 48-7, the subs came in.

Roy Zimmerman led his team to two more scores against the second squad, but it was too little, too late, and when it was over, the Bears had walloped the Steagles 48-21. Everyone was happy. At least everyone in Chicago.

28

On the one hand, he was tired and wanted to go to bed. It was late and he'd been drinking. On the other hand, he knew that no matter what the voice said, he wouldn't sleep. Not yet.

> *Quiet! Sleep! or I will make*
> *Erinnys whip thee with a snake.*

Priscilla. He rolled the name around in his mouth like a piece of sugar candy.

> *Thy heart shall burn, thy head shall ache,*
> *And ev'ry joint about thee quake;*
> *And therefore dare not yet to wake!*

He stood in the shadows and sucked on a cigarette and waited. He watched one go by. Then another.
They were all Priscillas.

<u>29</u>

"Great!" giggled Gloria. "Just great!"

She had the Sunday *Times* open and was poring over the latest Dear Priscilla column.

"Willie the Web-footed Wonder!" she hooted. "That's a scream!"

She folded the paper and put it on her desk. "I don't know who Priscilla is, but she hits the nail right on the head. I'm thinking that maybe I'll write her a letter myself."

"You need some advice?" said Fish. "Ask me. I'll give you some advice."

"Okay, smart guy," said Gloria. "Here's my problem. I'm working with a couple of lazy bums who keep trying to look down my blou—"

"Everybody in my office," yelled Stanley Sherman. "Now!"

Gloria jumped up from her chair like her girdle was full of ants. The rest of us—me, Fish, Ned, and Vince—ignored him of course. Gloria looked at us in confusion, then ran into Stan's office.

"What the hell?" yelled Stan. *"What the hell?"*

"You—you called us in," stammered Gloria.

"Are you crazy? Get the hell out!"

Gloria backed out of the office, taking the kind of small steps with which one retreats from the dangerously insane. I looked at her with a lopsided grin. Then Fish laughed out loud, and Ned and Vince whooped in tandem.

"I'm not telling you again! Get your sorry asses in here!" bellowed Stan again. *"Right now!"* Gloria looked from me to Fish and back again, uncertain as to what was expected. Then she turned to go back into the office.

"Hang on," Fish said, feeling sorry for her. "Not yet."

"What...?"

"If you sonsofbitches don't get in here right now, you'll all be walking a beat!!" screamed Stan.

I looked through his open door. The captain's face was beet-red and he was tossing a handful of papers into the air.

"Okay," I said. *"Now* we can go in."

"I don't get it," whispered Gloria.

"Third time's a charm," I said, as the five of us headed for the office.

We all managed to find a reasonably clean spot to stand. Gloria, on her initial entrance, had kicked over some old pimento cheese sandwiches, stepped on one, and, now noticing the cheese sticking to her shoe, backed up to the wall and tried to scrape the orange-colored goo off onto the molding.

"Have you seen the papers?" Stan said, holding up the Monday morning *Chicago Tribune.* On the front page was a picture that someone had managed to snap of the police line beside Rubenstein's Grocery the morning that we found the first body. The headline said "Chicago Duffle Killer At Large."

"I just got a call from the commissioner. The mayor's office is getting two hundred telephone calls an hour. The city's in a panic. Headless women chopped up and left in army duffle bags isn't the mayor's idea of Oktoberfest. That's the good news."

I looked over at Fish, then to the chief.

"What's the bad news?"

"There's another body—this one in Stanford Park in the bushes by the swimming pool."

"Popular place for stiffs," mumbled Fish, the cigarette in his mouth jumping like a fishing lure.

"What?" barked Stan.

"We had a murder over there a little over a week ago," I said. "Colored kid killed his girlfriend."

Stan nodded absently, then looked at me and Fish. "You guys have anything yet on this Duffle Killer?"

"We know that one of the dead girls isn't Betty Anderson from Oneonta, Alabama," I offered.

"Brilliant," said Stan in disgust. "How about the letters to Dear Priscilla?"

"The paper threw a teaser out there for us in one of her letters, but we haven't heard anything back yet," said Fish.

"That's it?"

"We think he's a big guy," said Fish. "Strong."

"We don't think he's getting the duffles from the army," I said. "I called Fort Sheridan and talked to the quartermaster. The army stencils those bags as soon as they come in and he hasn't noticed any theft. This guy's getting them somewhere else. Probably on the street."

"Anything else?"

I shrugged and Fish shook his head.

"As of now, you're all on the case. Kingston—you, too. Finish up what you're doing. And find out when Tilly's gonna be back in. Everything else gets passed on to the 22nd. Cahill, you're lead man on this one." He waved a dismissive hand. "That's it. Find this guy—and quick."

"We might as well all go," I said. "We'll take two cars. Gloria, you come with us."

"I'll ride with Ned and Vince," said Gloria, glaring at me while buttoning her coat. "They don't have holes in their roof." Fish shot me a grin from under his Homburg. Ned, Vince, and Gloria were out the door in a couple of minutes. It took me a minute longer, seeing as I was almost finished typing a report for Fish and wanted to get it off our plates.

"What was *that* about?" I asked, clattering away at the Underwood. "How come she didn't want to ride with us?"

"Because you let her blunder in Stan's office after the first yell," laughed Fish.

"Huh?" I stopped and looked at Fish. "It's a rite of passage. We all got yelled at the first time."

"Ah, but we're men. We love to see someone get chewed out and we don't mind getting chewed all that much. She, on the other hand, will view it as a colossal betrayal. She'll think that you should have given her a heads-up instead of letting her make a fool of herself."

"You're joking." I felt myself getting hot under the collar. "She told me she wanted be treated like one of the boys."

"Maybe before you banged her. Now, it's different. Make no mistake, my large friend, you are in the doghouse. I am very wise in the ways of dames."

I finished the report and yanked the page out of the typewriter in frustration, accidently tearing it and one of the carbon copies in half.

"Dammit!"

"You've still got one of the carbons. You can type it for me later," said Fish magnanimously. "And don't worry about Gloria. She'll get over it. Anyway, it was a one time thing—remember?"

We drove up to Stanford Park, circled the block, and saw Ned's car parked in front of the entrance to the swimming pool. There were two police cars up on the grass, blocking the gate. We pulled in behind Ned.

The wooden fence surrounding the pool was about six feet high, and as we entered, we could see noses and eyes aplenty, all perched above grasping fingers of both children and adults, intent on pulling themselves high enough on the fence to view the grisly scene.

Ned was squatting on his haunches near the bushes closest to the deep end of the pool. The water had been drained about a month ago in anticipation of winter, and now the pool had about two feet of dead leaves rustling in the bottom. Vince was standing over Ned with his pad and pencil out, taking notes. Gloria wasn't to be seen. We walked over to the two detectives.

"Same as the first two?" asked Fish.

"Yep," said Ned, looking up. "A naked woman in a bunch of pieces. There's no head."

"Army duffle bag," said Vince. "At least it looks like it. No stenciling. Why doesn't he try to hide these things?"

"He likes the publicity," said Ned, looking down at the bag and poking at it with his shoe. "That's what I think."

"Probably right," I said. Vince nodded his agreement.

"Where's Gloria?" asked Fish.

Vince gave a wry smile and a nod toward the back of the field house. We looked over and saw Detective Kingston losing her breakfast in the shrubs.

"Can't say as I blame her," said Ned. "Pretty rough for a first case."

"You think the bag was brought in last night?" asked Fish.

"Maybe," said Vince. "Victim's not ripe yet, so I'm thinking she hasn't been here very long. We haven't questioned the grounds keeper. He's the one who found her this morning." Vince pointed at a middle-aged bald man sporting a huge mustache and wearing a Chicago Parks department coverall.

"Any other evidence?" Fish asked. "You know, cigarette butts? Draft cards? Signed confessions?"

Vince sniffed. "We do have an eyewitness."

"You're kidding!" I said, looking around. "Who is it?"

Vince looked at his pad. "Name's Earl Parker. He was hanging around the front gate when we drove up. Volunteered to tell us everything he knew and then some. Ned put him in the car and told him to wait."

Gloria appeared beside me, pale and shaken, but in control of herself.

"You want to pass on this and get a statement from Mr. Parker?" Ned asked. "He's in the car."

"I know where he is," she snapped. "He'll keep."

"Suit yourself," Ned said.

Fish knelt down, undid the bag, and peered inside. Then he held it open for me to see. "Seems like the same guy to me."

Gloria turned white again but stood her ground.

"Yep," I said. "We can get her over to the hospital morgue and see what the doc says, but I'm pretty sure I already know."

"White female," said Fish. "Brown hair, between the ages of nineteen and twenty-eight, approximately five-foot seven or eight, one hundred fifty pounds. Average."

"Average," I repeated.

The grounds keeper's name was Maguire, and he hadn't been into the pool enclosure for the last week.

"I just come in to clean out the leaves," he said. "Then once every couple weeks to check on everything."

"So you found her this morning?" asked Gloria.

"There were ravens hopping around next to the bushes. I went over to see."

"Did you open the bag?" asked Fish.

"Nope. I read about the other girl in the *Trib*. I saw the blood and knew right away what it was, so I called the coppers."

I nodded.

Earl Parker had a different story.

"I was walking by the pool after midnight and I heard voices on the other side of the fence."

"What were you doing here after midnight?" Ned asked.

"I was at a meeting," said Earl. He was a tall, thin, scarecrow of a man, wearing a threadbare overcoat, too-big pants held up by a pair of suspenders, and a beat-up fedora—a look that pegged him as one of Chicago's down-and-outers.

"What kind of meeting?" asked Fish. "Union?"

"Klan meeting." Earl's eyes were hollow but defiant. Fish's eyes, in contrast, were now narrow and beyond menacing.

"Before you kill him," I suggested to Fish, "let's hear what he has to say." Fish grunted.

"What?" said Earl Parker, sizing Fish up and deciding, mistakenly, that he was no threat. "Oh, I get it. You're a Hebe."

Fish looked at him without expression.

"Spill it," said Vince.

"Like I said, I was walking by the pool. It was after midnight. Maybe 1:30 or two o'clock. I heard some talking over the fence. I couldn't make out what they were saying, but then a nigger jumps over the fence just in front of me and I hear someone yell 'Ray, get your ass back here,' or something like that. That's it." Earl pondered for a moment, then flung a thin arm out in front of him and pointed north. "He ran off that way."

"Ray, huh?" said Vince. "You sure he said Ray?"

Earl shrugged. "It's what I heard. 'Course I can't understand their jungle-talk half the time."

"Where was your Klan meeting?" asked Fish.

"It's a secret, Jew-boy."

Vince and Ned grimaced and shook their heads. Twice in one morning. They'd seen this before and they knew what was about to happen. Gloria took hold of Fish's arm and pulled him aside.

"Please Fish, not today," she said.

Fish was tight as a drum. I could see it on his face. Now he seemed to relax. "Okay, I'll let it go."

"Damn right," spat Earl, sticking out his meager chest. "No little Jew-boy's gonna mess with me! None of you papist micks, either. I'm a true American!"

"Earl," I said, "you are beyond stupid. The only reason that I'd rather my friend not kill you is because there are too many people around and you're not worth the trouble."

"No trouble," said Fish. "No trouble at all." He pulled out his gun and put the end of the barrel against Earl's forehead, right between his eyes. Then he thumbed back the hammer and we all heard the ominous click in the still morning air as the chamber rolled and the cocked ·38 became the focus of Earl's gaze.

"Oh, Jesus!" said Gloria, under her breath.

Earl's eyes had gone wide. Fish considered for a long moment, then lowered the hammer. "Pfft," he puffed in disgust. "I can't refuse a lady."

"Consider this your lucky day," I said to Earl. "Now get the hell out of here, before I kill you myself."

Earl Parker watched us warily for a moment. Then he turned and walked off without a word.

"Thanks," said Gloria.

An ambulance roared to the entrance to the pool, siren blaring.

"You're welcome," said Fish graciously. He turned to me as Gloria walked to the car. "If I see that asshole again," he whispered, "he won't be walking away."

30

When we arrived back at the station, Sally Clifford was sitting in the chair opposite my desk.

"Uncle Russ wants to see you."

"I'm kind of busy right now. Can it wait?"

"I don't think so." Sally lowered her voice. "There's been another letter." She looked around at the rest of the squad, but they were quite busy at their own desks. Everyone except Fish, who was pretending industriousness, but was all ears.

I studied Sally for a moment.

"It's *important*," she said.

"Right," I said. "Let's go."

"Got another letter," I announced. "Fish and I will cover it. Ned, why don't you and Vince go down to the coroner's office and see if he has anything new to say. I'm betting not. Gloria..." I paused. "You want to go with them to the hospital?"

"No, thanks."

"I still think that the first body we found wasn't his first victim. Too neat and tidy. He seems to want us to find them, so I'm betting there aren't any more in the area—but what if he's new to Chicago?"

Gloria's eyes widened and she nodded slightly. "He might have done the same thing in another city."

"Maybe."

"Shall I call all the police departments?"

"Nah. Take too long. They'll want more information than they're willing to give out. Probably the best way to check is call the biggest newspaper and ask for the city editor. He'll remember if anyone will. Then, if we find something that looks promising, I'll get the commissioner to clear the way for us."

Ned and Vince looked at each other and nodded.

"Good idea," said Vince.

"Any suggestions on cities?" asked Gloria. She had a pencil in her hand and was already taking notes.

"Start big," said Fish. "New York—ah, hell, that won't work. Everybody's always getting chopped up in New York. They must have three of these a week."

"Call New York anyway," I said, then made my way down the east coast. "Boston, Philadelphia, Washington, Richmond, Raleigh, Atlanta. Miami."

"Detroit," said Ned. "Birmingham. Nashville, maybe? Memphis? New Orleans for sure."

"Kansas City," I added. "Louisville. Start with those and any others you can think of east of the Mississippi.

"I'll get on it," said Gloria. She reached for the telephone on her desk, picked it up, then stopped. "Hey," she said, as we walked out, "is this busy-work?"

"Hell, yes!" I called back over my shoulder.

Russell Stewart was behind his desk and talking on the telephone when we arrived at the office door. He waved us in and pointed to the two chairs. We sat down. Sally followed us in, then changed her mind, retreated to the hallway, and closed the door behind us.

"I don't care how you do it," said Russell into the receiver. "You get that picture! This newspaper lives or dies on its pictures." He hung up and looked at Fish and me for a hard moment. Then he slid open a desk drawer and took out an envelope. He slid it across the desk in my direction. It had the same scrawl as the others. Dear Priscilla, *Chicago Times*, Wacker Drive.

I picked it up. Paper was useless for fingerprints and anyway, how many people had handled the letter since it had been mailed? Post office workers, newspaper workers, Sally and Russell—who else? It had been slit on the end. I blew into the envelope, puffed it open, and pulled the letter free.

Dear Priscilla,
   It is time for us to meet. If you agree, reply in Wednesday's paper.
E.P.

I passed it to Fish without a word. He read it and then folded it and returned it to its envelope. Then he slipped the envelope inside the breast pocket of his suit coat.

Russell looked grave. "I heard there was another girl found this morning."

I nodded. "Down in Stanford Park. By the pool."

"Same guy?" asked Russell.

"We think so."

He raised his hands. "I gotta go with the story, you know. All the other papers will have it by tonight. Tomorrow at the latest."

"We know," I said. "We think that's what he wants. The publicity. Otherwise he'd hide the bags a bit more carefully."

"I agree. Anything else you can give me on this?"

"Not right now. As soon as we catch the guy, I'll make sure you have an exclusive."

Russell smiled. "I need pictures, too. If you go to arrest him, give me a call. We'll stake Pete Flambeau out somewhere close. Don't worry. He won't get in the way."

I nodded and stood. Fish was on his feet a second later.

"By the way," said Russell, "our circulation is now at four

hundred eighty-five thousand on the days 'Dear Priscilla' appears in the paper. I'll be happy to hire you full-time whenever you say."

"Nah."

"I'll pay you a three hundred a week."

"No thanks," I said.

"How about a couple more columns?"

"Nope."

"One more," suggested Russell. "Four columns. I'll up you to two hundred a week."

"Not interested," I said.

Russell's shoulders slumped in discouragement. "Okay, fine. But think about it. Promise me you'll think about it."

"Okay. I'll think about it," I said, knowing that I wouldn't. "Tell Sally I'll be dropping a column off tomorrow, will you?"

"Sure," said Russell, smiling like the farmer that planted a money tree.

"You aren't gonna call Pete Flambeau, are you?" asked Fish as we walked out of the *Times* building.

"Hell, no. He's a weasel."

"I bet I can guess where we're going next," Fish said with a grin. "And it's my turn to drive."

"Let's go then. Henry Clarence Goldberg Junior the Third is a busy man. He ain't going to wait all day."

"Sure he is. He's in jail. Ah... hang on." Fish looked at his watch. "I've got to be in court in about fifteen minutes. Let me drop you off."

"We'll get him tomorrow. Anyway, I could use a drink."

31

The Cook County Jail was not a pleasant place, a barbed-wire-covered institution sprawling out behind the Criminal Court building at 26th and California. We showed our badges, walked through the front gates and into what passed for a lobby, then were escorted by a guard to an interview room where we waited for a half-hour while another of the bulls went to get Henry Clarence Goldberg Junior the Third. The whitewashed room stank of fear and urine and unwashed bodies. There were a significant number of what I assumed were blood stains on the floor and walls. I sat in a metal chair at a metal table bolted to the floor. Fish leaned up against the wall and lit up a smoke. Then another. When he lit up his third, I joined him. He was lighting his fourth when the door opened.

Henry came in in shackles and cuffs, head down, shuffling like an old man. He wasn't the same boy we'd sent here a scant two weeks ago. He shambled over to the table and sat down before bothering to look up. When he did, he looked at us both for a couple minutes before recognition set in. Then a smile crossed his face.

"Hey, it's *you* guys!"

"Sure is, Henry," I said.

"I haven't had no visitors. I don't think my mother or sister knows I'm here. No lawyer either."

"Plenty of time for that later," said Fish. "Right now, you've got to answer some questions for us."

"Okay."

"You know a guy named Ray?" I asked.

"Yeah. I hate that Ray."

"What's his last name?"

"Whistler. Ray Whistler."

"He hangs around Stanford Park?"

"Yeah. Him and me used to hang around the park. Then he moved in on Josephine. Now I hate him."

"Where does he live?" Fish said.

"With his momma. Sometimes he stays at a flophouse when he's got some scratch. Sometimes he stays with his girlfriends."

"What's he look like?" I asked.

"Medium," said Henry.

"Listen, Henry," I said, "we need to find him."

"I might could help you, if you can get me out of here. I know where he hangs."

"Couple of hours. That's it," said Fish. "You don't find him, I'll shoot you trying to escape. You believe me?"

Henry beamed and nodded. "Can I get a Maxwell Street Polish?"

"Yeah." I said. "We'll get you two of them. Then you find Ray and we're bringing you back."

"I understand," said Henry.

It took a call to the captain, who in turn called the commissioner, who called the warden, who threatened us for fifteen minutes on general principal before we took Henry, now in irons, out the front gate and to the car.

"I sure appreciate this," said Henry. "I was getting tired of that food."

"You'd better get used to it," said Fish. "That's all you'll be getting for the next twenty-five years or so. That is, if they don't electrocute you first."

I put Henry in the back and handcuffed his irons to the door while Fish made himself comfortable in the driver's seat. By the time I'd come around the back of the car and gotten in, he had the engine humming and the car in gear. My door hadn't even closed before Fish pulled away from the curb and into the street.

"I need to get that article we talked about to Sally Clifford," I said, with a backwards glance toward Henry. He was staring out the window, seemingly disinterested in the conversation of two cops. I looked back at Fish. "Maybe you can help."

"Glad to. We can't go to the station, though. Too many people."

"I could sure use a typewriter at the house."

"There's an extra one in Stan's office. Maybe two. There's the one he never uses. And I thought I saw one under a lemon pie."

"It's probably got gunk all over the keys," I said. "How about the newspaper office? I'll bet Russell Stewart will give me one."

"I have a better idea. You can have mine. I'm not using it, that's for sure."

"I think someone in the squad will notice."

"Did I mention that it's broken and needs to go in for repairs?" said Fish.

"Ah. I see."

"I got a typewriter," said Henry from the back seat. "You let me go, I'll give it to you."

We decided to go with Fish's plan. He waited in the car with Henry while I went in to the station to purloin his typewriter. Ned and Vince were still gone and Stan was nowhere to be seen. I suspected he was in the john. Gloria was on the telephone, but gave me a smile, followed by a confused look, as I tucked Fish's old Remington under one arm, reached into my desk drawer for my file of letters, and headed out the door. Ten minutes later, Fish and I were sitting at my dining room table, watching Henry—still cuffed to the Packard—through the front window and thumbing through letters mailed to Dear Priscilla.

"I'll read," said Fish. "You type."

It didn't take us long to finish the column.

Dear Priscilla,

I'm trying to get my boyfriend to marry me, but I can't manage to find the right words. Can you help?
Signed,
Anxious to get Hitched

Gracious Reader,

Priscilla suggests those three little words that men love to hear. "Darling, I'm pregnant."

Dear Priscilla,

My husband makes a good living and he graciously gives me five dollars a week to run the household. Try as I might, between my medical expenses and our eleven children, I can't seem to make my allowance go quite far enough. I would like to take in washing and make a little extra money, but he says over his cold, dead body. How can I get him to change his mind?
Signed,
Stretched Thin

Gracious Reader,

It may seem a bit harsh to say, but it seems to Priscilla that your husband is a selfish, greedy, manipulative pig in need of having his suggestion (the cold, dead one) taken seriously. But if you don't want to go that far, perhaps you could explain to him that five dollars just doesn't go as far as it used to. Then, when he isn't looking, crack him in the head with a rolling pin and take his wallet.

Dear E.P.
I agree.

"Hmm," said Fish. "Succinct, but maybe a little too abrupt. And, logically, why would Dear Priscilla agree to meet with him? He's a serial killer."

"That's a good point," I said. "But I'm looking at it this way. E.P. asked her to meet him and he's expecting an answer. Could be yes, could be no. Those are the choices. Which one do you think is the more likely to draw him out?"

"Yeah, you're right," agreed Fish.

"One more thing working for us," I said.

"What's that?" said Fish.

"He's nuts."

32

"We'll get you a Polish, then head over to find Ray," said Fish. He cranked the Packard and pulled into the meager traffic of Canal Street.

"Suits me," said Henry, settling back into the rear seat. "Think I could get some new threads? These stripes aren't gonna do my rep any good."

"You aren't going to be out that long," I said. Then to Fish, "I've got to drop the column by Sally's on the way."

Fish nodded.

"Can I at least get a hat?" Henry whined. "I'd hate for Ray to see me without no hat."

"No," I said. "Now, shut up."

Henry sighed.

"Aw," said Fish, "let's get him a hat. He'll be dead in another month."

"Huh?" said Henry.

"Your trial is next Tuesday," said Fish. "Didn't they tell you?"

"Nope," said Henry. "Do I get a lawyer, or what?"

"Plenty of time for that later," said Fish. "Right now, we have to concentrate on finding Ray."

"I could concentrate better if I had a hat."

"Fine," I said. "We'll get you a hat. Now shut up."

"I'd like one of them round ones."

"Like a bowler?" said Fish.

"Yeah. Like that."

"We'll stop on the way back from Sally's," said Fish. "I know a guy..."

Sally wasn't home, but I shoved the envelope under her door. Five o'clock came early in late October, and the lights of the city were starting to glow in the dusk. There had been a few government enforced blackouts during the early months of the war, but now we were pretty much back to normal. The prevailing wisdom seemed to be that if the German U-boats were going to attack us, they'd probably head for New York or somewhere else on the east coast rather than navigate all five of the Great Lakes to get to Chicago. Chicago Power and Light was the order of the day, and most of the city simply threw a switch to chase away the shadows, but Maxwell Street was still lighted by gas. The lamplighters could be seen every evening, making their way from Douglas Park to the river. We drove slowly until Fish spotted his haberdasher, then pulled over. He rolled down the driver's side window and yelled across the crowd.

"Bernie!"

A young guy ambled up to the car window. He was wearing an overcoat and a fedora. His hands were stuffed into his pockets and tired eyes peered into the car from behind a pair of wire-rimmed glasses.

"You look awful," said Fish.

"The kid's got the whooping cough," said Bernie. "I ain't slept for about three days."

"Sorry to hear it."

"I haven't got your ten-spot, if that's what you're here for. My wife made me buy some medicine. You believe me, don't you?"

"Sure, I believe you. Next week."

"Next week for sure," said Bernie. "Or we could let it ride..."

"Sure," said Fish. "Be happy to let it ride." He pulled out his pad to make a quick note. "Let's see... boxing, right?"

"Yeah."

"I've got Joey Maxim against Buddy Scott at Marigold Gardens. Thursday night."

"Yeah," said Bernie. "That sounds good. I'll take Scott."

"Even odds," said Fish, flipping his pad shut. "Now, you can do me a favor."

"Anything you need," said Bernie.

"This boy in the back needs a hat."

"A bowler," said Henry. "A yellow one."

"Don't have a yellow one," said Bernie. "I have a black one. Or gray."

"Gray," said Henry.

Bernie stuck his head in the window and looked at Henry. "What size?"

"I dunno," shrugged Henry.

"Wait here. I'll be back in a minute."

"He's going to lose that sawbuck," I said. "Joey Maxim's not going down."

"Bernie's a loser," said Fish with a shrug. "Nothing I can do about it. Once you start betting the kid's medicine money..."

"Yeah," I said.

"How about you? You want a piece of Joey Maxim?" Fish asked. "It'd be pennies from heaven."

"Nope."

"I do," said Henry. "I saw him fight once at the fairgrounds."

"You have no money and no options," said Fish.

Bernie showed back up at the window with two hats and handed one of them to Fish. "Let's try the bigger one first," he said.

Fish swung around and plopped the bowler on Henry's head. "That fit all right?"

Henry raised one of his shackled hands, the one not cuffed to the door, and adjusted his new chapeau. "Lemme try the other one."

Fish snatched the first one off Henry's head and replaced it with a slightly smaller version.

"That's better," said Henry. "How do I look?"

"Like a man going back to jail tonight."

It was another half-mile down Maxwell to the corner of Halstead, home of Jim's Original sandwich stand. Every corner along the way had a guitar player, or a singer, or a band, each fighting for space in the glowing streetlights. We had to park a block away, so we left Henry handcuffed to the back door and got out of the car, intent on supper.

"I don't want no peppers on mine," Henry hollered after us. "Extra mustard."

"He's certainly getting demanding," Fish said. "Perhaps we should explain his position to him."

"I think it might make the evening a little more tolerable. You never should have got him that hat."

"Give us six Originals," Fish said, walking up to the counter. "Four dressed, two with no peppers and extra mustard."

"That it?" said the vendor.

"Two beers," I added.

We decided not to join Henry in the car for dinner. Fish went to get us a bench at a table while I walked over to the car to warn Henry not to spill anything.

"How am I not gonna spill something? I've got these irons on, and you've got one of my hands cuffed to the door."

"Fine," I said, pulling out a small key from my pocket. "I'm taking off the cuff. You get out of the car, I'll shoot you in the head. You spill anything, I'll break your nose."

Henry nodded and rubbed his wrists before taking the brown bag from my outstretched hand.

"We'll be sitting right there." I pointed to a bench by the stand. "And we'll be watching you."

"I ain't going nowhere," said Henry happily unwrapping one of his sausage sandwiches. "I've got a Jim's Original."

"I told you not to spill anything," I said, opening the door to the Packard and cuffing Henry's irons back to the door handle.

Henry Clarence Junior the Third was a certified pig. There were remnants of onions on the floor, mustard on the upholstery, and it looked like he'd wiped his hands on the back of the front seat when he was finished.

"Don't worry 'bout it," said Henry smugly. "I'm going to help you find Ray, remember?"

Fish turned in his seat and looked at Henry.

"Henry, I don't think you understand your position," he said.

"I understand it perfectly well. You need me to find Ray. I've been thinking about it. You need me and I'm gonna need something in return."

I opened the passenger side door and got in. Fish looked at me with a crooked grin. I put my arm up on the back of the seat and twisted around to look back at Henry. Then I uncorked, straightened my arm and hit him in the nose. It popped with the sound of a firecracker going off. I was right-handed, and sitting the way I was, I had to hit him with my left, but it was a good shot—a hard, straight left from the shoulder. He gave a yelp, jerked his head back, and covered his face with his right hand, the one that wasn't cuffed to the door.

Wha... wha..." he sputtered through the blood dripping from his ruined nose.

He took his hand away from his face and looked stupidly at the crimson pool in his palm. I took the opportunity to hit him again. It has been my experience that although a busted beezer is extremely painful, being hit *repeatedly* in the beezer is a life changing experience. There was no tell-tale "pop" this time, because there was nothing left to go "pop." Henry's eyes rolled back into his head and he glugged unintelligibly.

"You see, Henry," I said, "like many others, you have misjudged us. Yes, Fish got you a hat and we fed you, but we are not your friends."

I smacked him hard on the side of his face with an open hand to bring his eyes back into focus. "You'll take us to Ray," I growled, "and you'll do it now, or I'll bust your beak so hard that you'll part your hair every time you sneeze." Then I grabbed him by his hair and banged his face into the back of the front seat. Henry howled again.

"Hey!" said Fish. "Watch the upholstery!"

I shrugged. "We're going to have to get the car cleaned anyway. I mean, *look* at it! Mustard, blood, grease..."

"Yeah, you're right," said Fish in disgust. "Hit him again for me."

"No," managed Henry. "Don't hit me again. I'm sorry for the mess."

We turned back around and Fish punched the starter. I looked in the mirror. Henry was slumped in the back seat, still wearing his bowler, his nose spread across his face, and blood dripping down onto his striped prison-issue shirt.

"Where to, Henry?" Fish said. Henry didn't answer.

"I'm not going to ask again."

"Stockyards," muttered Henry. "Ray'll be at the Yards."

"You see what happens when you try to be nice to people?" Fish said to me as we drove off. "They take advantage of you."

33

The Yards employed more people than any other enterprise in Chicago, but by the time we arrived at the Union Stockyard Gate arching over Exchange Avenue, most of the thirty-thousand day laborers that populated both the Union Stockyard and Transit Company and the dozens of independent meat-packers had gone home for the day. Word was that The Yards employed double that many workers twenty years ago, but a lot had happened since then. Even with the majority of the work force heading for home for the evening, the saloons, restaurants, and offices were still bustling. The stockyards were a city unto themselves, comprising more than a square mile of real estate, from Halstead Street to Ashland and from 39th to 47th. It was no wonder that all of the neighborhoods for miles around smelled of shit. It wasn't so bad on the West Side—the breezes off Lake Michigan kept the stink at bay—but in the summer when the air was still, the stench was almost unbearable, even as far north as Lincoln Park. The South Fork of the Chicago River—the same river I watched from my front porch a few miles north—was called "Bubbly Creek" as it passed by The Yards. Tons of blood and entrails were dumped into its waters, eventually turning to bubbling gasses as it rotted on the bottom.

The limestone entrance to The Yards was more a monument

to capitalism than an actual gate, stretching across Exchange Avenue. The famous bust of "Sherman," the prize-winning bull that looked down on the workers and tourists from the top of the central arch was slightly misleading. Yes, there were plenty of cattle that passed though the yard, but what the Union Stockyard was known for was hogs. "Hog butcher for the World" was what Carl Sandburg called us. He was right. I had to memorize the poem in school and what I could remember of it fit Chicago to a T. At least, the part of Chicago I knew.

They tell me you are wicked and I believe them, for I have seen your painted women under the gas lamps luring the farm boys.

And they tell me you are crooked and I answer: Yes, it is true I have seen the gunman kill and go free to kill again.

The rest of it was bunk.

We pulled up to the gate and got out of the car, holding our badges up to the two guards at the gate. We needn't have bothered. I knew them both—off-duty beat cops supplementing their city paycheck.

"Hey, it's Merl! And Fish!"

"Albert. How're you doing?" I said, putting my badge back in my coat pocket. I nodded at the second cop. "Jimmy."

I had worked with Albert Burke and Jimmy White down at the 13th. Both were stand-up guys. They were wearing Union Stockyard uniforms, dark blue jackets emblazoned with the Stockyard Security patch on each sleeve, and trousers with a crisp white stripe running down the leg. Their ·38 Police Specials were in plain sight, holstered on their belts. Albert was the older of the two, being somewhere in his mid-forties. Jimmy was younger by half.

"I'm doing okay," said Albert. "This second job's going to kill me though. The little woman says we need a new car. The next-door neighbors got a Studebaker last year. Now you can't get a new one 'cause of the government crack-down, but she's not going to let either *that*, or my skinny paycheck, stop her."

"'Course not," said Fish. "A woman wants what she wants and it's your duty as a husband to buy it for her. Tell you what, you need a new car, you come to me first."

"Thanks, Fish. I appreciate that."

We could hear the noise of fifty thousand cattle, sheep, and hogs waiting nervously in the holding pens for transport to their final destination via either railcar or the killing wheel.

"You don't mind if we look around, do you?" I asked. "We have a guy in the car who says there's a suspect in here somewhere."

"Don't mind a bit," said Albert. "You need any help? There's an awful lot of territory to cover."

"We might need some," said Fish. "I think we can handle it, but if you'd tag along, we'd appreciate it. Our boy's going to point us right to the place. Merl had a word with him."

"Come right on in then. Give us a minute to get our car and we'll follow you."

"By the way, Jimmy," said Fish to the younger of the two cops, "I'm going to need that fiver by Friday. You'll come by the stand, right?"

"Yeah, Fish. Sure," said Jimmy, looking at his shoes.

"Don't forget, now."

"I won't," muttered Jimmy.

"I wondered why Jimmy was being so quiet," I said to Fish as we walked back to the car. "He usually talks to beat the band."

"He won't show up on Friday," said Fish. "I can always tell when they don't have the dough. I guess I'll have to have Little Eddie pay him a visit." He sighed. "I swear, this is a tough business."

We climbed into the car, started it up, and drove slowly through the main gate into the stockyard. Fish stopped and idled for a minute, waiting till we saw the lights of the security cop's car flip on, then continued. There were plenty of exits and entrances to The Yards, roads and rails and footpaths, and the only fences were the ones that kept the livestock penned in.

"Which way?" I asked Henry who was either pretending to sleep, or trying to get rid of his headache by resting his eyes.

"Huh?"

"Which way, Henry?"

"This don't look right to me. I'm not sure I can..."

I turned around in my seat and glowered.

"I mean, turn left at this road right here. I remember now."

Fish turned left and headed down a long corridor of hog pens.

"You know, these hogs will eat you," said Fish. "If you happened to fall into one of those pens by accident. I've seen it happen."

"Really?" I said, glancing at Henry in the mirror. His eyes had gone wide.

"Yep. It was that colored boy from Glencoe about three years ago. We were chasing him and he thought he could get away by jumping one of those fences. Didn't get half way across the pen before the first hog got him."

"Glad I didn't see that," I said.

"Yeah," said Fish, sadly. "We gave his momma what was left. A bloody sock and part of his schwantz. We left it on the mantle in a pickle jar. His dick, not the sock."

"You guys ain't gonna throw me to the hogs, are you?" asked Henry, terror clouding his voice. "I didn't mean nothin' before."

"Depends," Fish said. "Depends on whether we find this Ray Whistler soon, or if we have to stay out here all night. I'd just as soon get to bed early."

"Save a whole lot of trouble if the hogs got you," I said. "Wouldn't need to go through a trial or anything."

"I'll show you where Ray is," said Henry. "No problem." He sat quiet for a moment. "That is, if he's here."

"Henry," I said. "You'd better hope he's here."

"Turn right," said Henry, when we reached the end of the row of pens. "And turn off your lights."

Fish toggled the lights off and we drove ahead by the glow of the gas street lights placed every fifty yards or so along the dirt drive. There were ramshackle buildings on either side, offices once, or maybe storage buildings. Now they looked deserted.

"Stop here."

Fish stopped the car and turned off the engine. It sputtered to a stop. Jimmy and Albert were behind us and a moment later we heard their engine die as well. Their headlights followed suit.

"You gotta take me with you," said Henry. "I know the password. They'll let me in."

I nodded as I got out of the Packard, easing the car door closed behind me as quietly as I could. By the time I'd come around the front of the car, Fish had Henry uncuffed from the door, standing in the middle of the dusty road, rubbing his wrists. His nose and face were a mess and his hat was on crooked. He was still wearing his prison stripes, although, in the dark, the stripes were almost invisible due to the dried blood all over the front of his shirt.

"Dammit," whispered Fish. "I didn't know we were going to have to take him in with us. He looks like hell."

"We've got one of your jackets in the trunk," I suggested. "A yellow one."

"Aw, man," whined Fish. "That's my spare. I *hate* to walk around with blood all over me."

"It's for a good cause," I said, as I popped the trunk.

"How about his face?" said Fish, quietly. "We gotta clean him up."

"We've got a can of gas..."

"Ouch," said Fish. "That's gonna sting."

"Can't be helped," I said, taking the tin can of the trunk. "We need a rag."

Albert and Jimmy had left their car and were now standing beside the Packard watching with silent amusement.

"Turn around," Fish said to Henry, spinning him one hundred eighty degrees in the opposite direction. He flipped open his knife, cut a piece of material from the back of Henry's shirt and handed it to me. I poured some gas over it and leaned in close to Henry's face.

"Pay real close attention," I said. "I'm going to clean up your

177

face. It's going to hurt like hell. You utter one sound and Detective Biederman will cut your throat clean through. We can't have you yelling."

Henry's eyes widened to a pair golf balls.

"You understand? Not a sound."

Henry nodded.

"Fish," I whispered, "put your knife here on Henry's throat, so he won't be tempted to yell."

"Glad to," said Fish, happily obliging.

I took the gas-soaked rag and wiped it over Henry's ruined nose and face, cleaning away the blood as best I could in the dim light. Henry gritted his teeth and squinched his eyes shut as tears ran down his cheeks, but didn't utter a sound.

"There, you see," I said, finishing up and tossing the rag onto the ground. "Nothing to it." I handed him Fish's jacket. "Put this on."

Fish flipped his knife shut while Henry slipped his arms through the arm-holes and shrugged the jacket onto his meager shoulders. The jacket seemed to fit through the chest, but that was as far as it went. Henry's arms and hands hung down a good eight inches below the cuffs.

"Doesn't fit so good," whimpered Henry, his teeth still clenched together in pain from his recent bath.

"It'll have to do. Here—roll up the sleeves." I rolled each sleeve up around Henry's elbows.

"No cat wears a jacket like this," said Henry in dismay.

"It's your new style," Fish said. "Now shut up."

"Ray's gonna make fun of me..."

"Shut up," I said, "or I'll clean your face again."

Henry walked the four of us about two hundred yards further down the street, then turned down an alley in between two dilapidated buildings left over from the last century. They were clapboard and might have been white-washed at one point in their history. Even by the light of the full moon, now high enough in the sky to cast light into the narrow space, they barely qualified as gray. The holes that had been punched into the sides of the walls, probably by vagrants during the Depression when housing was impossible to afford, had been covered over by tin, cut to size and nailed to the wall. The ones that hadn't been covered opened into the blackness of unused warehouses and offices. At the end of the row, the alley was flanked by two buildings that weren't made of wood, but stone, or maybe cement—it was difficult to tell in the dark—and it was here that Henry stopped us and pointed to an iron door on our left. There was a sliding metal window about face-high and some light leaking out from underneath. The window was closed. Fish pushed Henry in front of the window and banged on the door. The rest of us stood on either side, out of sight.

Nothing. Fish reached in and banged on the door again. After a minute the window slid open and a voice said "What?"

"It's Henry. Henry Goldberg. Lemme in," said Henry.

"It ain't Henry," came a voice from further back in the room. "Henry's in jail."

"Looks like him," said the voice at the window. ""Cept he's uglier. What happened to your nose?"

"Just lemme in, Stink Eye," said Henry.

"What's the password?" said the voice.

"Ray Whistler's mother blows Egyptians," said Henry.

"Hey!" said the second voice. "That ain't funny!"

"Close enough," said the first voice, laughing. "C'mon in."

We heard a bar being slid back and the iron door swung open. I gave Henry a push and followed him in knowing Fish was right behind me.

The room was large and devoid of furniture save for a small pot-bellied stove set against one wall. There was another door at the far end. It was closed. The single, bright bulb swinging from a metal dome cast all the shadows outward from the game of craps that was happening directly beneath it.

I gave Stink Eye a hard shove as I came through the door and he tripped and fell backward against the stove, yelping as sparks flew into the room. Ray Whistler, who I presumed the other colored boy to be, was on his haunches with dice in his hand, too startled to move. I took stock of the eight people in the room in an instant. So did Fish. Two were women, whores probably, judging by their lack of clothes, and six were men. Ray and Stink Eye and two of the men were no threat. The other two—Italians, by the look of them—were.

"Evening boys," I said to the gamblers. "You're all under arrest."

The two Italians were from North Chicago and preferred not to be under arrest. Fish shot one of the greasers in the eye just as his gun was clearing his jacket. It was a good shot. I saw his horn-rimmed glasses pop and blood bubble out of the socket like a small geyser as his head snapped back and he fell like a sack of wet sand. The second guy was smaller, slower, and closer to me. He turned for the other door, at the same time going for his gun. I reached out, grabbed him by the hair with one hand and his right arm with the other—just at the biceps—then yanked him into the air by his scalp and twisted his arm behind his back until I felt the shoulder separate with a rip. His scream didn't last long, ceasing almost immediately upon his forehead's contact with the cement wall. Still holding him up by his hair, I slipped the gat from his shoulder holster. Then I dropped him in a heap.

The two men who were *no* threat had been kneeling beside the pile of cash under the lamp. Now they stood up, but didn't make any kind of move toward Fish or me. We'd met them before—Jeff Howard and Don Picarro, the two Bears rookies. Each of them had fingers on both hands taped up in splints.

"Oh, shit," said Don, the color draining from his face. Jeff didn't say anything.

"You boys learn slow," said Fish, shaking his head.

The two girls got to their feet as well; one white girl, one colored, both naked above the waist and not wearing enough below the waist to hide any kind of weapon. They huddled together against the wall like cornered mice, trying to make themselves as small and unobtrusive as possible. The security cops followed us into the room, guns drawn, but the excitement was over. Now Jimmy, the younger one, was staring at the whores as though he'd never seen tits before, which he probably hadn't. Not like these, anyway. The white girl gave him a shy smile.

"Are you going to... going to... arrest us?" stammered Jeff, lifting his bandaged hands in surrender.

"Hell, yes," said Fish, waving his gun in the air. "You're lucky I don't shoot you." He put his gun away, walked over to Don Picarro, pulled his hands behind his back and snapped a pair of cuffs on him. He repeated the exercise with Jeff Howard who howled when Fish gave one of his broken fingers an "accidental" twist.

"What about them?" asked Ray, looking at the two Italians. "Are they dead?"

"This one for sure," said Fish, giving the first one a kick.

"That was a good shot," said Albert, the old cop. "Right in the eye as he was going for his piece."

"Bah," said Fish with a disgusted shrug. "I was trying to shoot him in the shoulder. I'd have liked to keep one of them alive."

"How about that one?" said Jimmy, pointing to the one who'd had the mishap with the cement wall. "He still alive?"

"For now, but probably not for long," said Fish. "Merl isn't usually too gentle."

I looked down at the second Italian. His breathing was shallow and he wasn't moving. He might wake up eventually. Maybe not.

"Is there a telephone?" I said.

The colored girl pointed to the back room. "In there."

"Your clothes in there, too?" Fish asked.

"Yeah."

Fish nodded.

"Can we go get them?" asked the white girl, crossing her arms in front of her. "It ain't cold with that stove going, but it's getting a little embarrassing."

"In a second," said Fish. "Young Jimmy here's gettin' an eyeful. I doubt he's ever seen a girl in her birthday suit, or as near to it as you are."

Jimmy grinned and turned red, but didn't look away.

I opened the door to the second room. It was lit by an identical hanging bulb and metal shade. Another little stove heated the room fueled by the half-empty coal bucket that sat beside it. The room was warm. In the opposite corner was an old, cotton-ticked, badly-stained mattress with a couple of blankets thrown haphazardly on top of it. The girls' clothes had been folded neatly in two piles and placed on the top of an ancient dresser beside some lipsticks and a hairbrush. A mirror hung on the wall just above it. Across the room, on a small dining table furbished with two mismatched wooden chairs, was a telephone. I walked over to it and picked it up. Dial tone. I set it back on the cradle, gathered up the girl's clothes and took them into the front room.

"Here," I said, tossing the clothes to the girls. I turned to the two security cops. "We're going to need that back room to have a word with Ray and Stink Eye. Henry, too."

"No problem," said Albert. Jimmy nodded.

"We'll call for some backup." I nodded toward the rookies and the whores. "Can you take these four to the gatehouse and wait for the squad cars? Have them take these morons to the station."

"Sure," said Albert.

"Get 'em to call for an ambulance, too. We'll be along shortly."

34

"You see, Mr. Eye," said Fish, "you are what we call an irritant."

Stink Eye was sitting in one of the kitchen chairs, his hands cuffed behind him and locked to the slats, trying to look as tough as a man in his tenuous position could look. I had pulled his chair into the middle of the room next to the one where Ray found himself in a similar predicament. Ray, unlike Stink Eye, looked ready to cry. Henry was crouching in the corner, his back against the wall with his eyes squeezed shut and both hands on his hat.

Fish stood in front of the two men. "Mr. Eye," he said, "we need some information about a killer."

"I don't know nothin'."

"Oh, we know you don't. But Ray here does."

"No, I don't," said Ray. "I swears it."

"Let me cut to the chase," I said, as I pulled a pair of leather mitts out of my pocket. "Here's the way this works. If we tune Ray up, he'll probably just say any old thing to make us stop."

"Yeah," said Ray eagerly, "I would."

"If I was you," I said to Ray, "I wouldn't be cracking foxy just now."

"Yeah! Shut up, fool!" said Stink Eye, his cool exterior beginning to crumble.

"So you see, Mr. Eye," continued Fish," when Ray sees what's happening to you, he'll be more than happy to cooperate with us when his time comes. I can practically guarantee it."

"Nah," said Ray. "You don't scare me. Do your worst."

"You better be scared," said Henry. "Look at my nose."

I shrugged and pulled on my gloves.

"You wanna use my sap?" asked Fish.

"Nah. I like to feel the bones break."

"Wait a second," said Fish. "Don't start yet. I gotta make a call."

"Huh?" said Stink Eye.

"I gotta make a call," repeated Fish, picking up the telephone. He clicked the cradle a couple of times, waited for a second, then "Operator? Can you get me Dearborn 4-6543? Thanks, I'll wait."

"Who you calling?" asked Stink Eye.

"You know a man named Fat Washington?" asked Fish, waiting for the operator to connect him.

Stink Eye went as white as Moby Dick's ghost.

"Don't be callin' Fat," he said quickly. "There's no need."

"Au contraire," said Fish. He tapped a smoke out of a deck and lit it. "You're running craps on his territory. Not only that, but you invited the wops in. Fat Washington is *not* gonna be happy with you."

Stink Eye squirmed in his chair. "Ricca called me himself! How're you gonna say 'no' to him? He's the boss!"

Paul "The Waiter" Ricca had taken over the Outfit after Frank Nitti ate his gun last March. It had been big news. The Chicago Outfit had been on the decline since their glory days running liquor during Prohibition, but they were still eager to get their fingers into whatever pies they could. These pies obviously included those being baked in Fat Washington's oven.

"Ricca's going to jail," said Fish, still waiting on the telephone. "Didn't you hear? Some Hollywood movie deal gone bad."

"Don't matter," said Stink Eye sadly. "If it's not him, it'll be someone else."

"Hey, Fat," said Fish into the telephone. "This is Fish... Yeah. Just fine." He laughed at some joke unheard by the rest of us, then continued. "Yeah. That's a riot! Listen, you know a guy named Stink Eye?"

Fat Washington was indeed fat—five and a half feet tall and probably close to four hundred pounds. In addition to being fat, Fat Washington was generally mean and extremely disagreeable. He presented himself well enough; he was a light-skinned Negro with a shiny bald head, always dapper in white linen suits with a matching cane. His eyes were small and black and flat and when he smiled, he gave the immediate impression of a shark; a reasonable assessment, considering that he had filed his front teeth—top and bottom—to points. The diamond rings that circled his fat fingers were the real deal, as was his slow accent cultivated in his native Virginia that bespoke culture and refinement, but if you crossed Fat Washington, his outward gentility quickly faded. Fat Washington ran the territory from Cermak down to Garfield and west to McKinley Park. The stockyards were his.

"Say, Fat," continued Fish, "seems like your boy Stink Eye has been running craps in The Yards. Not only that, but he invited the Italians in to take a slice. Wondered if you knew about that?"

"I didn't invite them," said Stink Eye.

"No? Well then, you want me to shoot him?" asked Fish. "Oh... okay. Yeah... Merl and I killed a couple of them. No one I recognized. New guys. I don't think they were made."

Stink Eye slumped into his chair, all his moxie gone. "Damn," he said.

"All right then," said Fish. "I'll let you take care of it." He hung up with a smile.

"You're lucky I made that call, Mr. Eye," said Fish. "Fat Washington wants me to let you go. You know, as a favor to him. You aren't gonna get tuned up after all."

"No... no... wait," said Stink Eye. "You gotta take me in. I belong in jail."

"I don't think so," said Fish. "I gave my word."

"What about me?" asked Ray.

No red haze this time. Just business. I hit him in the choppers, not too hard, but hard enough to knock out a couple of teeth. He spit them onto the floor along with a mouthful of blood.

"We're going to start with you," I said.

Henry gave a heavy sigh from the corner and covered his eyes. "Man," he said. "You guys are meaner than a half-skinned possum."

Twenty minutes later, we knew what Ray knew. We also knew what Stink Eye knew thanks to Fish's promise to take him to jail.

Last night, Ray and Stink Eye were hiding by the fieldhouse in Stanford Park waiting to sell some dope to a couple of college boys.

"I seen him come into the park," said Stink Eye. "A big guy. Not as big as you, but big. He had a bag slung over a shoulder."

"I didn't see him," said Ray. "Listen, could you save those teeth for me?"

"Then he walks over, nice as you please," continues Stink Eye, "and dumps the bag in the bushes."

"Did you get a look at his face?" asked Fish.

"Nope. Too dark or he might've had some color on his face. Saw his hands though. That's how I know he was white. He had big hands. Big."

"Any tape on his fingers?" I asked.

"Nope. Then, when he leaves, me and Ray sneak over to look in the bag. You never know, y'know? Might be something." Stink Eye shrugged.

"Then what?" Fish said.

"Then Ray freaks out and starts screaming like a woman. He took off running down the street."

"No I didn't," said Ray out of swollen lips. "I didn't scream, anyways. Well, not like a woman."

Stink Eye smirked at him. "So I yell, 'Ray, get yo' black ass back here. You've got all the dope!' But he was already gone."

"What time was this?" said Fish.

"'Bout two o'clock in the morning," answered Stink Eye.

"And you didn't think to call us?" I said. "Dead girl chopped up in a bag, and you didn't call?"

"You're the cops," said Stink Eye. "This is white crime. Got nothin' to do with us."

"And the big guy was white?" I said.

"White as the robe he was wearin'."

"You thinking what I'm thinking?" asked Fish as we drove back to the precinct. Stink Eye and Ray were handcuffed together in the back seat. We'd cuffed Henry's irons to the door.

"Probably. Wasn't one of the rookies. Their fingers are busted. Could be our friend Earl Parker, the Klansman." I shook my head. "E.P."

"Yeah," agreed Fish. "Can't believe we missed that."

"Too easy," I said.

35

If any of the squad had gone home for the evening, they'd been called back in by the time we arrived with the trio in tow. Henry Junior the Third, Stink Eye Johnson, and Ray Whistler shuffled into the office with their heads hanging. Stan Sherman was leaning against the door jamb of his office, watching the proceedings. He looked slightly more rumpled than usual, which was, for Stan, going some. One of his shirttails had come untucked, his tie was half-knotted and seemed to have a corner of a cheese sandwich stuck to it, his pants were unzipped, and the shirttail that had managed to stay in his pants was sneaking lewdly out his zipper.

Gloria was standing beside Stan Sherman, also watching the proceedings, exchanging the occasional whispered communication with the captain. She'd obviously changed from her official departmental look before she'd been called back in and was now wearing a dark skirt and a red angora sweater—a sweater that fit her better than it fit the rabbit. Her blond hair was pulled into a ponytail and tied with a red ribbon.

"Hey!" said Fish, giving Stink Eye a slight shove in the back to get him moving. "Tilly's back!"

"Yeah," said Tilly. "I've had all the chicken soup and war reports on the radio I can take."

"You're not still contagious, are you?" asked Ned.

"Nah. It was German measles. Three days and you're cured. Those Krauts are nothing if not efficient. Itched like hell, though."

"Glad you're back," I said. "You up to speed?"

"Not on the murders. Not yet. But we can sure get these upstanding citizens processed."

The two girls were sitting on the bench against the wall waiting patiently for their turn. They'd been down this road before and knew the routine. The two rookies looked extremely uncomfortable, Don Picarro sitting in front of Tilly and Jeff Howard occupying the chair at Ned Mansfield's desk. Vince came through the back door carrying a box of donuts.

"Hey, you're back," he said. "How 'bout a donut?"

"Sure," I said. "I'll take one." Fish nodded in agreement.

"What have we got?" asked Tilly, pausing at his typewriter.

"Start with solicitation of a prostitute," said Fish. "Then add illegal gambling, money laundering, assaulting a police officer, resisting arrest, and attempted murder. If I can think of something else, we'll throw it in."

Don shook his head, but didn't say anything. Jeff turned white. "We didn't do any of those things except maybe the gambling part. Ida and Lois aren't even whores! They just came over to have a party."

Hearing their names, the two girls looked across the room at him, smiled, and gave a little wave. The colored girl blew him a kiss.

"What's good for the goose is good for the gander," laughed Tilly, resuming his typing. "You were there. You all get charged the same." He chuckled to himself. "Ida and Lois... that's rich."

"The colored girl's name is Minnie Mayfield," said Ned. "The white girl's Velma Harvey, although she sometimes goes by Genevieve. You'll both have the clap by morning."

"Seems a shame, doesn't it," Fish said. "After we had that little talk with you and all."

"*And* busted our fingers!" Jeff blurted out.

A deadly silence came over the room, and every pair of eyes settled on the hapless rookie.

"I mean..." he stammered.

Stan waddled over from his door. "*What* did you say?"

"I mean... umm..." Jeff Howard stammered again.

"He don't mean nothin'," said Don. "He didn't *say* nothin' and we don't *know* nothin'." He turned to Jeff. "Now shut the hell up and wait for Hunk."

Two hours later, the whole batch of them had been processed, booked, and sent over to the city jail, all of them except Henry. We had to take Henry back ourselves and make sure he was checked in. For now, he was handcuffed to a desk in one of our interrogation rooms.

"What have you got?" said Stan, once we'd all settled in to the remainder of the doughnuts.

"Not much," I admitted. "Stink Eye and Ray both said they saw the guy who dumped the body."

"Unless there are two of them," said Ned. Ned liked conspiracies.

"Sheesh," said Tilly. "Two of them?"

"I don't think so," Vince said. "There's been no sexual assault. Usually, if there's two of them, at least one of them is a perv. Hey, who's got a smoke?"

Ned handed him a deck and flipped him a book of lights. "You're going to be in Dutch if the government ever starts rationing coffin nails," he said grinning.

"This is Chicago," said Tilly with a snort. "The day I can't get a smoke is the day I move to Poughkeepsie."

"I agree with Vince," I said. "This was done by one guy and he's big. Big enough to carry a body in a duffle bag and throw it over a seven foot high fence."

"How about that KKK clown?" said Tilly. "Elmo Parker."

"Earl," said Fish. "Earl Parker. He ain't big enough."

"Pick him up anyway," said Stan. He reached down the front of his pants and scratched at something, then caught Gloria watching him and quickly pulled his hand free.

I gave a nod in her direction. "Did you call those newspapers?"

She looked at her pad. "I called *The New York Times, The Boston Globe, The Philadelphia Daily News, The Washington Post, The...*"

"Save the recitation," said Stan. "You find out anything?"

"I only talked to five editors—Boston, Atlanta, New York, Miami, and Memphis. The rest were in meetings or out of the office. I left messages. The ones I talked to don't have any recollection of crimes like these, but said they'd ask around."

"Who talked to the coroner on this last one?" asked Stan.

"I did," said Ned, looking at his own notes. "Same as the rest. Mid-twenties, brown hair, approximately one hundred fifty pounds, five-seven or eight. No sexual assault. Seven pieces. No head."

"We've got a nut case," said Fish. "Maybe we ought to call a shrink or something."

"Not a bad idea," said Stan. "Do it."

Ned spit into a nearby trash can. "Probably has issues with his mother."

"Probably has issues with his dick," said Gloria.

"We're trying to set up a meeting," I said to Gloria after the room had cleared. "Through Dear Priscilla. The column comes out on Wednesday, so hopefully we should hear something shortly after that."

"Then what?" asked Gloria.

"Depends. Maybe we send Priscilla to meet with him."

"Is she up for it?" asked Fish.

"Oh, she's up for it," Gloria said with a smile.

"I'll take Henry back," offered Fish. "It's on my way."

I uncuffed Henry's irons from the desk after prodding him

awake. "You sure? I'll go with you if you want."

"Nah. No problem. See you tomorrow."

"Hey," said Henry, "my trial's on Tuesday. You think you guys could get me a lawyer?"

"Plenty of time for that later," said Fish.

36

It was late and my house was a good mile walk from the station. I didn't mind—it gave me time to think. The temperature had warmed up considerably since yesterday, but I knew it wouldn't last. Indian summer. I took my coat off as I walked, then my suit jacket. If Chicago weather held true to form, we'd have two or three days of warmth, then—bang—winter. Of course, the chances of Chicago weather holding true to form were longer odds than even Fish would feel comfortable taking.

I turned north on Canal and wandered up the street, not paying any particular attention to anything until I reached my house, then noticed a car parked in front. It was the kind of car that would bring a smile to any face. A cherry-red convertible coupe with the top down. It was long, low, and rakish, and looked as though it were going sixty just sitting still.

"Like it?"

I looked up and saw Gloria sitting on the porch.

"Yeah," I said with a school-boy grin on my face. "This yours?"

"It was Daddy-in-law's. I decided I needed it more than he did."

I walked up and joined her on the porch, flopping into the other wicker chair. "Nice. What kind is it? I've never seen one."

"A 1940 Lincoln-Zephyr Cabriolet convertible. They only made three hundred-fifty or so."

"Fast?"

She nodded. "Oh, yeah. It has a V-12."

"It must have cost him a fortune."

"I don't think so," said Gloria, shrugging. Her hair was down now and rested on her shoulders, golden and dancing the moonlight. "Three thousand maybe. The kicker was that he couldn't get another one. That's why I wanted it."

"You've got a real mean streak," I said, with a smile.

"Want to go for a ride?"

"Why, yes. Yes, I do."

"Get us a couple of beers then," said Gloria. She dangled a set of keys. "And you may drive."

Just a one time thing, I thought. But Fish was right. She was under my skin.

We headed up Canal Street to Jackson, then turned right and cruised slowly through Grant Park before turning north on Lake Shore Drive along Lake Michigan at Gloria's suggestion. The lake was calm, the air was cool and just about perfect for a drive, and the quiet rumble of the engine purred like a great cat. Gloria had added a head-scarf to her ensemble. I'd put my suit coat back on, and my hat, and smoking a couple of Camels, we looked like movie-stars out for an evening.

"You're not mad at me anymore?" I asked.

"No," said Gloria. "It was an initiation, I suppose. Fish told me that everybody gets screamed at. He said you got railed at, but good."

I laughed, remembering. "Yeah. Stan screamed at me for about ten minutes straight. I couldn't get out of his office because the boys had taken the doorknob off as a joke. They finally let me out 'cause they were afraid Stan would go apoplectic."

"Apoplectic? That's big word for a football player."

"Well, I was an English major."

"Hmm," said Gloria with a smile. "Anyway, I'm glad to know you didn't get off easy."

We picked up a little speed as we passed the Chicago Yacht Club and the Naval Reserve Armory. The car growled softly as we took a small hill, then settled back to its comfortable purr.

"Where are we going?" I asked.

"Kenosha."

"Fine with me. What's in Kenosha?"

"I have a little house on the lake."

I looked over at her in surprise. "You have a little house...?"

"On the lake."

"How much money do you have anyway?" I asked.

"Lots."

"Me, too," I said. I threw my empty beer can up into the air and watched the glint in the mirror as it bounced along the road before disappearing into the ditch.

"Oh, I'm *sure!*" laughed Gloria. "I know what a city dick makes. You're lucky you have Fish for a friend, or you'd be sleeping in some fleabag hotel with an old bed and one chair—all your worldly possessions stuffed into a steamer-trunk."

I scowled.

"Hey, I don't mind," she said. "I'm sure you do the best you can. We do need to get you a new suit though."

I scowled again, this time harder, but then, hearing Fish's wise yet imaginary counsel in my ear saying, "Shut your big yap and don't blow it," I came to my senses, settled back into the glove leather of the driver's seat, and thought, *What the hell?*

"That's what Fish said, too," I said. "That I should get a new suit. I'm just strapped right now, what with the coat and the porch furniture."

"And the ankle piece," Gloria reminded me.

"Yeah."

Gloria smiled, then tossed her empty out of the car. "Light me up again will you?"

MARK SCHWEIZER

I held out what was left of my lit cigarette and Gloria scooted across the seat toward me in order to light a fresh smoke. She didn't scoot back.

"You want another?" she asked. She took a long drag and exhaled slowly. The lake air caught the smoke, and it was gone in an instant, a fleeting vapor, or a ghost almost seen, but not quite.

"No thanks," I said.

"Did you steal the coat?"

"Well..."

"That's okay," she said taking another drag. "I understand." She fiddled with the car radio and found a station, then turned it up.

"I love this song!" She sang along with the Benny Goodman orchestra in a husky, deeply sensual voice. I felt a tingle all the way to my ankle holster.

Things are mending now,
I see a rainbow blending now,
We'll have a happy ending now,
Taking a chance on love.

Lakeshore Drive came to an end at a place called the Saddle and Cycle Club. We made the turn onto State Road 42 and followed the shore line north.

"So," said Gloria, "do you mind if I treat you to a new suit?"

"Why should I mind?"

"Most men would."

I shrugged. "Not me. I don't mind a bit. Fish says his tailor would be happy to make me one in lavender silk."

Gloria shook her head. "Ouch. Lavender? You don't want silk. Silk is Fish's look. You need..." She looked me up and down, then put her hand on my leg. "You need a nice worsted for winter and maybe something in serge for summer."

"Two suits now?" I asked.

"Two or three." Her hand slid up my leg and she put her lips

196

on my ear and gave a small nibble. "Tweed," she moaned into my ear, sending a delicious shiver down my spine. "I'd love to see you in tweed." It was then I knew I wanted tweed. Tweed suits, tweed drawers, tweed socks, tweed shoes, and a tweed holster.

"Are you providing me these gifts in exchange for carnal or amatory favors?"

"You mean for sex, English major?"

"Uh huh."

"Yep," she said. "Do you mind?"

We stopped at Highland Park and picked up some beer. Kenosha was sixty or so miles north of Chicago just over the Wisconsin state line and Gloria informed me that there was nowhere in Kenosha to buy suds—not at this time of night.

"It's not quite 10:30," I said. "It just feels later." It *did* feel later. It had been barely eight hours since we picked Henry Junior the Third up at the jail. A lot had happened since then.

"Wouldn't matter if it was 6:30. Nothing's open. It's a small town. Not like Chicago."

"How far?" I asked.

"We're about half way. Another thirty miles. It's a beautiful night for driving, though."

"I have to agree with you there."

She snuggled up under my arm as we wound our way up the coast. Her hand had found its way back onto my leg.

"You may have to give me a little room," I said. "I have to down-shift."

"I'll shift for you. Step on the clutch."

"Okay," I muttered, searching for the pedal with my left foot. "But just so you know... that's not the gearshift."

Gloria Kingston's house was just south of Kenosha, right on the shore of the lake. We pulled up to a Craftsman style stone cottage with a low pitched roof, exposed rafters, and brightly painted brackets under the eaves. The front porch was supported by two stone columns. It was a storybook house, a little bigger than mine, but not much. We walked up onto the porch and Gloria fumbled around in her purse looking for a key.

"Dammit," she said, finally. "I can't find it. I know I put in here before I left."

I dangled the car keys from my index finger. "Is it on here?"

"Nope."

"Do you have an extra one hidden somewhere?"

"No," she said. "I keep a spare car key under the left headlight in a magnetic box. No house key though. I guess we'll have to break a window."

"Hang on," I said reaching into a pocket for my pick. "I won't be a minute."

Gloria watched in consternation as I slipped the thin blade into the keyhole and had the door open in about five seconds.

"Sheesh. I've got to get that fixed."

"Have a deadbolt installed. These old locks aren't worth much."

"Hope no one else around here is as handy as you," she said pushing open the door.

Her house had a totally different feel than mine of course, the furniture not having been procured by Fish from a whore-house. The house bespoke of taste and refinement and old money and elegance. In spite of the obvious affluence, it was comfortable. There was a fireplace and a lot of expensive stonework. The floors were wood, polished to a high shine, and they complimented the woodwork and exposed beams throughout the cottage. I'd seen this furniture before. Stickley. Not cheap.

"Nice digs," I said. "Now I'm wondering about your main residence back in the city."

Gloria smiled, loosened her scarf, and tossed it on the sofa. "I just keep a little apartment. Nothing fancy. How about a walk on the beach?"

"Sounds great."

The beach was about a hundred yards from the front porch. The weather was still pleasant, but a little cooler here on the shoreline and sixty miles north of Chicago. The waves lapped gently against the rocks in a soothing lullaby. I took Gloria's hand and we walked.

"Why on earth would you want to leave all this to get shot at?" I asked. "Don't tell me you 'want to make a difference'?"

"Nope. I just got bored."

"Huh?" I leaned over and picked up a flat rock, then skipped it across a wave into the darkness.

"I just sat around all day. I couldn't get back into the society scene in Joliet. I've been... umm... excommunicated, for lack of a better word."

"Persona non grata."

"Exactly. So I moved to Chicago. I thought police work might be exciting."

"And is it?"

Gloria laughed. "Oh, yes. It's exciting. Don't you think?"

"Yeah," I agreed. "I guess so. Sometimes, anyway."

"Have you heard from Violet?" Gloria said, changing the subject. I felt a twinge in my gut. Guilt? Probably.

Gloria took hold of my arm and snuggled in. "Hey, I'm just asking," she said. "I know you're engaged. Tilly told me the first day."

I grunted. "Tilly doesn't know what he's talking about."

"He said that Violet told him."

"Jesus! Why would he tell you that?"

"Easy. He noticed that I was attracted to you and wanted me to know you were taken. I suspect he wants up my skirt himself."

"Him and every other guy in the squad. Hang on. He noticed that you were attracted to me?"

"And you call yourself a detective."

"Tilly's wrong. I'm not. Engaged, that is." I paused and thought for a moment. "Well, Vi might think we're sort of engaged. Pre-engaged, maybe. She's been talking about getting married a lot lately and I haven't exactly told her to forget it. But I never gave her a ring."

"Let me get this straight. You haven't asked her? Officially, I mean?"

"Nope."

"But she's been talking about getting married, and you didn't tell her no?"

"Right."

"Has she been talking about who's going to be invited to the wedding? What kind of dress she might wear? And you've slept with her?"

"Yeah."

"You're engaged," Gloria said.

"Huh?"

"By default. You didn't say 'no'. You're engaged. Don't worry about it too much. You're not going to marry her anyway."

I stopped and took Gloria by both hands, holding her at arms' length in the moonlight. "Now, how do you know that?"

She smiled the most beautiful smile I think I'd ever seen. "I can tell."

"Because I'm unfaithful?"

"No, that's not it." She looked thoughtful for a moment. "Well, that's part of it. But not the biggest part. You have no passion for her."

"How do you know?"

"Passion's not easy to fake. In the time I've known you, a passionate man would have already made six trips down to Peoria to visit her. You wait for her to show up and are sort of relieved when she doesn't."

"Yeah, I guess." I shrugged. "So it's obvious?"

"To me. Probably not to her. I expect she wants to get married. Could just as easily be to Fish as to you."

I chuckled. "Fish is already married."

"Really?" she said in surprise. "No one's ever mentioned it before."

"You'll know why when you meet her. Her name's Ziba."

"I can't wait." Gloria laughed. "How is she in bed?"

"Ziba?"

"No, silly. Violet. Unless you know about Ziba as well."

"I have no knowledge concerning Ziba. As for Violet, I'm not sure this is a fit topic for conversation."

"Sure, it is," said Gloria, pulling away and skipping a few paces ahead. She spun around. "Well? How is she?"

"She's great."

"Great?" Gloria giggled.

"Good. She's good. Or, if not exactly good, at least... cordial. And sort of willing. Sometimes."

The rocks echoed with Gloria's lilting laughter. *"Cordial?"*

"Yes. Cordial. Very cordial. And polite... although perhaps lacking in the enthusiasm department," I said. "She a good girl. Respectable."

"Eyes closed tight, lights off?" asked Gloria, walking backwards two paces in front of me. She held out both her hands and I took them. We walked that way for a few steps.

"Maybe."

"Maybe?"

"I couldn't tell. The lights were off."

Gloria let go of my hands and circled around behind me. I kept walking. Another giggle, this time in my ear. "Was she a virgin?"

"I didn't ask, but I'm sure she was."

"Oh, you're engaged all right!" Gloria said, coming up on my left side and taking my arm. "Seriously engaged! How many times?"

"In one night?" I asked. "Or overall?"

Gloria snickered. "Oh, please! Overall."

"Two nights."

"Nightgown?"

"Flannel."

"I would have guessed heavy cotton," Gloria said. "White, ankle length with a high neck. But I can see flannel. Is she pretty?"

"You asked me this before."

"You didn't answer. You said 'pretty enough.' So... is she pretty?"

I shook my head. "Not really. But she's very domestic. She can cook. She can sew. And she'd be great with kids."

"I like her," said Gloria thoughtfully. "I know you like her, too. The real question is, do you love her?"

"I *should* get married. Settle down. Have a family."

"That's not an answer."

"Here's the answer. It's like Fish said. People can grow to love each other. Maybe I should have told her 'no' right off, but I didn't. If I gave Violet any indication that I'd marry her, I will."

Gloria smiled at me. "That's a good answer. Maybe you'll get married after all."

"But not yet."

"No," she said. "Not yet."

37

Gloria drove us back to Chicago. We'd gotten up early and done our bit for the war effort by showering together, happily discovering that water conservation had jumped high on our list of priorities, although I doubted that Eleanor Roosevelt would approve. We left Kenosha at five o'clock, stopped for breakfast in Waukegan, and still made it back to the city by 7:15. Gloria dropped me off in front of my house.

"See you in a bit. I've got to go change clothes."

"Me, too," I said, closing the car door.

"The other gray suit?"

"Yeah," I laughed.

"We'll remedy that soon enough."

"Cahill! You're late. Get your sorry ass in here!"

I'd just sat down at my desk and was rummaging through my top desk drawer, trying to find some matches. The first cig of the day dangled off my lips and my lungs ached for some smoke.

"You got any lights?" I asked Tilly, as I gave up the search and started trying my jacket pockets.

"Nope," said Tilly. "I'm quitting."

"You say that once a month. C'mon," I growled, "first coffee, now cigarettes. I know you've got some hidden here somewhere."

"This time I'm serious. Clara read somewhere that fags'll kill you."

"You won't live long enough for the fags to kill you," I said, giving up on my jacket pockets. "Where's Ned? He'll have a light."

"Cahill!" came the second bellow.

"Ned's not here yet."

"What are *you* doing here so early?"

Tilly shook his head in disgust, pulled out his handkerchief, and mopped his brow. "I'm so far behind on my paperwork, I'll be typing till Thanksgiving. Goddamn, it's hot in here. And it's not even 8:30."

"Indian summer is just when the pestilential gusts from Lake Michigan are most likely to get you. Just ask Bessie. Gotta keep those windows nailed shut." I resumed rummaging.

"I'll bet that Stan has a light," Tilly suggested. "And I gotta talk to you when you get out."

"Cahill, you sonofabitch!" came the third bellow.

I shrugged and eased out of my chair. "Guess I'll go ask him."

"I got a call this morning at six o'clock," said Stan as I appeared at his door. "Woke me up."

"Yeah," I said. "That's tough. You got a light?"

Stan looked over the piles on his desk. "How the hell should I know?"

I sucked hard on the unlit cigarette, hoping for a whiff of tobacco, then gave it up.

"So this woman calls me up at six, all hysterical."

"Yeah?"

"She's related to some congressman. Sister, I think." Stan looked down at his desk and pushed through a few papers looking for his notes, then threw his hands in the air. "Ahh... I don't know which one. Anyway, this woman says that her daughter is missing. She was supposed to call home when her train got here from Bloomington. She never called."

"Bloomington, Indiana?"

"Illinois."

"Huh. You think it's the Stanford Park girl?"

"Timeline fits. Anyway, the mother's been reading the papers and is worried sick, and after calling every bigwig in the city, finally gets hold of my number. *At six o-goddamn-clock in the morning!*"

I spotted a box of matches peeking out from under a file folder, and helped myself and lit my smoke.

"Ah," I said, inhaling deeply. "Much better. Now what's this about a dead girl?"

"You ain't one goddamn bit funny," said Stan. "I don't know if the third body is this woman's daughter, but she'll be here in a couple of hours. She's taking the Wabash, same as her daughter did. Arrives at Dearborn Station."

That got my attention. "Dearborn Station. Same as the second girl. The one with the missing finger."

Stan nodded and leaned back in his chair. He folded his arms across his ample chest. "Same as her."

"What's up?" Tilly said.

"Missing girl's mother is coming up to talk to us."

Tilly slumped in his chair. "Jesus. I hate this part."

"Yeah," I agreed. "What'd you want to see me about?"

Tilly looked down at his desk. "Listen," he started, "I know I've been out of pocket for a week, but I heard some stuff from some guys downtown."

"What stuff?"

"Stuff about Gloria Kingston."

I gave him a hard look.

"Look, I know she saved Lee's life and I got nothing bad to say about that. She's my partner for God's sake. I like her. I like her a lot. She works those telephones like nobody's business. But she doesn't belong up here. She hasn't put in her time." He paused, took a deep breath, and lowered his voice. "The word is that she was sleeping with the commissioner before she got jumped up to detective."

My gut knotted up and I took a deep breath, processing what Tilly was telling me. I took another, then asked, "You got some proof of that?"

Tilly shook his head slowly and put on his best hangdog expression. "No sir. No sir, I don't. I'm just telling you because..."

I felt my ire growing. "Yeah?"

Tilly looked uncomfortable. He reached up and loosened his tie. "Because, Merl, it might come back and bite you is all. Sure, she was in the right place and got off a shot at that gunner and, thank God, took him out. Good, bad, whatever, we'll stand up for her because of that. The whole squad. I'm just saying..."

I relaxed. Tilly was a standup guy. "I'll be careful," I said. "Anyway, like you said, she's your partner." I looked at him for a long second. "You know about...?"

Tilly raised his hands. "Hell, yes. The only person who doesn't is Stan."

I shook my head with a grin. "You guys are all jealous," I joked.

Tilly loosened his tie and gave a little smirk. "Maybe a little. You tell Vi yet?"

I gave him a look that I was sure he'd remember for the rest of the day.

"Her name's Rachel," said the woman, stifling a sob and pushing a snapshot across the desk at Tilly. "Same as mine. She was supposed to telephone when she arrived in Chicago. She never called."

The woman that Stan introduced to us as Mrs. Dunne—the sister of our esteemed U.S. congressman William Rowan—had arrived shortly after ten o'clock. We'd been waiting for her, but weren't prepared for the enormity of her histrionics.

Gloria put a hand on her shoulder and offered her another tissue, but didn't say anything. Rachel Dunne the elder was an attractive woman in her early forties, or would have been, save for her puffy eyes, unwashed matted hair, sunken features, and a general pallor that spoke of three days of angst and worry.

"It's her, isn't it?" she said in a flat monotone.

"We won't be able to tell from this photograph," said Tilly, obviously uncomfortable for the second time this morning. "You didn't happen to bring something of hers that might have a fingerprint on it, did you?"

Mrs. Dunne shook her head.

Vince turned to Stan and whispered, "Maybe she could go home and get something."

"It's two and a half hours back to Bloomington. And that's not counting the time waiting for the train," said Stan. "If there's another way, find it."

"Maybe she had some other... umm..." Tilly paused, not sure how to continue.

"Identifying marks," said Ned. He was scratching notes on his pad.

"Oh my God," whispered Mrs. Dunne.

"Like a birthmark or something," said Vince.

Mrs. Dunne shook her head, squeezed her eyes shut, and bit down on her knuckle.

"Did she ever have an operation?" Gloria suggested.

"She had her tonsils out when she was ten," said Mrs. Dunne.

"Tonsils won't help," Fish said. "We need something lower. Like maybe she had that thing removed." He pointed at his right side and looked puzzled for a moment, then brightened. "Her liver."

"Or maybe her appendix," corrected Gloria.

"Yeah," agreed Fish. "That."

Mrs. Dunne started crying. "It's her. I know it's her."

"Jeeze, Fish," Ned whispered. "Show a little compassion."

"Sorry," said Fish. "I just meant that we wouldn't be able to check to see if she had her tonsils out."

Gloria winced, pulled another tissue out of the box, and shoved it in front of Mrs. Dunne just in time for the next sob. We all waited for several minutes while she got herself under control.

"Rachel was in a car wreck last year," she finally managed. "She broke her left arm in two places."

"Did the doctor take an X-ray?" I asked.

Mrs. Dunne shook her head. "He just set it."

"It shouldn't matter," whispered Gloria. "If the arm's been broken in two places, Doc Everette should be able to tell."

"Upper arm," asked Ned, still taking notes, "or lower?"

"Lower. Here." She pointed to a spot just below her elbow. "Do I need to go identify her?"

"Not yet," Stan said. "It wouldn't be prudent. We'll check with the coroner and let you know."

"I'm not going back to Bloomington until I find out if it's Rachel or not."

"Detective Kingston will take you to breakfast," said Stan. Gloria glared at him behind his back. "I'm sure the rest of us can find out fairly soon whether the girl we found is your daughter."

"We'll go see the doc," I said, grabbing my jacket off the back of the chair. "Give us an hour or so. C'mon Fish."

38

"Which girl?" said Doctor Everette.

"The last one," I said. "Her mother said she broke her left arm in two places last year."

"She's in the cooler. I'll get the arm." He stopped for a moment, took a long drag on his cigarette, and stroked his grizzled chin. "Hang on. Those arms are cut in half at the elbow."

"Lower half," I said.

"Ah," said the doctor with a nod. "The ulna then. Or perhaps the radius. Maybe both."

"Yeah," said Fish. "What you said."

"We need to get it X-rayed," I said. "Find out if it was broken. It may be the quickest way to identify her."

The doc shook his head. "Could be a problem. We only have one X-ray machine and it's not working. We can't get it fixed. No parts. The military's been stealing... I mean 'requisitioning' them."

"Could we take the arm to another hospital?" I asked.

"Sure," said the doctor. "If *their* machine's working. Either way, I doubt you'll get it back for a couple of days. They're not going to be quite as helpful as I am."

"Nuts," said Fish. "We need to get back."

"I've got a better idea," said the doc. "There's a shoe store right across the street."

"So?" I said.

"So they have a fluoroscope machine for fitting shoes."

"That'll work?" I asked.

"Same thing as an X-ray. I'll get you the arm and a box to carry it in. Better yet, gimme a smoke and I'll go with you."

We were met at the door of Cunningham's Fine Shoe Emporium by an elf of a man wearing a vested suit, a high collar and tie, brown shoes polished to a mirror finish, and spats. His salt and pepper hair was slicked back against his scalp and he looked at us with disdain through a monocle. Years of waiting on customers told him who was going to buy and who wasn't, and it was obvious to him that we were in the latter category. That, and the fact that, besides two other clerks, we were the only three men in a store bustling with women.

"You Cunningham?" asked Fish.

"No. I bought the store from Mr. Cunningham before the war," the little man said. "My name's Robinson. May I help you?"

"We need your fluoroscope machine," said the doc, the smoke from his cigarette billowing in the face of the owner.

Robinson waved the smoke away from his face in disgust. "It's strictly for customer use," he said, then pointed to the four-foot tall box in the middle of the store being manned by a handsome young salesman in shirtsleeves. "As you can see, there's a queue. We are the only shoe store in the city with the Adrian Special Fluoroscopic Shoe Fitting machine, a machine that gives you visual proof in a second that your shoes fit correctly. The Adrian Special Shoe Fitting machine has been awarded the famous Parent's Magazine Seal of Commendation."

"Thanks for the advertisement," I said. "Now, show us how it works."

"As I said before..."

Fish flashed a badge at him. "Show us," he said again.

Robinson acknowledged defeat, lifted his hands in

acquiescence, and gestured toward the wooden contraption.

"Sorry, ladies," said Fish, as we made our way to the front of the line. "Police business."

"I've been waiting for twenty minutes!" complained the next woman in line, a fat, sweating, walrus of a woman with a bad permanent wave in her bleached hair.

"Then you won't mind waiting a couple minutes more," said Fish. He handed her his box. "Here. Hold this, will you?"

"What's this?" she asked, making a sour face. Fish ignored the question.

"How's it work?" I asked the salesman.

"You put your foot in here," he said, pointing to an opening in the bottom of the box. "Then I can look in the viewer and look at the position of your foot inside the shoe. The fluoroscope allows us to see straight through to the bones and see if the shoe is allowing them to align properly."

"What are these?" I asked, pointing to two other viewers on top of the box.

"Well, up to three people can look at a time," said the good-looking salesman. "A trained professional such as myself, the mother, and the child as well, if he's tall enough."

"We have a trained professional of our own," Fish said, nodding at Doctor Everette. "He'll be happy to take your spot."

"This is safe?" I asked.

"Perfectly safe," Mr. Robinson assured us. "Go ahead and put your foot in. It's totally painless."

"We don't need to see our feet," I said. "Doc?"

The doctor turned to the walrus woman holding the box, took off the lid, and pulled out the severed left arm. The woman shrieked and fainted. Fish, closest to the action, didn't bother to try to catch her and she dropped like a stone. The rest of the line disappeared quickly into the racks of shoes.

"Here," said the doc, thrusting the arm at the salesman. "Stick this in the shoe slot."

The salesman had gone pale, but to his credit, didn't follow the fat woman to the floor. He gingerly took the arm, knelt in front of the Adrian Special Fluoroscopic Shoe Fitting machine as if in supplication, and offered the x-ray machine its latest sacrifice—fingers first.

The doc lowered his gaze onto the main viewer, an oblong, black piece of plastic that fit around both eyes and was designed to block out the light. I took the second viewer, the one reserved for the parent. Fish made do with the small one. We huddled around the machine and gazed into the darkness. Then, as our eyes adjusted and focused to the eerie glow, we could clearly see the bones in the fingers of the victim's hand.

"Wiggle them around a little," said Fish. The salesman obliged and gave the arm a half-hearted shake. "Weird," said Fish. "You can see right through the skin."

"Her digits seem to be fine," said the doc. "So is the wrist. The ulna and the radius look good. I don't see any breaks, old or mending."

"So it's not her," I said.

"Hang on," said the doc. "We haven't seen the whole thing yet. This machine can only look at about ten inches." He looked down at the salesman, now turning a lovely shade of frog-belly green.

"Flip that arm around, will you? Stick the other end in the slot."

The salesman did as he was told, taking hold of the fingers, swallowing hard and trying to look away.

"Ah," said the doc, peering back into the eyepiece. "Look there, about an inch from the amputation—a definite break in both the bones. Doesn't look as though the doctor set it too well, either. That would have given her some trouble down the road."

"Yeah," said Fish. "But not as much trouble as having her head cut off."

39

We broke the news to Mrs. Dunne, but in fact, she already knew. Gloria took her, sobbing, back to the train station and stayed with her until the 12:30 southbound train arrived. Detective Kingston arrived back at the squad room at the same time as two other visitors.

Hunk Anderson held the door open for Gloria and she gave him a smile and a quick "Thanks," as she came in. Woody Sugarman followed them through the door.

"Hunk!" said Fish. "Good to see you again."

"Hiya, Fish." The coach nodded to me as well. "Merl."

"Good to see you, Hunk," I said. "You, too, Woody."

"Hi, Merl," said Woody, giving Gloria a big smile.

"Can you give me any inside information on Sunday's game?" said Fish. "It's the Dodgers, right?"

"You know damn well it's the Dodgers," answered Hunk. "I should probably ask *you*. I'll bet you know more about the New York teams than my coaches."

"I'd be happy to give you what I've got, of course, but I'll need something in return."

"I can't do that," laughed Hunk. "I'd be fired so fast I'd think I was coaching Michigan again."

"Yeah," said Fish, with a sigh. "I understand. As far as

Brooklyn's concerned, Pug Manders has a knee injury and probably won't start. He'll play in the second half, though."

"Huh?" said Hunk.

"Dean McAdams will play, but he's got a strained shoulder. Ken Heineman is back. He's a good passer. Put Fortmann over center and use Bronko outside. The Dodgers will end up last in the East Division. Don't worry about them too much. You'll win easily."

"*What?* How do you know all this stuff?"

"It's my business to know," said Fish. "Now, how can we help you guys?"

Woody and Hunk both looked around as if there was someone else they should be talking to. Stan was in his office, and the door was standing open, but Hunk decided he should start with me.

"I need those two rookies. Don Picarro and Jeff Howard. Can we work something out?"

"I'm pretty sure we can," I said. "You know they're betting on dice and they're getting in pretty deep. Not just here, but with the Outfit up north."

"I'd heard that, yeah. I mean, I didn't know before they got arrested. Then I heard." Hunk looked over at Woody and gave him a steely look.

"What?" said Woody. "I'm supposed to rat out every guy that shoots craps or calls up a whore?"

"They'll be in the mob's pockets, they keep on," said Fish. "The league finds out, you'll have to forfeit games, maybe refund ticket money. Nobody wants that."

Hunk nodded thoughtfully. "I got it. The club will advance them the money to get square and hold it out of their paychecks. They do it again and they're out of football."

"They understand that?"

Hunk nodded. "I've explained it to both of them. Emphatically."

"I'll talk to the captain and see if we can't get them sprung by afternoon practice," I said.

"I appreciate that," said Hunk. "Will there be a record of the arrest?"

"Nah," I said. "We can take care of that."

"Thanks. By the way, do you know what happened to their fingers?"

"No idea," said Fish. "Maybe they had them in too many pies."

"You guys want a cup of coffee?" Tilly asked.

"I wouldn't mind," said Hunk.

"Me neither," said Woody. "Got any donuts?"

"Nope," said Tilly. "Coffee's over there." He gestured toward the glass pot sitting atop a small double burner on a table in the corner. The last two inches of Tilly's coffee had the look and consistency of licorice soup and was gently bubbling like one of the California tar-pits. Woody Sugarman looked askance at the brew, then shrugged and poured a cup for Hunk and one for himself. He took a sip without changing expression. The same couldn't be said for the coach.

Hunk, Tilly, and I started talking football while Fish went into Stan's office to expedite the two rookies' exit from the Chicago penal system. Tilly was firing questions at the coach when I noticed that Woody had taken his cup of sludge over to where Gloria was sitting and leaned against her desk.

"Hi," he said. "I don't believe we've been introduced. I'm Woody Sugarman."

"I know," said Gloria. "I'm Gloria Kingston."

"You a secretary?"

"Detective."

"Wow! I've never met a woman detective before. You ever go out with professional football players?"

"Occasionally."

"How about Friday night?"

"Sorry. I can't Friday."

"Saturday?"

"Don't you have a curfew Saturday?" asked Gloria.

"Oh, yeah," said Woody, shooting a nervous glance toward his head coach. "Next week?"

"Why don't you call me?" Gloria said, jotting a number on a piece of paper and handing it to him.

"What was *that* about?" I said to Gloria, when the two men had departed, Tilly and Fish had gone to lunch, and a gentle snore was coming from Stan's office.

"What?" said Gloria, the picture of innocence.

"Giving Woody Sugarman your telephone number."

"I don't recall that you and I are an exclusive item. If I remember correctly, you seem to be engaged."

"Yeah... well..."

"And he's very handsome, isn't he? Not as big as you, of course, but very well-built. And those movie-star looks. What girl could resist?"

I growled.

"Calm down," Gloria laughed. "I didn't give him my number. I gave him the number for army enlistment."

"You know the number for army enlistment?"

"Sure. Every girl has a fake number she gives out."

I just shook my head, marveling at the depth of my ignorance.

"Now you tell me something. How come Stan has me either on the desk or baby-sitting grieving mothers?" she asked.

I shrugged. "You're the best at working the telephones. Nobody better. And who else was going to sit with Mrs. Dunne? Ned? Vince?"

Gloria crossed her arms and looked disgusted. "Huh."

"You, umm, doing anything tonight?" I asked.

She brightened a bit. "Are you asking me on a date?"

"I guess so. "

She thought for a second, then shook her head. "Not tonight, thanks. I bought a new book today so I think I'll just get a newspaper and curl up with Dear Priscilla and this little literary treasure."

She reached into her handbag and pulled out a hardback book. "It's called *Congo Song*," she said, reading the front cover. "By Stuart Cloete."

"Never heard of him."

"And you call yourself an English major. Listen to this... 'Alone in a society of men on the equator, Olga Le Blanc is occupied by her lovers, her tame gorilla, and her own good looks.'"

I laughed. "So, sort of like *Gone With The Wind* except with gorillas."

"It's a romance."

"Ah, a romance. Will you identify with the heroine, Olga Le Blanc?"

"Maybe," she said with a smile.

40

"I would say," said Dr. Timothy Clementine, head of the Illinois Neuro-Psychiatric Institute, "that this man has a hatred of women."

Tilly rolled his eyes. "Gee, Doc, that's good to know."

"Shut the hell up, Tilly," said Stan.

"He's probably schizophrenic. Definitely psychotic."

"What's that mean?" asked Ned.

"He's mentally ill. Maybe he hears voices. Maybe they tell him what to do."

"So he's nuts," said Tilly.

"He's cutting up women and stuffing them in sacks," said Gloria. "Of course he's nuts."

"Any chance it's a woman doing this?" Stan asked.

"Practically none."

"Okay," I said. "Who are we looking for?"

"I'd say you're looking for a Caucasian male. Could be any age at all, although I'd say he was strong and in good shape."

"Not a colored guy?" said Stan.

"I don't think so," said Dr. Clementine, looking at the sheet of information we'd given him about the victims. "He's acting out something. All these women look alike and none of them were raped. If I had to guess, I'd say they all looked like his mother.

Dr. Freud would argue for some kind of phallic issues as well."

Gloria and I shot each other a look.

"Could there be two of them?" asked Ned hopefully.

"I seriously doubt it."

Ned sniffed.

"He probably possesses a superficial wit and charm, but he's quite aggressive and prone to fighting. He's impulsive, although he also plans carefully."

"Sounds like you, Merl," said Fish with a smile.

"Yuk yuk," I said.

"Also, I'd say he was probably abused as a child. Maybe sexually. Almost certainly physically and psychologically."

"What color hair does he have?" asked Ned, his sarcasm evident.

"That's easy," said Fish. "Brown."

"Huh?"

Fish shrugged. "Go with the odds. Simple Mendelian genetics. Brown hair is dominant—blonde recessive. Red or black are possibilities, but improbable. If the father and mother both had brown hair, there's a seventy-five percent chance that the kid has it as well. If the father had blonde hair, it's fifty-fifty. Same odds with the paternal grandfather so that narrows the chances slightly in our favor. Since brown is the second most common color in the world after black, with a brown-haired mother, I'd go with brown. I'd give seven to four and win most of the time."

"How do you know this stuff?" asked an incredulous Gloria.

"Pays to know the odds," said Fish modestly. "A Jewish guy once bet me that I couldn't guess the color of his kid's hair. His hair was jet black and his wife was a brunette."

"Did you win?" asked Gloria.

"Two large."

"So you guessed brown?" said Vince.

"Hell no! I guessed red."

"What?" said Vince.

"He wouldn't have bet me if the kid's hair wasn't red. I don't know if there was an orangutan in the woodpile or not, but the kid's hair was definitely red. It pays to know the odds, but it pays more to know people."

"Glad I asked," said Ned. "How do you know the mother had brown hair?"

"Well," explained Fish, pointing at his crotch, "if the victims all looked like his mother..."

"Got it," said Ned with an understanding nod.

"What about Priscilla?" I said.

"Who's Priscilla?" asked Dr. Clementine.

"Dear Priscilla in the newspaper. He started writing her letters telling her about the 'presents' he was leaving her."

"Dear Priscilla in the *Times*?" said Dr. Clementine. "I *love* her! She's the best thing since Wonder Bread."

"Yeah," I said.

The doctor shrugged and gave a soft whistle. "Could be anything. If he's writing her specifically, Priscilla might be the name of his mother. Maybe an old girlfriend. Of course, he might just have chosen her at random from all the Agony Aunts in the paper."

I nodded. "Maybe."

"When did he start writing her?"

"We don't know for sure. We think a couple of the letters were tossed. We paid attention to the third one because we'd just found the first body."

"Of course," said Tilly, "there may be other bodies we haven't found."

"I don't think so," said the shrink. "He wants you to find them. That's why he sends the letters."

"But Dear Priscilla has been an ongoing column for a couple of years now. Why'd he just start the killing?" Stan asked.

"Maybe he recently moved to town," said Vince.

"Maybe he's been killing all along and decided to advertise," said Gloria.

"Maybe his mother just died," said Ned.

"Maybe one of Dear Priscilla's letters finally pissed him off," said Fish.

41

"Bad news," said Fish, walking over to the table with two beers in his hand. McGurty's didn't usually cater to a lunch crowd, but apparently Chicago's Indian summer had brought out the noon barflies—our presence notwithstanding. As far as lunch, the only food to be found was some peanuts still in the shells, boiled sometime during FDR's first term. I'd make do with the beer. Fish was less finicky.

"Seymour Weissman's been arrested. I just heard it from Joe."

"For?" I asked.

"Hoarding silk. Smuggling art treasures out of China. Espionage. You name it. The feds have their hooks in him, but good."

"Is he going to name names?"

"He'll sing like Nelson Eddie after a night with Naughty Marietta."

"You in trouble?"

"Nah. He'll name names, but mine won't be one of them. Weissman ain't stupid. The bad news is, no more suits till I find another tailor."

I took a long draw. "Gotta be a hundred tailors on Maxwell Street."

"A tailor with a stockpile of silk," corrected Fish.

"That's gonna be tough," I said.

"I'll be all right for a while. I might even be able to hold out until the war's over. However, you, my friend, won't be getting a silk suit anytime soon."

"That's okay. Gloria's buying me some new threads."

"Really?" said Fish, cracking a peanut shell and tossing the two nuts into his mouth.

"Yep. She's quite rich, you know."

"Yeah, I know. I saw her driving that sled around town a couple of days ago. Nice car!"

"I'm going to be a kept man for a bit," I said, "'cause I'm a poor city dick."

"You certainly are," said Fish. "You and your one time thing. You want another beer?"

"Nah. There's something I've been thinking about, though."

"Yeah?"

"Remember when Stink Eye said the guy carrying the bag was wearing a sheet?"

"Yeah."

"Well, that's just stupid. Nobody would dump a body in the park wearing a sheet, even if he was in the Klan. That neighborhood, you go around in a sheet, you'll be shot."

"Huh," said Fish, nodding his affirmation.

"He'd be too obvious, too noticeable. Plus the bag's too heavy, too slippery, and too hard to maneuver from under bedclothes. I carried out that body we found at Soldier Field. Lugging a hundred and fifty pounds of dead meat will wear you out. I can't image doing it wearing a sheet and trying to navigate out of two little eye-hole cutouts."

"Good point," said Fish. "So Stink Eye was lying."

"I believe he was."

"Then we should go and pay Stink Eye a visit."

"Let's call Fat Washington and see if he'll go with us," I suggested.

Fish smiled.

Fat Washington didn't much care for prisons, having spent a good deal of his youth trying to get out of one, but he didn't mind going with us since he really wanted to have a chat with Stink Eye. His black and cream Rolls-Royce Phantom was waiting in front of the jail when we pulled up and his chauffeur, dressed in a smart black and cream uniform with brass buttons—the same black and cream as the Rolls--epaulets and a snappy hat, was waiting by the car door at Mr. Washington's pleasure. He opened it as soon as we were near enough to get a good view of the opulence of Fat's trappings. Fat stepped out of the car and placed a white derby carefully on his glistening chocolate pate. He held out a diamond bedecked hand to his man and Fat's white cane suddenly appeared in the chubby fingers, his rings flashing conspicuously in the sunlight.

"Thank you, Godfrey," said Fat Washington. "Wait here, will you? We shan't tarry." He looked over at me. "Merlin, it's good to see you again. It's been too long."

"Not long enough for me, Fat," I said. "Why so polite? You taking etiquette lessons or something?"

"How nice of you to notice," said Fat with a sharp-toothed smile. "Miss Ruby says that my manners could, just possibly, stand a bit of improvement."

"Certainly couldn't hurt," agreed Fish. "How is Miss Ruby?"

Miss Ruby was Fat Washington's live-in companion and ran Fat's whorehouse at the corner of California and Garfield. She'd been hauled in more than a few times for cutting up the faces of girls who tried to skim a little extra cream off the top of the bottle. Her favorite instrument of chastisement was a jagged piece of glass. Slower to heal—nastier scar.

"Why, she is just fine," said Fat in his slow, elegant, Virginia drawl. The words oozed out of Fat's mouth like cold maple syrup from a Log Cabin tin. "I shall tell her you asked after her."

At five and a half feet tall, Fat Washington was about Fish's height. At five and a half feet wide, it was no contest. Fat's vested, white-linen suit, snow-white four-in-hand and matching pocket handkerchief had Fish's silk coat beat by half. Still, Fish was no slouch in the fashion department. If anyone was feeling outclassed, it was me.

"Please do," said Fish. "Give Miss Ruby my very best."

"I shall. Oh, I *shall*. I trust Mrs. Biederman is well?"

"As well as any querulous harpy can be expected to be," answered Fish.

"Excellent!" said Fat, having no clue what a "querulous harpy" was. "Perhaps we should go in and have our chat with Mr. Stink Eye?"

"I can think of nothing I'd enjoy more," said Fish politely. He took off his homburg and made a sweeping gesture up the front steps. "After you, Mr. Washington."

Fat Washington tipped his hat. "Why, thank you, Detective Biederman."

I rolled my eyes. All this feigned civility didn't impress me. These two would kill each other in a heartbeat if justification and opportunity presented themselves. I knew it and so did they.

"We'd like to speak with a Mr. Stink Eye," said Fish to the guard sitting at his desk reading a Captain America comic book.

"Stink Eye who?" came the guard's reply, not bothering to look up from his reading material.

"How the hell should I know?" said Fish.

I reached across the desk and tilted the mag so I could see the cover. Captain America versus the Nazis. The guard glanced at me in irritation.

"Stink Eye Johnson," I said. "Actually, Floyd Johnson. Goes by Stink Eye."

"Huh," muttered the guard as he dropped the comic into a desk drawer and peered up at us. "And who the hell are you?"

"Detectives Cahill and Biederman," I said, pulling out my badge. Fish did the same.

"And who's this?"

"This is Mr. Washington," I said. "We all need to speak with Floyd Johnson. Preferably in an interview room."

"*Fat* Washington?"

"Yeah," said Fish. "You got a problem with that?"

"Is there a warrant out on him?"

"Not this week," I said.

"Gotta frisk him," said the guard warily.

"Please feel free," said Fat Washington, raising his arms into the air and performing a slow, hippopotamian pirouette. "I have nothing to hide."

"And you have to leave that cane out here."

"Absolutely," said Fat.

"Guns, too," said the guard to Fish and me.

"We know the drill," I said, pulling the ·45 from my shoulder holster. My ·38 had been relegated to the glove box of the car. The ankle piece stayed where it was.

We ended up in an interview room down the hall from where we met with Henry Junior the Third. It was identical to the first room, right down to the blood stains on the floor, and stank just as badly.

"Got a smoke?" I asked Fish. "Left mine in the car."

"Please," said Fat, "try one of mine. They're Turkish. I think you'll find them surprisingly smooth."

He reached into his breast pocket, pulled out a gold cigarette case and held it open.

"I'll try one," said Fish.

I shrugged. "Sure," I said. "I never had a Turkish smoke. Maybe it'll kill the smell in here."

Fat nodded to us as we took the cigarettes, then slipped the case back into his pocket while, at the same time, his other hand appeared with a gold lighter.

"These aren't poisoned, are they?" I said, taking a long drag.

"Detective, I do believe I should be offended," chuckled Fat Washington. "Poison? Where's the fun is that?"

Fat stepped back beside the door and rested his bulk against the wall. Half a fag later, Stink Eye was brought to the room in shackles, then shoved roughly through the doorway by a bull who seemed none too happy to be taking time out of his busy day to deliver a prisoner. Stink Eye tripped into the room and caught himself on the side of the metal table bolted to the floor. He looked pretty miserable, but then the Cook County Jail wasn't exactly summer camp on Lake Michigan.

"We meet again, Mr. Eye," said Fish. "Have a seat."

"Don't got nothin' to say to you," said a belligerent Stink Eye. But he pulled out a metal chair and sat down.

"That's why we brought a friend of yours along with us," I said. Stink Eye had his back to the door and hadn't seen Fat Washington when he stumbled in. Now, fearing the worst, he turned his head slowly, and seeing Fat grinning at him like an avaricious shark, lost a good deal of his color along with his attitude.

"Afternoon, Stink Eye," said Fat Washington politely. "I've been wanting to see you."

Stink Eye started shaking. "Ricca called me himself! I told these guys, but they wouldn't listen. I couldn't say no to Paul Ricca!"

"Ah, Stink Eye," sighed Fat heavily. "If only you had come to me first, none of what's going to happen to you and your family would be necessary."

"Ricca tol' me they'd give you your cut," said Stink Eye in desperation. "*Tol' me hisself!* He said it would be no problem."

"Yeah, that's a real sad story," I said, pulling out a chair across the table from Stink Eye. The metal legs scraped angrily on the concrete floor. I sat down and gave him my most pitying look. "Here's the deal. Fat's gonna kill you, that much is a given."

"But I don't want to die," whispered Stink Eye.

"I don't much care," I said with a shrug. "We might—*might*— be able to talk him out of killing your momma and your two sisters."

"What about me?" said Stink Eye. "Can't you give me protection?"

"How about if we make Fat promise to kill you quick?" said Fish. "Maybe shoot you in the head. It'd be a whole lot easier than what's in store for you now."

Fat clasped his hands in front of him and rested them on his stomach. He wasn't smiling any more.

"There's a reason why Fat Washington sharpens his front teeth," I said. "Want to guess what it is?"

Tears ran down Stink Eye's cheeks.

"Do the right thing," I said. "Think of your momma. Think of your sisters."

"Awright," whimpered Stink Eye. "What do you want to know?"

"You told us the guy you saw carrying the duffle bag was wearing a sheet. That wasn't right, was it?"

Stink Eye shook his head. "There was another guy. A little, runty peckerwood wearing a sheet. He was struttin' around like a banty rooster just looking for trouble. When I shined him on, he pulled a piece on me—waved it under my nose makin' some threats, then wandered off. If I'd had my gun, I would have shot him right there, but I didn't. So I just thought I'd get a little payback."

"Was he wearing a hood, too?" asked Fish. "Or just the robe?"

"Just a white robe. Patch on the front."

"What time was that?" I asked.

"Probably about a half hour before the guy comes in with the duffle. Maybe one, one-thirty."

"Then what?" I said.

"Me and Ray are waiting around to sell some dope to a couple of rich white boys. Then we see this goon come in with a bag slung over his shoulder. He was carrying it like it was nothin'. Big guy."

"Did you get a good look at him?"

Stink Eye shook his head. "Nope. Too dark. He was just a big white guy."

"What was he wearing?" asked Fish.

"Black pants. Black sweater or something. He had one of those knit caps on—like they wear in the Navy."

"Then what?" I said.

"Then he tossed the bag into the bushes and disappears. Just disappears! Me and Ray went over to see what's in it and when we open it, Ray screams and takes off like he's Sambo and the tigers are after him. I yell, 'Ray, get yo' ass back here,' but he was gone."

"That's it?" said Fish.

"That's all there was. I didn't wait around 'cause I didn't have the dope. Ray had it all. Next morning all hell breaks loose."

"Anything else you want to say?" I asked as I stood. The legs of the chair screeched on the floor as I pushed it backward across the concrete.

Stink Eye put his head on the table and gave a sob. Then he looked up at Fat Washington. "What about it, Fat?" he said. "Will you kill me quick? Shoot me in the head?"

"I don't think so," said Fat. "It's the principle of the thing. Try not to dwell on it. Fair's fair, though. I won't kill your momma."

"How about my sisters?"

"I can't promise. Best thing would be if they were both good looking."

42

I awoke Friday morning with a lot on my mind and three dead girls was only part of it. A big part, granted, dogging me and nagging at me like a fishwife, but still only part. I showered, shaved, and shouldered into one of my gray suits—the one I judged as the cleaner of the two—slathered on some Wildroot, checked both my guns, donned my hat and overcoat, and started walking toward the station. I turned onto Maxwell Street, walked into Big Shirley's diner, sat down at on a red-leather covered stool at the counter, and ordered a cup of joe.

"You want some eggs or sumpin' wid dat, Hon?" said a waitress, a sprightly crone named Mattie that I'd seen working at Big Shirley's for every one of the ten years I'd been in Chicago.

"No thanks, Mattie. How long have you been working here, anyway?"

"Since we opened—1918, right after the war," she said proudly, pouring my coffee. "How long is that?"

"That'd be about twenty-five years," I said, taking a sip. "Long time."

"Been married almost twice that long," said Mattie. "If you count all three marriages. Of course, I'm double counting the time I was married to two men."

"Only fair," I said with a smile.

I finished my cup of coffee, dropped a nickel on the counter, and left my unused ration coupon book as a tip. I was heading up Maxwell to the station, when I found myself walking right into the Western Union office on the corner of Clinton. It took me about three minutes to send a telegram to Vi at the lab telling her that this wasn't a good weekend to come visit. We were working overtime on the case. Might be true, I thought, but as I turned down the street, part of me wondered why I did that. The other part knew.

"I've got something," called Gloria. "The crime editor of the *New York Times* remembered a murder in Newark about five years ago. Same as ours—young woman, seven pieces, no head. The remains were found at the Hudson River docks, stuffed into a big hotel laundry bag. They never identified her."

"Sounds like our boy," said Tilly.

"One problem," said Gloria. "They caught the guy."

"What stinks in here?" said Stan, waddling out of his office.

"It *could* be that you never open the windows," said Ned.

"Nah, that ain't it." Stan walked over to the coffee pot and finished what was left of our Friday morning start-up brew. "Something else." He sniffed the air.

"It's Merl's Wildroot," said Fish. "I told him to quit wearing it. We have enough trouble sneaking up on the bad guys as it is."

"What do you mean they caught the guy?" said Tilly, his attention back on Gloria.

"Caught him, made him confess, and electrocuted him. Some poor retarded kid that was working in the laundry room at the Robert Treat Hotel. The laundry bag with the body parts inside had the hotel's name on it."

"Dead end," said Stan, glumly.

"I've got more," said Gloria. "There was another murder in Philadelphia in '40. Same thing, but that time they had a colored kid in custody. He was killed trying to escape. The official line is that he confessed, then tried to grab an officer's gun."

"Hey Vince, weren't you in Philadelphia around then?" said Fish.

"Harrisburg," said Vince. "I don't remember hearing anything about it."

"Never made the paper," said Gloria. "They hushed it up. That's what the *Times* editor told me. He was working at the *Inquirer* in '40."

"Okay," said Stan. "Then we have maybe the same guy killing in Jersey and Pennsylvania."

"If it's him, he's been at this a while and he's moving around," I said. "But there should be a string of bodies in each place. Not just one."

"Maybe he was just getting warmed up," said Fish.

"You guys find that Elmo Parker guy yet?" said Stan.

"Earl," I said. "Earl Parker."

"Yeah. Did you find him?"

"Nope," said Vince. "He just disappeared. We can't find hide nor hair of him. No address, nobody that knows him... nothing."

"Find him," said Stan over his shoulder as he trudged back into his office. "Today."

Ned and Vince decided that, since it was Friday and the weather was beautiful, they'd walk over to the Stanford Park area and, being highly trained detectives, see if they could detect Earl Parker, while at the same time managing to catch Willie Pep, the Featherweight boxing champion, in an outdoor exhibition on the corner of Maxwell and Union, and perhaps have a nice lunch.

"I've got to get down to the shoe-shine stand," said Fish. "Business doesn't slow down just because we have a killer on the loose. You want to come along?"

"Better not. I have some typing to do before lunch." I lowered my voice. "Sally dropped a new folder of letters by my house this morning before I came in."

"Oh, yeah," said Fish with a grin. "Good luck."

Gloria and Tilly dodged the mess in Stan's office while he called the police departments in Newark and Philadelphia for more information on the killings. I knew the two detectives would have to get the particulars. Stan was just the introduction.

I opened my folder of letters and read the one on top.

Dear Priscilla,

My husband has just been arrested as a Nazi sympathizer. They must be mistaken. Fritz has never sympathized with anyone. In fact, he's the most unsympathetic man I've ever known. I've offered to tell the judge this, but Fritz said "Stumm!" which, over the years, I have come to take as "shut your big yap." Now his German friends are hanging around the house giving out secret handshakes and goose-stepping all over the yard while putting a finger under their nose like a mustache. I think they're having meetings in the basement, but I'm scared to go down there. I really need your advice.

Signed,

Perplexed but Patriotic

I chuckled and flipped to the second letter. Sally was getting the hang of picking these.

Dear Priscilla,

I think I'm in love with a man I work with, but he's going to marry someone else. It all started when he saved my life and we ended up in bed. I've only known him for two weeks. I thought it would be a laugh, but now I'm falling for him. What should I do?

Signed,

Jamaica Jill

I stopped cold and glanced over at Stan's office. I had to think for about a second, but a second was all it took. Jamaica Jill. Gloria Jill Kingston. It wasn't a difficult leap to make and I made it with about a mile to spare. In love? This was a new wrinkle I had to consider and I caught myself smiling at the thought of it.

But what was she doing writing to Dear Priscilla? One thing for sure. Dear Priscilla wasn't answering this one. I wadded the letter up and tossed it into the wastebasket, then put a piece of bond into the typewriter and fired off a quick answer to "Perplexed but Patriotic" as well as the next letter in the pile.

Gracious Reader,

It's time for you to wake up and smell the schnitzel! You obviously have an infestation of dummkopfs in your basement. Priscilla suggests that you call the FBI immediately and have them come spray the area for pests or you may be joining Friendly Fritz in the big house where men are men and the women are men, too.

Dear Priscilla,

My boyfriend and I just came up here from St. Louis and he makes some money playing guitar and harmonica down on Maxwell Street. A girl at my office gave me two tickets to "Oklahoma," the new musical play. I'm trying to get him to go with me. I hear it's just the kipper's knickers! Priscilla, he just won't go. How can I make him see that there is more music out there than just "the blues?"
Signed,
Befuddled

Gracious Reader,

Unfortunately I must agree with your beau on this one. If Priscilla hears "Oh, What A Beautiful Morning," on the radio one more time, she will have to bite down on her Etiquette Book just to keep from plunging scissors into both her eardrums. "The corn is as high as an elephant's eye" indeed! When was an elephant last in Oklahoma? Mr. Hammerstein might well have said "The corn is as high as that drunk who walked by," and made more sense--seeing that the last time I was in Oklahoma, almost everyone I met was sozzled before noon. To quote Voltaire (and I frequently do): "Anything too stupid to be said is sung," and that goes double for "Oklahoma!"

I took the paper out of the typewriter, marked it "Friday," folded it carefully, and put it into my breast pocket. Then I glanced toward Stan's office and figured I might have time for one more. I took a look at the next one in the stack.

Dear Priscilla,

My husband is such a dear! I was going through the glove box in his car looking for a lipstick I thought I'd left in there, and I found six pair of nylons! I had a birthday last week and he'd forgotten to give them to me. Poor dear. He's been working late hours and has been under so much strain.

Anyway, when I took them into the house and tried them on, they were WAY too big. I checked the size and they're a large/extra-long. Priscilla, I'm barely five feet tall and wear a size small. I'm sure this was just an error, but I don't want to tell him, because he went to all the trouble to get them for me. We really can't afford them and you know how hard it is to get stockings these days. They even have seams in the back! He's such a thoughtful man!

How can I tell him these nylons are the wrong size without hurting his feelings?
Signed,
Still In Love

Gracious Reader,

I'm afraid that when they were giving out brains, you must have thought they said "grains" and said "Make mine oatmeal." It is now obvious to everyone in Chicago (except you, dear) that your loving husband is busy buttering the crumpet of a large woman with extra long legs. Still, all is not lost!

Priscilla would advise taking the six pair of stockings down to the USO center on Washington Boulevard and trading them. You can easily get five pair for six in the correct size. Then you may feel free to thank your husband for the lovely gift and mention that if you find another such gift, you will take the fountainhead of his perfidiousness into your own hands, and not in a good way.

If his appalling behavior continues, Priscilla recommends the liberal use of saltpeter, available at your local apothecary. Eggs are a good place to start. Eggs for breakfast, soup for lunch and a nice casserole for supper. Just sprinkle it on. He'll never feel a thing. For years!

I folded the letter, wrote "Sunday" on the back, and slid it into my pocket beside the other one. Then I dropped the file folder of letters into my desk drawer and locked it. Gloria and Tilly came out of Stan's office a moment later.

"I'm going to the crapper," said Tilly. "Be back in a few and we can start calling these guys." He grabbed a folded newspaper off his desk, stuck it under his arm, and headed toward the bathroom. I knew we wouldn't see him for a while.

"Okay, Mr. Gentility," Gloria called after him. "Thanks for announcing that. After you get back from the crapper, I'll sign us up for dinner at the Ritz!"

"Shut the hell up!" yelled Stan from the bowels of his office. Gloria winced and sat down behind her desk.

"You two get anything?" I asked.

"Yeah. Stan talked to the chiefs and we've got some telephone numbers. They'll tell us what they can, but like I said before, these cases have already been closed."

"Maybe it's enough to know that they happened and that our guy is moving around."

Gloria nodded. "And maybe he'll keep on moving."

"Yeah," I agreed. "I'd sure like to catch him though."

"Are you doing anything tonight?" asked Gloria, changing the subject.

I shook my head and gave her a smile. "Nope. I telegrammed Violet at the lab and told her not to come this weekend. I said we had a lot of work to do on the Duffle Killer case."

"Hmm. How is she?"

I shrugged. "Fine, I guess. I got a letter yesterday, but it was dated more than two weeks ago. Postal delivery has been awful for the past few months. She seemed pretty exited about going to Springfield for the wedding weekend."

"So," said Gloria, "the Wildroot Hair Creme is for me then."

"Well, I actually put it on before I decided to send the telegram," I said, remembering the crumpled letter in the wastebasket.

"Does it wash out?"

"Eventually."

"Two showers?"

"Three usually does it," I said. "Or four."

"Then we'd better get started early," said Gloria with a heart-stopping smile. "I'm off duty at six."

"I'm heading out now. Gotta go over to the *Times* and see what's happening in the Dear Priscilla department."

"Ooo," Gloria gushed. "If you meet Priscilla, tell her I'm her biggest fan! And see if you can get an autographed picture for me."

"I've never met her—just her secretary, Sally Clifford. Apparently, Priscilla stays incognito. I'll see what I can do though. Meet you at the house?"

"A little after six. See you then."

43

He tossed the butt onto the cement and ground it out with his shoe. A second cigarette dangled from his lips a moment later. He snapped his lighter open, struck his thumb against the flint and when it lit, cupped the flame against the breeze while sucking the smoke deep into his lungs. Donned in a dark overcoat with the brim of his hat pulled low over his eyes, he resembled three-quarters of the men in the train station.

He allowed himself to shut his eyes and drift for a moment, but only a moment. The voice was singing to him with more regularity and he embraced it, as he did now. It was his older sister's voice; his sister, who had read the lullaby in a library, thought it just the thing for her little brother, and so memorized it and sang it to him almost every night.

> Quiet! Sleep! or I will make
> Erinnys whip thee with a snake,
> And cruel Rhadamanthus take
> Thy body to the boiling lake,
> Where fire and brimstones never slake;
> Thy heart shall burn, thy head shall ache,
> And ev'ry joint about thee quake;
> And therefore dare not yet to wake!
> Quiet, sleep! Quiet, sleep!

Now she was back and the lullaby was back as well.

> *Quiet! Sleep! or thou shalt see*
> *The horrid hags of Tartary,*
> *Whose tresses ugly serpents be,*
> *And Cerberus shall bark at thee,*
> *And all the Furies that are three*
> *The worst is called Tisiphone,*
> *Shall lash thee to eternity;*
> *And therefore sleep thou peacefully.*
> *Quiet, sleep! Quiet, sleep!*

44

The Chicago Times building was, as usual, a beehive of activity. Wondering if it ever slowed down, I went into the lobby, tipped my hat to the guard, and climbed the stairs to the third floor where, hopefully, I'd find Sally Clifford anxiously awaiting my latest missives.

"You're late," said Sally, in a hushed tone. "I'm supposed to have this in by noon!"

"Sorry. I got tied up," I said, pulling both pages from my coat pocket. "The good thing is, I've also got Sunday's column written, so no more complaints."

Sally rolled her eyes. "A deadline's a deadline."

"Yeah. Listen, did we get any answer from our Wednesday letter?"

Sally shook her head. "Nope."

"If you do, bring it right to the station. Someone will know how to get hold of me or Fish."

"Okay." She opened the folded pages and started reading. Sally was a tough audience. If I could make her smile, these were good letters. I watched the edge of her lip lift just the slightest bit. It'd have to do.

"I'll get these to type right away," she said. "You shouldn't come over here, you know. You're supposed to drop these off at my apartment."

"I know. But there's a murder investigation going on and Dear Priscilla's a big part of it. I still have a good excuse."

"Are you going to solve it soon?"

"It all depends."

45

Fish and I walked into McGurty's at five on the nose, prime drinking time on a Friday, and the barflies were already standing two deep.

"Hey, you mugs!" called Oscar McGurty, spotting us in the crowd. Joe was working the other end and both of them were busier than three-legged beavers.

"I've got your set ups right here. Push your way in and get a smell from the barrel!"

It was a good-natured crowd and we didn't have to throw many elbows to get hold of our drinks. I tipped my hat back on my head, picked up my double scotch and threw it down. Fish preferred to sip his. He'd be singing Shabbat in a couple hours and always said that he needed to keep his wits about him or he'd forget where he was in the service. I, on the other hand, was off-duty. I tapped my glass on the bar for a refill and Oscar was Johnny-on-the-Spot.

"Merl!"

I recognized the voice behind me and looked over my shoulder. Bronko Nagurski was making his way up to the bar amid back slaps and general well-wishing from an admiring crowd. He nodded affably, and shook the hands that were thrust at him, then, finally reaching the bar, wedged his way in between Fish and me and gave Oscar the high sign.

The talk at McGurty's was about the game on Sunday. The Bears were undefeated and the season only marred by the opening game tie with the Green Bay Packers. The weekend looked beautiful for the Bears. The Brooklyn Dodgers hadn't scored a point in four games. The general consensus was that if the team played up to last week's potential, they'd score fifty points against the hapless New Yorkers.

I put my glass to my lips and turned around, leaning my back against the bar, resting my elbows on the counter, and surveyed the crowd.

"Hey Fish! You're not gonna make any money *this* week!" laughed a big man. Fish, who had turned around as well, smiled and lifted his glass in a mock salute. Most of Fish's customers had no idea how he worked his magic. The Bears could win big or lose big. Fish would make his nut.

"Tell you what," said Fish, magnanimously. "Make no mistake, I'm sincerely rooting for the Bears, but I'm in a charitable mood. I'll take the Dodgers plus two-touchdowns. If the Bears win by more than fourteen, you can all think of me as Santa Claus."

"You're kidding!" said the big man. "I'll take part of that!"

"Me, too!" said another.

Bronko and I escaped from the bar with a full bottle of scotch in my hand, just as Fish disappeared behind a wall of Bears fans, who saw easy money from a man who'd been taking their hard-earned wages for years. Bronko, who had managed to grab a handful of shot glasses, pointed to a table that had been recently vacated as the gullible scrambled to get a piece of Fish's action.

I shook my head and sat down. "They never learn."

Bronko snorted. "We'll kill the Dodgers. Two touchdowns ain't nothin'."

"Maybe. But you can be sure Fish is getting some side action. Once he has them going, he's got them right where he wants them."

"Yeah," agreed Bronko. "Hey, did you hear about the rookies?"

I shook my head.

"Picarro got drafted into the army. Hunk would have kept him out till the end of the season, but it seems that George Halas got a telegram outlining the problem and cut the punk loose. He's on his way to basic training tomorrow. Good riddance."

"Owners can do that. How about the other guy? Jeff Howard."

"Traded to Detroit."

"That didn't take long," I said.

"No, it did not," laughed Bronko. "I don't know who sent the telegram, but those two were not well-liked."

I saw Sid Luckman walk in the door. A few fans saw him as well, and he received the same welcome that Bronko had enjoyed. Then he spotted us at the table and walked over.

"How do you get a drink in this place?" he asked. "Looks like a mob scene at the bar."

"Fish is taking the Dodgers plus fourteen," I said. "He's got all the action he wants."

"Fourteen?" said Sid. "That's crazy. We're gonna kill those guys. They haven't scored a point all season. Now, how am I gonna get a drink?"

I motioned for Sid to sit. "It's your lucky day. We just happen to have a bottle and some glasses."

"Lucky, indeed," said Sid with a grin as he pulled out a chair and joined us.

"I hear you're going to break your passing record," I said as I poured a couple of fingers for the quarterback.

"Should do," he agreed. "I'm having a good year so far. I threw ten touchdown passes all last year. So far this year, I've already thrown nine. Still, it's a long way from Ishell's record of twenty-four."

Bronko and I nodded in agreement. "He had an amazing season last year," I said, "but amazing or not, the Packers still didn't win the championship."

"Yeah, well, neither did we." Sid took a sip of his drink and made a face. "Scotch? I hate scotch!" He took another sip. "Anyway, we should have a good crowd. The weather's supposed to be great on Sunday. Hey, you want to see the game from the bench? I've got a couple of passes."

"Absolutely! That would be great." I looked at the crowd still surrounding Fish—a sea of men waving five and ten dollar bills above their heads. "You mind if I bring Fish?"

"Nah. Fish is great."

"Even though he's betting on the Dodgers?"

"All the better," laughed Sid. "I'll be happy to watch him squirm."

I was waiting for Gloria on the front porch at six. She was late, but I didn't mind. I sat in my wicker chair, pulled some smoke into my lungs, and watched a barge plodding like an old dairy cow down the river accompanied by a tug nipping at its heels. The barge's long, mournful horn was answered regularly by sharp bursts from the tug until both sounds were finally lost in the din of the train that thundered by moments later.

The red convertible pulled up to the curb, its white canvas top now up shielding its driver from the fickle Chicago climate that had abandoned Indian summer as quickly as it had embraced it. The door opened and a pair of legs emerged, followed by some delicious curves, and finally the rest of the package. I smiled in spite of myself.

"Did you get me a beer?" she said, skipping up the walk.

"Well, I got *me* one," I answered. "But I put yours back in the Fridgedaire 'cause I didn't know for sure when you'd arrive."

"Don't get up," she said sarcastically when she got to the top of the stairs. "I'll get it."

"Thanks. Would you get me another one, too?"

I dodged her purse by at least three inches, stood up laughing, and grabbed her around the waist to keep from having to duck the missile again.

"I'm kidding," I said. "Sit down. Have a smoke. I'll be right back."

When I returned to the front porch, Gloria was relaxing with a cigarette and watching the back end of the barge disappear into the twilight. I handed her a cold can of suds.

"Nice," she said.

"Very nice," I agreed.

"What are we doing tonight?"

"Well, first thing, I've got to get this Wildroot out of my hair."

Gloria nodded and took a long pull on her smoke.

"Then, if you want, we've been invited over to Fish's house for supper."

Gloria's face lit up. "Really? That's great! I've been wanting to meet Fish's wife. What's her name again?"

"Ziba."

"Ziba," Gloria repeated. "When are we supposed to be there?"

"Fish said we should meet him at the synagogue at eight. Then we'll follow him to his house."

"Are we going *into* the synagogue? Are these clothes okay?"

I looked at her. She was wearing her office attire—a khaki suit and light yellow blouse, stockings and high heels—and looked great.

"Yeah," I said. "Perfect. Don't worry about it."

We both took a sip and sat for a moment listening to the sounds of the river. Gloria sat back in the chair and crossed her legs.

"Hey," I said, "do those stockings have seams in the backs?"

"Of course. Why do you ask?"

"Just wondered. I guess they cost more with the seams."

"A lot more. Some women who can't afford stockings draw the seam up the back of their legs with an eyebrow pencil."

"You're kidding."

"Nope. The other thing about seams is, they have to be on exactly straight. Right up the back. If they're crooked, people assume that you spent the night out and either didn't have time or were too hung-over to put your stockings on straight in the morning."

"People assume that?"

"Well, *female* people," she said with a laugh. "Why are you interested in stockings?"

I shrugged. "Something came up. I just never really thought about them before."

Gloria finished her beer with a flourish and changed the subject. "If we're going out, you'd better take a shower. You smell just awful!"

I grinned.

"And I think you're going to need some help washing that stuff out of your hair."

"Yes, I think I might."

"How long do we have?"

"Maybe an hour and a half," I said.

"Not much time," said Gloria with an impish smile. She stood up and took my hand. "Better get started."

46

We took Gloria's car to *Congregation Achavas Achim* on Newberry Street where Fishel Biederman was busy canting the service. Standing on the steps in the front of the synagogue, we could hear Fish's beautiful tenor coming from behind the doors, a muffled, melancholy melody that spoke of centuries of history and heartache. I opened one of the heavy wooden doors and motioned Gloria into the anteroom, and as we entered, Fish's muffled song became a brilliant anthem. We didn't understand a word of what he was singing, of course, but we exchanged a smile in appreciation of Fish's talent.

"Wow," Gloria whispered. "He's really good." I nodded.

We had arrived at eight and the service went on for another ten minutes. Then, abruptly, it was over and people started coming out of the synagogue. They were chatting among themselves and most gave us a friendly smile or a wave as they walked past us, out the doors, and into the cold air of the evening. When the crowd had cleared, we glanced in, saw Fish standing on the dais, and gave him the high sign. A minute later he joined us.

"That was just beautiful," Gloria said. "What I heard, anyway."

Fish brightened at the compliment. "When did you get here?"

"About ten minutes ago," Gloria answered.

"Too bad! You missed my best stuff! You should have heard

the *L'cha Dodi* tonight. It would have made you want to spit that wafer out of your mouth, slap the priest, and convert to the one true faith." Fish gave Gloria the once-over. "And, quite frankly, we could use a looker like you on our team."

Gloria laughed. "It's a shame I missed it then. I've been looking for a new direction. I was thinking maybe of Methodism."

"Don't do it!" said Fish. "I know all about those weasels. I bought a car from a Methodist once. Catholics are bad enough, but Methodists... pah!" Fish pretended to spit onto the tiled floor and rub it away with his shoe.

"Isn't Ziba expecting us?" I asked.

"Oh... yeah," said Fish. "She is." He turned his attention back to Gloria. "I must warn you though, she doesn't keep the Sabbath in the same way as you might expect."

"So, what does she do?" asked Gloria.

"Well, for one thing, she starts drinking at sundown and doesn't stop until I hide the liquor. "

"Oh, stop it, Fish," I said. "You know perfectly well she doesn't."

"I'm looking forward to a traditional Sabbath meal," said Gloria. "You know, with the candles and the unleavened bread and wine and prayers and everything. I've never been to a Jewish person's house before."

"There's something you should know," said Fish. "Ziba's not exactly Jewish."

"She's not?" Gloria looked over at me.

I rolled my eyes. "I think she's a Methodist," I said.

We followed Fish to his house in Lincoln Park and parked on the street behind the Packard. The Biederman home wasn't the largest house on the street, but it was certainly bigger than anything I'd ever live in, Dear Priscilla or no Dear Priscilla. Fish made a beeline up the front walk to make sure that supper was in the works, and we followed at a more leisurely pace.

"Nice house," said Gloria. "It reminds me of my ex-in-law's."

"Yeah," I said. "A bit much for me, but I like visiting."

"Anything I should know about Ziba Biederman before we get to the door?"

I shrugged and smiled. "She won't be what you expect."

"Oh, really! And how do you know what I expect?"

"Doesn't matter. She's not what anyone expects."

Fish left the front door open for us and we walked into a foyer that spoke of opulence without the ornate trappings that were often overdone by people too anxious to impress. The floor was marble, the ceiling two stories high, and the lighting arranged to highlight the art adorning the walls on both sides. We stopped and looked at one of the paintings. Actually, Gloria stopped, and I pretended to be interested.

"Wow! A Matisse!"

"Yeah," I said. "You know this stuff?"

"Well, sure. Everyone knows Matisse."

"How about this one?" I pointed to the framed mess on the opposite wall.

Gloria walked across the smooth marble and looked closely. "Kandinsky. Holy smokes! And a Klee watercolor. Where did Fish get these?" She moved from one painting to the next, her astonishment growing. "A Picasso!"

"Here and there, I suppose," I said. "He doesn't pick it out since he knows as much about art as I do. Ziba's the aficionado. She used to go over to Paris a couple of times a year before the war. Now she gets stuff smuggled out I think. She has contacts."

Fish appeared in the foyer, all smiles. "You like the collection?"

"Oh my, yes! It's amazing. The artists that I recognize are household names. The others probably will be."

"Yeah," said Fish. "Ziba has a good eye for talent. Most of these she bought fifteen or twenty years ago when she could get them for a song and a roll in the hay. The newer ones were a little more pricey. And now it's tough getting stuff out of Paris. Still..." He gave a smile and shrugged his shoulders. "That Picasso? Three hundred francs in 1928. Of course, I suspect that Ziba also slept with him. He really should have given it to her. Still, it was a good deal."

Gloria was speechless.

"We've got a Salvador Dali in the kitchen," said Fish. "He came over for dinner about ten years ago. The painting's okay, but what a prick!"

"Come in to supper," came a voice from the dining room. "It's ready."

People who had never met Ziba Biederman always stared when they first encountered her. Towering over Fish from a height of six-feet two inches, she was pole thin—a pale broomstick topped by a black mane. Ziba was always dressed, summer or winter, in tight black slacks and a form-fitting, black sweater. She occasionally wore pearls, as was the case this evening. If she was going out, she'd frequently wear a black beret, but since we weren't, she wasn't. She *did* have her signature long black and silver cigarette holder in her hand and was gesturing with it to the servant in charge of supper.

"Cela sera tout, Suzanne. Attendre dans la cuisine, s'il vous plaît."

"Have a seat," said Fish to Gloria and me. "Supper's not exactly kosher, but it'll have to do." He introduced Gloria and Ziba. Gloria extended her hand. Ziba ignored it.

"I didn't know you two were coming until Fishel left for the synagogue," Ziba said to me, her irritation evident. "I hadn't planned anything."

"My fault, I'm afraid," I said, pulling out Gloria's chair and seating her with great aplomb.

"Yes, I suppose it is," said Ziba, taking her seat as well. "Fishel wouldn't dare invite guests without giving me a week's notice unless he was goaded into the invitation."

"Exactly right," I said. "He was definitely goaded."

"Don't try to placate me with your so-called charm," said Ziba, coolly. She gave Gloria a hard look. "I'm not one of your easily impressed floozies."

Gloria's eyes narrowed. "I *beg* your pardon."

"No need," said Ziba, waving a dismissive hand. "I give it freely. You're obviously not party to this collusion. These are male machinations and far beyond you." She tapped her chin with a long, carefully manicured finger. "I'm sorry. Do you know what I mean by 'machinations?' I mean they are in cahoots."

"I know what 'machinations' means. I'm *not* an easily impressed floozy."

"I never said you were, darling," said Ziba, managing to look innocent and confused by the accusation. "I expect it takes quite a lot to impress you." She cocked her head and looked thoughtfully at Gloria. "Are you feeling all right? You're quite flushed. Would you care to lie down?"

"She's fine, Ziba," I said, trying to interject some of my so-called charm. "We've been under a lot of strain working on a case."

"Yes, Fishel told me about it. Terrible thing. Do you have any suspects?"

"Nope," I said.

Ziba smirked, put her cigarette holder between her lips and leaned in toward Fish for a light. He obliged.

"So, it's business-as-usual for Chicago's finest," Ziba said through a puff of smoke.

"Yep," Fish agreed.

"Now just wait a min..." started Gloria, but I interrupted.

"Business-as-usual is about right," I said. "This guy's tricky as one of your Frenchmen on a double date." I tasted one of the appetizers. "Mmm. Are these artichokes?"

"Yes. Artichoke tarts. It's a new recipe Suzanne is trying."

"Delicious," said Fish, downing his in one bite.

"Just what are you implying?" demanded Gloria.

"He's implying that the artichoke tarts are delicious, dear," said Ziba. She turned to me and whispered loudly, "It would facilitate the dinner conversation if your current paramour could *faire l'attention.*"

Gloria's face went from flushed to bright red.

"We have several leads," said Gloria through gritted teeth. "It won't be long until we catch this creep."

"I'm sure you're right, dear. I have no doubt that, as a woman, you're doing your best to keep up. It must be difficult."

Gloria bristled. "What I meant was that *I* have uncovered several leads..."

"That's just wonderful, dear," said Ziba, as if she was talking to a six-year-old. "But if you come across a real clue, be sure to give it to one of the detectives."

"But—I—you—I—" Gloria stammered furiously.

Ziba smiled and got to her feet. "Don't feel badly, dear. Sometimes I have trouble making complete sentences when I'm conversing in Portuguese." She looked at me and shrugged. "It's difficult in some languages, trying to get the noun and verb to agree, não é? Excuse me for just a moment. I need to see about the soup." We watched her disappear into the kitchen.

"Whew!" I said, exhaling in relief. "That went pretty well."

"Yeah," said Fish, dabbing his forehead with a napkin. "All things considered, she was positively charming." He grinned at Gloria. "I think she likes you."

"I need a drink," said Gloria, as we returned to the car after we'd said our thank-you's and good-byes.

"Yes, I thought you might. I have some scotch at the house."

"How about gin?"

"Gin, too."

I opened the passenger door and helped Gloria in.

"Is she always like that?" she asked, after I'd gotten in behind the wheel.

"No. Sometimes she can be quite caustic."

"Really? Caustic, you say? I say she's a *witch!* I gather the Biedermans don't have a lot of repeat dinner guests."

"On the contrary. They have a lot of parties and it's a very tough invitation to get. You should be flattered. Ziba's very influential in art circles. Being insulted by her is considered to be the latest word in swank."

"Huh?" Gloria looked confused for a moment, then thoughtful, as if her brain was trying to retrieve some forgotten bit of information, then her mouth dropped open. "Hang on," she said. "Ziba? That wasn't Hephzibah Brandeis, by any chance?"

"You've heard of her?"

"Of *course* I've heard of her! Are you crazy?" She slugged me in the arm. "Hephzibah Brandeis," Gloria started numbering Ziba's accomplishments on her fingers. "Art critic, writer, feminist... She's won the Pulitzer Prize. Twice! She one of my heros! Why didn't you tell me?"

"What's to tell? Fish was married to her long before I joined the force. They've been married about twenty years. He's insanely devoted."

"Wow," said Gloria, settling down into her seat and hugging herself with both arms. "I've had supper with Hephzibah Brandeis. Not only that, she insulted me! What a night!"

"I could try to make it even more memorable," I suggested.

"That's so sweet," said Gloria, reaching over and patting my cheek. "Sweet and pathetic. But I guess you can give it a try."

47

"Pris! Send that worthless whelp down here!" The old woman's voice held no affection and never had that he could remember.

"He's coming, Gran," his sister yelled back. She made them call her "Gran."

He shook his head at his sister, eyes filled with terror, but didn't speak, instead chewing his lower lip until blood ran down his chin.

"You'd better go on. Get it over with." Pris made her eyes go big and smiled with her little bow lips. She gave her dark hair a flirtatious toss—a mannerism that she'd picked up from Betty Compson at the picture show and had been practicing in front of the mirror.

His shoulders were shaking now, but he stood up, left the table, and walked slowly across the kitchen toward the basement door.

"Get yourself down here you little bastard, or I'll take the wire to you!" came his grandmother's voice from the bowels of the cellar.

He knew from his sister that he actually was a bastard. She was older than he by six years and spoke often about "her" father and "their" mother. He didn't remember either of them, but knew that Pris' father had left and no one knew who his father was—no one except the shade Pris called "Mother Priscilla," to whom she spoke during prayers, loudly asking for forgiveness in his name for killing her in childbirth as surely as if he'd "cut open her belly with a fish knife."

He was big for his age, but his size didn't help his tremors as he descended the steps into the dank of the basement where his grandmother did the butchering. It was illegal, of course, since they lived in the city, but they were country folk and Gran would bring home a lamb or some other small farm animal every few weeks. He didn't know where she got them.

Now he stood beside the filthy wooden table. His grandmother snarled at him.

"Go on. Don't always be such a goddamn baby. Pick up the knife."

He did as he was told, noticing the weight of the blade as gravity tugged the point downward. He tightened his grip on the handle.

"The first thing," his grandmother said, "is to cut its throat."

He looked down at the animal on the table and bit harder into his lip. The dog gave a small wag of his tail and tried to lift his head, but he'd eaten something bad, probably rat poison, Pris said, and was going to die anyway. He was a big black dog and Pris never liked him, but he'd found the mongrel, named him Teddy after Teddy Roosevelt, and fed him scraps from the table.

"About time you learned how to slaughter a pig," Gran had said one day at breakfast.

"You shouldn't waste a pig on him," said Pris. "He should learn on something else."

"Got nothing else," Gran said. Then Teddy got sick.

"Cut its throat," ordered Gran. "A slit throat's better than dying from whatever that mutt got into."

He'd watch Gran do this before. Now he lifted the dog's head and ran the blade ran easily across its throat. The blood ran across his fingers and down into the fur of the dog's neck.

He laid the head gently onto the table and stepped back. Gran shoved him out of the way, then grabbed hold of the carcass and dragged it to the end of the table, letting the head hang off the edge and the blood pool into an old metal milk bucket.

"Take the head off first," she ordered.

Gran had a particular system and she didn't deviate, having learned it from her Gran, she said. The head first, then the pelt if need be. She never skinned a pig, but she'd skin a lamb or a goat in nothing flat. Three quick cuts and she'd yank the animal out of its skin like it was wearing nothing more than a housecoat. Then take off the back legs, then the front legs, jointed. The guts last.

He cut the head off the dog with some difficulty, then watched as Gran showed him where to open the fur. He let her do it, and the skinning, too, pretending to pay close attention. The bloody pelt was wadded up and tossed into a washtub.

"Back legs, front legs," she said, giving him back the knife. She had blood up to her elbows and the front of her apron was covered in shades of crimson and rust as the new stains mixed with the old. He did as he was told and as he finished, heard a noise behind him. He turned and saw Pris standing on the stairs watching him. She was smiling.

"The guts," said Gran. She pointed at the abdomen of the carcass. "Start low and cut up to the ribs. Then pull everything out."

He stood transfixed, blinking in the light of the lantern, watching his sister's smile become a grin and then something more. He suddenly understood why Teddy had gotten sick.

"You hear me, boy?" said Gran. "The guts."

The knife slipped from his hand and banged against a rock on the basement floor. His eyes were locked on his sister's. He didn't move.

"Pick up the knife, you little shit," growled his grandmother.

"Give him the wire, Gran," said Pris, her face dancing with delight. "Give the little bastard the wire."

48

I stopped by the squad room to check in on Saturday morning, even though I was off

"Howdy, boys," I said. "Anything new?"

Ned and Vince were working. Tilly was off. Stan was nowhere to be found.

"We found Elmo Parker," said Vince.

"Earl," corrected Ned. "Earl Parker."

Vince shrugged. "Doesn't really matter. He didn't do it."

I pulled out my chair, sat down, and lit up a smoke. "Fill me in."

"We found him locked up down at the 22nd Precinct. Been there for five days. A cop saw him waving his gun around and dragged him downtown."

"And?" I said.

"And it seems he's a frequent visitor." Vince checked his notes. "He was also locked up from Wednesday, October 6th to the next Wednesday. That'd be the 13th. So he couldn't have done the first girl we found—not if she was fresh like the doc said."

"Also," added Ned, "he's never been out of the state that we can find. He never lived in Pennsylvania, Ohio, or anywhere else."

"Plus, he's a pantywaist," said Vince. "He couldn't carry a

fifty pound sack of fertilizer, much less a slimy duffle full of meat weighing three times as much."

"What did you do with him?" I asked.

"We left him in the tank at the 22nd. Who knows? We might need to throw him to the sharks later."

"Okay," I said, standing up. "At least Stan'll be happy. I'm outta here. You guys on tomorrow?"

"Yeah," said Vince. "I am."

"I traded with Tilly," said Ned. "I've got tickets to the game."

I met Gloria for lunch.

"You think anyone at the station suspects that we're seeing each other?" she asked me. "Except Fish, I mean."

"Yep," I said. "Everyone. Well, everyone but Stan."

Gloria looked concerned. "Can I ask you a question?"

"Sure."

"Do you think that Ziba was right?"

"I sincerely doubt it. What are we talking about?"

Gloria frowned. "I've been unofficially on the desk since..." She thought for a moment. "Well, more than a few days anyway. Do you think I should call a 'real detective' if I find a clue?"

"Hell, yes!" I said with a laugh. "Call me immediately. I love clues."

"I'm serious," said Gloria.

"Take everything Ziba says with more than a few grains of salt. We're all on the desk in case you hadn't noticed. You're great working the telephones. You've probably come up with more clues so far than the rest of us combined."

"Yeah, thanks." She brightened. "Anyway, let's get you some new suits. I know just the place."

49

What was supposed to be a beautiful day for football turned out to be one wretched Sunday. The clouds had rolled in early and the rain started coming down at about nine o'clock. It was still coming down in fits and spurts at 1:30 when Fish and I arrived at the stadium.

"My God, this is awful," said Fish, flipping up his collar against the wind. "If I didn't have a vested interest in this contest, I'd be sitting at home relaxing in front of a roaring fire, sipping cognac, while a bevy of scantily clad French maids scurried to and fro with their feather dusters gaily whisking everything in sight."

"Yeah," I agreed. "And I'd be happy to join you. I always enjoy a good whisking."

We weren't standing in any lines waiting to get in like the poor saps huddled around the turnstiles. I had our sideline passes and we walked right in the players' entrance and onto the field. It was cold, wet, and miserable. The grandstands looked forlorn, small pockets of people gathering here and there as they jockeyed among the empty benches, forsaking their assigned seat for a better view. These were the die-hards, the loyal following that would sit through a monsoon to cheer the home team on to victory. They were dressed in raincoats and carrying umbrellas, prepared for the worst. They weren't disappointed. Fifteen minutes before game time, the sky opened up and even the folks in slickers ended up drenched and shivering.

Fish and I had umbrellas, but no rain gear, and we were standing in what felt like a gale. I'd worn an old overcoat and my old fedora. Fish was more fashionably attired. The rain had decided to stop coming straight down and was now coming at us from various angles, changing as soon as we positioned our umbrellas for the latest onslaught.

"Dammit!" said Fish, as his umbrella turned inside out. He yanked it back into shape, but a couple of the tines had snapped and it flapped like a wounded crow. I handed him mine and pulled my hat down tight.

"Thanks," he grunted. I shrugged. I didn't mind so much. I'd been wet before at a ball game. Besides, Fish's yellow silk suits didn't look so good after they'd been soaked.

"So," Fish said, "how's that one-time thing with Gloria working out?"

"I thought it'd be a couple of laughs. Now, she says she's in love."

"She said that?"

"Well, not in so many words. And not to me."

"To who then?"

"Dear Priscilla."

Fish pursed his lips. "Uh oh. Did you give her any advice?"

"Nope. Threw the letter right into the trash. Anyway, apparently," with as much sarcasm as I could muster, "I'm already engaged."

"You saying you didn't know?"

"Hell no, I didn't!"

Fish laughed. "Everyone else knew. We might as well have all gotten engraved invitations. You see, this is why you're the sidekick. The big galoot."

"Yeah, well..."

"So now you're engaged to one girl but in love with another."

"I'm probably in love with Vi," I grumbled. "Gloria and me, we were just having some fun."

"Don't try to bullshit me," said Fish. "What're you gonna do?"

I shrugged. "Marry Violet, I suppose."

"Yeah," said Fish with a nod. "That's what the galoot would do."

At two o'clock—game time—the crowd was as thin as the Brooklyn Dodger's chances of winning this contest. Brooklyn hadn't managed a point all season and Chicago was the scoring leader in the Western division of the NFL. The rumor was that the Brooklyn franchise wouldn't be back next season. They had a few good players but mostly, the squad consisted of a lack-luster crew of mugs that had plenty of desire, but no real skill.

The teams had put off taking the field for as long as they could, deciding against the pre-game warm-up ritual. Then, just as the players had resigned themselves to the worst and jogged onto the sidelines, the rain came to a stop.

The players lined up for the kickoff, the black and orange hometown Bears on one end of the field, the red and white Dodgers on the other. The gridiron still had a hint of green, although the grass had definitely lost its summer verdancy, and for a brief moment, the snapshot of the field and the two teams lined up to begin the contest looked like a picture postcard. The look lasted exactly one play. After the opening kickoff, it was almost impossible to tell who played for which team, who the referees were, or, in fact, whether the brown lumps in the middle of the soup were downed players or simply giant clods of mud kicked up in the ruckus.

"Jeeze," I said, after the opening, sludge-covered carnage. "This is going to be a long afternoon. I wouldn't even know who to hit."

George Musso came off the field peeling his leather helmet from his head like the skin from an orange and trotted by on the way to the bench. "Hit everybody," he said. "Let God sort 'em out."

The rain started up again.

The ten thousand fans that weathered the first half of the game were treated to some good football. The Bears scored first with a field goal and then Sid Luckman added to his touchdown total by tossing a bulls-eye to George Wilson who caromed off a couple of defenders for an eighteen-yard catch and run. In the second quarter, the Bears had added another field goal and then Dante Magnani broke loose on a seventy-nine yard gallop from scrimmage. With only a missed extra point to mar their effort, the Chicago team went into the dressing room at the half with a 19-0 lead.

Fish and I followed the team in at half-time, principally to get out of the weather. It had rained for most of the first two quarters and was still coming down.

"How many of these fans do you think will stay till the end?" asked Woody Sugarman, wiping mud off his face with a towel.

"Depends on how much money they have riding on it," said Fish.

"I heard you were betting against us," said George Wilson, with a wide grin.

Fish shrugged.

"I hate to see you lose money, Fish, but this one's in the bag."

"I fear so," said Fish, putting on his most dejected face. "Do me a favor though. I've got a couple side bets going. Don't catch anymore touchdown passes."

"I'll try to drop a few," said George with a laugh.

About half the fans had left by the time the two teams took the field again. The ones that stayed weren't disappointed. In short order, the Bears had another opportunity to score when Musso blocked a punt and fell on it at the Dodger eighteen-yard line. On the next play, George Wilson made the catch of his career. Luckman pitched up a prayer and Wilson, falling backwards in the end zone, threw up his left arm like an outfielder reaching for a line drive and came down in a wave of mud holding the football in one hand. The defender took one look at the upraised trophy and kicked a giant puddle in disgust. Then he yanked off his leather helmet, threw it into the muck and stomped around like he was hunting snapping turtles. The referee blew his whistle and threw a mud-covered flag, but it didn't much matter.

"Great catch!" I said and elbowed Fish in the ribs. "Did you see that?"

"I did," said Fish.

"Does that mean you lose your side bet?"

"No. That means I *win* my side bet," said Fish with a self-satisfied smile. "I just wanted to make sure that George Wilson put forth every effort to catch one more touchdown pass. That's number eleven for Sid Luckman."

"Detective Biederman, I salute you," I said.

Wilson trotted off the field, his eyes and gigantic smile the only features visible in a sea of black. He looked like Al Jolson in a football uniform. "Sorry, Fish," he said with a laugh. "I couldn't help myself."

Fish looked mournful and nodded. "That's okay, George. Maybe next time."

The score was now 26-0 in favor of the home team and there was a lot of back-slapping taking place as George Wilson toweled off.

"I'll be back in just a minute," said Fish. "Here, hold this umbrella, will you?"

I took the umbrella, but the rain had begun to let up. There were just a few drizzles now, but the chill of the afternoon had already seeped through my wet overcoat. I was shivering, but happy. This was football.

Fish returned in short order and I handed back the umbrella.

"What's the deal?" I said. "You've got something cooking."

"I most certainly have not. I was just congratulating the trainer on a job well done.

"Something's up," I said. "I know that look. And the Dodgers haven't even scored a first down all afternoon."

"That's certainly true," agreed Fish. "And yet..."

"And yet?"

"The opera's not over till the fat lady sings."

Coach Luke Johnsos suddenly decided that, for the first time this year, and since the game was in the bag, the subs needed a little playing time. With the second team in, Pug Manders and

Ken Heineman of the Dodgers ran down the field on alternating plays, ending the scoring drive with a twenty-five yard pass. They were the first points that the Dodgers had scored all season. Hunk angrily put the first team back in, but the damage had been done. The New Yorkers finally had a taste of success and they were a different team. They stopped Chicago on the next two possessions, and almost scored again. It was Ray Nolting that dragged Heineman down from behind by the trousers to save another touchdown on a forty-two yard punt return.

Late in the fourth quarter, the Dodgers caught fire, and ran and passed their way down the field, reaching the Bears' six yard line. The defense rose up and held the goal for three plays, but on fourth down, the Dodgers drove the ball over the line and kicked the point after. 26-14.

Hunk Anderson was throwing a fit on the sidelines and the rest of the Bears were not taking kindly to being scored on by the worst team in the league. They whipped down the field in six plays for the score. The kick made it a nineteen point game. 33-14.

I looked over at Fish, intently studying the action. He had been sitting pretty when the score was 26-14, his fourteen point spread easily covered. Now there were only forty-five seconds left in the game.

The Dodgers returned the kickoff to the Chicago forty-four. On the first play, a Bears' lineman was offsides and when the referee's whistle blew, the rest of the defense relaxed. The Dodgers went ahead with the play, a screen pass that went fifty-six yards for the score.

Hunk was livid. He threw his hat into the mud, picked it up, and threw it down again. Luke Johnsos screamed at a referee, cussing him like a brother-in-law. The whole bench was in an uproar. It was no use. Every coach drilled his team to finish the play, whistle or no. After Brooklyn naturally refused the penalty and the point was kicked, the score was 33-21. The game ended one play later on a nice but useless kick-off return. The Bears had won their fourth game in a row but Fish had beaten his spread.

"I've got to get out of these clothes," I said on the cab ride home. "I'm freezing! How much did you win, by the way?"

"Counting side bets and layoffs, exactly three thousand, four hundred twenty-two dollars."

"Not a bad day."

"Not bad at all," said Fish.

"What did you say to the trainer? You know, when you walked over to him after Wilson's catch?"

"I suggested that, if he were of a mind, he might mention to Coach Johnsos the wisdom of putting the second team in for a couple of defensive possessions. No need in getting your starting players hurt in a game already won—especially since the conditions were less than optimal."

"And he did?"

"He had reason to agree," said Fish. "And sometimes it only takes a little bit of momentum to swing a game."

50

It was cold. It was rainy. It was Chicago in late October.

I walked into the station with a cup of coffee and a bag of donuts. Tilly and Gloria were at their desks, both of them on the telephone. Stan was in his office, talking loudly to himself. I didn't see Ned or Vince. They'd been on the weekend schedule and even though Ned switched with Tilly, he still had Monday off.

"Did you go to the game?" asked Tilly.

"Yeah."

"Pretty wet, huh?"

"Pretty wet. Good game, though."

"Hey," said Tilly, with a blink. "Is that a new suit?" Gloria flashed me a quick smile through her telephone call.

"Yeah. What do you think?" I tapped a lucifer out of the pack, stuck it in my mouth and patted myself down for a light. I found it in my pants pocket.

Tilly nodded his approval and took a drag on his own smoke. "Dark blue. Nice cut. You look sharp."

"Hey, Clark Gable," said Stan, standing at his door. "As soon as Biederman comes in, get your asses in here." Stan was dressed in his usual baggy suit. His mustache was drooping more than usual and his side whiskers hadn't been trimmed for a couple of weeks. "Also, there's a message for you to call some woman named..." He pulled out a piece of paper from his pocket and read the name. "Fannie Higgins."

"You have a number?" I dropped the bag of donuts on Tilly's desk and went over to my phone just as Fish came into the squad room.

"Nah," said Stan. "Says you have the number. Says she works at..." He checked his paper again. "Northern Regional Research Laboratory in Peoria."

"Morning, detectives," Fish called, hanging up his coat and hat on the rack. "Lovely morning, isn't it?"

"It's a miserable morning," said Gloria. "I'd rather be in Cuba."

"Yeah, me too," said Fish, walking across the room and taking a donut. "I love Cuba. Eighty degrees, good cigars, beautiful women, clubs, sailing, gambling... it's a paradise."

I gave a chuckle, picked up the receiver, and gave the information to the operator.

"Stan wants to see us," I said to Fish, waiting to be connected.

"Yeah, fine," said Fish. "Take your time. I need another donut and some coffee first."

Tilly's phone jangled and when he answered, the yelling was loud enough to make its way past Tilly's ear and all over the squad. "Yeah," he said. "Calm down. Yeah, okay. Go into the basement and turn off the water. No. Behind the furnace. Okay. I'll be there as quick as I can." He dropped the handset heavily back onto the cradle and let out a long breath. "Emergency at home," he sighed. "A water pipe busted and Clara's screaming like a banshee. Cover for me? I'll probably be gone till late afternoon. I can fix it, but I've gotta go get the stuff."

"No problem," Gloria said, as Tilly picked up his coat and headed for the front door.

The operator connected me with the lab and a female voice came on the wire.

"Northern Regional Research Laboratory. May I help you?"

"Violet Donovan, please. It's a police emergency."

"One moment." The line went silent for a few moments, then

the voice came back on. "Miss Donovan hasn't come in yet. May I take a message?"

"How about Fannie Higgins?"

"Just one moment." Silence again, then, "Hello, this is Fannie."

"Hi, Fannie. This is Merl Cahill in Chicago returning your call."

"Oh, hi, Merl! Thanks for calling back."

"Sure. What's up?"

"I found your telegram first thing this morning when I came in. The one you sent to Vi on Friday."

"Yeah. I just asked the operator if I could speak with her, but she hasn't come in yet."

There was silence for a long moment. "Merl, she hasn't been in for two and a half weeks."

"What?" I said, confused for a moment. Then I felt a blanket of dread drop over my shoulders and I fell back into my chair.

"She should have been back to work last Monday, but all the girls thought she'd decided to stay in Chicago with you. That's what she was hoping for, anyway."

My mouth went dry and my stomach dropped. "I... I don't get it," I said, hoping there was an explanation.

"She left Peoria two weeks ago last Thursday. She was going to surprise you. She would have been on the late night train."

"Two weeks ago?"

"Well, two and a half. Thursday night after work."

I got quiet and closed my eyes as I mentally checked the calendar. October 7. "I gotta go," I finally croaked and hung up the telephone.

"What?" said Fish.

I put my head in my hands. "Vi came in on the train two weeks ago last Thursday night. Dearborn Station."

Gloria looked at me, puzzled, then realization closed in and she lost all her color.

"Goddammit, Merl," said Fish. "*Goddammit!* We've got to go see Everette."

"The first girl we found," said Fish. "Bring her out."

The grizzled coroner shrugged and lit a cigarette. "Okay," he coughed. "Keep your pants on." He waddled out of the room and disappeared through some double swinging doors.

"Is there anything we can use to identify her?" Fish asked me. "Birthmark? Freckles?

"I don't remember," I said. I didn't. Couldn't.

"You saw her naked, right?" asked Fish. "Up close?"

I shrugged. "Not really. Well, a few times, but it was dark."

"Yeah," said Fish glumly. "Look carefully. You might remember something."

Dr. Everette pushed a gurney through the double doors and into the bright light of the examining room. His white hair was wild and his lab coat was stained with the stuff of nightmares. He sucked on his cigarette like he was siphoning gas.

"Here you go," said the doc. "You need me in here?"

"Nope," said Fish.

After the coroner left, I picked up each limb and looked it over carefully. Nothing.

"I never knew her to wear nail polish," I said. Fish looked at me but didn't answer.

I studied the torso. As hard as I tried, I couldn't see Vi in the disjointed corpse. White. Bloodless. Nothing seemed familiar. The belly was rounder. The skin had blemishes. The breasts were wrong, lower and further apart than I remembered. It wasn't until we rolled the torso over that I knew. Seeing the two moles on her right shoulder blade brought it all back.

"Oh, Jesus," I said, bile rising to the back of my throat. I swallowed, clenched my teeth, and gripped the table. "That's her."

Fish put his hand on my shoulder. "For sure?"

"Yeah."

As soon as I knew it was Violet, I saw her in the dismembered body. Vi knitting me a scarf, Vi making me a present of the

Wildroot hair tonic on a hot July afternoon and laughing about how she'd be able to find me in a crowded train station, Vi closing her eyes while we made love, Vi trusting me. My hands went to the pounding in my head.

I stepped away from the table and fell back against the wall, then slid down the damp bricks, inch by painful inch, my ruined knee screaming before finally giving way and dropping me heavily on the wet cement floor. My fingers dug into my skull—hard, painfully hard—and I heard an awful groan come up from deep inside my chest.

"Goddammit," said Fish, taken aback. "Goddammit. There's gonna be hell to pay."

I waited for the haze—the haze that had been part and parcel of my anger for as long as I could remember. I finally removed my hands from my head and sat there, looking up at the table for several minutes, aware that Fish had backed away, but was watching me intently. I felt my neck and shoulders tense, then relax. The haze never came.

I held out my hand to Fish, who helped me to my feet.

"Yes," I said softly, taking a deep breath, feeling the knot that had started in my neck settle just below my heart and start to burn. "Hell to pay. Yes, indeed."

51

Fish and I went to McGurty's. It was ten a.m., but I wasn't going back to work, and Joe McGurty had a morning crowd that drank as much as his night owls. A rougher group, coming off their factory shifts.

"Double scotches," said Joe, setting up the drinks as soon as he saw us come in.

I walked up to the bar, slugged down the glass and tapped it on the counter. "Keep 'em coming."

Fish sipped his. "I don't suppose we have any new leads."

"Nope." I pulled up a bar stool and sat down. Fish did the same. Joe filled my glass again and the hooch disappeared just as fast.

"You might want to slow down just a bit," said Fish.

"I don't think I do." I tapped the glass on the bar again. McGurty's was dark, even at ten in the morning. I pulled my hat lower over my eyes and rested my elbows on the counter.

Fish shrugged. "Yeah. Okay. We going back to the squad room later?"

"Not me. Not today." I squeezed my eyes tight and smacked myself on the side of the head with my fist, trying to rid myself of the image burned into my brain. No use. I kept seeing Violet's belly, rounder than I'd remembered, but now jaggedly and permanently carved into my memory. "She was pregnant, Fish," I said. Then softer, "She was pregnant. That was my kid."

"Oh." Silence. "I forgot about that." More silence. "There wasn't anything you could have done to save her, Merl."

I felt a hand grip my shoulder from behind. Then a voice. "You're in my seat."

I looked up into the mirror behind the bar and saw a big lanky, raw-boned guy who'd obviously just finished his shift. He was wearing canvas bibs over a dingy white union suit, a thug cap, and heavy work boots with his pant legs tucked inside. A three-day growth of beard covered his face and a smoke dangled from his lips. To most people, he'd be an intimidating figure. I wasn't in the mood.

"Buzz off." I looked down to see if my next drink had arrived. It had.

A finger poked into my back. "Maybe you didn't hear me, Nancy. You're in my seat."

I heard laughter from behind me. The mug had his friends with him. I looked up into the mirror and saw the reflection of three more men just like him.

"You tell him, Jesse," said one.

"Yeah, who does he think he is? This is *our* bar."

"Look at that suit!" came another voice. "I'll bet he's wearing a girdle underneath!"

"Hang on, Jesse," said a nervous Joe McGurty. "There's plenty of room. You don't want to be messing with..."

"Shut up, Joe," said Jesse. "This here's my spot, that's my seat, and no bum from uptown is gonna come in here and take it."

Fish shook his head and took another sip of his drink, but didn't turn around. He was watching them in the mirror.

"Beat it," I growled, my back still to the object of my growing irritation.

"Listen, Merl," said Fish, trying to be helpful. "Might be good for you to let some steam off. There're only four of 'em." I shook my head.

"Haw haw!" came a cackle from one of the palookas. "Only four of us."

I felt a hand hit me in the back of the head. "Time to move, Nancy," said Jesse. "And tell your girlfriend that if she wants a real man, give me a call. I'll be happy to give her the slap and tickle."

Fish shook his head sadly and took another sip of his drink.

I got up off the barstool, calmly took off my suit jacket, handed it to Fish, and turned around. The one called Jesse hadn't seen me standing up. Now he did. So did the others. Jesse was about six feet tall and looked to be in good shape. He had the face of a street fighter—a couple of scars, a beak that had been broken a few times, fists the size of hams, and a permanent snarl. I looked about the same, except that I was bigger and meaner. I expected to feel the rage, expected the heat crawling up my neck, and the knot in my shoulders. It didn't happen. It took me a moment to realize this and when I did, I looked over at Fish. My partner and I had been together long enough for him to know what was coming. Dozens of times he'd seen my jaw set, my eyes go from gray to black, heard the snarl that started low in my throat. None of that happened. He peered into my face, and look of concern crossed his brow.

"Jeeze," Joe whined, shaking his head. "Don't bust up my bar." The rest of the patrons backed away.

"Oh shit!" whispered one of the men. "That's Merlin Cahill."

The man called Jesse was in a tight spot. He was the tough of his little band and couldn't back down, so he did the only thing left to him—he threw a right cross at my head. It was a punch that landed just under my left eye, but it was a pulled punch and I knew it even as it was coming in. He'd held his shoulder back and there was no force behind it. I didn't even try to throw up a block, just gritted my teeth and let my head rock back with the force of the blow. I waited a second for the red haze. Nothing. Then I returned the favor, another pulled punch with maybe a bit more steam than was called for, but I figured he owed me a little something for interrupting my drink.

Jesse staggered back a couple of steps and shook his head to clear the cobwebs. "Damn!" He blinked twice, spit some blood out of his mouth, and looked me in the eye. "We square?"

"Yeah," I said, and turned back to the bar.

"C'mon," Jesse said to his boys. "That's Merlin Cahill. He's all right."

I watched in the mirror as they walked to the door.

"Did you see that?" said one of the boys as they left the bar. "Jesse just traded punches with Merlin Cahill!"

"And lived to tell about it," said Fish, glumly. "I was hoping to shoot somebody."

"He's not the one I'm after," I said. "It'd do no good to kill him." I finished my third drink in one gulp.

"You didn't get any blood on that suit, did you?" said Fish, as the bar settled back into its routine.

"Probably," I grumbled.

"I was just kidding. I've got your jacket. It's as good as new," said Fish.

Joe looked me over carefully. "Nope," he said with a smile. "I don't see any blood. It's your lucky day."

"Yeah. Lucky." I tapped my glass twice on the bar. "Keep 'em coming."

It was around noon, I think, when Fish dragged me home. I remember him helping me up the steps. I remember tripping over one of the wicker chairs and busting my noggin, and I remember it didn't hurt. I remember falling onto the bed.

And that was all.

52

She held her gun in front of her like she'd been taught at the academy, chest high, one-handed, arm bent, elbow in. She'd left her handbag in her car. The .38 wasn't particularly heavy, but it had a kick, and if she needed both hands, she'd be ready. After several thousand rounds at the range, she had a feel for it and she wasn't worried, not about that part of it. When the time came, she'd shoot and not think twice.

It was cold on the roof, seven stories up, and she'd come up the fire escape, taking her time as she climbed, letting her breathing adjust at each floor landing so she wouldn't be gasping for air when she reached the top. Even so, she could feel her heart pounding in her chest like she'd climbed the thing with a forty pound pack on her back. Fear.

At six o'clock in the evening, the building was empty and locked, but she'd found the fire escape without any trouble. The sun had dropped behind the skyline and the lights in nearby offices were starting to blink off. Dusk was turning to night in a hurry.

She stubbed the toe of her shoe on an unseen vent pipe and cussed in a most unladylike fashion. The roof was awash in shadows cast by refrigerator-sized metal housings—she didn't know what they contained, and couldn't care less—and she moved quickly from shade to deeper shade, looking frequently over her shoulder. She stopped to compose herself, then saw him, stepping out of one of the shadows to meet her, not three feet away.

A faint nimbus of light settled on his face and she lowered her gun in confusion.

"You? What are you doing here?" she asked.

It came to her a split second later.

53

"What have we got? Anything?" I asked, easing the squad room door open and doing my best to ignore the throbbing behind my eyes. It was early, but I'd awakened as soon as the sun streamed in the bedroom window and, after taking a shower, had spent the better part of an hour walking around and thinking. Thinking about Violet, thinking about the case, and, despite my best efforts, thinking about what Gloria and I had been doing while Vi was in pieces in the morgue.

It was these thoughts that steered me toward the bar, but I decided that I'd be better off at the station house than Mr. McGurty's establishment. Also, McGurty's didn't open until ten. Ned, Vince, and Tilly were already at their desks when I walked in, even though it wasn't quite 8:30. Stan was in his office, early as usual. We all suspected that he'd been sleeping there for the past week and taking sponge baths in the washroom ever since he confided in us that Bessie had been reading some book called *Kamasutra*. He was scared to go home.

"We heard about Vi," said Tilly. "Um..." He looked at me sadly. "We're all real sorry."

Ned and Vince nodded. They all looked at the floor for a moment, then Ned looked up and said, "Ouch! Where'd you get the shiner?"

"Some guy in a bar," I answered. The mouse under my eye had jumped up during the night. I rubbed at it and winced.

"Huh," Ned grunted. "Well, I guess you didn't kill him, 'cause we'd have heard something. Anyway, we don't have much more than we did before. We know this guy is big, we know he's white, and we're pretty sure he's done this other places."

"Newark and Philadelphia to be exact," added Tilly.

Stan waddled out of his office and tossed a file folder on Ned's desk. "Also Washington D.C., and Cleveland. This came in this morning from downtown. They put the word out as well." He folded his hands in front of him and squared up in front of me. "Sorry about your girl. That's tough. Real tough."

I nodded but didn't say anything.

"Same deal?" said Ned. He picked up the folder and flipped through the file.

"Same deal," said Stan. "Only one body in each place though."

"Only one that they found," said Vince.

"What else?" I said.

"This guy hates women," said Ned, "or so says the psychiatrist. We also figure that he picks these girls up at Dearborn Station, kills them, cuts them up, and stuffs the pieces in an army issue duffle bag." He looked over at me with a pained look on his face. "Everything except their heads. Sorry, Merl. I don't mean anything..."

I waved him off. "He's not only big, he's strong," I said. "His initials may or may not be E.P. And he's got this thing about Priscilla, probably an association with the name. Maybe his mother... grandmother..."

"Aunt, sister, mother-in-law, ex-girlfriend, ex-wife..." added Ned.

"Current wife," sniffed Stan.

"All these girls look about the same," said Vince. "Brown hair, one hundred fifty pounds, five foot seven or eight."

"Where's Biederman?" asked Stan.

"It's only 8:30," I said. "He usually doesn't come in till nine."

"He was here early," said Vince. "I suggested he might go out and telegram the Peoria police. Get one of them to give Vi's mother the bad news."

Vince looked over at me and I gave him an appreciative nod.

"You see the paper this morning?" said Stan. He threw his folded copy onto Ned's desk. "Apparently, we're a bunch of idiots with our thumbs up our asses! I want everybody here. Where's Kingston?"

I shrugged. "Don't know."

"Who's got her number?"

"I've got it," said Tilly. "I'll give her a call."

Fish came back in at 9:15. Sally Clifford came in one minute later.

"Uncle Russ wants to know what happened. You were supposed to call him," she said. "That was the deal."

I looked at her and shrugged. "What are you talking about?"

"The letter to Dear Priscilla."

"What letter?" Fish asked.

"I brought it to the police station around four yesterday," said Sally. "It came in to the newspaper in the afternoon mail. When I found it, I took it to Uncle Russ and he sent me right over. You were supposed to call him."

"Where's the letter?" I asked.

"I gave it to the lady cop."

"At four?" I said.

"Yeah. At four. Yesterday."

"Get Stan," I said to Vince. The whole squad room was listening now.

"Who else was here?" I asked.

"Nobody else."

"I came back in at three," said Tilly. "Gloria told me you guys thought one of the girls might be Violet. I went over to the morgue, talked to Everette and got the bad news, then back to lean on the grounds keeper at Stanford Park. McGuire. Turns out he's got a sheet as a peeper."

"After I dropped Merl off at his house," Fish said, "I started working the duffle angle. Up and down Maxwell, looking for some black market surplus."

"I was off yesterday," said Vince. "Ned, too." Ned nodded his agreement.

Stan walked up. "What's the deal?"

"Miss Clifford here gave a Dear Priscilla letter to Gloria yesterday around four o'clock."

"I was here," said Stan. "I didn't see you."

"That door was closed," Sally said, pointing at Stan's office.

Stan looked around. "Well, where is she?"

"Not here and not at home," said Tilly. "She didn't answer her phone."

"What did the letter say?" I asked.

"I wrote it down." Sally pulled a folded piece of paper out of her purse, and handed it across the desk. I opened it. It was Sally's handwriting.

Dear Priscilla,
*   I will meet you on Monday at six o'clock on top of the*
Oliver Building.
E.P.

"And you gave the letter to Gloria Kingston?" I asked.

"I guess that's her name. She showed me her badge."

"Good looking blonde?" Tilly said.

"Yes."

"Did she say anything?" I asked.

"She said she'd take it over to your house and give it to you."

"And that was at four?"

"Yes."

"Wasn't she on the desk?" asked Ned.

Stan shook his head. "Not officially, no."

"So she had two hours to find us," Fish said.

My guts knotted and I felt a smothering cloud of dread envelope me for the second time in as many days. "She might have tried," I said. "Then decided to go by herself."

"Aw, Jeeze," Tilly said, dropping his head into his hands. "Why would she do that?"

I was afraid I knew.

54

The Oliver Building was on Dearborn Street right smack downtown in the middle of the movie palace district. The Roosevelt Theater, the Oriental, the Wood, United Artists, and the Chicago were all within a two block radius. City Hall was a block west of the Oliver and Marshall-Fields cornered it on the opposite side. The old building that had once housed the Oliver Typewriter Company was ornamented in a cast iron exterior decorated with typewriter-related motifs. The upper floors were covered in wide windows flanked with narrower, double-hung panes, each central window still advertising the Oliver Typewriter Company in gold and black painted letters even though the company had been out of business since the late '20s. The doors were locked, the recent tenants out of business thanks to the war.

Fish hadn't said anything on the way over. He parked the Packard outside the Roosevelt Theater. A large poster advertised *Thousands Cheer* with Kathryn Grayson. I'd seen it with Vi. I didn't care for it, but we'd laughed that I didn't mind watching Bette Davis selling war bonds before the singing and dancing started. Seeing the poster, I thought of Violet stretched on the coroner's table, then mentally pushed the image away and tried to focus on Gloria. Somehow, that was worse. I tasted ashes in my mouth.

Fish, Ned, Vince, Tilly, and I piled out of the car. The front doors of the Oliver Building were locked tight, so we made our way around the facade and spotted Gloria's red Cabriolet parked on the street opposite the fire escape. I walked over to the convertible, rested my arm on the canvas top, and looked through the driver's window. Gloria's purse was open on the floorboard of the passenger side. I went to the hood of the car, ran my hand under the left headlight and found Gloria's spare key, then opened the door, took out her purse and rifled through it. No gun, but the letter that Sally had given her was in an envelope and stuck neatly in a side pocket. I handed it to Fish. He pulled out the letter and opened it.

"Exactly what Sally Clifford wrote down."

"Yeah," I answered.

"There's something for you in here, too," he added in a low voice.

"Later," I said, and Fish tucked the letter and envelope away.

We all looked at the fire escape. The retractable ladder that ran from the second floor to ground level was still extended and hung a foot above the pavement. I looked up and counted seven floors, then grabbed hold of the first rung and started climbing.

"Quite a climb," said Vince, the second one up. Fish was bent over and had his hands on his knees. Tilly, too. Ned had plunked himself down on a metal vent cover. I was puffing, but upright, and already looking around.

It didn't take five of us long to find the blood—a lot of blood that led us, in a smeared trail, from the tall elevator housing near the center of the building to its edge. There wasn't anything else. Just blood. I felt the muscles in my neck knotting and saw the red haze drift across my vision. I took a couple of deep breaths and looked down at my hands, clenched and white-knuckled, recognizing the rage seeping underneath my veneer of control.

I blinked the mist away and looked, with the others, at Gloria's car, a toy on a miniature street, eighty feet below.

"How'd he get the body down?" asked Tilly softly, voicing what we all now knew to be true. "If he'd thrown her off, we'd have seen gore everywhere."

"Rope," said Fish, bending over and pulling some strands of hemp from the edge of the copper rain gutter. "He just lowered her over the edge, then went down the escape."

I nodded, but didn't say anything. Couldn't say anything.

"She might not be dead," Vince said hopefully.

We all looked at him and he shrugged.

Fish put a hand on my arm. "Sorry, Merl."

"Me, too," said Tilly.

"We still don't have any evidence," said Ned. "Not a finger-print, not a shoe-print, not a witness. Nothing. Even if we knew who was doing this, we couldn't get him to trial."

"I will find this sonofabitch," I said quietly. "They can put what's left of him on trial if they want."

The others looked into my face and backed away. All except Fish.

55

Tilly, Ned, and Vince took the Packard back to the office. I climbed into Gloria's car, started it up, and waited for Fish to get in beside me.

"What a lousy, goddamn day," said Fish.

"Yeah." I didn't feel like chit-chat.

"There was a note in with the letter from E.P. It's got your name on it."

"Okay," I said. "So read it."

Fish opened the envelope and took out a half-sheet of paper. "It says 'I banged on your door, but there was no answer. I can't find Fish. I'm so sorry about Violet. We need to get this guy so I'm going.' She signed it."

I shook my head. "She could have called one of the other guys."

"Maybe she had something to prove."

Silence, then Fish said, "Why didn't she shoot him? You think he snuck up on her?"

"I don't think so. He wanted to meet Priscilla. Needed to. He wouldn't have ambushed her."

Silence again. We turned onto State Street and headed south.

"You want to take some time off?"

I shook my head.

After a while, I said, "You think he ambushed her? Maybe I'm wrong."

"No, you're right," said Fish.

"Well, if he didn't get the jump on her, why didn't she shoot him? She was a hell of a shot and she sure didn't hesitate in that dust up at the bank."

"Maybe she knew the guy," suggested Fish.

"Where would she know him from?"

"Dunno," said Fish. "She's been in Chicago three years. Another cop? There's some big cops working downtown."

I nodded. "If it was someone she knew, someone she recognized, or a guy in uniform, she'd hesitate, maybe."

"Maybe," agreed Fish. "But this guy has lived all over the country in the last five years. Washington, Cleveland, Philadelphia, Newark..."

"But maybe he didn't live there. Maybe he's lived here all along. There was only one body in those places."

"Damn!" said Fish. "Didn't think of that. Traveling salesman?"

"No," I said, as I puzzled it around in my head. "It doesn't wash. The Dear Priscilla column has been going for years. Why would he start writing to her now?"

"Probably because he just started reading it," said Fish. "Because he just moved here."

"She'd been here for three years," I said. "Plenty of time to meet a lot of people."

Fish thought for a moment. "But if this guy just moved here— let's say a few weeks before the first murder—she'd be new to him as well."

"So, let's say, someone that she might have met in the last two months."

"That hardly narrows it down," said Fish. "Do you know anything about her personal life before she hooked up with you?"

I shook my head.

"You knew about her and the commissioner, right?" said Fish, his eyes straight ahead. "Tilly filled me in."

I glanced over at him. "Yeah. He told me."

"Huh. Could be sour grapes. It's not everyday that a skirt with only three years seniority gets bumped to detective. Bound to be some talk. Still and all, she wasn't a bad detective. Sure as hell saved Lee Hogan's bacon."

I thought about that for about two blocks.

"I liked her," I said. "I liked her a lot. Loved her, maybe. Hell, I dunno. It probably wouldn't have worked out, but she was..." I searched for the right word, then gave up with a shrug.

"Yeah. You two were great together. She knew you were going to marry Violet?"

"She knew. Said it was just fun and games between us. Well, at the beginning."

"It turned into something," said Fish. "Me and Ziba could tell."

I gave a nod and gripped the steering wheel tighter, feeling both anger and sadness come over me in alternating waves.

Fish changed the subject. "Let's say it was someone she knew from work," he said. "A cop."

"Maybe. She's only been with the 26th for what, two weeks? Where was she before that?"

Fish gave a shrug. "Don't know. We could ask."

"You and I knew she was going to be the one to meet this guy if he agreed to it. But no one else—not even Stan."

"We're pissin' in the wind. Could just be a psycho that got her before she could drill him."

"I don't think so," I said. "That shoot out behind the bank put her on notice. She wouldn't have hesitated."

We took the long way back to the station and arrived well after the rest of the squad.

"You have a trial at one o'clock," said Tilly as we walked in. "The D.A. just called."

"Whose trial?" Fish asked.

Tilly checked his notes. "That colored kid. Henry Goldberg something-or-other. You need to be there, too, Merl."

I nodded. "Yeah. Okay." I felt like a zombie from one of those horror flicks.

"The D.A.'s not happy. You both missed a pre-trial briefing yesterday."

"We got a confession, for God's sake," snapped Fish. "How hard could this be?"

"You fill Stan in on Gloria?" I asked.

"Yeah," said Tilly. "He cried like a baby."

56

I dropped off Gloria's car at my house. Fish picked me up in the Packard and we headed for the courthouse. We walked in at ten till one and were immediately accosted by an assistant D.A., a jerk by the name of Milton McConnell. I knew his father. Milton came from a long line of jerks.

"I called you both yesterday," he whined. "You were supposed to come in. I got this case..." He looked down at his file. "Henry Clarence Goldberg Junior the Third. Second degree murder."

"We were busy yesterday," said Fish, taking a deck of Luckys out of his pocket and tapping one out. "Besides, you've got a confession." He put the cigarette to his lips and lit it with a gold-plated Zippo I hadn't seen before. I didn't ask for one, having switched back to Camels, the cigarettes that doctors recommended. I'd had enough of Fish's free Luckys to last me a while.

"Yeah, I know. He already pleaded guilty. This is the sentencing trial. I need you to tell the judge what a rotten little bastard he is. Mayor Kelly wants to crisp as many of these murderers as we can before next August. It's part of his law-and-order campaign. Election year coming up."

"Yeah, I get it," Fish said. "Y'know, Henry's not such a bad guy, as murderers go. He just made a mistake."

"I kinda like him," I added. "He's a pain in the ass, but he helped us out on another case."

Milton McConnell made a face and pointed a scrawny finger at us. "You screw this up and you'll answer to the mayor."

"Don't you mean *you'll* answer to the mayor, Milton?" I said. "By the way, does Henry have a mouthpiece?"

"Of course he does. I mean... I'm *sure* he does." Milton looked around anxiously. "You told him to call a public defender, right? I assumed he'd waived his right to counsel."

"Nah. He asked for a lawyer at least three times that I can remember," I said. Fish nodded in agreement.

"What? Why didn't you say something? Why didn't you get him a lawyer?"

"Not our job," I said. "We already had the confession."

Fish smiled. "Plenty of time for that later," he said.

"Whew!" said Fish as we came out of the courtroom. "That judge was *not* happy with Milton."

"No, he was not," I agreed.

We waited outside until the bailiff brought Henry out the double doors, still in chains, and wearing his black and white prison stripes. He shuffled across the tiles, head down, but brightened when he saw us.

"How're you doing, Henry?" said Fish.

"Okay," said Henry. "I get a new trial."

"Better than the chair," I said. "And now you'll get a lawyer. If I were you, I'd make a deal, maybe settle on fifteen years or so. The D.A. won't want any publicity on this one."

Henry nodded sadly. "Fifteen years in the big house?"

"You're a goddamn murderer, Henry," said Fish. "What the hell do you expect, a ticker-tape parade?"

57

By the time we arrived at McGurty's the word had spread and the cops were drinking toasts to a fallen comrade. We heard that Lee Hogan gave the first one, and although some of the toasts had to do with dames on the force and why didn't they stick to secretarial work, mostly they were made with respect. It didn't matter that she was a skirt. It didn't matter that most of them didn't even know who she was. She'd been a cop and one of them. Tilly was her partner and on the hook for the first drink. After that, every man bought his own and whatever the squad wanted as well. We pushed our way up to the bar.

"You singing at the funeral, Fish?" asked one of the uniforms.

"We haven't found her yet," said Fish. "I expect I will, though."

"You could change the words to *Danny Boy*, I guess," said another cop, pushing a drink into Fish's hand. "Oh, Danny Girl, maybe."

"Maybe," said Fish.

I had my drink and was shouldering my way to the back of the bar when I heard my name, turned, and saw Danny Fortmann and Sid Luckman sitting at a table by the wall.

"We heard about Violet. Sorry about your loss," said Danny. "Truly. C'mon, have a seat."

"Yeah, sit," said Sid. He pushed a chair out toward me with

his foot and I sat down. Fish had spotted us and was coming over.

"We gotta get this guy," I said. "I want him."

Danny took a sip of his beer. "Any leads?"

"Some." I shrugged my shoulders. Fish sat down at the table.

"You think he's enlisted?" asked Danny. "What with the duffle bags and everything?"

"He could be," said Fish. "But those duffles weren't tagged by the army and are available all up and down Maxwell Street. I got the names of maybe ten dealers. Black market army duffle-bags are a hot item."

"Yeah," said Sid. "We have a stack of them in the training room. They use them for footballs, extra pads, just about everything."

"Huh," I said. "No kidding? Didn't used to."

"Army surplus," said Sid.

"Big guy," said Fish, looking at me. "And strong."

We all took a sip of our drinks, then traded looks around the table.

"You guys know anyone with the initials E.P.?" I asked.

"On the team?" said Danny. He thought for a moment. "Nope. Why?"

"Just something we're working on," I said.

"Hey, you mugs," said George Musso, walking up. "I got us a bottle."

"Then you are most welcome," said Fish. "Pull up a chair."

"You know anyone with the initials E.P.?" asked Danny.

George pursed his lips. "On the team?"

"On the team, or maybe someone on the periphery," I said.

"Nope." He shook his head.

"Gloria wouldn't have known 'em anyway," Fish said, more to himself than anyone else. "We need to check the police rolls when we get back. Find out where she was working before she was assigned to the 26th."

"Only E.P. I've ever heard of in Chicago is E.P. Sweetwater," said George.

"Who's that?" I said.

George poured himself a couple fingers of scotch and took a drink. "Sweetwater canned hams, Sweetwater franks, Sweetwater hash…"

"Oh, yeah," said Danny. "Sweetwater Farms. Chicago's finest. It's not really a farm. They have a processing plant in the stockyards."

"E.P.'s the old man," said George. "Worth a fortune. I met him once. He's probably close to eighty now."

"I doubt he's our guy," I said.

"Hey, you know what?" said Sid, picking up the bottle. "Woody's related." He poured a couple of fingers. "Jeeze! I hate scotch!"

"Woody's related to who?" I asked.

"To Sweetwater Farms. He told me once that he didn't need to play ball. He was fixed for life."

"Woody Sugarman?"

"Yeah. He's a grandkid or something."

I turned to George. "What's E.P. Sweetwater's first name?"

He closed his eyes in contemplation, then opened them. "Elwood," he said. "Seems to me it's Elwood. Elwood P. Sweetwater." He looked over at Sid and Danny. "That sound right?"

They thought about it for a moment and then nodded.

"It strikes a chord," said Danny.

"Cleveland, Washington, Philadelphia," I said. "All cities Woody played in."

"Was he at practice yesterday?" Fish asked.

"We're off on Mondays," said Danny. "We practiced today, though. Woody was there."

"What are the chances that Elwood 'Woody' Sugarman's middle name starts with a P?" I asked Fish.

"I'd give you even money," said Fish with a snarl.

I felt the hair go up on the back of my neck. "That *sonofabitch!*" I said as I stood up. "Get everyone. Party's over."

58

Woody's middle name was Phineas. Not a name you'd give a kid unless there was some family history to back it up, and even then it practically guaranteed getting him beaten up a couple of times a week. Once the Bears' front office confirmed it, it didn't take long to get a search warrant. Judge Leo Fitzpatrick, a McGurty's regular who routinely laid claim to the table next to the john every afternoon from about three o'clock when he adjourned his court, until his wife had supper ready at eight, was happy to scribble a pickled signature on a search order that Fish and I walked over from the station.

We drove over to Woody's address on Tilden Street, a couple of blocks south of Jackson. The house was a medium-sized clapboard, nothing fancy, a house like a thousand others on the West Side—two stories, a small front porch, probably a dank basement, and an attic full of junk. I'd planned to move in quietly, and so Fish and I arrived at the address ahead of the others with little fanfare, the Packard a silent harbinger of law and order. Tilly, Ned, and Vince, all riding in Vince's car, drove up a minute later, but that was as far as "quietly" went. The other four black and whites, each carrying two officers, were glad to get a chance to try out their sirens.

"Hey," said Fish. "How come we didn't get to use our siren?"

"Stealth," I grumbled. "We're trying to catch him unaware."

"Oh, I see. Well, maybe he's deaf."

The folks who were outside enjoying the early evening, and even those who weren't, couldn't help but notice our arrival, and before we'd finished banging on Sugarman's door, the neighborhood porches were well populated.

"Police! Open up!" called Vince. No answer. The uniforms didn't waste any time pounding the door down. Two of the beat cops covered the back and we went in fast and hard. No one was home.

"See what you can find," I said. "Look, but don't take anything. We'll come back later if we need to."

We walked down the hall and spread out. Fish, Tilly, and I ended up in the kitchen. It was only extraordinary in its lack of individuality. It could have been a kitchen in any home in the Midwest. A large sink. Empty. Cupboards, empty. No refrigerator, instead an old icebox, empty. Kitchen table. No dirty dishes, no clean dishes, no sign that anyone used the kitchen at all. Tilly found a door, opened it, and disappeared.

"He sure doesn't eat here, does he?" said Fish.

"Single guy. Probably takes his meals out."

"Clean, though." Fish tried the spigot at the sink. The water came on immediately. He turned it back off.

"You might want to come down here," called Tilly.

Fish and I looked through the door where Tilly had disappeared, then climbed down the rickety stairs into the clammy, dimly lit cellar.

"Stinks," I said.

"I know that smell," said Fish.

"Yeah."

The bulb, hanging from a cord in the middle of the room, threw shadows across an old wooden table, eight feet long and half as wide, scarred with a thousand cuts, each gash stained dark with the mottled russet of dried gore. Hanging from the end of the table, on an iron hook, was an ancient metal bucket, the kind that you'd use to milk a cow, cleaned, or at least rinsed out, after the last use. Recent use, I thought. There was no dust in the bucket and dust was plentiful.

The table had been wiped down as well, but the perfunctory clean-up was as far as the hygiene went. There was no mistaking the blood caught in the corners, the joints, and nicks of the table, or the dark stains soaked into the dirt on the floor.

"Look at this," said Fish, pointing to two long, well used, butcher knives stuck into a rafter about a foot above his head.

"Jesus!" said Tilly. "You think this is where he does them?"

"Maybe," I said. I pulled one down and tested the blade with my thumb. They'd been sharpened countless times over the years, and this blade had an obvious concave dip along the edge. "Sharp, but this isn't what he used to cut them up with. He'd need something bigger."

"Animals?" said Fish.

"Or worse," I said. "He might have killed the girls here, but the bodies were dismembered with something else." I pictured Violet here in this basement, scared or dead. I hoped dead. Would her head be down here as well? I gave an involuntary shudder and pushed the thought away. Time for that later. I concentrated on the knife. "There'd be too much hacking with a blade like this, sharp as it is."

A voice came from upstairs. "We found some empty duffle bags. In the closet. Something else, too. You gotta see this."

"Coming," I hollered back and stuck the knife back into the beam.

Fish, Tilly, and I climbed the stairs back up to the kitchen. Ned and Vince and two uniforms were bending over the kitchen table.

"What?" I said.

"Letter," said Ned.

"To Dear Priscilla," added Vince. "Found it in the kitchen table drawer. Stamped and ready to mail. Pencil, paper, envelopes, and stamps are in there, too."

The officers made room and the three of us shouldered in. It was the same handwriting as the others. A scrawl, really. Dear

Priscilla, *Chicago Times*, Wacker Drive.

I picked up the envelope and tore off the end, then blew it open and dumped the letter onto the table. Fish picked it up.

Dear Priscilla,
You betrayed me. This one is on your head.
E.P.

"*Shit!*" said Ned. "He's got another girl."

"You think he'll bring her back here?" asked Vince.

I shook my head. "He doesn't cut them up here. Kills 'em maybe, but then he takes them somewhere else."

"Like where?" said Ned.

"Like somewhere he can work alone and take his time. Like somewhere he has a key to. Like somewhere with a meat saw."

"Somewhere like Sweetwater Farms," said Fish. "Goddammit!"

"He won't go in till after the last shift leaves," I said. "But he'll be there tonight." I pulled my watch out of my pocket. 6:45.

"Shift changes at five I think," Ned said. "At least it did when I was working at Armour."

"Maybe they have different hours now," said Vince. "You know, war effort and all."

"Maybe," I said. "He's there. I can feel it. Let's go."

59

The Yards were five miles south, straight down Halstead Street. Fish issued a stern warning to the flatties about the need to arrive at the gate relatively unanticipated.

"You turn on those goddamn sirens again and I'll shoot you in the asses!" Fish hissed. "You bunch of stupid buttons! I ain't kidding!" He pulled out his gun and fired into the kitchen ceiling a couple of times for effect, bringing some plaster dust down on their heads and knocking out one of the lights. They were eighty percent sure he meant it. So was I.

"Me and you," I said to Fish as we tore down the street. We barreled through the intersection at Roosevelt, horn blaring, barely missing a Model T farm truck who's driver had thought it advisable to meander through the intersection with its lights off. "Goddamn hayseeds," I growled, then turned back to Fish. "Me and you. The other guys wait outside."

"They're not gonna like it," said Fish, flipping his revolver open and reloading.

Fifteen minutes later, the imposing limestone gate at Halstead and Exchange, the official entrance to the Union Stockyard and Transit Company, loomed in front of us, glowing weirdly from the combination of the incandescent glow of electric lights and the fog that had rolled in from the lake. At seven o'clock, the sun had long set, but the activity at the stockyard didn't seem to have slackened. The bars and hotels, visible from the gate, were bustling. In addition, there were union workers going to and fro, carrying lunch pails, bundles, skeins of rope, or one of a hundred other things. Some of the killing yards and meat-packing plants operated full bore till ten or eleven, then shut down, some went all night, some just ran during the day. Schedules depended on which union was in charge, who paid what to whom, and what deals had been brokered under the table.

We were met by Albert Burke and Jimmy White, the off-duty cops from the 13th precinct.

"What's up, boys?" said Albert with a grin. "Got another crap game?"

"Not this time," I said, getting out of the car. "Can you tell me where the Sweetwater Farms processing plant is?"

"Sure," said Albert. "We've got maybe twenty or thirty meat-packers at the Yards, but they're one of the big ones." He turned and pointed down a long row of buildings. "Head that way about half a mile. Look for a sign on the right. Can't miss it."

"Thanks," I said.

"They're closed up, though," said Albert. Jimmy nodded in agreement. "Workers go home at four. The doors lock at six. Part of a new union deal."

"You got a key?"

"Yeah."

"Lemme have it," I said, holding out my hand.

"I dunno..." said Albert. He pushed his hat back on his head and scratched his brow. "You got a warrant or something?"

I took hold of his shoulder and pulled him close. "Albert," I said again, this time a hoarse whisper, "give me the *goddamn* key."

He looked into my face and lost a good deal of his color. "Yeah. Sure. No problem."

"You guys need any help?" asked Jimmy White.

"Not this time," said Fish. "Stay put."

We left the eight coppers with the security guards. They needed no convincing, happy to head over to the General Sherman Bar, about a hundred steps from the gate, and wait for our call. The detectives were a little more obstinate.

"Bullshit!" said Tilly. "She was my partner! I'm going in."

"You ain't keepin' us out either!" said Vince. Ned nodded his agreement.

"Fine," I growled. "But when it's time for you to leave, you leave. And if any of you kill him, I'll shoot you myself."

All three looked at me and saw what Albert saw. They nodded.

Sweetwater Farms was a big operation and comprised several buildings. We used Albert's key to go into the main office, then wandered through two more complexes, all devoid of any people, before discovering where the actual butchering work was done. We entered through a set of double steel doors at one end of the structure, a steel building with twenty foot high, girdered ceilings and concrete floors. We couldn't see the whole room as the only lighting was provided by the emergency system—low wattage bulbs humming inside small wire spheres, hanging every dozen feet or so far above us— but the space was vast, or seemed to be, judging by the echos. We could hear the faint clicks of cooling machinery, the scurrying of rats, our own footsteps, a hundred different sounds you'd never notice when the factory was in full operation.

We froze as the half-darkness was broken by a flickering yellow bulb, some eighty feet ahead of us and above the equipment, but still low enough to cast its glow in a small circle. The sudden illumination was followed by the high-pitched whine of a meat saw coming to life.

We all had our guns drawn and hustled as silently as we could, making our way in between electric saws, chopping blocks, hooks, and vats of animal parts waiting to be emptied after midnight by the cleaning crew. The floors were sticky, the air was sticky, and we could all feel the ungodly blood-stench in our pores. I heard Ned gag behind me and drop off, retreating as silently as he could. I doubted he was heard above the noise of the saw.

Fifty feet, forty, thirty. Four of us now. We were hidden by the shadows and the noise of the saw as we hurried toward the glow from the one light bulb and the sound of the butchering. Directly in front of us and shielding us from view, was the caged machinery that ran a huge conveyor belt. Huge meat-hooks hung from the giant chain that began in the cage and disappeared up into the gloom.

We gathered and pressed our backs against the metal mesh. I made a two fingered motion to Tilly and Vince, non-verbal instructions we'd perfected over our years together, and they nodded. We quickly checked our guns one last time, took a breath as one, and moved around either side of the enclosure, Fish and me coming from one corner, Tilly and Vince the other.

Woody was a big man. He had his shirt off and was wearing a dark-brown leather apron that covered his chest and the tops of his trousers. He glanced up from his work and saw the four of us move into his light, a yellow corona cast on the floor that centered on the meat saw. He froze for a split second. Then, in one motion, cut the power to the saw, jerked the body off the table and swung it in front of him, face out, his left arm under the arm of the naked girl and across her breasts. Her feet dangled several inches above the floor and she jerked like a broken marionette when he hoisted her a few inches higher to use her as a shield. The girl's head, rolling indeterminately with the sudden motion, slumped forward.

"It's not Gloria," I said quietly to Fish. "That's another girl. He got another one."

"Stay back!" yelled Woody.

"Or what?" replied Fish.

"Or I'll kill her," hollered Woody. "She's just drugged right now, but I'll kill her!"

"She's already dead," whispered Fish. *"I think."*

"Yeah," I said.

"I'm getting out of here and I'm taking this girl with me."

"Can't let you do that, Woody," I called.

"You put your guns on the floor, right now, or I'll cut her throat, I swear to God!"

"I don't see a knife," Tilly whispered.

"Chances are he's got one," hissed Fish. "I wouldn't bet against it."

"All right," I said, so Woody could hear. "We're putting our guns on the ground."

"You know what you're doing?" whispered Fish.

"Hell, no."

I bent my knees and lowered my ·45 to the ground, keeping my eyes on Woody the whole time. The other three did the same. When I stood up, though, I had the Walther PPK palmed in my right hand. Ankle gun.

"Now kick 'em over here," ordered Woody. We gave the guns half-hearted shoves with our feet, moving them out of our immediate reach.

"There you go," I said. "Now drop the girl and leave."

Woody had other plans. He pulled his right hand from behind his back and came out with an automatic that he had stuck in his waistband. It leapt in his hand with a flash and a crack and I saw Vince twist and go down. His next shot was at me. I felt a tug at my left arm, then burning. Tilly and Fish dove for cover as I came up with the PPK and fired three quick shots at the lower leg of the girl. One of them got through and lodged in Woody's knee. He howled with pain and dropped the body. I heard an explosion from the shadows on my right, followed by another. Ned had snuck in and gotten a couple clean shots at Woody as soon as he dropped the girl. I saw his gun hand erupt in blood as the automatic flew into the air and skittered across the floor. Woody fell as his leg buckled, clutching his ruined hand with his good one.

"That was either a hell of a shot, or you're damned lucky," I said to Ned. "Probably both. Good thing. I would have hated to have to kill you."

I walked over to Woody, now snarling like an animal on the

cold cement floor. His knee was bleeding and his gun hand was missing most of two fingers and part of a thumb. I grabbed him by the hair and yanked him to his knees.

"You and me, Woody. We're gonna have a talk." I let him fall back to the floor, then lifted the ankle gun and shot him in the other knee. His wail echoed through the building. I put my gun in my pocket, lifted him by his scalp once more, and hit hard him in the mouth. Silence.

"Vince okay?" asked Fish, collecting Woody's automatic and the other guns.

"He's breathing regular," said Ned. "Looks like he took one in the side."

"I'm all right," said Vince, rolling over and sitting up with some difficulty. He prodded his right side. "I think the bastard shot me in the liver."

"That'd be a shame," said Fish. "You couldn't drink anymore."

Ned was kneeling at his side, bending over him and helping him off with his jacket. Vince pulled up his shirt to get a closer look and groaned.

"Nah. It's not your liver," said Ned. "He hit something, though. Blood's dark. I don't like the look of this."

"How about you?" Tilly asked me.

I shrugged out of my jacket and looked at my arm. "Flesh wound. Through and through, I think. Give me a rag or something to tie around it."

Tilly obliged, turning to Fish and happily tearing a lapel off his yellow silk jacket.

"Hey!" said Fish.

"You've been rolling around on the floor, Fish. Just look at it! You won't be wearing this thing again," said Tilly.

Fish nodded glumly.

"Take Vince out of here and call an ambulance," I said, while Tilly wrapped my arm. "I'll be along."

"This girl's already dead," said Ned, bending over the corpse Woody had dropped. "Been dead for a while."

"Thought so."

"But you didn't know for sure?"

I shook my head and walked over to get Woody's coat and shirt, both hung neatly on meat-hooks. "I figured that if she was alive, she'd rather have a couple of slugs in the leg than have me blow her head off. She looked to be unconscious anyway." I rifled the coat and came up with a badge. "Detective's buzzer. From Ohio."

Ned nodded. "Sonofabitch." He looked at the gun in my hand. "A Walther, eh? I almost got me one of them. Those krauts make a nice gun. What about Sugarman?"

Woody had come to and started mewing through what was left of his teeth and broken jaw. He couldn't make much of a sound though. Not without causing himself incredible pain. Not yet.

I looked at Ned. Then Tilly and Fish. "It's time for you to leave," I said. "I'll bring the girl out when I come."

I watched them make a litter for Vince out of a piece of dirty canvas while I stripped to the waist and helped myself to a leather apron, one of several hanging on iron pegs in a neat row. Woody, in a last, desperate effort, had crawled across the floor, getting maybe twenty feet before I walked over, caught him by the pants cuff, and dragged him, whimpering, back to the table through a trail of his own blood. I turned on the saw and listened for a long moment. The gentle whir of the flywheel turned to a high-pitched whine as the blade picked up speed. Then the red haze descended.

The other detectives were almost out of the building when the real screaming started.

60

We called Stan and he met us at the station. Vince was going be all right, but wouldn't be back in the squad room for a couple of weeks. The doctor took a slug out of his side. It had missed all his vitals, but nicked his appendix, which the doctor removed just for fun. "Easier than sewing it up," he'd told us. My upper arm took a few stitches on either side and a dose of sulfa powder. Fish and I were back in the station around midnight. Tilly and Ned were there waiting for us. Stan came out of his office as soon as he heard us come in.

"You look like hell," I said to Stan. I stubbed my cigarette butt out on the corner of the desk.

"And you don't? I have an excuse. I haven't slept in a week. Can't go home," he grumbled, falling heavily into one of the wooden office chairs in front of my desk. It creaked ominously. "Bessie's gone crazy with this Kamasutra thing. I've seen things you could only imagine in your worst nightmares! I walked in last night and she was naked, upside down on the davenport, waiting for me. I said 'Bessie, you need to shave and put your teeth in.' She didn't think it was funny."

Ned guffawed and Tilly snorted coffee out his nose. Even I managed a smile.

Stan groped through his pockets for a smoke, but came up empty. None of us offered him one. He sighed heavily. "Okay, spill. What have we got?"

I took off my hat and tossed it onto the desk. "Woody Sugarman had a lot to say," I said. "In fact, he was very talkative after a while. Most of it didn't make any sense."

No one said anything, waiting for me to continue.

"He killed Gloria and threw her in Bubbly Creek—the river behind the stockyards. He said he didn't cut her up like the others."

"There's so much shit in that river, she'll never come up," said Ned. "It's like a meat sewer. I heard that the bloodworms were a foot thick in the bottom of that thing." He shook his head sadly. "Jesus..."

I nodded. "He told me he didn't know it would be Gloria. He was waiting for Priscilla—thought she'd help him. Give him some advice."

"What was that about?" asked Fish. "The whole Priscilla thing?"

"Like I said, he didn't make much sense," I reiterated. "He said Priscilla told him where to find the girls."

"So, the shrink was right," said Fish, between drags on his cigarette. "He was daffy."

I nodded. "It wasn't him, he said. It was Priscilla that was calling the shots. He brought the girls home, killed them, and cut them up afterwards, but she made him do it."

"Schizophrenia," said Tilly, with a knowing nod. "He was listening to the voices."

"He was doing what Priscilla told him. At the same time, he was trying to meet her so she could tell him how to stop."

"Christ! What a nut job!" said Stan. He let out a sigh and ran a hand through his greasy hair. "Tilly, tomorrow you and Ned get some dope on this guy. Something we can give the press. Find out about his family. Talk to the Sweetwater Farms people. His grandfather's alive as far as I know. Merl, you and Fish go take apart his house and see what you can come up with."

We nodded. I picked my hat up off the desk and put it on my head.

"Did you take him downtown to booking?" asked Stan.

"Who?" I said.

"Woody Sugarman."

I looked at the other three detectives. Fish snorted.

"Nope."

"Oh," said Stan. "Yeah. It's just as well." He ran a meaty hand over his tired face and sighed. "Where can we pick the body up?" he said. "Maybe we can get a photographer over there in the morning, take a few snaps for the papers, and take some of the pressure off."

"Bottom of Bubbly Creek," I said. "He fell in while I was apprehending him. It'll be in my statement. You're not gonna need a photographer."

"Too bad," said Stan. "Would have been nice to wrap this up neat and tidy. The politicians are going to want something concrete." He was quiet for a moment, thinking, then said "What about the girls' heads?"

"I'm guessing they're in Bubbly Creek as well," I said.

Fish and I were still jacked-up and decided that since there was nothing especially pressing, a midnight breakfast was in order. Rita's wasn't exactly jumping and we found ourselves looking at two orders of flapjacks and two steaming cups of joe about ten minutes after we arrived.

"You want me to sing at the funeral?" asked Fish. "Gloria's, I mean."

"Yeah. That'd be fine. When is it?"

"Haven't heard yet, but we gotta have one, body or no. That comes from the commissioner. She have any people?"

I shook my head and took a sip of coffee. "She told me she didn't. Her brother was killed last year at Guadalcanal. Both her parents are dead."

"I guess you might as well be in charge of the service then," said Fish.

I shook my head again. "Nope. You do it, will you?" I speared a forkful of pancakes, swirled them in a lake of syrup, and pushed them into my mouth.

"Yeah. Okay. What song did she like? *Danny Boy* probably wouldn't be a good choice."

"You know," I said, following the pancakes with a sip of coffee, "she liked that one that Helen Forrest sang. *Taking a Chance on Love*. The Benny Goodman version."

"I know that one," said Fish, with a big smile. "We'll even hire a band."

"That sounds good," I said. "I've got to go down to Vi's funeral day after tomorrow. Her family's in Peoria. She's got a lot of friends there, too. That Bible class she was teaching, high school... I'm the grieving fiancé."

"No," said Fish. "You're the good-hearted galoot. Did her mom like you?"

I shook my head. "Couldn't really tell. I only met her once. Seemed to go okay."

"You going to tell her you solved the case?"

"Yeah, but I don't guess that's any consolation right now."

Fish finished his breakfast without comment, took a sip of coffee, then asked, "You gonna take the Cabriolet down to Peoria?"

"Hadn't thought about it."

"Might as well drive it for a while," said Fish. "Since Gloria had no family..." He steepled his fingers. "If someone shows up, you can always give it back. If not, in a year or so, when the registration is due, there won't be much of a question."

"I'll be happy to keep it maintained for the estate."

"She have a house in the city?" asked Fish.

"Apartment. I never saw it. She did have a nice beach house up in Kenosha. She got both the house and car in the annulment, so the ex-family has no claim."

"Is there money as well?"

"Yeah, a lot."

"I expect," said Fish thoughtfully, "that she really wouldn't want it to go into the city's coffers."

"I expect you'd be right."

"I know a lawyer who deals in last wills and testaments. Let me talk it over with him. The money may be tricky, but the house and the car should be no problem. Wills are found all the time, and if they've been drawn up by competent attorneys, they're tough to dispute. You have a key to the house?"

"I can get in."

"We should go up and look at it sometime. Plus, if the money's right, you can keep the house and the car. I'd be happy with the cash."

I nodded. A good partner, Fish.

61

We drove up to the Tilden address late the next morning and found Woody Sugarman's house as we left it, including the broken front door hanging half off its hinges.

"You think anyone came in last night?" asked Fish. "Or maybe earlier this morning?"

I shrugged. "Didn't seem like there was much to take." I pushed parts of the broken door aside and shouldered my way past the wreckage. We walked into the hallway. The first room on the right, accessible from the hallway, was empty save for a neglected fireplace, filled with soot and ashes. The room opposite, across the hall to the left, had a beat-up sofa, placed on an angle, in front of another fireplace.

"Pretty dismal," said Fish. "Maybe he should have gotten some furniture from a whorehouse."

The kitchen was as we left it. I reached for the door to the basement, then stopped.

"You hear that?" I asked Fish.

Fish cocked his head, then drew his gun. "Radio?"

"Singing maybe. Where's it coming from?"

"Can't tell," said Fish, looking around.

I eased the basement door open, but a loud creak accompanied the action. I winced at the sound, and looked down into the darkness. Silence.

"Where's the light switch?" asked Fish.

"I don't remember. Maybe a pull-string on the bulb," I said. "Tilly came down first yesterday. Here, gimme your lighter."

I flicked Fish's Zippo open and carried it in front of me as I went down the steps. I could feel Fish right behind me. The old planks bent and groaned under my weight, something I hadn't noticed the night before. The Zippo didn't throw much light, but it was enough to get to the bottom of the steps. I held the lighter above my head as I reached the bottom and looked toward the table in the middle of the room.

"There's a pull-string," I said. "I'll get it."

It was three steps to the table, then a reach, and a tug, and the yellow bulb cast its swinging shadow across the ancient pine boards. Immediately, something felt different, *was* different. I blinked, trying to sort out the images. Not the table, not the bucket. I looked for another second, then realized what it was. One of the knives we'd left sticking in the beam was now planted in the table top, its point buried in the wood, casting its jittering shadow across the surface like a manic sundial. I looked up to where the two knives had been the night before. The other was gone as well.

A scream, like a howl from the pit of hell, ripped through the semi-darkness, and I saw an apparition jump up from behind the table. It was a witch—a harpy—eyes wild, teeth bared, dark hair flying in every direction. She plunged the butcher knife at my chest and I felt the blade slide into my flesh like a burning coal. I gave a bellow, staggered backwards, and fell to the floor, even as I saw the flashes from Fish's gun and the cellar echoed with explosions.

"Merl!" yelled Fish, still pointing his gun at the woman, now twisting and moaning in a heap on the other side of the table. "You all right?"

"Goddammit," I coughed. "Butcher knife. She got me, pard."

"I'm not jokin' around here," said Fish angrily. "You dead or what?"

"Nah, I'm not dead. Hurts like hell though." I pulled the blade out of my chest with a grunt and pressed my hand hard against the wound to stem the bleeding. The knife had gone into the hollow below my shoulder blade and managed to sneak between a couple of ribs. I took a deep breath and felt white-hot agony shoot down my left side.

"I don't think she got my lung. I'm still breathing okay."

"Dammit!" said Fish. He walked around the table and emptied his gun at the form writhing on the floor. Three more shots, then silence, broken only by the sound of Fish's heavy breathing.

"Who the hell *was* that?" he finally whispered, looking down at the woman.

"You guys down there?" came a voice from upstairs. "What's going on?"

"Yeah!" hollered Fish. "Get your asses down here. Merl's hurt."

I sat on the front steps with Fish and Ned and waited for the ambulance. The piece of tablecloth I held tightly against the wound was quickly reddening, and I felt woozy, but okay. The woman's body was still in the basement. Fish might have missed with his first shot, but his second and third were usually good. The last three were guaranteed.

"Dollar to a donut that was his sister," said Ned. "Her name was Priscilla. We talked to E.P. Sweetwater, the grandfather. He said that Woody had a sister living with him and that they were both raised by a woman who got them from an orphanage. The woman's name was Sugarman. As soon as we found out we humped over here as fast as we could."

"Why were they in an orphanage?" asked Fish.

"E.P.'s daughter got pregnant. She wouldn't say who the father was and this was the second time. He disowned her and the kids. Then she died and they went to the orphanage."

"Let me guess. Her name was Priscilla, as well," I said.

"You got it."

"So he was trying to get advice from his mother..."

"On how to stop his sister," Ned said. "At least that's how we figure it. What a creep show!"

"Don't matter much now," said Fish, spitting on the walk. "She's dead and he's dead and good riddance."

"Woody discovered the family connection and contacted E.P. Sweetwater about six years ago," said Ned.

"We should call Pete Flambeau and get him over for snaps," I said. "I told Russell Stewart we'd keep him in the loop. Give him first crack at the story."

"I'll call him," said Fish.

Tilly came out on the porch with a croaker sack. "I found the heads. They were in a couple of steamers in the attic."

I looked at the burlap sack in his hand and suddenly felt very tired. "That Vi?" I asked.

"Best you don't know," he said. "Let me take care of this. I've got to bring the rest of them down. There're a lot of 'em."

The ambulance drove up. I stood with a wince and almost made it to the back doors of the bus before collapsing.

62

I was resting in a hospital bed in St. Luke's when Sally Clifford came in. She was the eleventh visitor of the day, having been preceded by Fish and Ziba, the rest of the detective squad, Bronko, Musso, Danny, and Claude Everette, the coroner, who was anxious to see if I was in need of his services. Thankfully, I wasn't and he slipped me a couple of smokes.

"I heard you missed your fiancé's funeral," Sally said, primly sitting on the starched sheet at the foot of the bed. "I'm very sorry."

I nodded. "Me, too. I should have been there. Fish, Stan, and Tilly went down to Peoria in their dress blues. They stood for me."

"That's good," said Sally. She squirmed uncomfortably and chewed on her lip. "Today's Wednesday," she finally said.

"So?"

"So, I need a column."

I sniffed. "I'm almost dead here. How about some respect for the city's finest?"

"*I need* one. Uncle Russ has everyone working the Duffle Killer story. Holy smokes! Pete even got some pictures, but I don't think that the paper will print them."

"What pictures?" I asked.

Sally hesitated.

"It's okay," I said. "Tell me about the pictures."

"The basement, the table, the knives in the beam..."

"There weren't any knives in the beam," I said. "Not when we went back."

"Oh, Pete put 'em back for the snaps. It's a great shot. Those pictures will keep circulation up for weeks!"

"Then you don't need me to..."

"Yes we do! Uncle Russ says this is perfect! The Dear Priscilla connection... the sister being named Priscilla..."

I looked at Sally for a long moment and made a decision. "Nah. I'm done."

"*What?*" She looked panicked.

"I'm done. No more Dear Priscilla. I quit."

"*You can't quit!* What am I going to do?" she asked. "I've got to have a column."

"Write it yourself. I won't tell. You know the style. Do it for a few weeks, break the news to your uncle, and tell him you've been covering for me. Chances are he'll keep you on. Hey, it could be your big break."

Sally smiled and thought for a moment. "Might work. Will you help? I mean, just as long as you're laid up?"

I paused for a moment, then said, "Yeah, okay. Read one to me."

Sally waggled her shoulders and sat up straight as she pulled a letter out of an envelope. Then she read in a voice that couldn't have been chirpier if it had belonged to the red, red robin:

Dear Priscilla,

My boyfriend is crazy jealous. Whenever we go out together, he wants me to dress nice and I do, but as soon as another fellow notices me, he tries to pick a fight. I might also mention that my bosoms are quite abnormally large. Do you have any advice?
Signed,
Embraceable

I looked out the window. The leaves were tumbling from the trees and the sky promised a breathtaking, cool autumn day. Football weather.

"I'd tell her this," I said. "Gracious Reader..."